NO REGRETS

Buck could see his father, *their* father, in Ellie's face. He saw himself as he had been two decades ago, when he was young like her. Vital. Alive. Before they locked him away. Could it be that, making him feel this new emotion? Or was it the luminous quality of her skin, the rich tumble of hair, those remarkable eyes?

Buck ordered a second drink, tense as a stretched wire, watching Ellie sipping champagne, biting into the piece of cake. She touched her grandmother's arm affectionately, her voice too low for him to hear what she was saying as she handed Miss Lottie a beribboned gift package . . .

He heaved a regretful sigh. His plans were thrown into chaos. The old woman must die. But Ellie Parrish Duveen would be his.

Also by Elizabeth Adler

Private Desires
Peach
The Rich Shall Inherit
The Property of a Lady
Fortune is a Woman
Present of the Past
The Secret of the Villa Mimosa
The Heiresses
Now or Never

writing as Ariana Scott

Indiscretions
Fleeting Images

About the author

Elizabeth Adler was born in Yorkshire. She is married with one daughter and has lived in Brazil, the USA, England, France and Ireland.

No Regrets

Elizabeth Adler

CORONET BOOKS
Hodder and Stoughton

First published in Great Britain in 1997 by
Hodder and Stoughton
a division of Hodder Headline PLC
First published in paperback in 1997 by Hodder and Stoughton
A Coronet paperback

10 9 8 7 6 5 4 3

British Library Cataloguing in Publication Data

Adler, Elizabeth
No regrets
I. Title
823.9'14 [F]

ISBN 0 340 68466 6

Printed and bound in Great Britain by
Clays Ltd, St Ives plc

Hodder and Stoughton
A division of Hodder Headline PLC
338 Euston Road
London NW1 3BH

Revenge is a kind of wild justice,
which the more man's nature runs to,
the more ought law to weed it out.

Francis Bacon (1561–1626)

Prologue

1971

The cushiony leather seats in the back of the white Bentley convertible were Eleanor Parrish Duveen's favourite colour. Red. They were also extremely hot. It was early afternoon, but as she was only five years old, she wasn't much good at telling the time.

Ellie's father was sitting next to her mother, who was driving. His arm was flung lazily across the back of her seat and he was singing 'Onward Christian soldiers' at top blast in a loud but pleasing bass baritone. He threw back his head, belting out the verses of the hymn to the sky and the trees and the astonished birds, while her mother laughed gaily at his antics. Occasionally, he turned and glanced at Ellie, throwing her a grin and a conspiratorial wink as he escalated the volume for her benefit, making her mother laugh even harder as she negotiated the dangerous bends leading down the mountain.

The hot California sun beat down on Ellie's red curls. It was so hot she thought it would shrivel her brains.

She retrieved her straw hat from the floor and crammed it on her head, pulling it over her eyes, trying to shut out the sun. A yawn took her by surprise and she slithered further down in the hot red-leather seat, wishing they wouldn't insist on having the top down, however scorching the weather. The only time her father put it up was when it rained, and then they left California and 'escaped' to Europe.

Today, they had lunched at the old staging-post, hidden down in a valley of the Los Padres mountains. It was a place Ellie loved, where fake-cowboys barbecued steaks and quail and corn, and sang songs and strummed guitars. Her father sang along, waving his beer glass aloft in time to the music. Then her mother got up and danced, swirling her long gauzy skirts and clapping her hands over her head like a Spanish gypsy girl.

Ellie was fascinated by her mother's stomping little feet encased in expensive white-lizard cowboy boots. She thought she was a wonderful dancer and her father was the greatest singer. Even though her mother laughed every time he started on 'Onward Christian soldiers', which he always did after he'd been drinking.

Sometimes Ellie overheard other people's comments about her parents. 'Mad', they said. But they were the ones who didn't know them, and about their social connections, and how rich the Parrishes were. Those who did know smiled and called them 'eccentric'. They said they were true party-people, rich 'hippies', jet-setters. If there was a great party anywhere in the world, they would be there.

'Why not?' Romany Parrish Duveen would reply when asked why she felt the need to fly six or seven thousand miles across the world for one night's entertainment. 'Life is meant to be fun' was Rory Duveen's motto, and one he lived by.

The lunch had been long and Ellie had eaten to much. Her stomach stuck out from the quantity of food and her eyelids were heavy from the effects of it. She slithered down in the hot red-leather seat with her chin sunk onto her chest and her eyes closed. The sun beat on her eyelids sending brilliant flashes of purple and red as she half-dozed. Somewhere in the background she could hear her mother laughing and she thought it was the most delightful sound in the world. When her mother laughed, everything was right with Ellie's world.

'Ooops', she heard her mother exclaim, when the big Bentley wobbled skittishly as it took the curve.

Ellie half-opened her eyes. She peered over the edge of the car, over the edge of the road at the yellow-dried grass and jagged rocks in the ravine below. Her mother straightened the wheel and the big convertible rolled smoothly on down the steep mountain road. Ellie sighed contentedly and closed her eyes again.

'*Onward Christian so-o-o-o-ldiers, Marching as to war, With the cross of Jesus Going on before . . .*'

Her father's strong voice and her mother's laughter bounced from the mountain peaks, echoing round the valleys until Ellie thought it would wake even the sleeping rattlesnakes.

Then, 'Ooops,' her mother said again as the Bentley did another little shimmy. She turned and looked questioningly at her husband. Their eyes met, and it was as though they were drowning in each other's gaze. He didn't miss a beat: '*Onward Christian so-o-o-o-oldiers . . .*'

He was still singing, loud and clear, when the big car suddenly flung itself into a violent spin.

'Ooops', her mother yelled, laughing as she tried to straighten out. She was still laughing when the big car hurtled over the edge, bouncing from the rocks, deep into the canyon. Because wasn't life all a joke? And maybe death, too?

1

Present Day

The Hudson Sanitarium was built into a stretch of rocky land overlooking the river, as far upstate New York as you could get using a paved road. It consisted of a central red-brick administration block with smaller satellite wings where the patients were housed. Dark green ivy climbed the walls and circled the barred windows where, in springtime, starlings and sparrows made their nests, finding a snug haven from the howling winds and ravenous predators.

Those patients who were still able to tell the difference and understood what their surroundings were like, did not feel quite as happy as the sparrows. Besides the barred windows there were locked doors, security alarms, and armed guards. The nurses were burly men who could wrestle a patient to the ground if necessary, and even in the women's wing, the female nurses were chosen for their stature and strength, as well as their ability to distribute medication and keep control. The Hudson was a private maximum-security facility for violent and deranged patients. It was a place where families, fearing for their own safety, had committed them.

The man in room 27 was considered lucky by the other patients. His room was on a corner and had two windows. Admittedly, both were barred and set high in the wall, but they let in more light and a glimpse of the trees tossing in the everlasting wind. In this small, isolated half-world where

5

most patients wore cheap, well-worn clothes, he was remarkably well-dressed. He wore smart button-down shirts and chinos in summer and cords and neat sweaters in winter.

He had a seemingly inexhaustible supply of cigarettes, and even had special foods, pizza and chicken and ribs, sent in from the nearby township of Rollins. It was also rumoured that he paid a guard to keep him supplied with secret bottles of vodka, and to dispose of the empties. He was, those patients said who still had enough wits left to them to know the difference, a rich man.

Patrick Buckland Duveen did not agree with their assessment of him and his luck. It was not lucky to be incarcerated in the Hudson Sanitarium. It would have been called a lunatic asylum not so many years ago, and for its violent clientele a room there was as much a prison cell as any high-security jail. His 'privileges' were not due to his personal wealth, nor to the charity of his family. They were to appease the conscience of the woman who'd had him committed to this place, locked in like the 'crazy animal' she had called him, insulting him in her stern, unafraid voice.

The fact that she was not afraid of him was one of the reasons he had felt compelled to kill her. Too bad he'd not succeeded.

'You should go to jail,' she had stormed at him, while her guards held him down, his face pressed into the rich, soft carpet at her feet. 'But I will not allow you to disgrace our name.'

She had told the police she would not press charges against him, but that he was a proven danger to the public and she intended to have him committed.

The eminent doctors who were her friends had come hurrying at her command. They agreed he was dangerous, a born killer. 'A madman, you could see it in his eyes.' And those three doctors calmly signed the documents that had put him away in this place, for ever.

In Buck Duveen's book, decent clothing, the occasional pizza and bottle of vodka – chosen not because he preferred it but because of its lack of detectable odour on his breath – plus a room with two barred windows and an armed guard on every floor, did not make up for a lifetime of missed pleasures. He missed the restaurants, the bars, the booze and the women. And he missed *power*. He had spent twenty years without it and he craved it like a child wants candy.

One cloudy, blustery morning in early April, he was marched from his room through the green windowless tunnels they called transit passages, with an armed guard on either side, his hands cuffed safely behind his back because he had been known to try to fight his way out, to the office of the Chief Administrator.

Hal Morrow was sitting behind a large teak desk piled with papers. He could smell Duveen's strong breath-mint before he even looked at him. He took him in, quietly, for a few minutes, noticing how fit he looked. He was a tall, well-set-up fellow, of – he checked his papers – Duveen was forty-two now. He had a fine head of copper-red hair, dark eyes, narrowed against the unaccustomed light, and a lean-jawed, handsome face with the pale skin of an incarcerated man. He also had the wiry physique and strong hands of a peasant.

Morrow glanced at the file again. Those same hands had been used to attempt to strangle the woman who had put him in here, as well as, it was suspected, two other women, both prostitutes. No evidence had ever been found to link him definitively with those last two cases and he had never been prosecuted for them. Nor for attempting to murder the older woman, but that was because she had chosen not to press charges. In Morrow's view, she'd given Duveen a break because he undoubtedly would have done time in a maximum-security jail.

Buck Duveen was a psychopath: attractive, charming, unemotional, ruthless. And clever. New guards at the Hudson facility always said you couldn't meet a nicer guy: pleasant, softly-spoken, intelligent. He'd taught himself Latin and Greek, read Juvenal and Plato in the original. He quietly tended his garden, an immaculate plot in the large park-like grounds, where he grew only flowers. Beautiful, pampered flowers, with never a bug to be seen because he annihilated them the very minute they appeared. His roses were a picture, heavy blossoms locked in the neatest little prisons of clipped box hedges. He grew flowers for every season, except the long, hard winter when the earth lay under a blanket of snow for months on end.

If you didn't remind yourself where you were, you would have thought he was the easiest guy to get along with. In fact you might even have enjoyed his company. Except just when you were lulled into thinking he was okay and began wondering what he was doing in here anyway, he took you by surprise.

He'd almost succeeded in strangling a guard who got too close with him, began to treat him as a friend instead of an inmate. He'd leapt at him in a frenzy, fastening his hands round his neck with such ferocious strength it took three men just to get him off. Even when they'd knocked him unconscious they still had to prise his fingers from the guard's neck. He was strong as an ox and crazy as a loon, they said.

Whenever he got violent, they put the strait-jacket on him, locked him in a windowless cell and stood guard outside, listening to him howl his rage at them, and at the woman who had put him in here.

After a few days he would fall silent. 'I'd like to be released from here, if you don't mind,' he would say, so politely. And he would be. But this time in handcuffs and leg-irons. He would be taken to his own room and locked in there, observed through the grille in the door. Mostly, he would just sit at his desk, choose a book of Latin poetry, or a gardening magazine he subscribed to, and begin quietly to read. He was the model inmate once more.

Buck Duveen watched Morrow, his eyes hooded, face impassive. He knew he was smarter than Morrow. And cleverer than the psychiatrist whom he saw on a weekly basis, twisting the man's smug scientific brain around by feeding him the information he knew he would like to hear: about erotic dreams, fantasies, visions. He would watch him scribbling his notes, nodding his head approvingly, and he would be laughing inside because he knew he'd fooled him.

But he wasn't clever enough to escape, though he'd tried a couple of times, and it gnawed at his innards like a cancer. He needed to take his revenge on Charlotte Parrish, the old woman who had put him here. He wanted everything she had, everything that should belong to him.

He brooded over it, night after long dark night, in the cold of winter when the wind howled like the crazy inmates, and in the steamy summer when he prowled naked within his four walls. Trapped.

One day he would get her. But then there would still be another obstacle. He didn't know what had happened to the child, Ellie Parrish Duveen, only that she must be a grown woman now. Young and ripe.

He had conjured up her red-haired image thousands of times, alone in that cell. And thousands of times he'd played with the idea of what he would do with her when he finally got her. It made him howl with laughter and the guards patrolling the corridors stiffened to attention, cocking their heads to one side, listening.

'There goes Buck Duveen,' they said. 'Must be full moon again.' Then they went on their way and left him to his crazy, solitary laughter.

Hal Morrow studied the papers in front of him, considering what he was about to do. The Hudson Sanitarium was a private institution. The inmates' expenses were paid by their relatives who wanted them out of the way, out of their lives, and as far from them and civilization as possible. When those fees went unpaid, as they were now in Duveen's case, he had no choice.

He looked up, met the man's eyes. He said, 'Duveen, you will be leaving here today. You're a free man.'

Duveen's head shot up, his usually dead eyes glittered like polished dark stones in a beam of weak sunlight. He thought quickly about why? How? Where he would go? What he would do? And just as quickly he decided not to ask. Better not look a gift horse in the mouth.

A grin spread across his still-handsome face. 'And about time too, you fuckin' old bastard,' he snarled. Cocky with freedom, he turned on his heel, heading for the door.

'Just a minute,' Morrow barked. Duveen stopped but he did not turn round, and Morrow heard his exasperated sigh.

'We have been informed by the attorneys in charge of your case that no further money is available to keep you here. However, there is the sum of three hundred and twenty five dollars left in your account with us. This will be given to you in cash, along with your social security card and any other personal documents. Your possessions have been packed and you will be driven to the nearest rail station.'

Duveen tilted back his head, staring at the ceiling, waiting for him to finish. *Three hundred bucks*, he thought. *A hundred and fifty for each decade he had spent in this place. Fifteen dollars a year . . . and they would consider him a rich man just to have his liberty . . .*

'That is all,' Morrow dismissed him. 'I wish you good luck in your new life, Duveen.'

He did not reply and Morrow watched him go, walking with that confident swagger that had never left him in all the years he'd been in here. Morrow knew he had no choice but to do what he was doing. The financial spigot that had supplied the funds for Duveen had been turned off by the old lady's attorneys. And the state institution didn't want to know. He sighed again, regretfully. He hoped he was doing the right thing.

Back in his room, the handcuffs were removed. Whistling 'Dixie' under his breath as he always did when he felt elated, Duveen quickly changed his clothing, putting on the neat white button-down shirt, the Brooks Brothers tweed jacket, the soft beige cords and tasselled loafers. He combed back his hair and felt he must look pretty good. He couldn't check because no mirrors were allowed in case the inmates smashed them and used the shards as weapons.

An attendant had already packed his bag. He hefted it, smiling at its weight. The old lady had kept him supplied with enough clothes for a proper social life even though one did not exist. He took a last glance around as he left the place that had been his home for so many long years. There was no glimpse of emotion in his stone-dark eyes. But he would not forget.

Once again the guards escorted him, un-handcuffed this time, down the green windowless corridors to the administration building. In the front office a middle-aged secretary handed him his papers and a plastic wallet containing the three hundred and twenty-five dollars.

She slid the receipt across the table, looked up at him and said, 'Sign here please, Mr Duveen.'

His dark eyes burned into hers, sly with sensuality. It was as if he were looking at her naked, and she blushed, instinctively clutching her hand to the collar of her white blouse to cover herself.

Duveen's lips twitched at the corners, just enough so she knew he knew what she was feeling. Then he signed boldly, *Buck Duveen*. He pocketed the money and the papers, and said mockingly, 'You don't have to worry, honey, I like 'em younger and sexier than you.' Whistling 'Dixie' again, he strode out the door and into the waiting Yukon wagon.

Two guards rode shotgun with him as far as the station, just so he wouldn't hijack the driver and steal the Yukon, he guessed. As though he would be that dumb. They had always underestimated him here, but now the world was about to find out what a clever man he really was. Especially those nearest and dearest to him.

He'd had a long time to figure out what he would do. There had been many long nights when he'd planned and plotted and dreamed of how it would feel. He could almost taste it, like the slick sharp flavour of good bourbon on his tongue. Revenge was going to be so sweet, so very, very sweet.

2

Ellie Parrish Duveen backed the taxicab-yellow Wrangler out of the garage of the tiny Santa Monica house she called home, and headed down the hill toward Main Street. Like the jeep, her house was old and decrepit. Since the last big earthquake, none of the walls quite met at the corners and the bedroom floor trembled when she walked across it, but it did have a view of the ocean, and getting up in the morning was so much easier with the sun glittering on the waves just two blocks away. Besides, it was cheap. Something that mattered very much to her.

Main Street was at a standstill and she fretted behind the wheel, checking her serviceable steel watch anxiously. As usual, she was running late. Keeping an eye on the traffic, and without the benefit of a mirror, she dusted powder onto her freckled nose, swept black mascara onto her copper lashes, and added a slick of deep mocha lipstick. Years of being late had made her an expert at the quick traffic-lights fix-up. A spritz of *Eau d'Issey*, a quick flick through her red hair with a brush, and she was ready to face the day. Taking a sip of coffee from the paper Starbucks cup, she put the car into gear as the traffic moved off again. Life, she decided, was just one big rush, and no matter how hard she tried she was always just a couple of beats behind.

Ellie was twenty-nine years old, with her mother's misty blue-grey eyes and curly red hair worn long and flowing down to her shoulderblades, except when she was at the café she owned in Santa Monica, and then she skewered it beneath a black baseball cap with *Ellie's Place* inscribed on it in green silk.

She was tall and slender, though not model-thin, with long legs and embarrassingly large feet that her grandmother always said, teasingly, she needed in order to keep her anchored safely to the ground. Her nose was straight and freckled, she had a big smile that began in her eyes and ended at her generous mouth, and a faint scar ran across her forehead, all the way into her scalp.

She was smart and sassy, alone in the world but for her grandmother, Miss Lottie, and she was determined to be a success. After college, and then culinary school in New York and a stint in a Michelin-starred restaurant in Paris, she had come home and learned the restaurant business the hard way, from designing her tiny storefront premises to battling downtown bureaucrats for the necessary permits; to dealing with building contractors who didn't keep their promises and left her weeks behind schedule and over budget. But she didn't regret a minute of it.

The café had been open for just over a year and she worked hard six days a week, which left very little time for a private life. She did the ordering, kept the accounts and, along with her best friend Maya, served the food, opened the wine and cleared the tables. She also cooked up a storm whenever the temperamental chef quit, which he did every few weeks, as well as baking her own bread and her famous *tarte tatin* that was the specialty of the house. Plus, she had been known to clean the place at the end of a long night, when the crew failed to show. She was practically a one-man-band, and she loved it.

She would tell new customers maybe they cooked fancier at Wolfgang Puck's glamorous *Chinois* a few doors away, but 'Ellie's' was cosier and cheaper. 'I'm your local bistro,' she'd say. 'You can drop in here any time, no need to dress up. Just a glass of wine and some good food . . .

Ellie's Place was ticking over, not making a fortune yet but enough to keep her roof over her head and to stay open. She was, she would remind herself determinedly at the end of yet another long, hard day, doing all right.

Snagging the only free parking spot, she jumped from the Wrangler, shoved a quarter into the meter and sprinted, long red hair flying, half a block to the café. She stopped for a minute to look at it. It was cheerful, painted forest green with lace café curtains on a brass pole, and *Ellie's Place* in gold script on the window. The old-fashioned bell tinkled musically as she opened the door.

Inside was like an old Parisian bistro, with smudgy mirrors on the walls, a sprinkling of fresh sawdust on the floor, an authentic zinc counter, inexpensive cane chairs, crisp white tablecloths and fresh daisies crammed into yellow pottery jugs.

It was a Monday, and her day off, but there were still things to be done. She checked the tiny kitchen. The cleaning crew had done their stuff; the floors gleamed, the big steel refrigerators and stoves shone, everything was in its place. She glanced, half-longingly, at the marble work-station where she did the baking. She kind of missed it on her days off, getting her hands into the pastry, working with food instead of managing a business, but she'd learned early on that she couldn't be two people at once. And, despite her talent and her training, for the moment that had meant hiring a chef.

Opening the refrigerator she removed the stacked boxes containing the left-over food from the previous night, plus the rosemary olive bread she'd baked herself. Laden, she staggered back to the car, tripped over her feet and lost her backless brown shoe. 'Oh shoot,' she muttered. Ellie never cursed, because her grandmother had taught her a lady never did. Balancing precariously on one leg, the boxes shifting and sliding, she felt around for the shoe with her bare foot.

'You look like a stork without wings.' Maya Morris pulled her red Pathfinder into the kerb and leaned out the window, laughing.

Maya was Ellie's best friend, and her co-helper at the café. She was blonde and gorgeous and she was never up this early in the morning. 'You might help instead of laughing.' She shot Maya a glare, clutching the boxes to her chest, her bare toe pointed.

'Or maybe a ballet dancer.' Maya climbed from the car. She was on her way to yoga class and had on a black leotard and sneakers, and not much else, and she was stopping traffic. She slid the shoe onto Ellie's foot. 'And I'm the fairy prince who turns into a pumpkin at midnight.'

'Cinderella's *coach* turned into a pumpkin and she married her prince.'

Maya put her hands on her hips, looking at Ellie, still clutching the sliding boxes. 'Fat chance you have of marrying a prince, or anyone else. You're a woman married to your work. Anyhow, where are you going?'

'To see Miss Lottie.'

Maya nodded; now she knew why, instead of her usual jeans, Ellie was wearing the ice-blue flowered skirt and a deeper blue skinny-knit top. And her mother's pearls – the ones taken from her throat after the automobile accident that had killed her. She dropped a kiss on her cheek. 'Give her my love.' She got back in the car, wishing Ellie would get herself a date. It was all work and no play for her.

Ellie dashed back to the café, locked up, then drove, too fast as always, to the Santa Monica homeless shelter where she dropped off the food, hoping it would help, if only a little bit.

Checking her watch, she climbed back into the jeep, wondering where the time had gone.

As she headed north on the 101, Ellie thought worriedly about her grandmother. Miss Lottie lived in a rundown old mansion in Montecito with just a housekeeper to help. She was well in her eighties and her mind wandered erratically. She could lose decades between one thought and the next, but then she would recall, in perfect detail, the time she had bought a hat in Paris in 1939 – though there were moments Ellie suspected she simply chose to be vague, when there was something she just didn't want to discuss.

'Old age has its advantages, my dear,' Miss Lottie had said smugly, when Ellie exasperatedly accused her of it. 'I brought you up properly after your poor mother died. You've flown the nest, I have no more responsibilities. Now, I'm without a care in the world.'

Ellie only wished it were true. Meanwhile, the traffic was hell and she was going to be late. Again.

3

Lottie Parrish's 'cottage' stood on twenty prime acres of land in the affluent little resort township of Montecito. Ten minutes further north was Santa Barbara, site of the old Spanish Mission and a campus of the University of California. And just over an hour and a whole life-style to the south, lay the great smog-scorched urban sprawl of Los Angeles.

Beach houses and Spanish *casitas* hugged the curve of the bay, shaded by palms, and orange and lemon and fig trees. Tropical-hued bougainvillaea sprawled in abundance in shady gardens and along Coast Village Road, which was lined with little boutiques and restaurants, and tourists. But for all the activity down in the 'town', life up on Hot Springs Road might not have changed since the thirties, when the grand Italianate mansion had been built by Charlotte Parrish's father.

Waldo Stamford, a Boston Yankee, had fallen in love with the tiny, flower-bedecked coastal community. He'd built his house out of imported cream limestone, with a columned arcade, tall french windows leading onto shady patios, fountained courtyards and gardens copied from a Palladian villa in the Veneto region of Italy. Each of the twelve bedroom suites had its own bath and sitting room, with green wooden shutters to close out the afternoon sunlight. And each had been fitted out with every luxury, from European antiques and priceless rugs, to gold faucets shaped like dolphins and the very best Irish linen sheets. Which in those days were changed every morning by uniformed maids, and washed and ironed in their own laundry, a special building hidden in the birch woods near the back gates.

Waldo and his young daughter, Lottie, had entertained lavishly, filling the house with what he called 'amusing riff-raff' and flamboyant movie stars, as well as 'proper' people, meaning California's rich tycoons and gentry. But now Miss Lottie, as she was always known affectionately, never entertained.

Miss Lottie was still in her room, supposedly getting dressed ready for Ellie's visit, but instead she was sitting at the antique Venetian desk with the intricate marquetry inlay. An old green celluloid visor that her father used to wear for his poker games shaded her eyes, and she was busy at her personal computer. She had her own Internet number: http:/www.misslottie7AOL. com, and corresponded with any number of strangers, some of whom seemed to have become friends, especially a Rabbi Altman in England, whom she was particularly fond of. To her delight, she also seemed to have become an Agony Aunt.

Dear Al, she typed, quite speedily for someone using only two arthritic fingers. *Thank you for your message on my E-mail. I'm sorry to hear of your problem with your paramour, and this is what I think you should do. Marry her at once. Make an honest woman of her. Settle down, have children. This is what life is for, believe me, I know.* She signed it, *Sincerely Lottie Parrish*, then added at the end, *Shalom*.

It was a word of peace she'd learned from the Rabbi, and she liked to use it because it expressed her feelings towards the people she never saw, but who confided their innermost secrets to her.

Maybe it was because she was old, she thought, watching the *Opus 'n Andy* screensaver cartoon flickering across the screen, but they seemed to believe she had a special wisdom, when all she was really doing was talking common sense. She thought it surprising how little that was used these days. Now it was all technology and psychology with not much in between.

She'd bought the computer when her old lawyer died. She just couldn't get along with the new fellow who'd taken his place, and she'd decided to manage her money herself. A nice, very clever young computer expert had come in for a week to teach her how it all worked, and to her surprise she loved it. Unfortunately though, it hadn't been good for business.

Miss Lottie's suite of rooms was at the top of the grand staircase. It had tall double doors and panelling taken from a French chateau, painted a faded lilac, her favourite colour. French windows led out onto a marble balcony, and the green brocade canopied bed was the same one she'd had as a young girl when she'd first come to this house. In fact, nothing much had changed. It was all the same as it had been when her father was here, and when her daughter Romany was still alive, and Rory Duveen. Now, she supposed it was shabby, but it still pleased her. It was still elegant, still beautiful, still home.

Sighing for the past, she picked up her cane and went to get dressed.

Half an hour later, she was waiting for Ellie on the marble-paved terrace, sitting in a high-backed rattan chair that was probably almost as ancient as she was, with Bruno, the old golden labrador, dozing beside her. Her back was as straight as the chair's, her silver hair was immaculately coiffed in a chignon, and her blue silk dress was carefully chosen to be appropriate for afternoon tea at the Biltmore. The jaunty little silk scarf at her throat disguised, she hoped, a little of the unfortunate sag that, no matter what face cream she used, refused to go away.

'A little vanity is good for a woman,' she'd told her house-keeper and old friend, Maria, when she'd been rebuked for wasting her money on such things. 'After all, when you're my age, it's about all you've got left. Besides, a woman should always try to look her best.'

Miss Lottie thought it a pity that her mind could no longer keep pace with her body. Sometimes she couldn't even remember what she did yesterday, let alone last week, though she could recall perfectly the house being built and the day she and her father moved in.

All the men who'd worked on the house had gathered on the grand terrace, where she was sitting now. Champagne was poured into saucer-shaped crystal glasses, then her father had distributed lavish bonuses, and they'd drunk a toast to the success and beauty of the new house. They'd called it 'Journey's End', and Miss Lottie had always supposed it would be where her own personal journey through life would end. Until a few weeks ago, when the lawyer and accountants had told her that, finally, there was no money left.

They'd come to see her, carrying bulky files and ledgers of accounts, and she had sat, bewildered, while they went over everything point by point, expense after expense.

Ellie was meant to be there but she'd called to say she would be late, and when she finally arrived pink-cheeked from hurrying, long red hair flying untidily as usual, Miss Lottie had already approved the termination of what they called 'the unnecessary expenses'. That meant the charities dearest to her heart. Old friends who'd fallen on hard times to whom she gave money, retired servants whose medical expenses she helped with, a children's charity. It had all flashed before her eyes in a blur and she'd sighed regretfully and agreed it could not go on.

'You have to think of yourself, Miss Lottie', the lawyer admonished her sternly. 'You'll probably lived to be a hundred, and you'll need whatever money we can salvage. You're just not a rich woman any more.'

Maria Novales walked along the terrace carrying a tray with glasses and a jug of freshly-made lemonade. Her sandalled feet made no sound on the marble tiles and Miss Lottie did not hear her. Maria watched her for a moment, thinking how well she looked today. But then, she always perked up when Ellie came to visit.

Miss Lottie was immaculate, as always, in her favourite blue silk. A couple of dusty old diamond rings gleamed on her slender fingers, and her silver hair shone in the sunlight. And she was wearing that silly old green visor again. She always wore it now, when she sat at her personal computer, surfing the Internet. It was that same darn computer that had brought her financial downfall, but she loved it. It kept her amused for hours into the night when she couldn't sleep, and Maria was grateful for that.

There was something about Miss Lottie's determinedly upright posture that brought to mind the word 'indomitable'. Not that she couldn't be a maddening old woman when she chose. And persnickety with it. And eccentric in her ways. But when you were as much a lady as Miss Lottie, you could get away with eccentricity and foolishness, and a tart tongue. Especially when you knew she didn't mean it, and inside she was just a sentimental old marshmallow.

'You should take off that silly visor,' Maria said. 'Before Ellie gets here. Or else she'll know you've been at the computer again.'

Miss Lottie snatched it off guiltily. 'I thought it was my hat.'

'Here's your hat.' Maria handed it to her. 'She's late, as usual,' she added, putting down the tray.

'Don't worry. She'll be here soon.'

Maria headed back to the kitchen. She had known Ellie since she was born, and she'd even shown up late for that event. She had not changed one little bit. 'Late' was in her genes.

Miss Lottie thought that Maria was looking old too. She used to be a small, round, smiling woman, with thick dark hair and shiny brown eyes and a golden skin. Now, like herself, she was all bones and her dark hair was threaded with grey.

Maria had helped her bring up Ellie, after the accident. And that was an event Miss Lottie had never forgotten. The image of that day lived in her fuzzy memory, clear as a new photograph. The day her beautiful, wild, darling daughter had died, along with her husband.

Taking a sip of the cool lemonade, she reminded herself to count her blessings. The sun was warm; the sky a clear blue. Bruno, her beloved old golden labrador, was sprawled by the fountain, chasing rabbits in his dreams. Her dear friend, Maria, was happy. And Ellie was coming to visit.

No matter what the accountants had said, somehow Miss Lottie didn't think life at Journey's End would change much. After all, it hadn't changed in sixty years. Why should it now?

4

Gravel spurted from Ellie's tyres as she finally swung into the long, poplar-lined driveway at Journey's End. She gave a sigh of pure happiness as the lovely old house came into view. No matter where else she might live, this would always feel like 'coming home'.

Of course, she'd known for years that her grandmother was not rich any more, but there had always been money in the Parrish family. That is, until Miss Lottie had decided to manage her fortune herself. Ellie had been shocked when Michael Majors, the lawyer, told her of the destruction Miss Lottie's stock-market gambling had brought. He'd explained what he'd done, and said there would be just enough to keep her grandmother in comfortable, if not lavish style. Then he'd asked if she couldn't persuade her to sell the property.

'A run-down mansion doesn't mean much on today's market, but the prime twenty acres in Montecito certainly do. You'll have enough to live in clover for the rest of your days, let alone hers,' he persuaded.

But Ellie would have none of it. Miss Lottie had lived at Journey's End for more than sixty years and that's where she would stay, even if Ellie had to work double hours to keep her there. Miss Lottie had looked after her when she was a child, now it was her turn.

The tall oak doors stood welcomingly open, and she shook her head worriedly as she strode into the flagstoned great hall, thinking how unaware her grandmother and Maria were of present-day dangers. Open doors invited robbers – or worse. But they had always lived this way and they never gave it a thought.

'Late again, Ellie.' Maria appeared, wiping her hands on a teacloth.

'Anybody would think I made a habit of it.' She swung Maria into her arms, whirling her round. 'Oooh, Maria. I've missed you. And you smell so good, of vanilla and sweetness.'

'That's just my soul you can smell, the goodness of it.' Maria's face was pink with indignation and pleasure. 'Anyhow, it's just some cookies I baked. I thought you might enjoy them, after work, when you have a few minutes alone.'

'You spoil me. And you know I'm just a brat.'

'Somebody's got to spoil you, brat or no. You look tired, Ellie.'

'I know. And don't tell me – I'll bet I'm untidy as well.'

Smoothing her windswept hair, Ellie bent to pet the dog as he lumbered to his feet, doing his best to gambol toward her. 'Sweet old boy, lovely dog. Who loves you, mmmm?'

'There you are,' Miss Lottie called. 'I've been waiting for you.'

'Sorry, Miss Lottie. It's the traffic.'

Her grandmother threw her a disbelieving glance, and Ellie laughed as she hugged her. 'Okay, partly traffic, and partly because I had some stuff to do at the café.'

'Nothing changes,' her grandmother said wryly. 'And somehow I suspect it never will.'

'Well, now I'm here, let's hit the Biltmore. I'm dying of hunger, and I'll bet you are too. Then I can tell you all my news, and you can tell me yours.'

'It's a good thing I still remember where the Biltmore is.' Miss Lottie pulled the wide-brimmed straw hat trimmed with pink roses firmly over her silver hair. 'And I also remember exactly where I got this hat. In Paris, in 1939, just before war was declared in Europe. Long before your time,' she added, retelling the hat story for the umpteenth time as she took Ellie's arm and walked down the steps to the car.

'I bought it at Madame Pepita's on the Rue du Faubourg Saint-Honoré. Fifty-five dollars it cost. And that was a small fortune then, I can assure you.'

'See, Miss Lottie. You can remember when you want to.'

Ellie helped her into the custom-built 1972 white Cadillac, whose only outings these days were to the Biltmore and back. Miss Lottie had always refused to own a Rolls. She said she bought Paris hats and English woollens, but her automobiles were always American.

'You have to support your country's economy:' she'd quoted her own father. Not that the economy was currently benefiting from her beliefs; she hadn't bought a car in twenty years. 'Buy good and it lasts,' was one of her other mottoes, and the old Caddy had proven that true, though it still had only twelve thousand miles on it.

The car purred smoothly down the drive, cushioned as a baby-carriage, and Ellie said, 'The Manager is expecting us. No doubt they'll roll out the red carpet for you.'

'Nonsense, Ellie. They see us every Monday. Besides, they understand a lady doesn't like a fuss.'

Still, Miss Lottie was pleased, and she patted her hair and adjusted the angle of her hat in the mirror, then polished up her old diamond brooch with a linen handkerchief. She wondered fleetingly who had given to it her, but the identity of the donor was lost in the mist of her faulty memory.

Secretly, she enjoyed the fuss they made over her at the Biltmore. After all, she'd been dining there for over half a century now. Besides, she and Ellie always had fun together, and maybe later she would persuade her to sleep over. Then it would be just like old times.

5

Buck Duveen bought a newspaper and a pack of Camel Unfiltered at the rail station. It felt strange, handing over the money, checking the change from the twenty, stepping onto the waiting train. He turned his head, half-expecting to see the armed guard behind him, ready to haul him off again, to tell him it was all a sick joke and he was heading right back into the hard-timers ward. But the only person behind him was a young woman in a blue suit, with a very short skirt and very good legs.

Buck stood politely to one side to allow her to get by and she threw him a casual smile of thanks. He grinned maliciously as he walked behind her through the railroad car. It wasn't politeness that had made him step back. He hadn't seen a real honest-to-god woman in years. The Amazons in the Hudson didn't count, though they would have done in a pinch, if he could have stunned one of them long enough to get his hands up her skirt. Now he could hardly contain his excitement, just looking at the movement of her taut little butt.

She stopped at an empty seat, took off her jacket and placed it on the overhead rack, giving him a further opportunity to linger. He'd seen young women on TV, but watching her was like the difference between reality and a porn magazine. Each had its place but he knew which he preferred. She took her seat and he nodded to her and went on his way.

He chose a seat opposite another woman, an older one this time but still attractive, in her early forties: short bouncy black hair, brown eyes, a fleshy mouth. Her fingernails were very long, squared off at the tips and painted dark red. He thought they looked predatory, like a vulture's claws. He imagined them digging into a man's back, instead of into the bag containing a ham sandwich.

She acted as if he were not there, opening her book, taking a bite out of the sandwich. Buck placed his newspaper on the table, took the pack of cigarettes and shook one out. She glanced up, frowning.

'Smoking is not allowed.'

'Excuse me. I'm sorry, I didn't realize.' He was polite, a gentleman. He put the cigarettes away and popped a breathmint in his mouth, and she went back to her book.

He did not open the newspaper. He sat facing her, his eyes fixed on her. It was a game he'd always liked to play and he wondered how long she would last.

The woman could feel his eyes, like heat on her skin. She glanced up at him, then away again. She shifted uncomfortably and held the book higher in front of her face so she wouldn't have to look at him.

Duveen smiled, that same knowing little curve of the lips he'd given the secretary when she'd handed him the money. He felt a surge of power as he watched her. It was a feeling he had not experienced in a long time, deprived as he was of human prey, and he knew himself to be glorious again. He had not lost his touch.

The woman snapped the book shut. She flung it into her bag along with the remains of the sandwich, grabbed her coat from the seat next to her and eased sideways out of the seat as quickly as she could. He watched every move, every fluid ripple of her body.

'*Pervert*', she hissed. And then she was gone, striding purposefully down the swaying train, away from him.

Duveen heaved a pleased sigh. He was back in biz.

In Manhattan, he checked into a cheap hotel near Times Square. He went out and bought himself a steak dinner and found a back-street bar where they stocked reasonably good bourbon. Then it was time to put his first plan into action.

Tanked up and humming with power like an electricity pylon, he found himself a hooker. He took her into a dark alley and had her up against the wall behind a garbage dumpster. While he was doing it he put his hands round her slender neck and began to squeeze. He had no worries about anyone coming into the alley and seeing him, because he was in control. He was invincible.

She gagged, fought back, so he punched her senseless. When he had finished, he let go of her and she slid to the ground. He took the knife from his pocket and carefully etched a deep cross into her forehead. Temple to temple, scalp to nose. It was something he liked to do, his personal mark. Hefting her easily in his strong arms, he flung her into the dumpster, took the bottle of bourbon from his pocket, and poured it over her.

He straightened his clothing, took out a cigarette, lit it, and tossed the lit match into the dumpster. Whistling 'Dixie' under his breath, he strolled back down the alley. He felt like a new man.

As he turned the corner, he heard the whoosh of flames. He smiled, that curious little smile. He'd always enjoyed fire.

He hung around a while, mingling with the crowds on the busy sidewalks, inspecting the sleaze-shops selling porn equipment and magazines, the theatres selling blue movies and the pimps selling their women. Ten minutes passed before he heard the wail of fire engines racing toward the alley.

He turned his footsteps back towards his hotel. It was only a warm-up, but he thought it wasn't bad for his first day's work in twenty years.

6

Homicide Detective Dan Cassidy was at his desk in the squad room of Manhattan's Midtown South, fiddling with the computer. There was no need; his notes were as complete as he was ever going to make them. Shutting it down, he turned his attention to his files. They were all in order. He opened the desk drawers and closed them again. They were empty.

Pushing back his chair, he prowled restlessly down the hallway to the vending machine and punched out his fifth cup of coffee of the evening. Leaning his rugged body against the wall, he sipped the sluggish brown liquid, wondering anxiously if he were doing the right thing. Didn't they always say you couldn't go home again? He shrugged off the misgivings. It was too late now.

Dan was dark-haired and blue-eyed, like his Irish ancestors, and built tall and rangy like his mother's all-Californian family. He'd grown up in Santa Barbara, a typical outdoorsy Californian; a champion swimmer in high school, on the rowing squad at UCSB, and an avid surfer and fisherman. He was a lean, hard-bodied, thirty-nine-year-old, attractive and with an ex-wife in LA.

They'd married young, when Dan was still in college. The break-up came a couple of years later and he'd wanted to put as much distance between himself and the past as possible. He'd needed a new direction, so he'd gone to New York and become a cop. He'd never regretted it. His colleagues knew him to be a tough, intuitive detective. A man who cared about his job, and cared about the victims. 'Dan's only failing is that he can't set the whole world to rights all by himself,' the Chief had complained, but he was smiling when he said it.

Two years ago, Dan had been badly wounded, shot in the chest while arresting a murder suspect. Only quick action by his colleague and friend, Detective Pete Piatowsky, had saved him.

Being that close to death had given him pause for thought. He'd been lucky this time, but what about the next? The answer was moot, because the injury left him with a stiffness in the right arm and shoulder that hampered his speed drawing a weapon. It didn't seem like much of a disability to him, but the Police Medical Board had disagreed and assigned him to permanent administrative duties.

Life as an NYPD detective was one thing, out on the edgy streets, doing his bit to clean up the city. Life behind a desk did not have the same appeal. And that's why, tomorrow, he would be on a flight back to California and a new life as the owner of a small winery he'd bought, not far from the town where he grew up.

He told himself he'd had enough of murder and mayhem to last him several lifetimes. He wanted to get back to the simpler life the countryside offered. Horses, dogs, chickens; small-town living. If it meant he had to become Farmer Dan to do it, then that's what he intended to be.

His father had died recently, and he'd bought the vineyard on a wave of memories and nostalgia with the idea of getting back to his roots. On bad days, he told himself he must be crazy and that Running Horse Ranch was doomed to failure. And on the good days he told himself he was a quick learner and willing to give it all he'd got. His time, his energy, his money – what he had left of it. And one day it would all pay off and be a big success.

He'd never actually visited the property, though when he first saw the ad he'd remembered the area from when he was a kid. And he wasn't a complete greenhorn. The year before he left for college, he'd earned tuition money working at a vineyard in Napa. He'd done everything from toiling in the fields to harvesting grapes; to working the crush and in the bottling plant. Interested, he'd hung out with the winemaker, observing the various processes. He'd experienced all the problems: the sudden frost that could wipe out a crop overnight if you didn't get out there fast – usually at three in the morning – and mist down the vines. He'd seen grapes shrivelled to hard worthless little raisins by disease. He'd fought flood and worked with the burning sun on his back. And most of all, he'd learned exactly how dependent a winemaker was on the weather. Good vines plus good weather equalled a good crop. It was a simple equation. He only hoped he could make it work.

The sunshiny photos of the property had shown a rolling landscape scattered with scrub oak, shady eucalyptus and bare-looking rows of vines. There was a little wooden house complete with a wrap-around porch, a red barn that housed the winery, and Spanish adobe-style stables set around a picturesque courtyard. It looked so good he had fallen instantly in love with it. Besides, it was cheap, a bargain they'd told him. With what he'd inherited from his father, his savings, and his disability pension, he could just about swing it. And now he was hoping, uneasily, that it was really as great as it looked in the pictures.

Heaving a half-regretful sigh, he wandered back into the squad room, just as the call came in about the burned-up body in the alleyway off Times Square. His adrenalin rose in conditioned response as he headed for the door.

'What the hell, I'll ride with you one last time,' he said to Pete Piatowsky, his partner of five years.

Piatowsky threw him a shrewd sideways glance. 'You're never going to make it, alone out there in the sticks. You can't even get yourself outta here and into the saloon for your own farewell party, you've still gotta hit the streets. What's the bettin' you're back in three months?'

'Five-to-one on two,' Dan heard someone yell over the laughter in the squad room.

Piatowsky's fair-skinned aimiable face split in a snaggle-toothed grin. If making book wasn't illegal, he'd have shortened those odds.

Dan was tall, but Piatowsky was a blond giant. He was forty-two years old, wore his thinning hair combed carefully across his high forehead, and his blue eyes had a deceptively mild expression. Dan knew him to be sharp as a razor, in synch with life on the streets. He was a good detective, as well as a good friend. And Piatowsky had saved his life. He owed him.

The sickening stench of charred flesh hit them as soon as they stepped out of the car. Death on the streets was never pretty and this one was stomach-churningly gruesome. The flames had not eliminated the cross etched deeply into the woman's forehead, curling back the blackened edges of the cut flesh like pages in a book, exposing her skull. And her eyes bugged from her head in the terrified stare Dan knew she must have given her killer at the moment of death.

The Medical Examiner arrived just after they did, leaning over the stinking dumpster, doing what he had to do. Dan didn't envy him his job, and he reminded himself again of the blue skies, the sunshine, the fresh country air that would soon be his.

'It wasn't the knife that killed her,' the ME said finally, 'Nor the fire. It was manual strangulation. Mutilation came after death, and the fire was an attempt to destroy the evidence.'

To their disgust, the Fire Department had washed away any possible clues with the fierce water-hoses.

'Whoever he is, he's a lucky bastard,' Piatowsky said wearily to Dan. 'Anyhow, why did he have to carve a cross on her forehead, after she's dead? What kind of a sicko is he? Some New Age Disciple, out to reform Manhattan his way?'

'It's his signature, an ego thing. My guess is he's done it before. You might check records, see what nut has just finished a prison sentence and hit the streets again.'

'Thanks a lot, buddy.' Piatowsky could have used that drink and the companionship of his colleagues in the nearby saloon, but he had a long hard night in front of him. 'Why don't you take your smart-ass FBI profiling outta here and go to your own farewell party.' He shook Dan's hand, slapping his shoulder affectionately. 'Wish I could get there, but as usual I'm stuck with the body.'

Now the time had come, Dan hated like hell to leave. 'I'll have that guest room all set for you in sunny California.'

'I'll bring my fishing rods – and the kids.' Piatowsky turned back to the crime scene.

Dan knew friends like Piatowsky didn't cross your path often in life. Straightening his shoulders, he walked into the crowds and the anonymous night.

He returned to the precinct, turned in his badge, shook hands all round and headed to the saloon to drown his regrets with his colleagues.

7

Ellie pounded her fists into the ball of bread dough, kneading it until it was smooth and elastic enough to satisfy her standards. Dusting it with flour, she covered it with a cloth and set it near the warm stove to rise. She cleaned off the marble work-top, fetched butter from the refrigerator, and began to prepare the pastry for the *tarte tatin*. The apples were already sliced, and the aroma of sugar syrup caramelizing gently on the stove filtered pleasingly through the kitchen.

It was eight-thirty in the morning and she had already been to the wholesale produce market at six to collect the day's vegetables. The chef, Chan, would take care of buying the meats, and later he would telephone her and they would discuss the day's specials. Depending on what he'd bought, she would write up the menus, then rush down to Kinko's to get copies made, dash back again and open up in time for the lunch trade at eleven, for which she did the cooking and Jake acted as server.

Jake was dark, handsome, and an actor. In LA everybody was really somebody else, Ellie thought. Even herself. She was a baker, and also a waiter and a manager and general Girl Friday. Anything but the proper chef she had been trained for, because lunches were mostly omelettes and soups and salads. Meanwhile, as usual, she would open up at nine-thirty and serve coffee and muffins, eggs and toast, a simple break-fast that brought in a nice bit of trade and added to the weekly takings. Except the darned coffee machine wasn't work-ing again.

The phone rang. Dusting her hair back with a floury hand, she picked it up. 'Ellie's Place'. Her deep sweet voice had a rising intonation that always made her sound as though she were happy to hear from whoever it was. Even Chan.

'Morning, Chan.' She steeled herself, waiting for the daily barrage of complaints from the chef.

'They had no veal this morning. D'you believe that? *No veal.* What kind of butcher is this, anyway? We get another supplier today, or I quit.'

'Chan, they are the only ones whose quality you say is perfect. So they don't have veal today. Why not try pork instead?'

'Pork? Mmm, maybe I do some ravioli, like Chinese dumplings, with a special hoisin sauce . . .'

'You got it, Chan. Just tell me what it's called, then I can go to Kinko's.'

'It is Ravioli Chan.'

Ellie rolled her eyes; what else would he call it? She wrote down the list of dishes he proposed for the evening's menu. 'See you later.' She rang off thankful to have stalled him from quitting for another day, then walked through the café, switched on the lights and turned the *Closed* sign to *Open*. It was, she thought, sighing happily, just another day.

Back at the work-station, she poured the caramelized sugar into the cast-iron *tatin* skillets, arranged the apple slices in concentric circles over it, then topped them with the pastry, ready to be cooked and served warm later that evening.

She was thinking about Chan. He was half-Asian, short, black-haired and dark-eyed, talented and temperamental, but he gave the French cooking an exotic edge that lifted it above the usual. His assistant, the twenty-year-old sous-chef Terry, with the short-cropped blond hair, bland blue eyes and solid methodical ways of his German ancestors, came from Minnesota; and Ellie thought he probably would have worked anywhere, just as long as he could stay in sunny California. 'I can't believe there's no snow,' he'd say, amazed, when everyone else was grumbling about the few days of rain.

There was also a dish-stacker, busboy, washer-upper, cleaner-upper, who changed so often they'd given up trying to remember a name; and whoever was employed this week was known, generically, as 'the kid'. Then there was Jake, who came in to help at lunchtimes, and whenever they were short-handed. And of course, there was Maya. She had been Ellie's friend since college and for a while they'd shared an apartment together in Venice, while they 'found' themselves.

Maya was a blonde goddess, a knockout, with a helmet of golden hair, whisky-brown eyes fringed with long dark lashes, and a voluptuous tightly-toned body which turned heads no matter how she disguised it in trailing skirts and long sweaters. Ellie said Maya attracted more customers to the café than the food, the four days a week she worked there. The other three days she was working on a screenplay. Something about evil this week, she'd said. Soon, she knew she would sell it, then she'd give up waitressing for ever.

'Then I'll just come and spend my money here,' she'd told Ellie. 'And I'll make sure to bring all my important new friends with me. You'll be made, just you wait and see.'

Meanwhile, they were both waiting, and waitressing, and hoping.

Dan backed his brand-new white Explorer into a tight spot on Main Street. The California sun blazed down, bronzed people in shorts and t-shirts whizzed by him on roller-blades or simply took it easy at sidewalk cafés, and the parking meter still had half an hour left on it. It was early April and he'd seen the weather back east on TV: they'd just had another two inches of snow. Feeling that life wasn't too bad after all, he strolled into Ellie's Place.

The red-haired young woman behind the coffee machine gave him a dazzling smile of welcome that seemed to spread from one pretty diamond-studded ear to the other.

'Be right with you,' she called. 'The coffee machine's acting up again though, so if it's caffeine you're after, you might want to try Starbucks. It's on the next block.'

'Juice is fine. It's eggs I really want, scrambled with a toasted bagel.'

'Okay.' She wrote the order and headed toward the kitchen in the back.

It was just a tiny store-front café done out like a Parisian bistro. The mirrors covering the walls were old and foggy, the bronze sconces were verdigrised, the tables were marble and the chairs cane. A scattering of fresh sawdust covered the tile floor and lace curtains hung from a brass rail half-way up the window, on which the name *Ellie's Place* was inscribed in green shadowed with gold.

Cute, he thought. Like the waitress. She came back carrying cutlery, napkins and a basket of fresh bread covered with a green-checked cloth, and he quickly amended that statement. You could never call a woman as tall as she was 'cute'. And she was no cookie-cutter California girl either.

She gave him another glancing smile as she set the bread in front of him and he noticed a smudge of flour on her cheek. Her eyes were the pale bluish-grey of opals, her nose was freckled and her red hair was bunched through a black baseball cap in a long curly ponytail. It was odd, but he felt he'd seen her somewhere before. He guessed it was because she looked a bit like Julia Roberts.

'Out here on vacation?' She arranged the table-mat and cutlery and folded the green-checked napkin. Her voice was deep and soft as melted chocolate.

'How do you know I don't live here?'

She put her hands on her hips regarding him. 'It's that east-coast pallor. It's a dead give-away. Most people out here have a tan, even if it's fake.'

Dan laughed. 'You mean I'll have to apply bronzer in order to qualify as a native?'

Her long legs covered the distance to the counter in three strides. She picked up the glass of juice and brought it to him. 'Oh, a couple of days at the beach and you'll be fine. Better watch it though. I know it's only April, but the sun is strong.'

He watched her walk back to the kitchen to get the eggs. 'How come you're so pale then?'

'That's my grandmother's doing. She always made me wear a hat when I was a kid, never let me sunbathe. She said with my red hair and freckles it would be like frying myself. And you know what? She was right. Now I'm older and wiser, I thank her every time I look in the mirror. No lines, no sunspots. I'm a lucky woman.'

Ellie smiled at him again as she put the plate of eggs in front of him. Back behind the counter, she cast him a speculative glance.

'Cute', she thought, if you could call a guy that rugged 'cute'. Deep blue eyes that looked as though they had seen it all; strong dark hair, a hawkish nose and blue-stubbled jaw. Lean, broad-shouldered, muscular.

She shrugged regretfully. She didn't have time for men anyway. A career girl was what she was now, and forever would be. She was determined to make her way in the world. Ellie's Place was only her first venture into the restaurant trade; she already had steps two and three planned.

Dan finished his eggs in record time. He glanced at his watch then went to pay his check. 'Thanks', he said with a smile, 'I enjoyed it.'

'Enjoy your vacation,' she called, as he strode to the door.

He stood on the sidewalk, hands in his pockets, taking in the street scene before getting into the white Explorer. Ellie thought he surely had a great walk, confident, sexy.

Putting the thought of sex determinedly from her mind, she concentrated on the problem of the coffee machine. She had already been on the phone twice yesterday, this would make the third call. Maybe today they would send someone out to fix it.

When Jake arrived, she had to dash to Kinko's with the menu. Then she had to go over the week's orders, find out why there was so much waste in the fresh produce. Then there would be the busy lunch trade. After that she would set up the tables for dinner and check with Chan to make sure he was coming in. She would help with the preparations, take a half-hour break for coffee and a muffin, go home, shower, change, and be back at five for the evening's stint as waitress, wine steward, dish-stacker, and any other job that nobody else wanted to take care of.

Sometimes she wondered if she was in the right business. Then, when she'd had a good week, or even a good day, she knew she was. And every night when she fell into bed, exhausted

– and alone – she told herself it would all be worth it and that one day she would be the owner and proprietor of a Michelin-starred restaurant.

So there was absolutely no time, or room, in her life for a cute, blue-eyed rugged guy just passing through on vacation. Or anyone else for that matter. She had her grandmother to take care of and she definitely didn't need a man to complicate her life.

8

Dan drove up the coast, enjoying the way the new car handled, slowing here and there to admire the scenery. The road curved alongside the ocean and he stopped to watch the surfers, remembering when he was sixteen and had spent as much of the year as he could in the water. His mother told him she wondered why his brain wasn't waterlogged, and then, when he'd married his high-school sweetheart at the age of nineteen, his father told him he was sure it was. Dan guessed he'd been right.

Running Horse Ranch lay just to the north of Santa Barbara in an area of gently rolling green hills, that in summer would be scorched to the colour of crusty french bread by the hot California sun. He drove past other wineries, admiring their orderly rows of vines, already bursting into leaf, and the attractive wine-tasting facilities set in manicured gardens, luring travellers to pause and picnic beneath shady oaks while sipping a glass of the house product.

Running Horse Ranch was not quite like that. He got out of the car, and stared at the slopes of shrivelled vines, then picked up a handful of earth, let it trickle through his fingers. It was dustbowl-dry and looked as though it would blow away in the breeze. The tangle of rose bushes at the edge of the rows of vines were an old-fashioned warning signal: aphids attacked the roses first, then the vines. These were covered in bugs of every colour – black, green, red, white.

He groaned out loud. It seemed the only thing he'd got right was when he'd calculated Running Horse would take all his money, plus whatever the banks would lend him, plus all his time and a lot of hard work.

Squaring his shoulders, he climbed back into the car and bounced over the potholes to the top of the hill to inspect his new home.

He'd thought he'd bought a neat little New England-style farmhouse, but this was more Addams Family than Norman Rockwell. The square wooden house hadn't seen a coat of paint in a decade and had faded to a dead grey. A sagging porch ran round it and every window was cracked. He stood for a minute, taking in the rusting remains of the tractor dumped in front, and the pile of debris swirling in a sudden gust of wind that shook the tall pepper tree, showering him with leaves. When the wind stopped, there was just silence. No birds sang, nothing moved. He thought it was a long way from the streets of Manhattan.

The porch steps creaked ominously as he walked across and unlocked the door, wincing when the hinges screamed in rusting agony. Years of dust covered the few bits of broken furniture and ominous trails of droppings led to holes in the baseboards. Standing at the bottom of the rickety staircase, gazing into the eerie shuttered dimness, he could just make out the broken banisters of the upper hall. He cancelled the Addams Family. This was more like something from Stephen King.

Pete Piatowsky's words echoed in his head. 'You're buying a pig in a poke, man,' he'd warned. 'You don't know what you're really getting until you get there.' Was he ever right.

Dan kicked the bottom step, dispiritedly. Wondering which he would have to tackle first, the vines or the house, he went out to look at the winery.

The big red barn housed tall steel fermenting vats, the crushing machinery, and stacks of mouldy-looking oak barrels. The bottling plant in the adjoining shed looked like a Disney cartoon and, like the house, everything was covered in a thick coat of dust.

Gloomily, he walked through the graceful arched gates into the stable courtyard. There was an old tiled fountain in the centre, and scarlet petunias and purple bougainvillaea tumbled picturesquely from clay pots. A long shady patio fronted the stalls, with a couple of old wooden benches meant for lazing away the hot afternoons. It looked exactly the way it had in the photograph when he'd lost his heart to it – a perfect rustic idyll. Betting gloomily that the fountain wouldn't work and the roof would leak and the whole place was about to fall down, Dan took a closer look.

To his surprise, it wasn't too bad. Sure, the paint was blistered and peeling, but the roof looked fine, and the six stalls were in good condition. Cheering up, he decided first thing, he would buy a couple of horses. He hadn't ridden since he was a kid, but they would make the place feel more like home.

He checked the irrigation system. It looked in good shape and he thanked god for that. Water was in short supply in California, and vines needed a lot of water. Without it, he might as well quit now.

There was a satisfied smile on his face as he circled the reedy pond in back of the house, planning on installing carp and mallards and maybe a couple of geese.

He strolled round the porch, saw exactly where to place his chair for that sundown drink and the view, and began to think maybe it wasn't such a pig in a poke after all. All of a sudden, he couldn't wait to tackle it.

He thought regretfully of the attractive young woman at the café. There would be no space in his schedule for romantic dalliance in the near future. Not with all this work to be done.

Arms folded, he surveyed his new home and his neglected acres, assessing the amount of money, water, time and hard labour they would need. He shook his head as Ellie's face and that big smile flashed before his eyes again. There would be no room for romance in his life for a long, long time.

9

The morning after the killing, Buck went into the Madison Avenue branch of the Bank of America. He smiled, satisfied, as he caught sight of himself in the plate-glass window. He might just have emerged from the portals of the Harvard Club, in his conservative tweedy jacket, his button-down blue shirt and glossy brown loafers. They always said a man's background showed, and his mother had surely brought him up to be a gentleman. He laughed out loud just thinking about her, and he was still smiling as he swaggered confidently to the counter, presented his ID and asked to see a current statement of his savings account.

'Certainly, Mr Duveen.'

The female teller gave him a pleasant smile, and he smiled back. No fooling around this time though, the way he had on the train, testing his power. Today, he was practising his charm. He was here on business and besides, he'd kind of gotten it out of his system. For a while.

He hummed his favourite tune while he waited, thinking how good it felt to know he was in control again. That he possessed such power. The greatest power of all, over life and death. This young teller didn't know how fortunate she was that he wasn't in the mood. His mind was on more important things. His future plans.

'Here you are, Mr Duveen.' She handed over the statement. 'Anything else I can do for you today?'

He checked quickly. He had exactly thirty-five thousand one hundred and twenty dollars. 'I'd like ten thousand in cash and the remainder switching to a cheque account right away.'

He signed the necessary papers, took charge of a temporary cheque book, pocketed the ten thousand and walked out onto Madison Avenue, feeling master of all he surveyed. Then he strolled round the corner to the Four Seasons, where he had a couple of drinks to celebrate. He had an excellent lunch of grilled sea bass and salad, pretending to peruse a copy of the Wall Street Journal while taking in the power-lunch scene.

He thought, idly, how he might change the lives of any of these heavy-hitters, in their European suits and Hermès silk ties. All he had to do was find out where they lived. The country house would be best . . . catch the wife alone . . . it was easy. The man opposite, for instance, with the blonde trophy wife half his age, diamonds, Chanel . . . He studied her, eyes half-closed, wondering what it would be like to have a woman like that, ripping off her expensive clothes, biting the diamonds out of her ears, the woman screaming, begging . . .

The woman felt the heat of his gaze and looked up at him. Their eyes met for a second, then hers widened in alarm. She stiffened, said something to her husband who swung round angrily.

Buck didn't even glance their way. He paid cash for his lunch, including a lavish tip, then walked past them out of the restaurant and back to Madison.

He inspected the windows at Barneys, then went to the men's department and bought himself some clothing suitable for California. A couple of lightweight Italian suits, pants, a jacket. The salesman guided him in choosing the right shirts, a couple of interesting ties, plus shorts and polo shirts, underwear and socks.

Three pairs of new loafers later, he discovered he'd spent a small fortune, but not to worry. Soon, there would be plenty more.

He went to a nearby luggage shop, purchased a couple of bags and put his new stuff right in them.

'Leavin' town in a hurry, huh?' the salesman grinned. 'Hope the wife isn't on your tail.'

Buck levelled an icy glare at him and the young man backed quickly away. 'Just jokin' buddy, just jokin'.'

Buck grabbed his cases and went out onto the sidewalk. A smartly-dressed woman had just hailed a cab and it swerved into the kerb. He elbowed past, using his suitcases to block her way.

'My God,' she exploded, 'I thought I'd seen everything New York had to offer, but this is too much . . .'

Buck grinned as he slammed the door, 'You ain't seen nothing yet, lady,' he promised. Then he told the driver to take him to Penn Station.

The train left for Chicago at six-thirty, so he went into the bar and had a couple more drinks. When he finally took his seat and the big locomotive pulled out of the terminal, he felt excited as a child leaving on vacation. He was on his way to LA, at last.

The only thing bothering him about going back to California was his mother. Over a couple more drinks, he had plenty of time to brood over her, and their life together.

10

Buck was known as a Mama's boy in the small town near Santa Cruz in Northern California, where they lived in a pin-neat Victorian house, painted yellow with white gingerbread trim.

People said Delia Duveen must have been in her forties when she had him, because all the other mothers at the PTA and Little League games were in their twenties and Delia looked three decades older.

And she never let that boy out of her sight. It was always, Buck come here, Buck do this, Buck do that. Buck was not allowed to play with other kids after school because he had to do his homework and his piano practice. And then there were the chores, bringing in the firewood and stacking the logs in the woodshed in the neat rows she liked, large ones at the bottom, small in the middle, and smallest and kindling at the top.

Saturdays, he got to mow the rectangle of lawn in front of the house, and then to wash her car, an immaculately-kept old Plymouth. And on Sundays, she drove him to church in that shiny, polished automobile.

He sat quietly beside her, short-cropped red hair combed flat to his head, wearing a dark-blue blazer and starched blue shirt, with his striped tie neatly knotted. Plump Delia wore pastel dresses in summer, and a nice tailored grey suit in winter, and she always wore a hat. Nothing *froufrou* and frivolously feminine, just a plain straw with a ribbon, or a dark felt with a feather. She bought new ones every season, but somehow they always looked exactly like the old ones.

Delia and Buck never ate supper companionably at the dinette set in the kitchen. That was only for breakfast. Evenings, they sat opposite each other in the small, over-furnished dining room, beneath the blaze of a mock-crystal chandelier, sipping plain water from a glass because she disapproved of soda pop, and anyhow would never have allowed soda cans on the table.

Her meals were carefully thought out, a different one every night of the week, she was proud to say. But it meant that each night of the week, Buck knew exactly what he was going to get to eat. And he didn't like any of it. The pot roasts with watery spinach; the grey fish under a blanket of gooey white sauce; and the everlasting jello with a blob of Reddiwhip – a different colour and flavour Monday through Sunday. He craved burgers and fries, tacos, ice cream and hot dogs.

Buck Duveen hated his home, he hated his food, hated his life. And he loathed his mother with an overpowering force that from a young age had made him itch to kill her. But to Delia Duveen and the neighbours he was the perfect son. 'Wish my boys were like him,' the neighbouring mothers said to each other when their own kids were wreaking havoc.

Buck's grades were good, he was a model student, and he worked hard. But inside he burned with a silent rage. At school he joined in the guy-talk of how far they'd made out on the back seat, about the parties and drinking and the fooling around. And he sheltered his massive ego behind a wall of pretend indifference.

He knew a liquor store in town where the owner was so old, it was easy to steal a bottle of vodka. He'd sneak it into his room, prop a chair under the door handle, because his mother didn't permit a lock, then lie on his bed, staring at the ceiling, knocking it back, neat.

He pictured his mother naked and himself with a knife in his hand, ripping her from end to end, seeing her guts spill out. He pictured the high-school sweethearts taking off their cute little sweaters for him, then screaming as he did unthinkable things to them. He pictured his strong hands around soft throats and a surge of power rippled through him. With the vodka in him, in his drunken fantasies, he *was* power. He was omnipotent.

He'd never really known his father, Rory Duveen. His mother had divorced him when Buck was three years old. She'd implied that she had no time for what went on in the bedroom. Not in plain graphic words, because Sex was a word with a definite capital S in her mind. S for sin. S for sickening. S for shame. So Rory had left. He'd given Delia everything he had: the house and all his money, in settlement. He wanted nothing to do with her or her child.

The only thing Buck remembered about his father was his singing in church. There was a particular hymn that was his favourite, because it was the kind you sang loud and strong.

> *Onward Christian soldiers,*
> *Marching as to war,*
> *With the cross of Jesus*
> *Going on before.*

Buck could hear Rory's voice in his head, see that cross he sang about . . . somehow it made him feel like a god, crusading for his rights. To him, the cross was a symbol of his power and masculinity. The sign belonged to him, and to his father.

Buck thought he would escape from Delia when he went away to college, down the coast at UCLA Santa Barbara. By now, he was a clever young man, tall, strongly-built with rich copper-red hair and deep-set dark eyes that shifted slyly away when he spoke to you. Still, he was attractive and he got himself a date the first week. She wasn't available for a second date though, told her friends he was 'creepy'. Same happened with another girl, then another. So he found himself a hooker, paid her twenty bucks. It was over in seconds so he beat her up, took back his money and kicked her out of his car.

Hookers were easy, he was the one in control. Except not sexually. Sometimes they laughed at him and it drove him into a frenzy of hate and violence.

Delia kept him short of money and he was working two jobs to pay his way through college. He felt demeaned by it, and by the shabby old wreck of a car he drove. He wanted Delia's money and he wanted rid of her.

One night, after a bottle of vodka, he saw the light. A voice in his head told him all he had to do was remove his mother from his life. Then he would be free, he would inherit the house and her money. He would be rich.

He made his plans carefully, going over them again and again. He even did a test run one night, driving from the campus at Santa Barbara and sneaking up to the house, though he didn't go in. No one was around, no one saw him. He knew it would work because everybody trusted him. Besides, he was smarter than the local police.

When the night of the killing arrived he was excited and happy. Everything went to plan. She never heard him come in, never spoke, never screamed. Only her puzzled eyes, bugging from her head, had fixed mutely on his, while his strong hands squeezed the life out of her.

In that moment of empowerment, when his energy buzzed through his veins in a single electrical jolt, he felt invincible. Submitting to an overwhelming compulsion, he carved the sign of the cross into her forehead. He looked at it, pleased. It was his signature.

Before he left, he jimmied the back door, ransacked the place, took the money from her purse so the cops would think she'd been robbed. Then he headed out of town.

The next morning, he drove back again. He stopped at the local store and told the owner, whom he had known all his life, he'd not really intended to come home this weekend, but he'd been calling his mom and gotten no reply. He was worried.

He called again from the payphone at the store. 'Hey,' he said, with a puzzled frown, 'it's really weird. She's always there. At this time of day, y'know.'

The store owner did know. Everybody knew Delia. Her movements were regular as clockwork.

Buck went home and 'found' the mutilated body. He called the cops, distraught, his voice choked with sobs. The evidence of a fight was all around: a table tipped over, vases smashed, her purse flung to the ground. The store owner corroborated his tale. And besides, Buck had planned his alibi perfectly. He told them he was at a concert in Santa Barbara the previous night, he still had the ticket stub in his pocket.

Buck was always a good kid, people said sympathetically, a

bit of a loner, but he surely looked after his mom. He was never even a suspect.

He inherited the house and the bank accounts. He wasn't a millionaire but the money was his to spend as he wanted. He bought a three-year-old Porsche convertible, a Rolex and some smart clothes. With his mother out of the way, he could play the big-shot he'd always wanted to be.

During the time Buck was in Hudson, what remained of that money had been held on deposit at a good interest rate that had brought him enough extra funds to pay for his pizzas and vodka. Now, it would be put to better use.

The hell with Delia, he thought, staring out into the dark night speeding past the train window. She'd only got what she deserved. The main function of her life, and her death, had been to show him his own power. He'd found killing easy after that. No need for much planning, the way he'd had to with her. Random killings, without motive, a stranger in a strange place, were almost impossible to solve.

He'd had the formula down pretty good, until the old woman had him locked up. Now her turn had come to join the élite. She was as good as his. And, like he had with Delia, he would take his time about it, plan things carefully. This time, he meant to really enjoy it.

11

Dan exited the freeway and halted at the Stop sign at the
turn to Olive Mill Road, in Montecito. The Explorer's engine
idled perfectly as he waited for the oncoming traffic to slow.
Glancing in the rearview mirror, he observed uneasily the
yellow jeep coming up too fast. He couldn't believe the driver
would just keep on going until, with a squeal of brakes, she
rear-ended him.

He thumped his fist angrily against the steering-wheel. He'd
had the car less than a week and the stupid woman had already
screwed it up. Had she been oblivious to the Stop sign? And
the traffic? Blood boiling, he leapt from the car.

'What are you? Blind?' he yelled. 'Or just crazy? Couldn't
you see me sitting at the Stop sign, waiting for a break in the
traffic? I guess you just meant to go straight through. And god
help anyone who got in your way.'

'No I did not,' Ellie yelled back hotly, climbing from the jeep.
'And you might at least be civilized about this.'

'Civilized? Lady, I've had this vehicle exactly five days! You
want me to be *civilized?*' He stared angrily at the dent in the
back of the Explorer, then turned and glared at her. She was
wearing baggy white shorts and a t-shirt, and, even angry, he
noticed that her slender brown legs went on for ever. Her red
hair whipped round her face in the breeze and she pushed it
back impatiently, then glared back at him.

He said, surprised, 'Oh. It's you.'

Ellie suddenly recognized him. It was the rugged blue-eyed
machoman. She wondered how she had ever thought him sexy.
'And it's you,' she said coldly. 'And if you don't behave in

a civilized fashion, I'll call the police.' He grinned at her, a mocking little smile that showed off his perfect white teeth and for some reason annoyed her.

He said, 'Lady, I *am* the police.' Then he remembered. He held up his hand. 'Delete that statement. I *was* the police. Now I'm just Dan Citizen who's mad as hell because his new car has been smacked up. Can you blame me?'

Ellie heaved a regretful sigh. 'Of course I can't blame you.' She looked disconsolately at the wound on the Explorer, then turned and gave the ancient jeep a kick. 'Oh, *you*,' she muttered, scowling.

Dan clapped an unbelieving hand to his forehead. And he had thought her 'cute' when he first saw her.

'I apologize,' Ellie said stiffly. 'My hair blew across my face just for that second. It's horribly dangerous, I know, and I usually tie it back when I'm driving. It was all my fault.'

She fished her bag from the car and took out a card. 'Here's my name and address. And my registration and insurance. I guess that'll take care of things.'

Dan looked at the name: Ellie Parrish Duveen. It had a familiar ring to it. She was looking expectantly at him and he said, 'Don't I know you from somewhere?'

'The café. You came in for eggs, no coffee.'

'But I know your name. I used to live round here when I was a kid. Didn't you go to surf camp one summer?'

She stared suspiciously at him. 'A long time ago.'

'I think I taught you to surf. You were just a little kid, long and stringy with a mop of red hair. I remember now, it was always getting in your eyes even then.'

Ellie inspected him warily for a minute. Of course, how could she forget . . . he'd been the heart-throb of the beach . . .

The big wide smile lit up her eyes as she remembered. 'We called you Danny Boy. I think I even had a crush on you. All the girls did, even though you were an older man.'

'I was eighteen years old. And you must have been about eight or nine.' They looked at each other, smiling. 'How time flies,' he said finally. 'And how about that *Danny Boy*?' he added, wincing.

'I seem to remember your Irish eyes were always smiling then,' Ellie retorted smartly. 'What happened since, to make you so angry at the world?'

He shook his head at the female way she'd just managed to twist things round. 'No man's eyes, Irish or otherwise, *smile*, when his brand-new vehicle has just been severely dented by another driver. Female and old acquaintance notwithstanding.'

She laughed then, a soft rich sound. 'Couldn't fool you on that, huh? I just thought I'd give it a try. It always works on Seinfeld.'

'This is real life, Ellie Parrish Duveen,' he reminded her, busily writing down his new address for her, and the name of his insurance company. 'Business is business.'

'Tell me about it.' She sighed dramatically. Then she read his address. 'Running Horse Ranch,' she remarked, surprised. 'It's been on the market for years. Don't tell me you bought it?'

'Yup. Why?' He was beginning to suspect he knew the answer.

She hesitated, avoiding his eyes. He obviously hadn't heard about the jinx. 'Oh, no reason. It's really pretty around there.' She glanced at the traffic circling them. 'We'd better get going. It was nice to meet you again, Dan Cassidy. Good luck with the winery. Maybe I'll be able to buy some wine from you before too long.'

'I'll take you up on that,' he promised, as she got back into the jeep.

He eyed her through the rear-view mirror as he drove off. Cute was definitely the wrong word. If she hadn't wrecked his new van, he would have called her beautiful. He sighed regretfully, then put her out of his mind and drove to the cottage he'd rented at the beach. Just until he got his property in shape. It shouldn't take long, a month at the most.

It wasn't until later, sitting alone on the deck of his newly-rented beach house, enjoying the view of the ocean, that he remembered who she was. One of the mega-rich Parrishes who lived in a palace up on Hot Springs Road. Lottie Parrish had been one of the society leaders in the area, head of all the smart committees, opening her fantastic house for charity balls and garden parties. He seemed to remember talk of a butler and uniformed housemaids and a French chef.

He wondered why Ellie was driving the beat-up old jeep when she could easily have afforded a new Mercedes if she'd wanted. He guessed she enjoyed playing at being a regular working girl, like everyone else. Except, remembering her opal eyes, and her voice, soft as poured chocolate, he thought, Ellie Parrish Duveen definitely was not like everyone else.

The next evening, he was out on his deck overlooking the ocean. He'd put in a long, hard day walking his property, all dried-out forty acres of it. He'd been told a manager was supposed to be looking after the place for the previous owner, but he'd disappeared, and it seemed to Dan no one had set foot on the ranch in years. That morning he'd taken out ads for a winemaker, and spoken to a building contractor about fixing up the house. Tomorrow, he would start work on getting the stables into shape.

He poured a glass of wine and stared moodily at the opalescent sky. The colour reminded him of Ellie Parrish Duveen's eyes. 'Ah, the hell with work,' he said, fishing her card out of his shirt pocket and dialling her number.

'Ellie's', she said. Just the single word in that soft voice made him smile with pleasure.

'Can I help you?' She sounded more than a little distracted, as though she had the receiver pressed to her ear and was doing three other things besides talk on the telephone.

'I just thought I'd let you know the Explorer isn't as bad as it first looked. Nothing the body shop can't hammer out tomorrow.'

'I'm glad to hear it, Danny Boy.' There was laughter in her voice. 'And so, I'm sure, will my insurance company.'

'I was just wondering . . .'

Ellie stopped inserting figures into the cash register and fiddling with change. She pressed the receiver closer to her ear, shutting out the background music, the chatter and clatter of dishes. She was smiling as she said, 'What *exactly* were you wondering?'

Maya stopped to listen, expertly balancing plates of salad with hazelnut vinaigrette. Was Ellie actually giving a man the time of day instead of her usual brush-off?

Dan said, 'For instance, can you tell me why, though Montecito is on the edge of the Pacific, the sun sets over the mountains and not the ocean?'

'That's because the coastline faces south at that point and the Santa Ynez mountains run east to west. Confusing, I know, for newcomers, but a fact of nature, Mr Cassidy. Anyhow, you can't fool me, you already knew that. In any case, what are you doing watching the sun set over the ocean? I thought you were inland, at Running Horse Ranch?'

He heaved a regretful sigh, remembering the way it looked. 'Unfortunately the ranch house needs a bit of work before it can be termed habitable, except by rats and gophers and a few swallows up in the chimney. Humans demand a little more in cleanliness and comfort. That's why I'm in a rented cottage on Padaro Lane, watching sunsets, all alone . . .'

'And lonely,' she finished for him, glaring at Maya who was still eavesdropping.

Maya rolled her brown eyes, intrigued, then hurried off to serve the salads. Ellie was definitely flirting.

Dan said, 'You've got it, Ms Parrish Duveen. And that brings me to my other question. I know you're a busy working woman . . .'

'And you're about to become a busy working man . . .' she was still smiling, hugging the phone.

'True. In the meantime, I guess even you must get a night off? I thought it might be a good opportunity to check out the competition. Say dinner at *Chinois*?'

Ellie laughed at the idea. 'Danny Boy, I'm no competition for them. I'm just a speck in LA's ocean of little cafés. *They* are the big leagues.'

Then she gave the stock reply that she gave any guy who asked her out these days. 'Look, I'm sorry, I just don't have any free time right now. Maybe later . . .'

Her voice trailed off, and he said quickly. 'Right. I understand. Work comes first.'

'Thanks anyway,' she added, a touch regretfully; but she could already see customers looking restless, wondering why their food had not arrived. 'I've got to go.'

'Sure. Anyway, it was nice to meet you. Again.'

'Goodbye,' she said, sounding edgy as she put down the phone.

Maya stood, arms folded, chin belligerently sticking out. She always kept a worried eye on her friend, but even she hadn't been able to penetrate the work ethic of the past year and persuade her to take time out for a social life. That's why she was excited when she caught on to the fact that Ellie was talking nicely, *to a man.*

'You showed him the door pretty firmly. Did I miss something? Or was someone asking you out on a date?'

Ellie nodded. 'He was.'

'And?' Maya held up a protesting hand; she already knew the answer. 'No, don't tell me. You said you were too busy. For god's sake, woman, you can't go on like this. Celibacy is okay, if that's what you choose, but at least share a few hours conversation with the guy. There's real life out there, Ellie. I mean, there's got to be something besides this.' She swept her arms wide, knocking over a bottle of wine. 'Now look at what I've done. It's all your fault!'

Ellie grinned, she knew Maya's explosive temperament, she'd lived with it long enough. 'I simply told him I was too busy right now,' she said, calmly picking up the bottle and getting a cloth to mop up the wine. 'And if you paid a little more attention to the customers, instead of eavesdropping on my conversations, you'd notice that table three is waiting for menus.'

Maya glared at her, then flounced off in a huff. 'The lamb couscous is off tonight,' she announced icily, venting her ire on the customers as she handed out menus. The three men at the table stared at her, astonished, and she grinned shamefacedly. 'But Chef Chan's Peppered Ahi is divine,' she added sweetly. 'I recommend it *personally*.'

She only wished she could have recommended a guy for Ellie, and a night out instead of the everlasting work.

12

Maya Morris had been Ellie's best friend since college. She had arrived in Phoenix from the east coast, a Manhattan Jewish girl through and through – blonde, beautiful, know-it-all, and with a fast mouth. And Ellie had arrived from the west coast, all tumbling red hair and long legs, perfect manners, clumsy, big-hearted, and with a wild look of new-found freedom in her wonderful eyes that spelled trouble, even to an *habituée* of 'trouble', like Maya. It was as though they recognised each other, instantly. They were soul mates, two of a kind.

In a couple of weeks, they'd found themselves an apartment off-campus and began to do what Maya called 'throwing parties' and what Ellie called, 'giving a little soirée' Which in plain terms meant everybody brought a bottle and those who were musicians played piano and guitars and anything else they happened to bring with them, as well as blasting rock on the hi-fi and dancing up a storm. After a month, the landlord threw them out.

Undaunted, they found another place, a house this time where the noise would be less noticeable, and anyhow the neighbours were fellow-students. Then Ellie, high on freedom, went out and traded in her Pathfinder for a Harley. Metallic-scarlet, flashy with polished chrome, and hot.

Maya was rocking slowly back and forth on the old floral swing-seat on the front porch when Ellie roared up.

'How about this?' Ellie yelled over the space-shuttle roar. 'Great, huh?'

Maya stopped her rocking. She had a splitting headache from the tequila last night and was not at her best. But, ever fashionable, she tuned right in. 'We'll need leathers.'

'Right.'

It was terrific, the way they knew each other's minds. If one did something, the other picked right up on it, no questions asked. Maya climbed on the back and they shot off downtown to the bike shop. An hour later they emerged, sleek as panthers in tight black leather pants, fringed jackets, boots, gauntlets and sinister black and silver helmets.

'Perfect,' was Maya's comment.

And that's how they became known as the 'Arizona State Hogettes', famous for their speed, their soirées, their sartorial splendour and general outrageousness.

All in all, they behaved like kids who'd never been away from home before, wild with freedom and completely irresponsible. Because they were bright, they got away with a minimum of classes, until the boom came down and the dean threatened expulsion, and Miss Lottie and Mr Morris showed up, furious.

They'd caught them as they zoomed up on the Harley, long hair streaming behind them in the wind, singing at the tops of their voices, shrieking with laughter as Ellie executed a neat u-turn, tight on centrifugal force, then screeched to a halt.

'Whoawhoawhoa,' Maya yelled, vaulting off the back. 'How about that, then?'

'How about that,' her father's voice repeated grimly from the porch.

Maya's eyes met Ellie's and they swung round, taking in Miss Lottie, regal and rigid with fury in a smart beige suit, and Michael Morris, icy-eyed and businesslike in grey pinstripes, standing on the ramshackle front porch, looking as out of place as Hells Angels at a presidential banquet.

'Shit,' Maya said softly, glancing at Ellie.

'We're in for it now,' Ellie muttered back. 'Think you can talk your way out?'

Maya shook her head gloomily. 'Not a chance. How about you?'

Ellie took a deep breath. 'I'll give it a try.'

She bounded up the front steps, beaming. 'Well, hi there, Miss Lottie. What a surprise.' She stopped, uncertainly. In all her life she had never seen her grandmother look at her that way, sort of hurt and disappointed, as well as angry. And she had never, *never* before, not put her arms round her and given her a big hug. Ellie did it anyway, while Maya watched, admiring her balls.

'Boy,' she murmured, when Miss Lottie did not hug back, 'are we in trouble.'

'I've come to take you home, Ellie,' Miss Lottie said coldly. 'Mr Morris agrees with me, that there's no point in you girls staying at college if you're not going to learn anything. And so, of course, does the Dean.'

'But Gran . . .'

'You're forgetting your manners, Ellie. Please say hello to Mr Morris.'

Ellie shook hands, smiling uncertainly at Maya's father. 'There's nothing for it but to apologise, to both of you,' she said humbly. 'Maya agrees with me on that.'

'Sure,' Maya mumbled in the background. 'Hi, Dad. Hi, Miss Lottie.'

She waved a limp hand, eyeing Ellie, hoping for a miracle.

'Gran?' Real tears stood in Ellie's eyes and she touched Miss Lottie's arm uncertainly. 'I didn't realize . . . I mean I didn't know how I'd upset you. I'm sorry, truly I am.'

She meant every word of it, Maya could tell, and tears pricked her own eyes. 'Oh, hell, Dad,' she said, hurling herself up the steps and into his unwilling arms. 'We only meant to have fun.'

Shaking his head, Mr Morris glanced down at his beautiful daughter. 'I guess you did, punkin,' he agreed. 'But somehow you just forgot about work.'

Then they had all gone out to lunch and Miss Lottie and Michael Morris had decided on a three-month probationary period, with mandatory good grades, and the pressure was off. Except this time they'd shouldered their responsibilities and gone to classes, worked nights in the library and gotten those decent marks. Then, since they did everything together, they had both fallen in love.

Maya's was a visiting professor from London, all tweeds and a pipe and argyle socks; and Ellie's was Italian, an artist in residence. Young, sexy and built like Michelangelo's David.

That had lasted a whole year, until their lovers returned to their respective countries and, to the girls' shock, their wives, leaving them devastated and in floods of tears.

'So much for men,' Maya had said bitterly. Then Ellie had pulled herself together. 'Think of it this way,' she'd said, 'we're free again. Have you ever been to San Francisco?'

And they'd shot off on the scarlet Harley, across the Arizona desert to California, free as birds and giddy with youth and enjoyment, for a final summer of total irresponsibility, before settling into their senior year and hard work and graduation.

They had fallen in and out of love several times since then, but only one was serious. Ellie had met Steve Cohen at a party in SoHo given by a friend of Maya's. He was tall and lean, handsome in a predatory sort of way, and an intellectual. And he'd swept her off her too-large feet. Overnight, Ellie changed from a slick, sexy dresser, to black turtlenecks and long black skirts. She'd dragged her hair back in a tight thick braid and wore Doc Martens at all times. It was all terribly exciting and sensual and she couldn't get enough of him.

Maya knew Ellie always led with her heart and, in typical fashion, it was head over heels, all or nothing; but she also knew he wasn't worth it. But she went right along with it, hanging out with the SoHo crowd, while Ellie went to culinary school, and she attended classes in creative writing at Columbia.

Ellie always said it was the New York winter that killed her plans of marriage to Steve. Either that or he was always too busy, pursuing a new career as an art dealer. It was his turn for an overnight change: from cords and leather-patched jackets to Hugo Boss and Calvin Klein suits. Either way, the winter storms kept them apart, and so did his new, upwardly mobile social life. Ellie was wounded, but typically she took it on the chin. The turtlenecks and long skirts were made redundant. Broken-hearted, she took off to Paris to gain culinary experience instead.

When she returned to California, Maya soon followed.

'Why put up with frost when the sun shines all the time?' She'd called Ellie on the phone. She was on a flight the next day and the two of them rented an apartment in Venice Beach, while they looked around at the world, and the men, and the job opportunities, and decided how to play out their lives.

Maya wasn't at all sure she'd found the answer yet, but Ellie certainly had. Whether it was because money suddenly became tight, or not, Ellie shouldered responsibility like a pro. With her background, brains and looks, she had a dozen different career opportunities. But Ellie knew what she wanted. Her own café.

It had taken her over a year of sheer, teeth-gritted hard work to pull it together, and that on a shoestring. But together it was. And Ellie was not about to let it fail, even if she worked all hours that God sent. And that, Maya thought, was where the problem lay.

When the café finally closed, she stayed on to help Ellie clear up.

'You want my advice, hon,' she said when they'd finished and were sitting over a glass of fruity merlot, hacking chunks off the wheel of Parmesan and sticking it on slices of baguette. 'Call him back. Say yes, I would like to have dinner with you after all.' She took an enormous bite of the Parmesan sandwich, rolling her eyes in appreciation. 'I promise you it's *easy*. And I know you'll enjoy it as much as I'm enjoying this.'

'Wanna bet?' Ellie chewed her sandwich morosely. She was too tired even to think about Dan Cassidy. 'I've just got too much to do.'

Maya shrugged, she knew when she was beaten. 'Okay, I tried. And I'll keep on trying. But we've got to get you out of this rut, woman, before you forget you *are* a woman. Anyway, I'm off, I'm meeting Greg at,' she glanced at her watch, 'Right now!' Picking up her purse she headed for the door.

'Who's Greg?' Ellie called after her, curious.

Maya paused, a hand on the door. 'Greg is a writer. A *published* writer. He's giving me some tips on structure.' She grinned. 'I'm not sure whether he means mine or his. He's also a very nice man with some very nice friends. Maybe you'd like to meet one of them,' she added hopefully.

'Goodnight, Maya.' Ellie pushed her out the door. 'See you tomorrow. Have fun.'

She was smiling as she carried their dishes back into the kitchen. But there was work to be done, and she would stay there until she'd finished it.

It was late, and Dan was thinking that a cosy cottage overlooking the ocean could be very lonely with no one else to marvel at the sunset. No one else to share the sound of the surf crashing, to sniff the clean salt air and say how great it felt after New York's traffic fumes and LA's smog. No one but him to admire the romantic moon riding high in a flawless, star-filled sky, and the silver path cast across the water, all the way to the horizon.

Moonlight and silence had not featured much in his life. He was restless, missing his job, the action, the big city.

It was not meant to be a substitute, but he decided that tomorrow, first thing, he would go to the local animal shelter and get himself a dog.

13

It was one in the morning before Ellie got home. Her back ached and her feet ached and there were tight little ripples of tension in her neck.

Kicking off her shoes, she thought wistfully of Dan Cassidy's invitation. Dinner out? The idea was laughable. *She* was the one who organized and served dinners. *She* ate hers in the café kitchen, not in smart restaurants.

Besides, she was afraid of getting involved. Too much was at stake. Everything she had and could borrow was invested in Ellie's Place, and that meant her whole life, her *future*. She was determined to prove herself, though to whom, she hadn't yet figured out. And most of all, she had to make enough money to take care of her grandmother.

Her little house was cosy and welcoming. There was a poky little entry hall with a small sitting room to the left, furnished with a few antiques from Journey's End. A pair of silver candlesticks stood on the beat-up-looking pine mantel with some framed photographs of Miss Lottie and Maria, and of course, Bruno. A pretty Venetian mirror hung over the mantel, and an antique French giltwood console with a large faience urn of jungle-red tulips, stood against one wall. There was a glass-topped coffee table piled with books, a bronze silk-skirted side table holding a nineteenth-century lamp with an amber shade, and half a dozen old paintings scattered across the walls. With a comfortable old cream-linen-covered sofa, a couple of chairs and small tables, the tiny room was crammed to the hilt. Not another thing could be squeezed into it.

On the other side of the hall, the walls of the dining area

were painted her favourite forest green, with the earthquake cracks showing white plaster in the corners. There was a round travertine marble table and half a dozen old wheelback chairs, a fake ficus tree in a terracotta pot, and more paintings.

An archway led into the little white-tiled kitchen which was immaculate, mostly because she never used it except to fix a cup of tea.

Stairs led steeply up to the one large bedroom and bath. Comfortable, lived-in, this was her place. The canopied bed had been her parents', only then it had been draped in Indian shawls and bright spangled sari fabrics in gold and orange and purple. Now it was more chaste in creamy gauze, and piled with pillows. She'd tossed several beautiful Persian rugs one on top of the other until they overlapped, in a pleasing mosaic of soft colour and pattern. The night tables were inlaid Italian marble and the lamps were simple urns with biscuit-colour shades.

There was an antique pine dresser with a silver tray on top containing her make-up, a bottle of *Eau d'Issey* – her favourite perfume – and a photo of her parents; and the comfortable pink chenille robe that she'd had since she was seventeen and couldn't bear to part with was tossed over the striped chaise near the window.

It was simple, pleasing, and it was all her.

She took a shower, pulled on an old Lakers t-shirt and a pair of white sweat-socks and sat in front of the mirror, patting cream into her face and inspecting it for wrinkles. Then she brushed her long hair, wishing it didn't curl, and wondering how she might look with a straight bob.

Wandering to the window, she stared out at her tiny glimpse of ocean reflected under a high-riding moon, imagining a date with Dan Cassidy. Dressing up, a good restaurant, a bottle of wine. Somehow it didn't seem to fit. Still, as she climbed wearily into the canopied bed, it wasn't a bad image to fall asleep with.

Closing her eyes, she recalled the clean jut of his jaw, the deep blue of his eyes and the way they had changed from anger to amusement when he'd recognised her. She told herself, yawning, he probably still thought of her as the freckle-faced kid he'd taught to surf all those years ago. And she fell asleep with the memories of those days filling her dreams, when life was fun and easy, and Miss Lottie was still her old self, and the sun seemed to shine perpetually on them.

The next-morning, she couldn't get that image out of her mind: a bunch of laughing kids at the beach and big handsome Danny Boy, the heart-throb of the coast, fishing them out of the waves when they wiped out. All that afternoon, while she was working, he lurked in the back of her mind. Finally, when it got to evening, she said the hell with it, picked up the phone and called him.

'Hi,' she said. 'It's the surfer girl who rear-ended you.'

Dan's eyebrows shot up and a pleased smile curled the edges of his mouth. 'You again,' he said, shoving the mutt off the chair for the tenth time. And for the tenth time it climbed back up again and sat there, tongue lolling. He stared at it, exasperated. That darned dog had a mind of its own. It also had a barrel-body perched on long skinny legs, a long plumed tail and shaggy, moulting black-and-tan fur. It looked like a moth-eaten fur cushion, but it also had a face exactly like the dog in *Babe*, and right now he could swear it was grinning at him. Suddenly, it gave a mischievous woof, wagged its plumed tail and sent everything crashing from the table.

Ellie held the phone from her ear, then asked, astonished, 'Was that a dog?'

It barked again and Dan said, 'Meet my new friend, Pancho. I couldn't stand watching the sunset alone.'

'That bad, huh?' Ellie was smiling.

'That bad,' he agreed hopefully.

'I was just thinking, the café is closed on Mondays. I usually drive up to see my grandmother. Why don't we have dinner? It doesn't have to be fancy, a barbecue on the beach would be fine.'

Dan laughed. 'You're talking to a city slicker here. I don't think I ever saw a barbecue in Times Square. I'm not sure I'd know what to do with one any more.'

'Then I'll just have to teach you, Danny Boy. You can't be a Californian and not know how to sling a steak onto

63

the grill. Don't worry, I'll bring the fixings, you chill the wine.'

'At least I know something about that.'

'You'd better,' she said, mockingly. 'Around seven then, Monday?'

He gave her the address and said sincerely, 'I'm looking forward to it, Ellie.'

'Me too.' She kept her voice deliberately cool. 'See you tomorrow, Danny Boy. Around seven.'

He waited for her to disconnect, then poured a glass of Cakebread chardonnay. Leaning on the deckrail, he watched the sky turn midnight-blue, until the ocean finally blended into the horizon. He hoped one day he would make a wine as good as the one he was drinking, and wondered where he could buy a barbecue tomorrow. Life felt pretty good.

'You really did it!' Maya, who'd been eavesdropping again, appeared at Ellie's elbow. 'I'll lend you my new Versace. Bright red and clinging. It'll look great with your hair.'

'What are you doing, buying Versace? You can't afford it.'

'Don't you know it's the Sales, woman? They're on everywhere. You want it? It's yours.'

'I'm bringing steaks, he's barbecuing them. Not exactly a Versace kind of night. But thanks anyway, I know your intentions were entirely dishonorable.'

'I just want you to have fun.' There was a wistful edge to Maya's voice, and Ellie could see she really meant it.

A little wellspring of excitement bubbled inside her, like champagne. She'd kept herself on the straight and narrow workpath for over a year now and the thought of a date and a little fun, away from the daily grind of the café, made her feel the way she used to when she was a kid and Saturday morning rolled round, with no school and a long lazy weekend to look forward to.

It was only one evening, but a beach house and a barbecue and Dan Cassidy sounded like a great recipe for relaxation to her. Though of course, romance was out of the question. Subdued, she hurried back into the kitchen to check on the chef and find out why the food was emerging so slowly. If she weren't here the whole place would go to hell in a night, she just knew it.

Much later, after Maya had left and the café was closed, she set up the tables for breakfast, enjoying the temporary peace and quiet. The traffic had slowed on Main Street, and the few passersby never even glanced at the darkened café.

Ellie poured a cup of coffee, then went and sat at a table by the window, gazing into the quiet night. The fog promised by the weatherman was rolling in, as it often did at this time of year, muting the street lights and muffling the city noise, drifting, silent as smoke. She found it soothing after her noisy, hectic day.

Her conversation with Dan Cassidy floated through her mind and she wondered if he'd heard about the jinx on Running Horse yet. She'd hate to be the one to tell him, but no wine had been produced there in years and they said it was a bad-luck place. She hoped for Dan's sake it wasn't true.

Sipping hot coffee, she thought of her mother, wondering wistfully if she would have approved of Dan. It was silly, she told herself, to still long for a mother to share things with. A mother she could ask, 'Am I doing the right thing with the café, and my dedication to succeed?' Or 'What d'you think about this guy?' After all, she was twenty-nine years old, independent and far more worldly-wise than Romany had ever been.

When she was a child, Ellie never realized they were rich, not until she went to school, that is. It was normal to live in a house with forty rooms, to have a butler and a cook, a housekeeper and maids, a chauffeur and a team of gardeners. She'd never known anything else. Besides, Maria and Gustave the butler and the rest of the household staff were her friends, a substitute family for the parents she'd lost, and the aunts and cousins she'd never had. There was just this big tearing gap in her life, where once there had been security. A mother and father. Romany and Rory.

For a long time after the accident, when she closed her eyes she would see their smiling faces again, hear her mother's light gay laugh, her soft voice telling her she loved her; and her father's deep one, singing her to sleep with a favourite Neapolitan song. But gradually their sharp images had faded, and all she was left with were their photographs. She would pore over them, alone in her room, reminding herself of her mother's smile and her father's red hair, knowing she was losing them. And it hurt all over again, because she wanted so badly to keep them with her for ever.

Even now, a grown woman, she missed them. She wondered how different her life might have been had they lived. It was a big unknown and she sighed, thinking about it. Not that her life had been terrible, far from it. Miss Lottie had been a wonderful companion. She'd been grandmother, mother, father, friend and loyal supporter. She'd shown up for the PTA meetings along with the young parents; she'd cheered on the sidelines at the softball games; sent her off to camp and written faithfully every day. She had even bailed her out when she was acting like an idiot, that time at college. Miss Lottie hadn't missed a trick in the parenting book. No one could have done it better.

But there was still something inside Ellie that yearned for the closeness she remembered at the Stagecoach Café, and in the big car, driving home. Just the three of them.

The memory of that day still troubled her. She recalled every detail: the hot leather seat, her mother's white lizard boots, her father's last smile and the wink he'd given her. At least, she told herself she remembered everything: but often, in her dreams, she thought there was something else. Something important out there, on the blackest edge of her dream. Something she could never capture, because just when she thought she'd got it, all she would see was herself sitting by the side of the road. Alone and crying, with the blood running down her face. And the silence all around her. The silence of death.

A shiver ran down her spine, raising goosebumps. She swallowed the hot coffee quickly and carried the empty cup into the kitchen. Making sure the alarm was on, she slammed the door and locked it. The old-fashioned bell tinkled prettily as she sprinted down the street to the multi-storey parking lot, into the jeep and home. She didn't sleep well that night.

14

Buck thought LA was hot, meaning more than just the sun was shining. He was sitting at a café table on Sunset Plaza, taking in the crowded lunch scene.

Things had changed in the couple of decades he'd been incarcerated, and he couldn't believe women like this existed outside of magazines. Tall blondes with long swingy hair and tight-muscled bodies; lustrous dark-haired women with bold eyes and long, long legs and short skirts; short-cropped red-haired women in ankle boots, tight white t-shirts and lacy skirts. It was a passing parade of Hollywood's finest, and it took his breath away.

Every now and then, a girl smiled at him as she pushed her way through the crowded tables, and he smiled confidently back. No one would ever dream he'd spent the last twenty years in an institution. With his new look, he fitted into the chic, casual crowd as though he belonged.

It was more than the expensive beige chinos, the light linen shirt, the suede Gucci loafers, and the rented convertible parked in the lot behind the café. Now, his red hair was a dark chestnut, courtesy of the smart hairdressing salon down the block. The new dark moustache suited his long lean face, and the cool, steel-framed sunglasses hid the heat in his eyes. He looked like a different man. Rich, sleek, good-looking. He looked like a Californian who had it all.

Finishing the iced *latte*, he paid his bill, popped a breathmint in his mouth, then swaggered his way through the crowd, smiling as a girl caught his eye. He felt the power buzzing through him again, heard the voice telling him he could be whomever he liked now. He could do whatever he wanted, have whichever woman he wanted, even the girl smiling at him. He turned purposefully away, his mind was fixed on business.

He was instinctively a man of the streets and he knew how to find what he needed. He drove downtown and took a stroll. He hadn't gone more than a couple of blocks before he was accosted.

'Coke, mister?' A voice called from the darkened doorway.

Buck's eyes darted quickly round; the street was almost empty. He turned to the man. He was black and big and menacing, but Buck was buzzing with power and had no fear of him. He had the switchblade palmed, ready.

'What if I told you I was a cop?' He grinned as he said it, enjoying the flash of alarm in the drug-pusher's eyes. He pressed the knife against his stomach.

The guy didn't breathe. 'I – I didn't mean nothin', officer . . . it's nothin' . . . I'll just get going.' Flattened against the wall, he slid sideways, and Buck laughed.

Suddenly the pusher reached for his gun. With the same speed and strength of the madman who had almost strangled his guard, Buck slammed the switchblade into his hand.

The man made no sound, not even a whimper. He just stood there looking at his bloody hand, and at the Glock 27 Automatic pistol lying on the step in the dirt and litter. He was trembling like a stunned steer in the abattoir, waiting for the death blow.

'You ain't no cop,' he gasped. 'What d'ya want, mister? Look y'can have all I got . . . it's yours man . . . Just let me go, that's all.'

Suddenly he was begging, pleading for his life. Buck was enjoying it. He would have liked to string it out further, but business was business.

'You give me the information I need. Maybe I'll give you your life.'

He pushed the tip of the knife against the man's ribs, just to remind him who was in charge here, and he sagged against the wall, his hand dripping blood onto the step. His jaw hung slack, his eyes rolled back in his head, and his voice was reedy with terror. 'You got it, man, whatever you want—'

'Identity cards, social security . . .'

'Alvarado Street, that's where you go – you can buy anything there, man. Twenty, maybe fifty bucks. Anything you want . . . green cards, driver's licences, fake IDs . . . heroin . . .'

Buck gave the knife another little push and a red stain grew quickly around the point of the blade. For an instant, he contemplated whether to finish the job, but killing men wasn't his thrill. Besides, he was in a good mood, and very much into his new charming role of the rich Californian. Which was only a preview, because as soon as he got his act together, that's what he really would be.

'Thanks', he said, still smiling, 'for everything.' Pocketing the Glock, which he considered a nice little bonus in their transaction, he turned and swaggered away. 'Consider yourself lucky I'm a gentleman,' he called over his shoulder, still laughing.

The pusher's knees gave way. He sank back into the doorway, clutching his stomach. His right hand bled steadily and the fingers hung, useless as sausages. 'Fuckin' psycho,' he groaned, scrambling to his feet and stumbling as fast as he could down the block, away from him. 'What's the fuckin' world comin' to . . .'

Alvarado Street was bustling. Buck didn't even need to look for the sellers. They found him, swarming over the car at the traffic light, holding their wares up to the window for him to see. Glassine packets of white powders and pills; bogus immigration green cards, fake IDs and passports.

Within a couple of hours, Buck had acquired the name and life of one Edward Jensen, complete with social security card, driver's licence, and the registration of a stolen and revamped BMW convertible.

He abandoned the rental car, which he would later report stolen, then drove the BMW to the Santa Monica Branch of the First National Bank, where he opened a checking account with one thousand dollars cash, and arranged for the remainder of his money to be transferred from the Madison Avenue bank. Then he took a room at the luxurious Shutters Hotel, right on the beach, where he showered and changed.

Combing his dark hair in the mirror, he checked his new

appearance. He was wearing a lightweight business suit, a crisp white shirt and an Hermès tie. He looked like a new man. A power-broker. Rich, conservative, attractive, successful. For the moment, Patrick Buckland Duveen no longer existed. And Ed Jensen lived.

Buck asked the concierge to book him a table at the Ivy in Santa Monica, where he had a leisurely dinner and a good bottle of wine. He was charming to the hostess, the table was a good one where he could watch all the action, and he enjoyed the gumbo soup and crab cakes. It was, he thought, satisfied, an excellent day.

He slept well, and the next morning, feeling better than he had in years, he swam several laps, then enjoyed a late breakfast.

He eyed the attractive young woman lounging by the pool speculatively. She was small and very slender and her dark hair was cut in shaggy bangs. As he watched, a nanny in a white uniform appeared, holding the hand of a little girl around five years old. She had curly red hair and blue eyes.

Buck's heart missed a beat. His hand began to shake and the glass of orange juice crashed to the ground.

The waiter came running. He eyed Buck's ashen face and said, alarmed, 'Are you feeling all right, sir?'

Bucks glazed eyes shifted to the waiter's worried face.

'I asked if you're all right, sir?'

Buck waved him away, impatiently. 'I knocked the glass over, that's all. Just clear it up.'

He never took his eyes off the child. Time had stopped, and he was looking at little Ellie Parrish Duveen.

'Margaux, come here, darling.' The illusion broke as the child ran to her mother, and he shook his head, letting out the breath that seemed to have stayed captured in his chest for an eternity. Sweat trickled down his back. For a minute, he'd believed it was her. Exactly the way she was the last time he'd seen her. A little red-haired, freckled kid, rigid with terror, clutching the arms of the big antique Chinese chair while the guards held him down at her grandmother's feet. A little red-haired freckled girl who stood in the way of everything he wanted.

The metal chair scraped harshly against the cement as he pushed it back and strode to the pool. He stood on the edge for a second, forcing himself to take deep breaths before he dived in. The cool water soothed his fevered senses, and he swam laps slowly for ten minutes before drying off and heading back to his room.

The waiter watched him go. 'Thought for a minute there, we'd have to send for the paramedics,' he grinned. 'Thank god he saved the heart attack for somebody else's shift, not mine.'

Buck felt better after a shower. He told himself he'd lost his grip, something he could not afford to do. It was ridiculous to think that Ellie Parrish Duveen still looked like a red-haired little kid. Besides, there must be thousands of little girls like that in California. He had to keep control of himself.

His reflection in the mirror reassured him that he was doing all right. He looked good, he looked the role, and best of all, he did not look like Buck Duveen.

With his new luggage in the BMW's trunk, 'Ed Jensen' drove up the coast. In Montecito, he swept grandly up the driveway of the Four Seasons Biltmore, handed the convertible to a valet, checked into an ocean-view room, then strolled into the bar and bought himself a double bourbon, to celebrate.

Excitement stirred in him like sexual exhilaration, as he looked around the familiar rooms. He'd been here before, but then he was humbler, less confident. Poorer.

He liked this rich life, it fitted him like a glove. When the Parrish money was his, he could afford to stay at the Biltmore for months. For ever, if he so desired. After all, he deserved it. He'd waited twenty long years. A whole fuckin' lifetime.

He relaxed in his comfortable chair, sipping the excellent bourbon, gazing out over the serene blue ocean. His plan was underway. At last.

15

It was Monday afternoon and, as usual, Miss Lottie was waiting for Ellie. Today was her birthday, and Maria had helped her choose the lilac floral dress with the matching little bolero jacket. Maria told her she'd had it for donkey's years, though to Miss Lottie it was as good as new because she didn't remember seeing it before.

She was wearing her pearls, which were exactly like Ellie's, the ones Miss Lottie had given her own daughter, Romany, on the occasion of her eighteenth birthday. She also had on her diamond rings and a scatter of old brooches, and the Vacheron gold watch she'd bought in Switzerland on one of their grand tours of Europe in the thirties, just before the terrible war.

'Something's wrong with you,' Maria had said to her this morning, when she brought her breakfast in bed and Miss Lottie mentioned the War again. 'You only seem to remember the bad things that happened.'

'I do not,' she'd replied indignantly, attacking her boiled egg with a silver spoon. 'I remember good things too. I always know when Ellie's coming. And when Bruno needs to take his pills.'

The old labrador rested his big head on the coverlet, his eyes fixed on the silver toast-rack. Miss Lottie slathered a piece of toast with imported French butter, unsalted the way she liked it, and held it out to him. Bruno dropped it, butter-side down, onto the carpet, an antique Aubusson, pale green covered with curlicues, roses and lilies. He ate it, then licked at the butter-stain.

'It's nothing,' Miss Lottie said guiltily, catching Maria's exasperated glare. 'Only butter.'

Bruno had two more bits of toast after that. She knew butter wasn't good for him and only made him fat, but she figured when you were as old as she and Bruno, a little fat didn't matter. Being happy did, even if the happiness was a small piece of toast.

But now, sitting out on the terrace waiting for Ellie, she was thinking about Europe again. She could remember that trip as clearly as a movie. The places they'd visited, the grand hotels on the Italian and Swiss lakes, the dresses she'd bought in Paris.

She sighed regretfully, pushing back the green celluloid visor. She'd been a young woman then, and had thought life would never change. That it would always be carefree and happy. Never imagining that she would be forced to live through the tragedy of the death of her daughter in the automobile accident.

Whenever that image crossed her mind, which it did frequently, she wondered why her brain had chosen to retain it when it had rejected so many other memories that were pleasanter. But she knew she would take it to her grave, though she had no recollection of the events following it. Not even of the funeral, though she knew there must have been one. And only the fact that she'd had to raise her granddaughter had kept her from crumbling into a bottomless pit of despair.

Images of the young Ellie flickered through Miss Lottie's mind in quick succession. The laughing child with her father's flaming red hair and large feet, and her mother's beautiful misty blue eyes. Ellie, six years old in a pink tutu, tripping over those feet in a clumsy pirouette – but she knew Ellie had *felt* as beautiful as a ballerina, and that was what mattered. Eight-year-old Ellie on horseback, taking a tumble and refusing to cry, even though they found later she had broken her arm. And the school essay she had written, titled 'My Parents', saying proudly that her grandmother was both her mother and her father, and she was sure she was better than everybody else's put together. Then there was homecoming, and High School graduation, and the long dresses and all the parties. And then college.

She remembered Ellie and Maya on the red Harley and how she'd laughed about it later, though of course she never told

Ellie that. Ellie had needed to learn a tough lesson: that nothing good comes without hard work, especially a college degree.

Then there had been the boyfriends, and the house full of young people. It had given her a new lease on life just when she ought to have been considering slowing down and maybe taking a world cruise, along with the other, old ladies. But not a chance, not with a live-wire like Ellie around.

Miss Lottie smiled, glad that not everything had been expunged from her faulty mind, and she still had a few treasured memories to sustain her. She thought that after all, Ellie was like Romany. She had her mother's zest for life and love, and her off-beat beauty. She only hoped she would be happy, too.

'Hi, Miss Lottie. Here I am.'

Ellie bounded up the steps to the terrace and Miss Lottie checked the Vacheron. 'And almost on time, for once in your life. Whatever happened?'

'Your birthday, that's what.' She knelt on the marble tiles and put her arms round her. 'Happy, happy, happy, darling Miss Lottie. Many happy returns. *Feliz cumpleaños, bonne anniversaire* ... oh, just the happiest of birthdays in every language you can think of.'

'*Feliz Navidad,*' Miss Lottie suggested helpfully.

'Happy Christmas, too, Gran, if you like.'

Miss Lottie threw back her head, laughing at her own silly mistake, and for a fraction of a second Ellie saw the girl she must have been.

'I may not always get it right these days,' Miss Lottie smiled, 'but it's close enough.'

'So, why are you wearing the eyeshade? Uhuh, don't tell me you've been at the computer again, shifting stocks around and losing your shirt?'

'Nothing so vulgar, dear. Besides, I'm not sure I have any stocks to shift around, or a shirt to lose. I just like to play with it. It's fascinating you know, what you can do on that machine. Why, it even talks back to you, and it leaves little messages. E-mail, they call it. Or maybe it's the Internet?'

'You've been surfing the Internet?' Ellie's jaw dropped. 'How on earth did you learn to do that?'

'The young man showed me. He was very competent, he knew his stuff, all right. I found it quite easy, and it's so amusing, making new friends, chatting to them on the machine. It's more amusing than the television programmes. All violence and sex.'

'Miss Lottie, you should wash your mouth out with soap at once. That word has never passed your lips before.'

'Oh really? Then how d'you suppose Romany got here? Via the cabbage patch? Don't be ridiculous, Ellie, of course I know all about sex. A lady doesn't talk about it, that's all.'

Ellie's eyes widened in astonishment. 'Gran, you never fail to surprise me.'

Miss Lottie grasped her silver-topped cane for support, as she got slowly to her feet. 'Sometimes I surprise myself,' she said, with a wicked little sidelong smile. 'Now, as ladies together, you can feel free to tell me all about your sex life. Experience counts you know, when you need help.'

Ellie felt herself blushing. 'Miss Lottie, I don't know where you're getting all this from. And anyhow, I don't have a sex life.'

'I told you, I get it from my friends on the Internet. I act as their advisor, sort of Ann Landers or Dear Abby, you know. And at your age you *should* have one. You can tell me why you don't, over tea.'

Ramming the green visor firmly over her eyes, she strode through the drawing room and into the hall. 'Bye, Maria,' she called. 'Bye, Bruno. See you later. And *shalom*.'

Ellie laughed, but she made a mental note to check exactly what was going on on Miss Ellie's Internet.

At the Biltmore, Buck gave the valet his keys. Humming 'Dixie' happily under his breath, he waited under the awning for his car. An old white Cadillac circled into the drive and the valet rushed to open its door, forgetting all about him. Buck watched as everyone fussed around. The Manager appeared, waitresses popped their heads round the door, and the reception staff thronged round.

Must be a politician, Buck thought, still humming softly. Or a movie star.

The Manager was helping an old woman out of the car, smiling at her, shaking her hand. Leaning on her stick, she walked slowly toward Buck. Her faded blue eyes lingered on him.

And time seemed to stop. The blood froze in his veins. He couldn't breathe, waiting for her to recognize him, to accuse him . . .

The Manager took her arm, she nodded a polite good afternoon, and walked slowly past him into the hotel.

Buck's heart was pounding somewhere in his throat. Fate, efficient as FedEx, had delivered his victim to him on a plate.

He closed his eyes, his strong fingers flexing; he could almost feel her buttery flesh bruising under his grip.

'Excuse me, but are you all right?'

He opened his eyes, and looked at the most beautiful woman he had ever seen.

She was very tall, gracefully elegant in a sunshine-yellow dress and strappy little sandals. Her long legs were tanned and her toenails lacquered a deep coral red. And her eyes, looking into his, were a delicate pale grey-blue.

'Do you need help?' she persisted, still staring anxiously at him.

'No, no, it's okay. I'm all right.' He pulled his wits together. 'Thank you . . .'

'Good afternoon, then.' Her long red hair swung prettily around her shoulders as she walked away, and Buck knew he was looking at Ellie Parrish Duveen.

His heart was doing double time. A pain cleaved suddenly through his chest, making him gasp, and he pressed a hand to it, feeling his heart jumping.

'Your car, sir.' The valet had the BMW's door open, waiting.

Buck shook his head, unable to speak. Turning away, he walked slowly back into the hotel and sank onto a couch, waiting for his heart to find its normal rhythm. He hadn't been prepared for this . . . he'd thought he would choose the moment . . . his mind was in chaos.

When his pulse slowed sufficiently and the pain had lessened, he followed Ellie into the pretty high-ceilinged room overlooking the ocean, where tables were set with pink linen cloths and tea was being served. Waitresses hovered near Lottie Parrish's table and the old lady sat there, regal as a queen, except for an old green celluloid eyeshade crammed over her eyes.

Ellie pushed back her chair and went around the table to her.

'Miss Lottie, there's no need to wear your eyeshade. We're indoors now.'

'I know we're indoors, Ellie. I'm not stupid.' She glared at her granddaughter and the waitresses giggled. With dignity, she removed the shade.

Ellie ignored them. 'Of course you do. And I'll bet you know exactly what you want to order.'

'Salmon and cucumber sandwiches, hot scones with Devonshire cream and strawberry jam. And Earl Grey. Not teabags, mind you. Tea simply doesn't taste the same out of bits of paper.'

Buck had heard her voice in his dreams for what seemed like a thousand years, which it might as well have been, incarcarated as he was in that lunatic asylum. And she had not even recognised him. He wondered whether it was because of his successful new image: the dark hair instead of the red; the moustache; the dark glasses. Or whether old age had simply blotted him from her memory. He shrugged. Either way, she was as good as his.

Taking the table next to theirs, he ordered tea, then pretended to read a newspaper, watching and listening.

Choosing a smoked salmon sandwich on crustless brown bread, Miss Lottie took a dainty bite. 'So, Ellie, what do you have to say? Why is there no man in your life? A lovely girl like you?'

Ellie sighed. This was obviously one subject her grandmother was not going to forget. 'I told you, I'm too busy, Gran, I'm a working girl, six days a week, endless hours a day. It's been like that for a year now and it's likely to continue that way, or at least, until I make enough to open a second café.' She laughed, just thinking about it. 'And then it'll probably get even worse. Seven days a week and all the hours that God sends.'

Miss Lottie thought Ellie looked so pretty when she laughed, so young and gay. She wished passionately that her grand-daughter didn't have to work so hard. 'I was thinking,' she said, carefully selecting a scone, 'perhaps we should sell Journey's End.'

Buck's suddenly nerveless hands dropped the newspaper. *Had the Parrishes come down in the world? What the hell had happened to all that money? It had flowed like water from an endless reservoir last he'd heard. That must be the reason they'd let him out, she couldn't afford to keep him there any more. Christ, what would he do now?*

He poured Earl Grey tea with a shaking hand, then stuffed a sandwich into his mouth. It choked him and he took a gulp of the boiling tea, gasping, agonized. He cast an angry gaze at the large noisy group at the next table; he could no longer hear the conversation.

'We've been over this before, and there's no chance,' Ellie replied, serenely. 'You can't sell the house.'

'I don't see why not? I could always go and live in one of those condos. In Beverly Hills, or somewhere,' she added vaguely. 'And you could open as many restaurants as you like. You might even find time to meet a man and get married, give me some grandchildren.' Miss Ellie smiled teasingly at her. 'I could call my friends, find out how their grandsons are doing. There's bound to be one or two still left unattached.'

'On the shelf,' Ellie said gloomily. 'That's what you think I am. Well, this should please you. I have a date tonight.'

Miss Lottie's eyes brightened. 'With a man?'

'Of course with a man.'

'So? Tell me about him? Do I know his family?'

'Probably not, but he's a local boy. He taught me to surf when I was eight years old.'

'A *surfer?*'

'Oh come on, Gran,' Ellie laughed. 'Of course he's not a surfer now. He was a cop. A homicide detective in Manhattan. Now he's bought a winery out here. Running Horse Ranch.'

'Running Horse?' Miss Lottie sifted through the faulty computer in her head. 'Never heard of it, but that doesn't mean anything. I've not heard of half the stuff I used to know. Is it a big success, then?' She nibbled on her scone.

'Not yet, but I'm sure it will be. He seems a very determined man. I'd bet that whatever it takes, he'll do it.'

'I like that about a man. Determination. But a *homicide cop?*' Miss Ellie shuddered. She watched *NYPD Blue* and knew what she was talking about. 'Ellie, dear, are you sure you're moving in the right circles? However did you meet him?'

Ellie licked the cream from the top of her scone, and Buck thought he could die of happiness, just watching her. He suddenly wanted desperately to lick the cream from her laughing mouth. He was fascinated by every move she made, the tilt of her head, her rich glossy red hair, the smoothness of her bare golden arm.

Ellie said, 'I smacked up his brand-new car, right here on Olive Mill Road. I'm surprised he even spoke to me after that.'

'Young people meet in such strange ways these days.' Miss Lottie shook her head, bewildered. 'When I was young it was all arranged. You went to parties and dances or the theatre with people you knew, or friends of people you knew. Nothing was hit and miss, the way it was with you and the homicide cop, literally, with the new car.'

She glanced up, surprised, as the Manager hurried toward her. Behind him walked the Pastry Chef, bearing a pink frosted cake in the shape of a gaily-wrapped package, with a single lit candle.

Everyone turned to watch as the wait-staff and the chefs gathered round and sang Happy Birthday. Then Miss Lottie, pink-cheeked with pleasure, blew out her candle and everyone, including the other diners, applauded. After that the Manager produced a bottle of champagne.

'As usual, it's our pleasure to see you here, Miss Lottie,' the Manager said, holding up his glass in a toast to her. 'Because Lottie Parrish and the Biltmore are institutions, and they have been here almost as long as each other.'

Buck fought back the overwhelming urge to leap at her, there and then. He'd fix his hands round her old throat and they'd never get him off, those pearls would be embedded in her flesh for all eternity. Trembling, he summoned a waiter and ordered a double bourbon. He gulped it down quickly, never taking his eyes off the two women.

In the past, when he was free, he took women as and when he wanted. They were never more than a commodity to him, breakable and expendable. His usual icy reaction, the way he thought, felt, everything was in turmoil.

He could see his father, *their* father, in Ellie's face. He saw himself as he had been two decades ago, when he was young, like her. Vital. Alive. Before they locked him away. Could it be that, making him feel this new emotion? Or was it the luminous quality of her skin, the rich tumble of hair, those remarkable eyes?

He ordered a second drink, tense as a stretched wire, watching Ellie sipping champagne, biting into the piece of cake. She touched her grandmother's arm affectionately, her voice too low for him to hear what she was saying, as she handed Miss Lottie a beribboned gift package. The old woman's face was alight with surprise and pleasure, exclaiming over the cream velvet robe her granddaughter had bought her.

'Too extravagant, but beautiful,' she smiled. 'You spoil me, Ellie.'

'It makes a change from you spoiling me, Gran,' Ellie kissed her, and they sipped tea, chatting a while longer.

When they finally got up to leave, Miss Lottie's gaze lingered on Buck, as she passed by. There was a puzzled little frown between her eyes as Ellie took her arm and they walked slowly from the room.

Buck saw that she held herself upright as a soldier, refusing to lean on the cane. She thanked everyone personally as she said goodbye, and there were smiles, and even a few tears, in the eyes of those who had known her the longest. He thought the Manager was right, and Lottie Parrish was a Montecito institution. But not for much longer.

He heaved a regretful sigh. His plans were thrown into chaos. The old woman must die. But Ellie Parrish Duveen would be his.

16

It's spring, Dan thought, gloomily, the time *'men's minds'* were supposed to *'lightly turn to thoughts of love.'* Was that quote Tennyson? Someone with the right idea, anyhow. Except his thoughts were not on love, but on what he was going to do to try to salvage Running Horse winery.

He rode the new mare, Honey, over his forty acres, stopping at the top of a slope where he could see the lie of the land. He looked round for Pancho, but the lazy hound was nowhere in sight and he guessed he'd slunk back to the stables. The sun blazed down and he slid from the horse, pulled off his t-shirt and stood, drinking in the silence.

A hawk hovered in the clear blue sky and a couple of rabbits bounced along a furrow. He thought their cute white scuts and quick movements were a dead giveaway to the hawk, poised above, ready to swoop. Maybe life on the ranch wasn't so different from life on the streets, after all. Predators and victims, sudden violent death on a fine afternoon. God, he was missing the action, though.

He rubbed the aching scar on his chest, thinking of Piatowsky, wondering what was going on. Maybe he'd give him a call later, and a progress report. Or lack of it.

The cellphone rang and he fished it from the back pocket of his Levis.

'So? How's Farmer Dan?'

He grinned. 'Are you into telepathy, or what, Piatowsky? I was just thinking about you.'

'Answer the question, Cassidy. How's it goin'?'

'Fine, fine. For a pig in a poke.'

Piatowsky whistled loudly, sending shockwaves down Dan's ear. 'You mean I was right?'

'You were right. And I'm standing here, in the glorious California sunshine, admiring my withered vines. I'll bet not a one of 'em's any good. Probably got to replace the lot.'

'It's gonna cost ya, huh.'

'It is. But it's beautiful. You should just see the stables, like an old Spanish adobe. And have I got a horse for you.' Dan glanced at the big bay mare, pawing the ground nearby. 'Come on out here, and you'll be Cowboy Piatowsky before you know it.'

'The closest I ever got to riding a horse is a Harley, and they tell me the Harley is less dangerous.'

Dan laughed and Piatowsky said, 'Listen, you old bastard, I miss you, out on the streets. Angela's taking the kids to visit her mom in Maine the end of the month, thought maybe I'd get out there to see your pig in a poke. Give you a hand with some of that work, ploughing and furrowing and all that country shit.'

Dan imagined his grin as he was saying it. 'Sure,' he said. 'I'll probably have the house fixed up by then too.'

'The house needs fixing also?' Piatowsky's voice cracked with laughter. 'I'm buying a new sign for your ranch. A flying pig with dollar signs all over it.'

'Thanks, friend. I miss you too.'

'I'll call, let y'know when to expect me. You sure it's okay, though? Seriously?'

'I'm sure. And I'm sure you're gonna love it. It's a jewel in the rough.'

'Yeah. I'll bet.'

'Give my best to Angela.'

'Will do. Take care out there, in the wild west. Oh by the way, remember the hooker, burnt up in Times Square? Never did find out who did it. At least not yet. But no one checked out of jail with the kind of profile you mentioned. Just wanted to let you know you were wrong. Maybe it's better you've become a rube, Farmer Dan.'

The phone clicked off and Dan shook his head, smiling. He looked at the beautiful curve of the hillside silhouetted against the blue sky, and listened again to the silence. Then he told himself he wouldn't swap it for New York's mean streets for a million bucks.

The bay mare he'd bought that morning from a horse ranch near Los Olivos was big, seventeen hands, and nine years old. She was whinnying and tossing her head, flicking her tail restlessly. He swung himself onto her back and said, 'Okay, okay, Honey, let's get going.'

She threw her head up again and did a little dance, testing him. Gripping her firmly, he shortened the reins, and said, 'Let's get this straight. I'm the boss, you're the horse. I ride, you obey. Got it?' The mare rolled her eyes, but she trotted obediently back toward the stables.

Dan breathed a sigh of relief. He couldn't have stood it if he'd bought another dud. First the crumbling house and vineyard; then Pancho, who could wreck a place in two minutes flat and stole food like the veteran streetdog he used to be; and then the mare, with a mind of her own, ready to throw him the minute he relaxed. He figured he wasn't doing so good as Farmer Dan. Not good at all.

Pancho was sprawled on the shady stable patio. He lifted his head and wagged his plumed tail in a lazy greeting, then settled back down to his snooze. The roof tiles gleamed coral in the sunlight, the purple and pink petunias and geraniums tumbled colourfully from their huge clay pots, and the old Spanish-tiled fountain tinkled prettily in the centre of the yard, thanks to a new pump. A couple of doves even fluttered in and out of it, taking a free bath.

Dan thought it looked just the way it had in those sunny photographs when he'd fallen in love with it, and he had to admit even now, with all the drawbacks, it stirred his heart.

He removed the saddle and bridle, gave the mare water and oats, then went to check the pretty Apaloosa in the next stall. He'd bought this one for her looks. Dapple-grey with a creamy mane and tail, she was young, just three years old, but she also had a sparkle about her that he liked, and an easy temperament.

'How're y' doin', Paradise?' She came to snuffle his hand and he fished a carrot from his pocket. The horse took it from his palm, crunching noisily. 'Sweet girl,' he said. 'Unlike your raunchy new sister out there. Got to keep her under control, teach her the ropes of civilized behaviour.'

He remembered Ellie accusing him of being uncivilized when she'd smacked up his car, and her kicking the jeep's tyres. He grinned, thinking she was a bit whacky, but cute with it. No, no. He corrected himself. Definitely not cute. He hadn't found exactly the right word yet to describe her, though beautiful had crossed his mind. Maybe not quite that, either, but whatever mysterious quality it was, he liked it. And her. And he was looking forward to meeting her again, tonight.

Wiping the sweat from his back with the t-shirt, he grabbed a Diet-Coke from the small fridge he'd installed in the old tack-room that he'd designated as his office, took a long cool slug, then walked back onto the patio, and perched on the mounting-block. He was contemplating his dusty boots and his lazy dog, wondering why he hadn't had any response to his ad for a manager, when Pancho suddenly leapt to his feet, barking madly at the man galloping into the stableyard on an old palomino.

A bottle of whisky poked from the man's jacket pocket, his denims were full of holes, and he wore a greasy red bandanna round his neck and scuffed leather cowboy boots with silver toecaps. A wide Mexican sombrero was clamped over his thick black curls and a bushy Zapata moustache almost hid his beaming grin of introduction.

Dan pushed back his baseball cap, astonished, as the palomino pawed the air in a flashy finale. 'You a circus act, or what?' he demanded, grinning.

'No, Señor.' The man leapt from the saddle, and beamed again. 'I am Carlos Ortega. Your new winemaster. I know everything there is to know about making the wines and I have the best "nose" on the coast. I have come to offer my valuable services to you.' He swept off the sombrero with a flourish and both he and the palomino bowed low.

Dan was laughing, but he could see Ortega meant business. 'And how did you hear I needed a winemaker?'

Putting back his sombrero, Ortega hitched up his jeans and

gave him a cocky grin. 'Let us just say I heard it on the grapevine, Señor.' And he threw back his head in a great shout of laughter at his own topical little vineyard joke.

Dan eyed the whisky bottle sticking from his pocket speculatively, but he also noticed his twinkling brown eyes and his air of *joi de vivre*. And *joi de vivre* was something Running Horse could do with a major shot of right now. He doubted Carlos Ortega knew a merlot from a sauvignon but, despite the bottle of booze, he kind of liked him.

'Put the mare in the stall and give her some water. Then come to my office and we'll talk.'

Carlos quickly did as he was asked. He took a seat opposite Dan in the bare but clean little space that had become his office. Placing the sombrero carefully across his knees, he stood the bottle of whisky on the trestle table between them.

'Señor Cassidy, I will not lie to you,' he said, suddenly serious. 'I am a good winemaker, maybe even great. I first came to California when I was a boy, to pick the walnuts, then the pistachios, then strawberries. Anything there was to be picked, I picked it. 'He shrugged and threw Dan a modest smile. 'Of course I was only twelve years old but I was big for my age, and nobody questioned me.

'When I was fifteen I went north, to the Napa Valley to pick grapes. I worked hard, I was intelligent, I was promoted from the fields to work in the winery. I learned everything I could. It interested me, you see, Señor. I loved the process of growing the grapes, the harvest, the winemaking. I loved the smell of it, so much so, that I would leave my bed in the night to come and see that my wines were fermenting properly. First I worked in the fields at Mondavi, then for Beaulieu, and then I went to a small vineyard, what they call a *boutique winery*, like Running Horse, Señor. The owner liked my interest, he apprenticed me to the master winemaker, and because I loved what I was doing I learned quickly. And I also learned I had a talent for it.'

His intelligent brown eyes met Dan's across the table. 'Señor, I became cellar foreman, then an assistant winemaker. I worked for top wineries, though never in the chief position. This,' he tapped the whisky bottle, 'was my undoing.'

Heaving a sigh, he replaced the sombrero and gave his moustache a wistful twirl. 'So you see, Señor Cassidy, I will not lie to you. But my little problem is my own and it will not affect my work. With me, Señor, the wine comes first.'

'You're not a wine drinker, then?'

Carlos shook his head. 'I only enjoy to create it, Señor. In my view, wine is a drink for señoritas and fancy men.' He patted his belly and threw Dan a conspiratorial grin. 'And there's nothing warms the heart more than good whisky. Unless it's a good woman.'

'And what makes you think, Señor Ortega, that I will take on an acknowledged drunk as my winemaker?'

Ortega leaned closer across the table. 'Señor Cassidy,' he said, smooth as silk, 'I do not think either of us has much choice. You need a winemaker. I need a job. You will not get another man of high calibre to come and work at Running Horse. It is badly run down, it has a bad reputation, they say there's a jinx on it, and a decent bottle of wine has never been produced here. But I know this land, the slopes are south-facing, the soil is light. Good robust wines can come from this soil, Señor, but to get them, you need an expert. Much money will need to go into new vine stock, and in bringing the vineyard up to standard. It is expensive and will take time. But I am not a greedy man, I do not demand high wages. I will work alongside you until we make a success.'

Looking levelly at Dan, he said, 'All I need is a roof over my head. The little house near the gates will do fine, I can fix it up good, it won't cost much. With enough for me and my family to eat, and for the occasional bottle of whisky. Only occasional, Señor, that I promise you. Later, when we are successful, then we shall renegotiate.'

He sat back in his chair, satisfied that he had presented his case to his best advantage, and this time it was Dan who threw back his head and laughed out loud.

'It's that simple, huh? I need a winemaker and nobody will work for me. And you need a job and nobody will hire you. It seems we're stuck with each other, Señor Ortega. It's a deal. Only no drinking on the job.'

The Mexican pumped his hand enthusiastically. 'Señor Dan, you will not regret it. I promise you.' He stood up, pocketed his bottle and swaggered to the door.

Whistling for the palomino, he leapt on its back and galloped out of the stable yard in a swirl of dust, the same way he had come in.

Watching the cloud of dust disappear down the hillside, Dan wondered if Carlos Ortega was a mirage, or whether he had really just hired himself a whisky-drunk as his winemaker. He shook his head, telling himself he must be crazy and that Carlos had better be as good a winemaster as he was a talker, because *he* sure as hell didn't know much about it.

A short while later Carlos came back, driving an ancient pickup with a dusty-looking brown mongrel standing in the back, and a plump young woman with long, shiny black hair sitting in the front, holding a baby on her lap.

Pancho ran at Cecil, the brown dog, barking ferociously, and Dan hauled him back by the collar as Carlos said, 'Señor, this is Florita, my wife. And this,' he swept the baby from her lap and held it proudly aloft, 'is my son Roberto Carlosito Ortega. An American citizen.' He raised his hand to his heart in a solemn salute. 'God Bless America.'

'And God bless Señor Cassidy for giving you work,' Florita added, shyly. 'I can work for you too, Señor. I can clean your house, do your laundry, cook for you. Anything you need.'

Dan laughed, he liked Carlos, he liked the whole family. 'And I say God bless you, Florita, for that,' he replied. Then, remembering the state of the house, he added. 'And oh boy, will you need it.'

17

Miss Lottie was upstairs in her little sitting room watching television. She was wearing Ellie's birthday present velvet robe, and her neatly brushed hair – a hundred strokes every night, all her life – fell around her shoulders in a silvery cloud. She was sipping a glass of milk, and there was a puzzled frown on her face.

'Maria,' she said, 'I think I saw someone I know today, only I don't remember.'

Maria was sitting opposite. Her slippered feet were propped on a faded green brocade ottoman, and she was drinking hot chocolate and munching her home-baked vanilla cookies.

'You saw a lot of people at the Biltmore. You've known them for years, Miss Lottie. It just slips your mind, is all.'

She shook her head. 'No, I don't even recall what the man looked like. When I first saw him I thought he was familiar. Then later, when he was sitting nearby, I thought perhaps I *should* know him.' She sighed, frowning again. 'Oh my useless brain, I've a good mind to have a computer disc installed up there.'

Taking a sip of the milk, she helped herself to one of Maria's cookies. 'I have the feeling it was someone important though.' She shook her muddled head, 'It's so annoying. It's like waking from a vivid dream and not being able to remember it, though you really want to. That's what my life has become now, Maria,' she added irately. 'Just a series of half-remembered dreams. Reality no longer exists.'

'Except when Ellie comes to see you,' Maria patted her hand comfortingly as she got to her feet. 'I'd better take Bruno out for his stroll. Can't really call it a "walk" these days.'

Miss Lottie's suite was at the top of the grand staircase, on the left, and Maria had the rooms to the right. Most of the others were closed off now, except for Ellie's just down the hall, which still looked exactly the way it had when she'd left for college. Miss Lottie wondered why Ellie had not stayed over tonight, then remembered she'd said something about a date. She wondered with whom?

She turned her attention to the TV and *NYPD Blue*. That was it, of course. Ellie's young man played a homicide detective on the television programme. Miss Lottie smiled, pleased that at least she'd got that right. But she still puzzled over who it was she'd encountered at the Biltmore. It was someone important, she was sure of that.

Buck had driven slowly past the gates of Journey's End twice already. He pulled onto the soft verge opposite, half-hidden in the shadow of the eucalyptus trees, then shook a cigarette from the crumpled pack of Camels. He lit it, staring at the elaborate iron gates. They were flanked by two enormous pink granite columns, thick as redwood trees, topped with a pair of winged griffins.

'*Guarding the rich woman's palace,*' he thought bitterly. And keeping out the rest of the world. Except him, of course. He would find his way in there, even if they kept it locked like a fortress. He wondered how many there were now, in the household. And if she still had an armed patrol? The house was not visible from the road, but a faint yellowish glow in the distance indicated that there must be outdoor lights for security purposes. He would have to check things out properly. He wasn't going to end up locked away a second time.

He imagined the old woman as he'd seen her today, so upright in her chair, no elbows on the table or dowager's stoop. Still living like she was a queen, everybody bowing and scraping . . .

Flinging the cigarette out the window, he started up the engine. 'Happy birthday, Miss Lottie,' he called mockingly as he slid past the gates. 'Happy fucking birthday. Better make the most of it. Because it's your last.'

The dark road spiralled down from the foothills but he took the bends at top speed, not caring. *You are invincible*, the voice in his head told him triumphantly. *You are smarter, better, stronger*. Besides, he knew all about them now. He had asked the waitress, when she'd brought him his check.

'Miss Lottie's a lovely lady,' she'd said. 'Everybody knows her, she's lived in Montecito longer than anybody else. Anyone who's still alive, that is.'

'A charming woman,' Buck had agreed, pleasantly. 'They don't make them like that these days. A true lady.'

The waitress smiled approvingly at him. '*And* she brought her granddaughter up the same way. Ellie's a real lady too, even if she does run a café in Santa Monica.'

'And where would that be?' Buck added a large tip, then handed it to her. She glanced quickly at it, pleased at his generosity.

'On Main Street. They say it's a nice little place and Ellie works real hard. I guess she has to, if the rumour's true there's no money left, and Journey's End will have to be sold.'

Buck's heart had turned to stone, but he'd still kept his smile. 'I guess it's not often a property like that comes on the market. No doubt there'll be plenty of buyers after it.'

The waitress shrugged, refilling his teacup. 'I don't know about that, sir, though they say it must be worth a fortune. Millions, I heard.'

Buck felt better knowing about the millions, and now he had a new plan of action.

He shifted gear and the BMW shot out of Hot Springs Road onto Coast Village, tyres screeching as he made a right, then a quick left onto the freeway, speeding south. He needed action. He needed to see where Ellie lived. He needed a woman.

18

The road was empty and the Highway Patrol not in evidence. He was in LA in less than an hour, then traffic slowed him down. He switched onto the 405, then the Santa Monica Freeway, and exited at Fourth Street.

A patrol car sitting at the traffic light brought him to his senses. He couldn't afford to get a ticket, the new driver's licence and registration looked good for everyday purposes, but he wasn't sure how well they'd stand up to police scrutiny.

He drove slowly down Main until he found it. *Ellie's Place* it said on the forest-green facia-board, and again on the window. He stopped the car and sat looking at it. A *Closed* sign hung over the door and no lights were on.

He got out and walked round the corner to the back of the single storey premises. Latticed steel covered the kitchen door and the window. Frustrated, he wondered where she lived. He would need to keep watch on her, find out. The thought filled him with excitement. Buzzing with power, he drove back to Sunset Boulevard.

Even on a Monday night, the strip was lively. Keeping an eye out for the cops, he cruised slowly as far as Hollywood Boulevard, checking the roadside action. There were plenty of women, any shape or size you wanted. With Ellie in mind, he chose a redhead.

He rolled the window down and leaned across, checking her out. She was tall and breasty in a skimpy black skirt and top, and black patent high-heeled boots. 'How much?' he said quickly.

She looked him up and down. 'Depends what you want, mister. You tell me, I'll tell you.'

'Get in,' he said, deciding. 'We'll negotiate on the way.'

She slid into the passenger seat. 'You want all night, I'm yours,' she said. 'Anything you like, a hundred bucks.'

He glanced sceptically at her. 'A hundred? I'd say more like fifty.'

She pouted, eyes flashing sullenly. 'It's a friggin' bargain,' she said, then yelled with laughter. 'That's me,' she added, chortling. 'A friggin' bargain.'

Buck did not laugh.

'Where we goin'?' she demanded, suddenly nervous.

'Any place. Just as long as it's quiet and there are no cops.'

She grinned, relieved. 'First, give me the fifty. Then I'll take you somewhere special.'

He didn't bother to negotiate.

He fished the wallet from his pocket and she eyed it greedily. 'Don't even think about it.' he said coldly. I'll have you locked up so fast you won't know what hit you. Except this time, you'll be doing more than just thirty days for hookin'.'

She shrugged and tucked the fifty into the top of her black patent-leather boot. 'No need to get nasty. Make a left here, then another. It's just an alley but it's quiet.'

Buck parked at the far end of the alley near the trash cans, then sat back while she took care of his needs. She was good at her job, her mouth felt like silk and rubber, her teeth like the scratching of demons, tearing at his soul.

He slid his hands round her neck and she jerked backwards, 'What y' doin? . . .' Panicked, she dived for the door but he was too quick. He had her by the throat and nothing would have prised him off. His face was contorted with the effort and sweat dripped into his eyes.

She choked and flailed around, clutching at his hands. Then she went limp. The tongue that had done such a good job on him a few minutes ago stuck out from her slack mouth like a swollen purple eggplant, and her bulging eyes were dark with congested blood.

Buck dragged her from the car and let her drop. Her wig fell off, revealing matted black hair. He aimed a kick at her; the bitch hadn't even been a real redhead. Retrieving the fifty from her boot, he pocketed it.

The alley was quiet, there was just a dim light at the end. He took out the switchblade and knelt over her. The knife made a little hissing sound as he slit the skin, etching the deep cross, from temple to temple, scalp to nose. There was little blood because her heart was no longer pumping it around, but he wiped the knife fastidiously on her short skirt, then got back in the car and drove out of the alley.

There was still no one in sight. When he got to the next intersection, he switched on his lights and checked his appearance in the driver's mirror. Smoothing back his hair, he thought he looked pretty good. Whistling 'Dixie' happily under his breath, he headed back to the freeway, and Montecito.

The bar was crowded. He took a stool and caught the bartender's eye.

'Double Jim Beam, Mr Jensen?' the barman asked.

'You got it, Al. Any chance of some of those pretzels?'

'Certainly, sir. You catch the Lakers game tonight?'

'I sure did.' Buck was never one to turn down an alibi when it was offered. 'Boy, they're tough to beat these days.'

He had forgotten about the woman he'd just killed, and he sipped the good bourbon, remembering how he used to dream about it in Hudson, how it would taste, so smooth, rich. And now he had it. He almost had it all.

19

Dan was out on the deck, playing with the new Weber barbecue. He'd dashed back from the ranch early, not wanting Ellie to catch him sweaty from the fields and smelling of stables. He was freshly showered, wearing Levis, sneakers, and a blue shirt rolled at the sleeves. And he ached in every muscle from the long horse-ride that afternoon.

He ran his hands through his still-wet hair, wondering why he was so keen to see her. It wasn't even really a date, just two old friends catching up on each other. Even though she was beautiful. There, he'd finally said it. Ellie Parrish Duveen was a knock-out.

A sudden image of Ellie as a child flashed into his mind; a photograph of a lanky, freckled redhead in a saggy bathing-suit, shivering on the windy beach, then plunging fearlessly into the waves. Had she had braces then, he wondered? No, she must have been too young, only eight or nine. Too young to date, anyhow.

As a cop, finding time for dates had been a major problem. A detective's hours were difficult and subject to change. He'd never understood how Piatowsky juggled marriage and four kids, but he'd held it together and had a pretty and devoted wife.

'It's Love,' Piatowsky had told him cryptically. 'Like, she loves me. And I love her. That's all there is to it. And maybe a bit of give and take.'

'I assume the "give" comes on Angela's part?' Dan remembered asking with a grin. He knew Piatowsky too well. He was at the precinct all hours of the day and night. He never let a case drop, not even for a day off.

Anyhow, being a cop hadn't done wonders for Dan's relationships. There were women of course; women he liked. Especially an assistant DA he'd met when he was in court, presenting a case against a felon he'd arrested. He had thought, for a while, she might be the one. But between his unsociable shifts and her busy schedule, spending time together had become more and more difficult, until there hadn't been much point to it any more.

So he'd gone on working out at the gym, getting up extra early to run, finishing the NY Marathon twice, respectably in the first quarter. He'd filled his apartment with music, and with books – true stories of derring-do: mountain climbing, solo ocean-crossings in small yachts, and treks to the North Pole, always thinking that maybe, some day, he would find space for an adventure like that.

The rest of his time was filled with work. He'd lived it and breathed it, and he'd almost died for it. But he still liked quiet dinners in charming little Italian restaurants, a good bottle of wine, and the company of a pretty, intelligent woman.

Ellie nosed the jeep down the quiet lane, looking for Pines Cottage. She had changed from the yellow dress into narrow white jeans, Converse sneakers, and a soft white shirt tied at her waist. As always, she wore her mother's pearls, and she'd taken the time to apply mascara and lipstick properly, instead of at the traffic lights as she usually did. In the back were two grocery bags with the steaks, salad, cheese, fruit, French bread and part of Miss Lottie's birthday cake.

She checked her watch. Two minutes before the appointed hour. Being early might be a first in her life, and she wondered whether she was acting too eager. He was just an old childhood friend, she reminded herself, then corrected that. Well, almost a friend; at least she'd known him, way back when.

Dan Cassidy had looked great at eighteen: abs like a washboard and zero bodyfat. Those deep-set Irish-blue eyes, with the long black lashes stuck together in little wet points, his chest tanned a deep golden brown and his lower half encased in a sexy black wetsuit that fit snug as a second skin, and had all the girls giggling.

She also remembered being clasped against that golden chest as he hauled her from the surf, after she'd been hit on the head by a board, and her throwing up seawater all over him. She must have swallowed a gallon of the stuff. 'That'll teach you never to do that again,' he'd said frostily, 'it's a good way to get yourself killed.' Ellie grinned; she surely hoped he didn't recall that little incident, it would ruin her image in a minute.

An old wooden board with 'Pines Cottage' carved clumsily into it, hung askew over a wooden gate. She parked the car, hauled the grocery bags from the back and pushed the gate open with her foot.

As she walked toward the roar of the ocean, the trees thinned out and she could see the house. It was small and simple, painted white with nautical blue trim, and a big old brass ship's bell by the door.

Shifting her packages to one arm, she tugged on the bell-rope, then took a step back, sniffing the clean salt air like a happy puppy. She decided she might as well enjoy this: after all it was just dinner with a friend. Even if he was cute.

Pancho leapt out as Dan flung open the door. Their eyes met. 'Hi,' they said, simultaneously.

Ellie looked down at the mangy dog bouncing all over her. He was the worst-looking mutt she had ever seen. She grinned at Dan. 'I'll bet you took him because you knew nobody else would.'

'He'd been at the shelter for months. Next week he was headed for the kennels in the sky. He looked at me, with those big brown eyes,' Dan lifted his shoulders, heaving a sigh, 'and now he thinks he owns me.' He grabbed the grocery bags from her. 'This was meant to be my treat, and I've let you do all the work.'

'Oh no. No, sir. This is where I quit and you begin.' Following him into the kitchen, she began to unpack the bags.

Pancho pranced on his hind legs, whining eagerly as he scented the steak, and she said severely, 'No chance, dog, even if you are a beauty.'

'You can't mean you think the mutt's beautiful?' Dan looked astonished.

'He looks like a moulting fur cushion, but then I'm a pushover for waifs and strays.'

'I hope you're not including me in that bracket.'

Ellie laughed, taking out the rest of the food. 'I thought it was the other way around. Ah, here it is.' She unwrapped part of the pretty pink cake that said 'Happy Birthday Miss Lottie' on it in silver, then stuck a finger in the frosting and licked it.

'Bad,' she admitted, rolling her eyes with pleasure. 'But I can't resist.'

'I bet your grandmother told you it'll spoil your dinner if you eat your cake first.'

'I thought you were going to say, "You can't have your cake and eat it."'

'I'm doing my best to prove that's not true. What about you?'

She sighed, leaning against the sink, 'I'm trying. I'm trying.'

She sounded wistful and he poured her a glass of wine. 'Iron Horse,' he said, 'a class-act winery. Taste it and tell me what you think.'

She gazed, too innocently, into his eyes, 'I think it's been a long time since I had dinner with a man.' Then laughing, she added, 'Of course, I get to have dinner with dozens of men, every night. But that doesn't count, if you know what I mean.'

'I know.' His eyes were still on hers. 'It's nice. Especially because you're an old friend.'

The wooden deck looked out over the ocean, with a flight of steps leading down to the beach. The tide was turning and a soft wind blew the hair back from Ellie's face as they leaned on the rail, drinking in the view. Noticing the scar on her forehead, Dan wondered, shocked, how she had got it. Then he said, 'Want to take a walk, before the sun sets?'

She had her sneakers off in a second and almost beat Pancho down the steps to the sand. Rolling up her pants legs, she yelled, 'Last one in's a sissy.' Then she took off down the beach.

He jogged after her, every muscle groaning with agony.

'Just look at the old man.' She was kicking up her heels at the edge of the waves, enjoying her freedom. 'Whatever happened to Dan, Dan, the surferman, with abs of steel and a butt to die for?'

He grinned. 'You've got a pretty good memory. How about that time you threw up all over me?'

He came up beside her, and she groaned. 'I was hoping you wouldn't remember.'

'Total recall. Except did you have braces or not?'

She shook her head, tossing back her windblown hair. 'They came later. I'm glad you don't have that memory to add to your hit list.'

'Maybe it's a wish list.'

She glanced sceptically at him, and he added, 'You were a cute kid, even then.'

'Liar,' she grinned. 'I was kind of like Pancho, chunky, with long spindly legs and big feet. Race you to the rocks,' she challenged, taking off again, her long hair streaming behind her. He huffed after her, limping.

She circled back, hands on hips, regarding him critically. Her cheeks glowed pink and her eyes sparkled. She felt the way she had on her first day of college, on her very first day of freedom – even if this was only one day.

'Uhuh,' she groaned, 'I knew it. It's whiplash and you're going to sue the hell out of me.'

He laughed. 'Rear-ending my new car had absolutely nothing to do with it. It's just that I rode a horse today for the first time in years, a frisky mare – almost as frisky as you, and twice as powerful. She gave me a run for my money and now I ache in places I didn't know I had.'

'They say horses can reach parts even bicycles don't.' She linked her arm companionably through his as they ambled back to the house.

'So what made you do it?' she asked suddenly. 'Give up the police?'

'A bullet had my name on it. I thought I was lucky, it didn't kill me, then they told me I'd be stuck in a desk job for the rest of my working days.' He shrugged, 'After that, the simple life suddenly seemed attractive. Back to the earth, small-town living. A man can get sick of having to deal with day-to-day crime.'

Ellie nodded, she could understand that. She sniffed the salt air, enjoying the warmth of his bare arm against hers, the maleness of him. It had been a long time between dates, she told herself, smiling. Though of course, this wasn't a real 'date' date.

He said, 'So? What about you? I remember you were a pretty ritzy family. The mansion on top of the hill? Family retainers to do your bidding. Old money.'

Ellie stopped and skimmed a pebble across the waves. 'That was then. Now I have to work for my living. My grandmother still lives at Journey's End, but only just, and without the retainers. Somehow the money just ran out before it reached me.' She pushed her hair from her eyes, looking at him. 'That's life, as they say.'

'No regrets?'

'Are you kidding?' she laughed. 'Of course I have regrets. For one, I'd like to be able to keep my grandmother in the way to which she has always been accustomed, without having to worry where the money is coming from. Two, it would have made my own life a lot easier.' Heaving a sigh, she added, 'But you know, I probably would have done exactly what I'm doing now. So I guess that says something. Like, if you want it badly enough you go for it, money or no money. Or else, that I'm an idiot working eighteen hours a day in a business that's only just ticking over.'

'Looks like we're in the same boat. Running Horse is a mess. It'll probably take years before I get it into shape. They tell me there's a jinx on it, and it's never produced a decent bottle.'

'Until you came along.'

'Until Carlos Ortega came along. My new winemaker. Either that, or he's escaped from the local circus.'

Ellie laughed when he told her the story of Ortega's arrival. 'But how can you trust a man like that?'

'Gut reaction. It's about all I have to go on these days, but I'd bet on him. And, as he shrewdly pointed out, I don't have too much choice.'

Pancho streaked ahead of them up the steps to the house, then darted past them again, on his way down. From the corner of his eye, Dan caught the flash of red meat in his jaws. He clapped a hand to his head, groaning. 'That darned dog has just run off with our dinner.'

Ellie peered over the rail. Pancho was lying in the sand, demolishing the last of the filet mignon. 'That is one thieving, conniving mutt you've got there, mister,' she said, awed. 'He chose his moment perfectly. He's pretty damned smart.'

Dan eyed him, exasperated. 'I can't send him back to the pound. He thinks he's mine now. He's even started to sleep on my bed.'

'You're a sucker, Dan Cassidy. You have to train them from day one, otherwise they peg you for a soft touch and you're a goner.' She grinned at the dog's happy face as he rolled over in the sand, waving all four paws in the air. 'He's awfully cute, but it's a good thing I bought bread and cheese. With a bottle of wine, who could ask for anything more?'

'I forgot to ask you,' Ellie said, in the kitchen, cutting the baguette into hunks. 'Weren't you married?' The minute it was out of her mouth, she wished she hadn't said it. The wine must be loosening her tongue. 'I take that question back,' she added quickly.

Dan leaned against the white-tiled counter, arms folded. 'I was,' he said, looking at her. 'And as a friend, you have a right to ask. And no, I'm not married now. It wasn't her fault, and I guess it wasn't mine either. It was kid's stuff, all romance and no reality, it could never have worked. That's when I went to New York and became a cop instead of a biologist.' He shrugged. 'No regrets though. I guess I was cut out to be a winemaker anyhow.'

'Just the way I'm cut out to be a restaurateur, and not an idle society woman. I have my father's genes, he was a wild Irishman, too.' She carried the basket of bread into the living room and set it on the coffee table. 'Maybe that's why I like you.'

Dan put the plate of cheeses down carefully. 'You like me?' He was laughing.

'Oh, I guess I like you enough,' she said, flirting with him. 'You're sort of okay, for the genre.'

He filled their glasses then sat on the floor next to her, helping himself to cheese and bread. 'Tell me about your father. And your mother.'

Ellie sipped the wine, thoughtfully. There was so much to tell – and yet so little. So few years together for her to remember.

'I know she was beautiful,' she said at last. 'I was only five when she died, but I can still remember her smile, and her perfume. Piguet's *Fracas*. It smelled like all the lilies in the world melted down into a bottle. It's so distinctive, I almost can't bear it when I catch a whiff of it on another woman. Just thinking of it now, it's as though she's in the room.'

20

The story of her parents was engraved on Ellie's heart, she'd heard it so often. When she was a child, it was her favourite bedtime story. 'Tell me again about my mother and my father,' she would ask, and Miss Lottie would repeat it one more time, often with tears in her eyes that Ellie would brush away with her small finger.

'When my mother was born,' she told Dan, 'my grandparents couldn't agree on who to name her for, so instead they named her Romany. Something Miss Lottie said she regretted ever after, because that girl lived up to her name. She was a wild gypsy of a young thing, always happy, giddy with the sheer pleasure of being alive and in love. And it seemed to poor, proper Miss Lottie, that from the age of fifteen Romany was *always* in love.

'When my grandfather died unexpectedly, she was left to bring up Romany alone. Her standards were strict and Romany was wild, but she always assumed she would calm down and marry someone suitable. But times had changed. It was the sixties and the young had turned the world as Miss Lottie knew it completely around. They lived for the moment. And on their terms.

'Then, when she was twenty-four, Romany ran off with Rory Duveen, penniless and a nobody. Plus he was fifteen years older, and divorced.'

'Why?' Miss Lottie had demanded, anguished.

'Because I love him, Ma,' her smiling, beautiful daughter had replied, her mist-blue eyes dancing with mischief, because she knew her mother hated to be called 'Ma' almost as much as she hated her unexpected new son-in-law.

'Anyhow,' Ellie told Dan, 'The damage was done. Romany had her own money, inherited from her grandfather, and the happy pair flitted around the world in a haze of marijuana smoke and well-being, partying and enjoying life. Because, as Rory always said, what else was life for?

'A few years later, Romany took time out to give birth to me and then they were off again, leaving me with Miss Lottie. Sometimes, over her protests, they would take me to Europe with them. Rory hated California in the summer, he said it was too hot.'

She lifted her shoulders in a little shrug, that somehow expressed her sadness. 'And that's the way life was. Until the day their white Bentley convertible threw an unexpected snit, and hurled them into a rocky canyon in the Los Padres mountains.

'It's so strange,' she added with a frown, 'I can see us on that mountain road, I can hear my father singing, I can see him turning to smile at me. I can feel the car doing this funny little shimmy . . . I can even remember them smiling at each other, his voice, still singing . . . and then they were gone.

'I was tossed out onto the grass and bushes at the side of the road. They found me later, still sitting there with the straw sunhat crammed on my head and a big cut on my face. But that was all.'

Dan saw her shiver. Wondering if it were the sad memories, or the mist creeping in, he closed the windows and then put a match to the fire. He gave her his sweater and Ellie snuggled into it, curling her coral-toed feet under her. The sweater felt good, soft and masculine-scented.

'I don't know why I'm telling you all this,' she said, looking at him across the coffee table, 'I've never really talked about it with anyone, except Miss Lottie and Maya. I figured it was nobody's business but my own. The odd thing is though, I have the feeling something is missing from that memory. It's on the edge of my mind, out there in the blackness of eternity.' She sighed wistfully, then added, 'But I remember their funeral as though it were yesterday.

'It was one of the biggest and most memorable in Montecito's

103

history, because Miss Lottie wanted it that way, for Romany. The church and Journey's End were covered in white roses, and she decked me out in a pretty white organdie dress, and shiny black mary-janes, as though I were going to a party.

'Crowds gathered at the graveside and a choir sang 'Onward Christian soldiers' while the two white coffins were lowered into the ground.

'I remember I cried when they sang. It just didn't seem possible that my vivid, life-loving parents could be gone. I felt so sure they were going to pop out from behind a tree calling, 'Surprise, surprise,' the way they used to when they came back from their travels.

'Still, it was a fact and Miss Lottie said we'd both better get used to it. But for a long time afterwards, in my dreams I heard the shriek of steel ripping apart and the sound of shattering glass. And then just that deep, endless silence. Even the crickets had stopped their chirruping, and the birds their singing. It was as though the whole silent mountainside had gone into shock.

'It wasn't until I was much older that Miss Lottie told me that, in ten years, Romany had frittered away the inheritance it had taken three generations of Stamfords to accumulate. Ten years of the high life, running round the world first-class on chartered planes and luxury yachts. It was de luxe all the way for them because, as my father always said, life was meant to be fun and what else could money buy, if not pleasure? That was their philosophy. They lived by it, and they even died by it. In a hundred-thousand-dollar automobile.'

'I'm sorry,' Dan leaned across and took her hand. 'That was a tough break, and you were so young.'

Firelight bathed them in a soft reddish glow leaving the corners of the room in darkness. From outside came the roar of the breakers, curving along the shoreline. Ellie felt suspended in time, as though she had stepped back and saw things clearly, events that had happened that she had chosen not to remember. Dan's eyes were dark with sympathy as she looked at him.

'I learned all about violence, that year,' she said quietly. 'First, with my parents, and then with my grandmother.'

She hesitated. 'I've never told anyone about this before, not

even my friend, Maya. Miss Lottie asked me not to, she said I
had to erase it from my mind like chalk from a blackboard, and
never speak of it again. I tried, but I've never forgotten it. And
how terrified I was.'

He took a sip of wine. Seeing the remembered terror in her
darkened eyes, he said, 'Do you want to tell me?'

It had been locked inside her for so long, Ellie knew it would
be a relief to speak of it.

'It happened a few weeks after the accident. Miss Lottie always
put me to bed herself and then she would read me a story. Of
course, I know now how hard it must have been for her, trying
to cope with Romany's death, putting on a brave face in front of
me, though I suspect she cried herself to sleep too. And I hated
being alone at night . . .'

Telling Dan about it, Ellie could see herself, alone in her
blue-and-white gingham room, in the narrow French sleigh-bed
that had been her own mother's when she was a child. The
curtains were not drawn and Miss Lottie had left the window
open as she always did, rain or cold, for 'health reasons', because
she said a child needed fresh air when she was sleeping. But the
branches of the juniper tree tapped scarily against the window
and Ellie couldn't sleep, so she did what she often did those
days. She climbed from the high bed and ran, in her bare feet
and pyjamas, along the hallway to Miss Lottie's room.

She turned the door handle and peeked in. No one was there,
so she trotted to the top of the stairs and looked down.

A fire blazed in the big fireplace in the hall, and the lamps
were lit. It looked warm and cheerful, and a lot less lonely than
her room. Clinging to the oak banisters, she walked slowly down
the wide shallow steps and through the hall. She knew where
Miss Lottie would be and she headed, like a homing pigeon, to
the library.

Often, those nights, she would sneak in and just sit quietly,
watching her grandmother while she opened her mail, or wrote
letters, or made telephone calls. Miss Lottie would pretend for a
while not to see her, then she'd glance up and catch her eye and
say, 'Now, be off with you, child. It's late. Come, I'll take you up
myself and tuck you in again, if you promise you'll go to sleep.'

Nodding solemnly, Ellie always promised, and the little respite in the calm of the library, with its ticking clock and the crackling logs slipping in the grate, and the sound of Miss Lottie's pen scratching across the thick cream notepaper as she wrote, somehow worked its soothing magic, and she slept.

Only not that night. Voices came from the half-open door and she peeked interestedly at the visitor. Unnoticed, she slipped into the room and took her usual seat on the oversized Chinese elmwood chair that Miss Lottie always called 'the Mandarin's chair'. Its smoothly-polished wood felt cold through her thin pyjamas and she shivered, watching the man and her grandmother, wondering what they were talking about.

Suddenly the man stood up. He towered over Miss Lottie. He was yelling at her in a hard furious voice. Ellie had never heard anyone speak like that before, harsh, angry words. Then he leapt at Miss Lottie, clasped his big hands round her throat. He was shouting at her, saying something over and over again . . . '*bitch, old bitch, I'll get you and I'll get what's mine . . .*'

Ellie clutched the chair arms tightly. Her mouth fell open in silent panic and her eyes were round with terror. She was shaking, unable to move, to speak. 'Gran,' she cried out at last, 'Gran . . .'

He turned and saw her. Their eyes met and she shrank back into the chair, transfixed by the naked evil in his. She began to scream.

Suddenly the door burst open. The men servants ran in, Gustave and the chauffeur. Behind them were the security guards, weapons drawn. In an instant, they had him down on the floor, his arms twisted behind his back, his face pressed into the carpet.

Ellie watched, numb with terror, while a guard held a gun at the man's head, and Miss Lottie walked slowly across the room and stood looking down at him. She was pale, trembling, angry. But she was not afraid.

Then Maria had come running in. She grabbed Ellie and carried her off, still crying, still terrified, to her room.

Later, Miss Lottie came to speak to her. 'It was just a crazy man,' she explained. 'He's gone now, and I want you to forget you ever saw him. He'll never bother us again. Promise me, Ellie, that you will forget tonight, and that you'll never speak of it to anyone.'

And Ellie had nodded, crossing her heart, promising.

'And until tonight,' she said to Dan, sitting opposite, watching her through hooded dark eyes, 'I've kept that promise. I was too young to understand what was going on, but I knew he was hurting her. She said, afterwards, it was just lucky I was there. And that I saved her.'

'Did you ever find out who he was?'

She shook her head. 'I told you, we never spoke of it again.'

He sighed, 'That was a hell of a year for a five-year-old. All credit to your grandmother for getting you through it.'

The log sputtered in the grate, and she yawned, exhausted. 'I've talked half the night away,' she said apologetically. 'Thanks for listening.' She reached for his hand. 'Friends?' She smiled into his eyes.

'Friends.' Her hand felt firm and cool in his. 'And as a friend, I'm not about to let you drive home. You've drunk too much wine, talked yourself out, and you're about the tiredest woman I ever saw. The sheets are clean and the bed is comfortable. And I guarantee it's all yours. Please, be my guest.'

Ellie shook her head, 'Can't,' she yawned. 'Sorry, it must be the sea air.' She slithered further down in the comfortable sofa, her eyes half-closed. 'I have to get back,' she mumbled. 'I'm expecting deliveries at the café tomorrow at eight.'

Dan grinned, she would be asleep before she even knew it. He walked into the bedroom and came back with a blanket. As he had guessed, she was out for the count. He tucked the blanket round her, letting his hand rest lightly on her soft hair for a second. Sleeping, she had the face of an innocent child. Awake, she was all woman.

He walked out onto the deck, gazing at the fading moon. Pancho flopped down next to him, put his nose on his paws and closed his eyes. But Dan sat staring out into the night, listening to the soft slap of waves on the shore, thinking about the woman asleep on his sofa. And of the tough road in front of him. It was a long time before he finally went to bed.

He woke her early, with coffee and toast.

Ellie leapt to her feet, running her hands distractedly through her tangled hair. 'What time is it?'

'Six. And take it easy, friend. There's time for coffee and a shower before you go.'

She smiled at the word 'friend.' Tilting her head on one side, she looked into his eyes. 'Thanks, Danny Boy,' she murmured.

All he said was, 'You're welcome, ma'am.' But he figured it might be tough, staying just friends with Ellie Parrish.

21

At about the time they were having their early-morning coffee, Buck was sprawled on a sofa in one of the Biltmore's luxurious terrycloth bathrobes, reading the advertising pages of *USA Today*, and waiting for room service to deliver his breakfast.

The gods were with him. The ad offering a business address and telephone answering service was exactly what he needed, and the fact that it was three thousand miles away, in Miami, could not have been more perfect. He got on the phone and made the arrangements. He could receive mail there and they would answer the phone in the name of *The Jensen Property Development Company*, and take messages. Not that he expected any, but in case anyone should check, he was covering all bases.

Room service arrived and he devoured the oatmeal blueberry pancakes hungrily, then dressed, packed his things and checked out of the hotel. Too long a stay would make him known to the management; people would observe him, get too friendly, ask questions. Besides, Journey's End might take a while to sell, and he wanted to conserve money.

Back in LA, he rented a cheap studio apartment on a narrow little street, just south of Sunset. The building was a transient one, full of young people on the move, and the furnished apartment was on the ground floor with a private entrance, which suited Buck just fine.

He dumped his bags there, then drove a few blocks until he found a quick-print shop where he ordered business cards in the name of the *Jensen Property Development Company*, with the Miami address and phone number.

After that, he drove west to Santa Monica.

It was early evening when he got to Ellie's Place. Again, he got lucky, a car was pulling out of a parking spot directly opposite and he slid the BMW in, cutting off the waiting green Accura. The driver mouthed an obscenity at him, but Buck ignored him. He slipped two quarters into the parking meter, then got back in the car and sat watching the café.

It was early, only just six, but already a couple of tables were occupied. A sexy-looking blonde was taking orders and bringing glasses of wine but there was no sign of Ellie. The passing traffic blocked his view and he glared round, frustrated.

He was parked directly in front of a bustling little gourmet sandwich bar that was getting a lot of lively action. And their window looked directly across into Ellie's Place.

He went in, ordered a mocha granita, then took a seat in the window. Sipping the iced drink, he concentrated his gaze on the café opposite.

Half an hour passed. He ordered another drink, wondering nervously what had happened to Ellie. Then he saw her, loping breathlessly down the street, long red hair flying. She was clutching a large box and dodging passersby expertly. As he watched, she shoved through the café door and disappeared from sight.

'About time,' Maya greeted her, from behind the zinc counter. 'I thought you must be making that coffee machine.'

'Sorry.' Ellie dropped the box onto the counter between them. 'But I had to do something or the customers will be deserting us for Starbucks. Anyway, this will do until the big machine is fixed.'

She dashed into the back to check the chaos in the kitchen. Chan was slamming woks and pots around, frowning, while Terry prepped vegetables. The 'soup of the day' simmered gently on the gas burner next to pans of sauces, and everything was smelling good.

'I gotta get another job,' Chef Chan greeted Ellie, scowling. 'This kitchen is too small.'

'Small is good, Chan.' She wrapped a spotless white apron round her waist and tied it firmly. 'You don't have as far to walk. In a big kitchen, your feet would be killing you.' Chan's feet were a sore point, he complained endlessly about them, clomping round in wooden clogs for comfort. Swinging her hair into a ponytail, Ellie pulled on the baseball cap, then hurried out front to greet her customers.

Maya leaned against the door, blocking her way. 'Not so fast, Ellie Parrish. First, tell me about last night?'

'Last night?' Ellie shrugged, grinning. 'Oh, it was good. Nice, you know. Being with an old friend.'

'What's all this old friend stuff? You were a kid when you knew him, and you were definitely not friends.'

'Well, we are now.'

'Hasn't he asked you for another date?'

'Maya, I keep telling you, this was not a date. We had a nice friendly dinner. He told me about his life, I caught him up on mine. Then I fell asleep and he woke me this morning with coffee and toast . . .'

There was a dazed look in Maya's whisky-brown eyes. 'Wait just one minute, woman. Are you telling me you stayed over? On the first date? My god, celibacy must have wrecked your brain. Either that or he knows which buttons to push. Ellie, I think you need serious retraining in dating etiquette.'

'We just talked, that's all. Or rather, I did the talking. He listened.'

'*Listening* is always a good ploy.' Maya scowled suspiciously. 'I don't trust this guy.'

'Believe me, it's good to be listened to for a change, instead of being lectured.' Ellie pushed past her, automatically checking tables, smiling greetings to a couple of regular customers, offering menus. The familiar nightly routine had begun.

'Just think what your grandmother would say,' Maya commented loudly as she passed her.

'Remind me to tell you later about my grandmother's lecture on my sex life, or lack of it,' Ellie whispered back, laughing as Maya's brows climbed into her hair in astonishment.

Buck walked across the road and into Ellie's Place. He glanced round, looking for her, but instead the beautiful blonde came toward him, menu in hand.

'Good evening,' Maya smiled politely. 'A table for two?'

He gave her a charming smile. 'I'm afraid I'm alone tonight.'

'Too bad, but you've come to the right place. Alone is not a problem here, and you'll enjoy the food.' She showed him to a table in the window and added, 'You can watch the passing show outside, it'll keep you entertained.'

He gave her another smile, taking the menu she offered him. 'You certainly know how to make a person feel welcome.'

'That's my job. I'll just tell you tonight's specials, then I'll leave you to look at the menu. And of our wines by the glass, I can recommend the Vieille Ferme in a red, or if you prefer white wine, the Fess Parker chardonnay.'

Buck was polite, charming. He ordered the red wine, the *soupe au pistou* and Shrimp and Scallops Chan-style. He nibbled on the good bread, waiting and watching.

He was half-way through the glass of wine when Ellie emerged from the kitchen. She threw him a smile as she served the table nearby. Buck quickly drained his glass. He caught her eye as she turned, 'Could I have another?' He held up the empty glass, smiling.

'Of course, sir. What were you drinking.' Her voice was sweet and soft as sugar.

'The red. I think she said it was the Ferme something . . .' he looked vague.

'The Vieille Ferme.'

'Wait a minute,' he said, pretending astonishment. 'Weren't you at the Biltmore yesterday? In Montecito?'

She looked puzzled. 'Yes, but . . .'

'You noticed I wasn't feeling well. You were kind enough to stop and ask if you could help me.' He looked warmly at her, 'A man doesn't forget an act of kindness like that. It's something that's rare these days, unfortunately.'

'Ellie's puzzled frown cleared. 'Of course, I remember now. I'm glad to see you've recovered, anyhow.'

'It was nothing, just too much sun, I guess.'

His smile was warm and friendly, and Ellie smiled back, though she hardly thought it could be too much sun he was suffering from. The man was as pale as a ghost.

'I'll get that wine for you right away, sir,' she promised.

Elated, he watched her walk back to the kitchen. Humming 'Dixie' under his breath, he waited for her to return, but instead the blonde brought the wine. 'This glass is compliments of Ellie's sir,' she said. 'Enjoy.'

Buck did enjoy. In fact, he couldn't remember enjoying a meal as much in his entire life. The food was good, but the fact that he had a grandstand seat, watching Ellie, made it even better; though he was jealous of every man who spoke to her that night, every smile she donated, free, with the food.

He took his time over coffee, and the customers had thinned out when he finally got up and walked to the counter to pay his bill.

'I hope you enjoyed your meal, sir?'

He held out the cash and Ellie took it from him. For a fraction of a second, her fingers touched his. It was like detonating a stick of dynamite.

'It was very good. And so was the wine. You're very generous.'

'We try to look after our guests, at Ellie's Place.'

'Thank you. And my name is Ed. Ed Jensen.'

'Hope to see you again, Mr Jensen.' She gave him that big smile and he waved a hand as he turned away.

He was well pleased with himself. Phase One was underway. Contact had been established.

Back across the road again, he fed coins into the meter and got back in the car, waiting. It was a slow night on the street and at ten the sexy blonde waitress left, calling goodbyes over her shoulder. He saw Ellie turn the *Open* sign to *Closed*, then she disappeared from sight.

Chan and the sous-chef had gone home half an hour before and Ellie was alone. She leaned against the counter, sipping a glass of water, thinking about Dan, wondering if she'd revealed too much about her private feelings last night. Baring her soul to him hardly made for great entertainment, and to prove it, he hadn't asked to see her again.

With a little 'who cares' shrug, she put down the empty glass, telling herself she didn't have the time, anyhow. Taking off her apron, she hung it on a hook, released her ponytail, and lifted her hair in her hands with a sigh of relief. Then she grabbed her jacket and bag.

As Ellie locked the door and strode rapidly down the street in the opposite direction, Buck made a quick illegal u-turn, and cruised slowly after her. After a couple of blocks, she turned right, heading for a four-storey carpark. He pulled into the kerb, engine purring softly.

A few minutes later, Ellie drove past in a bright yellow jeep. She halted at the intersection, indicating left and Buck swung quickly round in another U. He was right behind her as she took off down Main.

Fatigue settled over Ellie like a heavy grey blanket; all she wanted was to get home, take a hot shower and crawl into bed. Turning right, she drove a couple of blocks up the small hill, then made a quick left. It barely registered that there was a car right behind her.

She punched the garage opener and the temperamental door swung half-way up, then stopped. It stuck there, trembling, and she gave it another angry click, breathing a sigh of relief when it slowly shuddered open. She was out of the car in a flash, pounding up the stairs, flinging her clothes off as she went.

After the shower, she went to the window and leaned her elbows on the sill, listening to the softer night sounds. A cool breeze was blowing and in the distance she could hear the surf, though she couldn't see it because the night was overcast.

She thought of the pounding surf outside Pines Cottage last night, and the intimacy of the firelit room. Of Dan sitting opposite her, filling her wine glass and eating birthday cake; and of the shabby dog sleeping contentedly at his feet, its belly full of stolen steak. It was such a warm, companionable scene; she sighed with regret. Dan Cassidy was a very busy man. And she was a busy woman.

'"And never the twain shall meet",' she quoted, climbing into the canopied bed and closing her eyes, waiting for sleep to overtake her.

In the shadows across the street, Buck groaned with lust for her. The night was cool, but heat rushed up his spine. He was on fire.

He ran back to the car and drove to the studio apartment. Locking the door behind him, he stripped off his clothes in a frenzy. Minutes later, he was prowling the tiny apartment, wild as a caged animal, exactly the way he used to at the Hudson facility. Only this time there were no guards to observe him and say, 'Better get the strait-jacket. There goes Buck Duveen again. Crazy as a loon.'

22

Carlos Ortega was on his hands and knees, his face pressed to a single stick-like vine, inspecting it from bottom to top, branch by branch.

'You see this, Señor.' He indicated a frail-looking twig. 'These vines were budded, grafted onto the Cabernet Franc rootstock. Neglect and possibly bad weather spoiled them. The rootstock is good. If we baby them, treat them like little children, pamper them, caress them, love them, Señor. They will revive.'

He looked up beaming, and Dan said. 'You mean I'm going to have to *love* my vines as well as give them all my money. It sounds exactly like a bad marriage, Carlos.'

'No, no, Señor, it's not the same like loving a woman. These are your children. Is different.' He got to his feet, wafting dust from his knees with his straw sombrero. 'Is good news, Señor Dan. I'm already saving you money.'

Dan was on his knees, staring at the vine. He could feel the warmth of the earth under his hands, smell its sweet, flat odour, see tiny tufts of reddish-green growth that might almost be a bud. A surge of pride went through him. This was his land, his vines, his goddamn buds. Ortega was right, they were like his kids.

'How much?' he asked, getting back to basics before he became too poetic.

Carlos tugged thoughtfully on his moustache, considering. 'Good cabernet budwood, maybe ten cents each one.'

Dan brightened, that number didn't sound too drastic.

'For the whole hillside,' Carlos swung round, surveying the slope, 'Maybe thirty, forty thousand dollars.'

Dan sighed resignedly. He might have known it. In wine-making everything sounded reasonable until you added up the quantities. 'I guess I'd better make an appointment with the bank manager again.'

'Buying budwood is like making love,' Ortega announced, ignoring the mundane bit about the bank manager. 'You get to know your woman, you know her scent, it lingers in your memory . . . that is what you look for when you choose your vines. The rich aroma the wine produces that lingers in your nostrils.' He breathed in deeply, then exhaled, shaking his head with pleasure. 'First, Señor, you call the Foundation Plant Material Service at UC Davis. If they no have the right cabernet, we go to Napa. I know exactly the vineyard. Later, closer to harvest, we go taste the grapes on the vine. And I shall know if it is the best.' Carlos rolled his eyes, in ecstasy. 'We shall produce a beautiful cabernet.'

Dan surely hoped he was right. 'How soon can we graft?'

'July is good. Further north, it would be August, but here we have more warmth.'

Dan looked at the gentle slope, imagining it filled with leafy vines, burdened with luscious ripe grapes, ready for harvest. Already a half-dozen Mexican workers were spread out down the hillside, backs bent as they chopped out the weeds and cleared clogged irrigation pipes. Mariachi music blasted gaily from Ortega's rusty old pickup, where Pancho sat, tongue lolling, surveying the scene as if he owned the place. From the top of the hill, he could hear the whine of a saw as the carpenter tackled the sagging boards on the porch, and see Maria hanging out washing on a line beside the lean-to outside the kitchen. His horses were in the stables and in a few days he would be sleeping in his own bed. The place was almost beginning to feel like home.

Back at the office, the phone was ringing.

He picked it up on the run. 'Running Horse Winery.'

'Almost sounds like it's real,' Piatowski said.

Dan could hear the grin in his voice. 'It sure is. It just cost me another thirty thou today, maybe forty.'

'What the hell for, man?'

He sounded outraged and Dan laughed. 'For budwood, Piatowski. And you don't know what that means and I'm not about to tell you. Just trust me. Ortega says we'll have great cabernet.'

'Whoever Ortega is, if he's talking you out of thirty thousand bucks for buds he sounds like a terrific con artist. That's a lot of bouquets, fella.'

'Yeah, I'll tell my bank manager that. So?' Dan propped his booted feet on the desk and ran his hand through his dusty hair, thinking how great a shower was going to feel. 'When are you coming out?'

'I just want you to run this little nugget of info through your Californian sun-addled brain. Just before it atrophies, y'understand? I caught something on the computer this morning, I don't imagine you'll have heard about it on TV yet, other than just another murder, because the LAPD won't have given out any details. About a hooker murdered in an alley, not too far from Sunset Boulevard?'

Dan's ears pricked up as Piatowsky paused dramatically.

'There was a cross carved into her forehead, Cassidy. Temple to temple. Scalp to nose.'

Dan gave a low surprised whistle. 'It's the signature killer. I was right.'

'Unfortunately for the hooker, you were. And this one's in your neck of the woods, buddy. I contacted the LAPD, and the FBI, gave them the info on the Times Square woman, to compare notes. It's the same fella all right, he used the same knife, probably a switchblade. Seems like he's into his stride, and I've no doubt he'll do it again. Sooner rather than later.'

'When the mood is on him,' Dan added, thoughtfully.

'We're issuing warnings,' Piatowsky added. 'Much good it'll do. For the girls, it's business as usual, and hooking's always been a risky business. Anyhow, I thought when I get out there, I'll check in with the LAPD, see what's doing. A little collaboration, y'know.'

'When do you get here?'

'In a couple of weeks. Around the fifteenth. That okay with you?'

'I've got Honey ready and waiting.'

'Who's Honey?' Piatowski sounded suspicious and Dan laughed.

'Wait and see, Detective. I guarantee it'll be a surprise.'

'Yeah, I'll bet. Meanwhile, how are the women out there in sunshineland?'

'Dazzling,' Dan said, thinking of Ellie. 'Terrific, as a matter of fact.'

'Well, at least that was positive. I'll bet she's less expensive than the budwood. And more fun.'

'Bet all you like. But if you act civilized, I might let you meet her.'

'If she likes her men civilized, what's she doing with Daniel Patrick Cassidy, the scourge of Midtown South?'

'Get lost, Piatowsky.' Laughing, Dan put down the phone. He circled the fifteenth on the wall calendar with the picture of the John Deere tractor, wondering about the signature killer.

He'd have bet money on it being a just-released prisoner. One killing on the east coast, one on the west. Could be a long-distance driver? Or just some bum who'd hopped a Greyhound to satisfy his Hollywood fantasies? He shrugged; either way, it wasn't his problem now. He had four thousand pieces of budwood to worry about.

His hand lingered on the telephone. He could call Ellie, just to say, 'Hi, friend, how are you doing today? Thanks for coming by. And for providing the food, the conversation, the company . . . I loved having you sleep over on my sofa.'

He dialled her number.

Ellie's heart jumped when she heard his voice. 'I was just thinking about you.'

'You were?'

'I wanted to call to say thank you. I enjoyed myself.'

'Me too. And thanks for bringing the food. Sorry about the steaks and Pancho.'

She laughed, 'That's okay . . . next time . . .'

'About that *next time*,' he jumped in quickly. 'I know you're a busy woman, or I'd suggest sooner. But what about next week? I thought maybe you'd like to take a look around the vineyard.'

'I'd love that.'

She sounded as though she really would love it, and he added eagerly, 'We could have dinner somewhere, after.'

'Where?'

'How about Mollie's?'

Ellie laughed. 'Is she any competition for me?'

'Not a bit, she's Italian, not French. A trattoria, not a bistro.'

'In that case, I'd like it.'

'Good.'

Silence hung like a silken thread between them.

'And how is the rugged farmhand?' she asked softly, cradling the phone under her cheek.

'Hot and sweaty, with dirt under his nails.'

'Sounds like the real thing.'

'I'm getting there, with Carlos's help.'

'I've got customers. You can tell me all about it later. I can't wait to hear . . .'

'I can't wait, either . . .' he said.

He was still thinking of her when he dialled the number of UCLA, Davis, about the cabernet budwood.

23

Buck was back in Santa Monica at 6 a.m. parked on the hill at the end of Ellie's street. Rolling down the windows, he let the early morning air cool his brow, sipping Starbuck's coffee from a paper cup and reading the *LA Times*.

At seven, the yellow jeep drove past him. He followed at a discreet distance, just keeping her in view, all the way to the produce market where he parked and waited again.

A while later, Ellie emerged pushing a dolly piled with cartons of fresh vegetables. She loaded them into the back of the jeep, then took off again.

Buck was right behind her.

He kept watch for a week. By then, he knew her routine, knew her hours, where she went, who she saw and what she did. He knew she left the house at seven every morning and most nights didn't return until after midnight. He knew that she visited Miss Ellie every Monday and they had tea at the Biltmore.

It was just dark when he parked opposite her house. He was smartly dressed and looked like a prosperous businessman if anybody should see him, but there was no one around to notice. Hurrying across the street, he pushed open the little white gate and strode the four paces up the brick path to the front door. It took seconds to jimmy the lock, then he was inside.

He leaned back against the door, buzzing with excitement. A lamp was lit in the tiny sitting room on his left. He took a seat on the sofa and propped his feet on the coffee table, looking calmly round as if he owned the place.

A pretty Venetian mirror hung over the pinewood mantel,

adorned with a pair of old silver candlesticks and some photos. He got up to look at them, greedy for a glimpse of her, but none were of Ellie. An antique French giltwood console stood along one wall, with a faience urn filled with gaudy overblown parrot tulips. There was a painting of a Pre-Raphaelite maiden, who looked quite a lot like Ellie, and another of Journey's End, painted in the thirties when it was first built. Books were piled haphazardly on every surface. It was clean, but had the air of a room rarely used.

Disappointed, he walked back across the tiny entry hall into the dining room. A dozen gilt-framed paintings covered the walls and an open archway led directly into the minute white kitchen.

A mug of cold tea stood on the kitchen counter with an imprint of Ellie's lipstick on the rim. Trembling, he pressed his own lips over it, drinking her in with the Earl Grey. A shiver of ecstasy throbbed deep in his gut.

He could smell her scent, even before he reached the top of the creaking stairs. He stood in the bedroom doorway, his eyes closed, inhaling her. Then he opened them, and knew he was in paradise.

Clothes were flung carelessly across a chair, and a trail of discarded undergarments led to the bathroom. Kneeling, he ran his fingers over the lacy white thong, the flimsy bra. Then he picked them up and held them to his face.

When he came to his senses, he went systematically through her closet. He noted that her clothes were size six, and her shoes an unexpectedly large ten. He wrote down the name of her perfume, her bath-soap, lotion, powder. He saw that her favourite colour was blue, that there was Evian in her refrigerator, Fuji apples in a bowl, a half-full bottle of good French burgundy, Chateau de Peyrelle. He went through every cupboard, every drawer.

When he left, an hour later, he knew all there was to know about Ellie Parrish Duveen.

He put the car in the lot round the corner from Main. Then, stoked with power, he swaggered into Ellie's Place. The beautiful blonde greeted him again.

'Hi,' he said, 'how are you? It's Ed. Ed Jensen, remember? You helped me the other night.'

'Oh, sure, How are you, Ed? Good to see you back.'

'Alone again, I'm afraid,'

He smiled cockily at her and warning signals flickered suddenly in Maya's head. 'Too bad. How about the same table, by the window?' His harsh voice grated like sandpaper on her spine. There was just something about him, maybe it was the eyes, they didn't smile when his mouth did.

'Where's Ellie tonight?'

So that's it, Maya thought, catching on. He was interested in Ellie. Well too bad, Ellie would never look at a guy like this once, never mind twice.

'Busy,' she said briskly. 'Can I get you something to drink, *sir?*' Placing the relationship back on a formal footing, she handed him the menu, then brought the glass of red wine he asked for.

In the kitchen she said to Ellie, 'Who is this Ed Jensen, anyway? He seems pretty darn friendly with you?'

'Jensen?' Ellie lifted her eyes from the grill where she was about to burn a fine piece of Ahi tuna if she weren't careful. Chan had quit again and she was in charge. 'Oh, him. He's just an acquaintance. I bumped into him at the Biltmore, then he came here.'

'Yeah, well he's here again, and he's asking after you, like he knows you.'

Ellie grinned, 'It's my fame as a chef, and a restaurateur. Everybody wants to know Wolfgang, now they want to know me too. I guess I'm doing something right.'

'But this one's creepy, Ell. You know how sometimes you get that gut feeling?' Maya rubbed her stomach, frowning.

'I think he's from out of town.' She was busy with the fish. 'He obviously doesn't know too many people out here, I guess he's just lonesome.'

'Oh, sure.' Maya's voice had a sceptical edge. 'And that's probably exactly what they said about your everyday axe murderer. He was just lonesome.'

Buck ordered steak and *pommes frites*. After a good day's

work, he was in the mood for a hearty meal. He was disappointed when the blonde served him and still Ellie did not appear, but contented himself picturing her in her home, in her room, in her bed. He'd almost forgotten the grandmother in his overwhelming obsession with Ellie.

Lingering, he drank another couple of glasses of wine and was the last to leave the restaurant. Maya rang up his bill, then took his money briskly. Cash, she noted, not a credit card. Hmmm, this guy was leaving no traces . . .

'What's your name?' Buck was waiting for his change.

'It's Maya, *sir*.' Politely, she handed him his receipt and the change.

'Thank you, Maya, I enjoyed it.' He gave her that sly smile again, but she refused to lift her eyes from the cash register.

'Goodnight, Mr Jensen,' she murmured, still avoiding his eyes.

'Goodnight, Maya. And the name is Ed.'

He walked confidently to the door, then turned and grinned at her. Maya's cheeks burned. He'd known she would be looking at him.

Remembering his strangely cold eyes, she told herself he looked like a man who knew too much. Hurrying to the door, she locked it securely after him.

24

Promptly at four on Monday, Miss Lottie wafted into the
Biltmore for afternoon tea. She was wearing a linen skirt in
a colour she called 'fawn', a cream silk shirt, her pearls and the
Paris hat with the roses. Ellie was outside, talking to someone
who had admired the Cadillac, but Miss Lottie's arthritis was
bothering her today and she wanted to get to her table and
sit down.

Her cane tapped on the polished saltillo tiles as she walked
slowly through the lobby, nodding good afternoon to people
she knew. The tall dark-haired man caught her eye as he hurried
past, and she swung round, staring after him.

It was him again, the one she couldn't remember. A frown
creased her brow; when a man wore a moustache, it was so
hard to tell what he really looked like. Perhaps she should
have introduced herself, asked who he was? But of course, a
lady didn't do that sort of thing.

Buck was smart in a blue suit and an expensive tie. His pale
blue shirt was immaculate, his tasselled loafers gleamed and his
newly-dark hair was carefully combed. He caught up to Ellie
on the steps.

'Well hello again.' He reached out, caught her arm. 'We seem
to make a habit of bumping into each other.'

'Mr Jensen.' Ellie turned, surprised. 'I didn't know you
lived here.'

'I only wish I did.' He gave her a sincere smile. 'It's
like a little oasis of peace and quiet, after the whirlwind of
Miami.'

Ellie smiled, understanding. 'My great-grandfather felt exactly that way about it and he never went back east again. He bought his land, built his house, and here he stayed.'

'Lucky man.' Buck hesitated, as though he was reluctant to bring the subject up. 'Actually I'm in property development.' He fumbled in his pocket, then handed her his business card. 'As a matter of fact, I'm looking for a house here, and I heard a rumour there's a wonderful old mansion for sale. Then they told me it belonged to you.' He smiled warmly at her. 'Such a coincidence. But then, I'm a great believer in fate.'

'That old rumour again,' Ellie sighed, 'it's been going round for years. But Journey's End belongs to my grandmother, Mr Jensen, and anyhow, it's not for sale.'

'To be honest, my health is not what it used to be.' He put a hand on his heart, grimacing, and Ellie gazed sympathetically at him. 'What I'm really searching for is the home I was never fortunate enough to have as a child. Now, the grown man wants a *true* home. I'm looking for a place I would love and live in, until my own Journey's End. You would make me a very happy man, if I could just see it,' he persuaded. 'Who knows, one day you may change your mind and decide to sell. Then at least, you'd know it would pass to someone who loved it, the way you do.'

Ellie eyed him, uncertainly. He was polite, charming, a gentleman, it couldn't just be a pickup line. Remembering his ashen face last time she'd seen him here, her heart went out to him. Besides, he was right, one day she would have to sell, though it wasn't something she really wanted to think about now.

Impulsively, she agreed. 'Why not come by at five, and I'll give you a quick tour.'

Buck beamed, pleased with himself. It had been so easy. He still knew how to turn on the charm. Shaking her hand warmly, he said, 'Thank you, thank you. I'll be there at five.'

Dan drove up to the hotel and handed the keys to the valet, then suddenly he saw her. 'Ellie,' he called, surprised,' 'I didn't expect to see you until later.'

'Dan Cassidy!' He was walking toward her with that macho loping stride that had first set her thinking that he was sexy. 'Fancy seeing you here.'

Her face lit up with that special smile and Buck's eyes turned to stone. Flinging an icy glare at Cassidy, he said quickly, 'Goodbye, Ellie. Until later.' As he walked away, he wasn't even sure that she had heard him. She had forgotten he even existed.

Dan's eyes followed him speculatively for a second, his cop's antennae bristling. He shrugged it away, he guessed it was just that the guy had been standing too close to Ellie and he was jealous. 'Who's the dark-haired Lothario?' he couldn't help asking.

She smiled at the description. 'Hardly a Lothario – just an acquaintance, interested in buying Journey's End.'

He looked at her, surprised. 'Are you selling, then?'

'No, but people are always asking. I guess they've heard the rumour that Gran's lost all her money. Anyhow, what are you doing here?'

'I came to pick up a copy of the *New York Times*, they usually have it at the news-stand.'

'And I'm taking Miss Lottie to tea. I know she'd be thrilled if you'd join us. She'll think I have a boyfriend, at long last, so just ignore her if she starts wanting to know your pedigree and your prospects.'

He laughed. 'The answer's easy. Zero on both counts.'

Miss Lottie spotted Ellie coming into the restuarant, noticing that she was laughing, and she was with a man. A *handsome* man. Miss Lottie perked up.

'Gran, this is a friend of mine, Dan Cassidy. You remember, I told you about him?'

She favoured him with a smile as she shook his hand. 'Certainly I remember, Mr Cassidy. I thought your face looked familiar. You're the star of *NYPD Blue*, aren't you?'

Dan heard Ellie's sigh as he said, 'Unfortunately not, ma'am, but I was a New York policeman.'

'Ah, that's it. The homicide detective, I knew I was right.' She waved him to a seat. 'I hope you're joining us for tea?'

'Ellie kindly invited me.'

'Good, good,' Miss Lottie poured tea from a silver pot with a shaky hand. 'I hope you like Earl Grey and scones.' Turning to Ellie, she said in a loud stage-whisper, 'I like his eyes.

Trustworthy, like a labrador's.' She beamed at Dan again, 'Such a pity you weren't here last Monday, for my birthday. There was a splendid cake. And champagne.'

'Dan bought the Running Horse Winery, Gran,' Ellie reminded her. 'He's working hard getting it back into shape.'

Something clicked into place in Miss Lottie's faulty mind. 'But isn't there a jinx on that place?' she asked, surprised, and Ellie groaned. 'Anyhow, it's a fool's game, farming,' she continued, sipping her tea. 'Always dependent on the weather and the gods.'

'Ellie's promised to come out and take a look at it, this evening, Miss Lottie.' Dan was enjoying himself.

'Has she indeed?' She threw a speculative glance at her granddaughter. 'Well, you must have something about you, Dan Cassidy, if you can prise my granddaughter away from that café. All she ever does is work.' She glanced at Ellie again. 'You'll have to bring your young man to visit me at Journey's End, Ellie, then we can talk more about what he does.'

Ellie rolled her eyes at Dan in an I-told-you-so look, and he grinned back at her.

Across the room, Buck drained his glass and signalled the waiter to bring another Jim Beam. Jealousy turned into anger as he watched them laughing together. He was locked out of their world. Gulping the bourbon, he reminded himself that in a little while he would be with Ellie. He smiled, that secret little smile. Phase Two of his plan was in motion.

25

Ellie was waiting on the stone-columned portico when Buck drove up, promptly at five. She had changed into jeans and a white polo shirt, and her hair was caught back loosely in a blue ribbon.

Buck caught the clean, sharp scent of her as she came down the steps to meet him. 'I hope I haven't kept you waiting?' He handed her the enormous bunch of roses he'd brought. They were big and pink and perfect, with no scent. She thanked him, surprised.

He stood for a moment, looking at the garden, taking in the balustraded terraces, the enormous fountain spouting water musically from the mouths of bronze dolphins; the formal Italian gardens with the reflecting pools, and the ancient shade trees dotting the emerald lawns. Shaking his head as though he couldn't quite believe its beauty, he said, 'This place is paradise.'

Ellie smiled, pleased. 'I think so, but then I was brought up here, and to me it's the best place in the world.' She glanced covertly at her watch as they walked up the steps, already regretting inviting him. She was seeing Dan at six and she wanted to get this meeting over with as soon as possible.

Buck felt that electric buzz of power as he stepped through the door of Journey's End, an invited guest in the house from which men with guns had dragged him, screaming in a strait-jacket. 'You've done it,' the voice in his head yelled triumphantly. 'You're back in control again.'

Exhilaration had him on the balls of his feet, ready for

action. Whistling 'Dixie' under his breath, he followed her into the house.

Taking off his dark glasses, he stowed them carefully in the top pocket of his jacket, then smoothed back his hair, looking round.

Nothing had changed. The same Savonnerie rugs, the same beautiful Venetian antiques, the Flemish tapestries. And Waldo Stamford's enormous full-length portrait dominating everything. Even the white roses in tall crystal vases could be the same, and the peachy scent of pot-pourri.

Ellie had given the house-tour more times than she could remember. They often had groups round: the historical society, antiquarians, magazine writers, newspaper columnists. By now, she was as expert as a museum guide on its history and contents. Hoping he wouldn't notice, she whizzed him through at top speed, not allowing him time to linger.

'The hall floor is limestone,' she told him briskly, 'from a quarry near Bordeaux. It was chosen by my great-grandfather specially for its warm, slightly pink colour. The oak staircase is Jacobean, from an English manor house, and the great baronial fireplace was carved right here, on site, by Italian artisans, working from photographs of a seventeenth-century Venetian one. There would always be a huge log fire in it on Christmas Eve,' she added, smiling fondly at her memories, 'with garlands of fresh bay and holly swagged around the walls and along the banisters. An enormous tree stood right here at the foot of the stairs, piled with presents, and Miss Lottie would serve hot spicy punch and Christmas cake to the local carol singers.'

Buck's eyes were everywhere, taking in every detail. He thought how easy it would be to break a pane in the french windows and slip the old-fashioned catch. Everything depended on how efficient the alarm system was, and what kind of security they had now.

He said inquisitively, 'It must take an army of servants to keep up this place.'

She shook her head. 'It's impossible to do that now. There's only Maria, the housekeeper, and the ladies who come in a couple of times a week, just to try to keep up the house. You'll need to bear in mind, Mr Jensen, that when you finally do buy a large house, the upkeep might ultimately cost more than the purchase price.'

He laughed, pleased with the information she'd given him about Maria. 'I'll certainly do that.'

They were out on the terrace, walking toward the old lady. Quickly, he put on the dark glasses.

'Gran,' Ellie said gently, 'this is Mr Jensen. I'm just giving him a tour of the house.'

Buck stood in front of his persecutor, the woman who had taken twenty years of his life away from him. He had no fear she would recognize him. '*Look at her*,' the mocking voice in his head said triumphantly. '*See how old she is, how frail and weak. Now you are in charge. Now, it's your turn.*'

Miss Lottie had been dozing. Startled, she sat up too quickly. Her head swam, her glasses slipped down her nose, and the book she'd been reading slid to the floor. The dog lumbered to his feet, barking loudly . .

'Good to meet you, ma'am.' Buck was in his role of polite gentleman.

'I didn't know we had visitors,' Miss Lottie said, flustered, as Buck bent to retrieve her book then placed it on the little table next to her. The dog growled softly in the back of his throat.

'Bruno, stop showing off,' Ellie said, astonished, but he growled louder.

Buck took a quick step back and Miss Lottie shook her head, puzzled. 'I think I must have been dreaming.'

Ellie handed her her spectacles. 'Then we won't disturb you any longer, Gran. Come on Mr Jensen, let's finish the tour.'

Miss Lottie's eyes followed him as he swaggered confidently back into the house. There was something about the way he walked; she could swear she knew him from somewhere. Her eyelids drifted down and in a minute she was dozing again. It had been a long day.

Ellie threw open the door to the library. 'When I was a child, this was my favourite place.' She ran a hand over the smooth polished wood of the Chinese chair near the door. 'I used to sneak in here at night when I was supposed to be in bed. I thought Miss Lottie didn't see me, but of course she knew. I would sit here and watch her at her desk, writing letters. How big the chair seemed then, it almost swallowed me up.'

Buck remembered the little red-haired child, her mouth open in a scream, terror in her eyes.

'There's a pair,' Ellie went on. 'They're seventeenth-century Chinese, made from elm wood. We always call them the Mandarin's chairs because they came from a wealthy Mandarin's estate, in Shanghai. The inlaid rosewood desk is Italian, and the rug is eighteenth-century Turkish, badly faded now from the sun, but still beautiful.'

A pulse ticked nervously in Buck's cheek. Swept back into the past, he walked to the desk, and stood looking at the place where they had held him down. The musty smell of the rug was in his nostrils again; its red colours filled his eyes like blood, he was screaming, cursing her. And Charlotte Parrish was standing over him. Tall, icy, unafraid. Master of all she surveyed. He took a deep breath. Now he was master of *her* fate.

With an effort, he jolted back to the present. Ellie was saying, 'Come and see the ballroom, Mr Jensen. We had such wonderful parties there. My great-grandfather welcomed two presidents and their wives to this house, as well as William Randolph Hearst and Marion Davies of course; and Ronald Coleman and Charlie Chaplin.'

Buck followed her through the main rooms, seeking access, and opportunity. He remembered the alarm system, it was the same antiquated one as before. It must have been there for thirty years and he'd bet it was never used now.

Ellie glanced at her watch. 'I'll just show you the kitchen before you leave, Mr Jensen. They simply don't make them like this anymore.'

The enormous kitchen looked exactly the way it had since the sixties with a black-and-white tiled floor, white-painted cabinets, massive steel stoves and a range of ovens. Tall windows were set high in the wall, and, on a hook next the back door, Buck spotted a large brass ring with a bunch of keys, each with a label.

'Can you just imagine this kitchen when there was a chef, and half a dozen maids and a butler?' Ellie said. 'Even then, it never seemed crowded. Why, my little kitchen at the café would fit comfortably into the butler's pantry.'

Buck's eyes glittered; he had to get those keys. 'I wonder,' he said, politely, 'if I might have a drink of water?'

'Of course. Or maybe you'd prefer a Diet-Coke?'

'That would be fine.'

As he had hoped, Ellie walked into the butler's pantry to find a glass. He was at the door in a flash, and the keys were in his hands. The writing on the labels was large and three of them said 'Kitchen.' He'd hit paydirt, the old lady had more keys than she knew what to do with. Sliding a key off the ring, he put it in his pocket. He was standing by the big scrubbed pine table when Ellie came back with the cold drink.

He hated to leave her, hated to leave Journey's End. Her spun-sugar voice as she said goodbye wrapped around his heart like a soothing blanket, and the touch of her hand left a searing imprint in his memory, one that he would dwell on later, alone.

Driving back out the big iron gates, he couldn't get her image out of his mind. He was in love. Soon, he would make her his princess. He would give her everything she wanted, she would forget everyone else when she was with him. Though of course, only he would ever see her.

Smiling, he patted the key in his pocket. It was going to be easy.

He was whistling again as he headed back to the hotel, and the bar. He had earned a celebratory drink. Phase Two was complete and the deed was as good as done.

26

'This is it.' Dan stared proudly at his rows of neatly-cropped vines.

The bare sticks were trained like an army of little soldiers into perfect rows, curving over the hillside into infinity. 'Impressive.' Ellie threw him a mocking grin. 'Not a grape in sight.'

'Wait till next year, then I think the proper word to use will be burgeoning.'

'*Burgeoning*?'

'As in growing, flourishing.'

She stared sceptically at the skinny, dead-looking branches. 'Aren't we being a little optimistic here?'

Dan shook his head, exasperated. 'You're a toughie, Ellie Parrish Duveen. Okay, so I bought this place like a kid at a party, sticking the tail on a donkey. Pure guesswork. But the fact is Running Horse failed because they planted the wrong grapes for the soil. We're starting cabernet here, on the south slopes, and chardonnay on the other side of the hill.' He shrugged, 'Anyhow, it was all I could afford, but I look at it this way, if I make a success of it, I got a bargain.'

There was something magical about it though, Ellie thought, wandering through the rows of vines, gazing at the serene pastoral view. In the distance, she could see the road curving round the bottom of the hill, and opposite, under a clump of oaks, black-and-white spotted cattle were bunched together in the shade. The setting sun warmed her back and a light wind tossed her hair around. Eyes closed, she listened entranced to the special 'silence' of the countryside: the soft moan of the wind sweeping over the hill; a whirr of wings as a bird took flight;

secret rustlings in the grass. Taking deep breaths of the clean fresh air, she wanted to bottle it and take it home with her.

'This is how it must have been, years ago,' she whispered, her eyes still shut tight, 'Before there was traffic, and planes and ghetto-blasters. Nothing but slopes of vines and silence, for miles.'

Dan heard it first. He held up a warning hand as her eyes popped open. A minute later Ortega's rusty pickup crested the hill, mariachi trumpets shrilling from the radio. They glanced at each other, laughing, as he jumped from the pickup and strode toward them.

'Señorita.' Doffing his sombrero, he gave her a beaming smile, then took her hand and held it to his lips. 'It is a great pleasure to meet such a beautiful woman. The Señor has kept you a mighty big secret.' He winked at Dan.

Ellie had to laugh. 'Thank you, Señor Ortega, I've heard a lot about you too.'

'Of course.' He put on his modest face. 'The Señor will have told you I am the best winemaker in the county. And now I work with him, we shall make a wonderful cabernet. *This* Running Horse will be "first past the post" in the wine stakes.' His moustache bristled and his white teeth flashed as he laughed again at his own topical little racehorse joke.

'I was just about to show Ellie the winery.' Dan grabbed her hand and led her back to the car. She turned and waved to Ortega. He bowed low, still smiling.

'You think that's a great act,' Dan told her, grinning, 'wait till you catch him on the palomino.'

It was cool inside the red barn, and silent. Dan ran an appreciative hand over his sleek new barrels. 'These are American oak, not French. It'll give a softer, more subtle oaky finish to the wine. Of course, there'll be no harvest here this year, but we're buying in grapes and we'll put out our first vintage. Zinfandel. It's good hearty stuff, fruity, rich. It won't be a long-lasting wine, but a wonderful mouthful and not expensive. It'll be a good work-out for us.'

Ellie peered into the freshly-cleaned steel fermenting vats; she inspected the bottling plant that looked as though it came from

135

a Disney cartoon, then wandered through the lofty space at the front of the barn which, Dan told her would become the tasting room.

'One day, visitors will flock here to try our wines, and taste our delicious food,' he said.

She spun round, hands on her hips, her eyes challenging him. 'What food?'

'Oh,' he shrugged nonchalantly, 'just a little French café, nothing grand you understand ... casual, comfortable, with excellent food and the best bread and *tarte tatin* in California.'

Her eyes lit with amusement. 'Hah, some hope Mr Cassidy. My next restaurant is going to be up-market, I'm aiming for that Michelin star, and this time I'll be the chef.'

'Just dreaming,' he said with a regretful grin, grabbing her hand and leading her toward the stables. 'Just dreaming, woman.'

Pancho dashed at her, prancing on his hind legs, 'This is cupboard love,' she said. 'He remembers I'm the sucker who brought the filet steak.' She sleeked his rough fur, glancing surprised at Cecil, lurking behind him. 'Now you have two, and I don't know which is worse-looking.'

He showed her round the property: the glossy horses in the picturesque stables; Cecil and Pancho running wild around the place: the team of Mexicans recruited by Carlos working their way rhythmically along the furrows. New stock had been bought, the earth was being revitalized with the proper nutrients, and Dan told her that was where a great deal of his and the bank's money had gone.

'At least it's beginning to look like a winery again,' he said, picking a red rose from the bush and handing it to her.

Tucking it into her hair, Ellie thought how much he seemed to love what he was doing. He was such a physical man, and she could tell he enjoyed the hard work; he loved getting his hands in the earth, back to his farming roots.

She was silent on the drive back to Montecito, her head tilted back, her eyes closed, thinking about the life Dan had chosen, far from the city's stresses and pleasures. Maybe there was something to it, but it wasn't for her. She was a city girl now, through and through. She was making her own way, on the big screen of LA.

She was yawning from a surfeit of fresh, unsmogged air when Dan parked and they walked across Coast Village Road, into Mollie's.

Looking at her across the candlelit corner table, with her long curling red hair and pensive expression, Dan thought she resembled a woman in a Whistler painting. Except in real life she was a sunshiny person. Or was she? He knew nothing about her life, except for the deeply personal confidence she had shared with him that first night at the beach house.

'Do I really know you?' he asked. Ellie's eyes widened in surprise, and he added, 'I feel like we're old friends, but I know so little about you.'

'I thought I'd told you everything.' She took a sip of the Chianti he'd ordered to go with the Italian food.

He leaned closer, across the table. 'There's a big empty space between the kid on the beach and the woman sitting opposite me. What happened in those years? Where did you go to college? Who are your friends? Have you ever been in love?'

She eyed him warily, head tilted to one side, half-smiling. 'That's a very personal question.'

'Where you went to college is personal?' His pseudo-innocent expression made her laugh.

'I'll answer that one. Arizona U. in Phoenix. That's where I met Maya, my dearest friend. It's also the place from where we almost got ourselves thrown out. We were only saved from absolute disaster by Miss Lottie and Maya's father. Ah, we were wild in those days, crazy kids having their first taste of freedom.'

Dan laughed when she told him the story of her college career; it was quite different from his own, more serious one, as a married student with the impossible romance and even more impossible dreams.

'Of course, I fell in love there.' Tasting the lobster ravioli, she made a rapturous face. 'This is heaven.'

'You were in love?' His eyes were on her delicious mouth.

'Mmmm, once or twice.' The Italian with the Michelangelo

body seemed eons away, another lifetime, another world. 'But I guess I sublimated those feelings when I bought the red Harley.'

'You bought a Harley as a substitute for sex?' He was laughing at her now.

'Mr Cassidy.' Her lashes covered her downcast eyes, demurely. 'We all know there is no substitute for that.'

His sigh of relief was exaggerated. 'I'm glad to hear it.'

'Though of course, it doesn't even enter into our personal equation.' This time, she wasn't joking around. Reaching across the table she took his hand in hers, held it to her lips, dropped a kiss on it, then returned it to him. 'I'm just so glad to have you as my friend.'

His blood pressure lifted a few notches, maybe he wouldn't wash that hand again, like a teenager in love. 'Of course not,' he agreed, even though he didn't mean it. 'I just don't get it,' he added.

'Get what?' She spooned up the last of the sauce. 'I really have to compliment Mollie on this dish, it's wonderful.'

'You should try her red mullet, she has it flown in specially from Italy, on Fridays. And what I don't get is exactly what makes you tick. I mean, why are you so driven? What motivates you to make this café such a success, to devote all your time, all your energy, your *life* to it?'

Ellie sat back, her face serious, considering the question. 'It's like I have to prove something to myself,' she said honestly, after a minute. 'That I *can* do it, that I *can* succeed. That because I was raised in a privileged background, doesn't mean I can't make it on my own. And for me, that means the big screen. You know, LA or New York. I want to be up there with the best, with my name in lights like on Broadway. I want them to say, "there goes Ellie Parrish," just the way they do about Puck, or Vergé, or Ducasse.'

'You want to be a star.'

'I admit it,' she said flatly. 'And I want to make a lot of money. Mostly so I don't have to think about it, and so I can keep Miss Lottie in the style to which she is still accustomed.'

'And what will you do, with all that money?' Somehow, he didn't think money was her main motivation.

'If I make really a lot, you mean? That's easy. I'd use part of it to open special kitchens, like in the Depression. But not just for soup. I'd serve good simple, nutritious meals to kids who go to school hungry every morning. To kids who have to pretend they've forgotten their lunch because they're too ashamed to say they don't have any lunch. To kids who go home after school to an empty house and no dinner on the table, or to a parent out of it on drugs. I've never known what being hungry is like, being seriously deprived. I just feel it's my duty to repay some of the goodness of my life, let it spill over into theirs.' She shrugged, looking apprehensively at him. 'I didn't mean to sound preachy.'

'You didn't.' The young waiter came with the tiramisu she'd ordered, and two forks. 'I think I like you, Ellie Parrish,' he said. 'Even though you still haven't told me about being in love. *Seriously* in love?'

She heaved a sigh, scooping up the delicious creamy dessert. 'You don't quit, do you?'

'Not when it's a subject that interests me.'

She grinned, thinking about Steve Cohen, and how young she had been then, and how naïve. 'I've only been seriously in love once,' she admitted, telling him about the long skirts, and the braid and the Doc Martens, and Steve's almost overnight tranformation from intellectual to upwardly mobile executive in a Hugo Boss suit. 'He ditched me and broke my heart,' she added, then laughed. 'But you know, it's a funny thing, hearts seem to patch themselves right back up again, if you let them.'

A yawn surprised her. 'It's all that fresh air,' she apologized. 'I'm a big city girl, I'm not used to it any more.'

'You could always stay the night?' He was an optimist by nature.

'Thanks, friend,' she squeezed his hand across the table, 'but this time I really must get back. Thanks for showing me the ranch, I loved it.'

His dark-blue eyes linked with her opal ones. 'Come again,

when the house is finished. Stay for dinner this time? How about next week?'

She nodded, smiling. 'I can't make it Monday, but what about Wednesday? I'll take the night off, specially.'

'Great. This is getting to be a habit.'

Ellie thought so too, but it was one she liked. Being with Dan Cassidy was as seamless as being with a friend she'd known all her life.

'See you Wednesday then,' she called, climbing into the old Wrangler.

He was leaning in the window, looking at her. The scent of fresh clean air still clung to him, and impulsively she put her hand to his face and drew him towards her, then kissed him on the lips. It was a light, friendly little kiss, nothing important, she reassured herself.

'Goodnight, Danny Boy,' she murmured, backing the jeep too quickly out of the tight parking spot. There was a crunch as it hit his Explorer.

Dan slapped a hand to his head, like a man in pain. 'Jesus, Ellie! Not again!'

'Sorry.' She poked her head out, inspecting the damage. 'Oh well, you already know my name, and my insurance company. And after all, what's a little dent between friends?'

Dan could hear her laughing as she took off.

27

Buck reconnoitred his enemy's position, circling Hot Springs Road in the daylight hours until he was familiar with every twist and turn, every house, every horse trail. He observed the comings and goings of the neighbours, the delivery vans, the workmen; knew what time women took their children to school, what time they returned. He noted the cruising police cars and the frequency of the various private security patrols. He also knew there was no longer a security patrol at Journey's End. And that many of the people in the neighbouring houses were weekenders from LA, and that Saturdays it became busier, with parties and valet parking and action.

He'd acted impulsively before, not thought it out, not made his plans. This time, it would be perfect. After a week, he knew the routine, and that things were very quiet week nights.

After darkness had fallen, he drove up Hot Springs Road, past Journey's End, and turned into a narrow riding trail, half hidden by trees that ran behind the property. He was doing a test run, just the way he had when he'd killed his mother.

He was wearing a black tracksuit, black Reebok Walkers and black gloves, and carried a backpack with his tools. Guided by the thin beam of a tiny flashlight, he walked along the trail until he came to a pair of tall, rusting iron gates. He shone the flashlight up until he spotted the big padlock. He sighed, he might have known it would be locked up like a fortress. Eyeing the wall, he decided against trying to climb over. It was too high, it would be difficult and too time-consuming on the way out.

However, he'd anticipated just such a problem. Taking the

small bolt-cutter from the backpack, he got to work on it. It took only seconds before the chain and padlock dropped into the grass at his feet. He looked up, sweating. In the distance, he could hear dogs barking.

The gate couldn't have been used in years and it squealed rustily as he pushed it open, slipped inside and closed it carefully behind him.

He was in a copse of birch trees. He hadn't anticipated the all-enveloping darkness and it disoriented him, made him nervous. He stood for a minute, getting his bearings, letting his eyes adjust. He would have preferred a little light and made a mental note to check the phases of the moon.

Taking a compass from the backpack, he shone the flashlight on it. He knew the house lay due east, on a rising knoll. Threading his way carefully through the trees, he plotted his course.

A long, low building appeared out of the darkness and he skirted it cautiously until he came to a window. The thin beam of his flashlight showed a large, empty room, with deep old-fashioned pot sinks and antiquated laundry machinery.

Taking out a pad and pen, Buck made brief sketch of the terrain, noting the location of the laundry. Then he continued on his way.

He was out of the trees now and on an overgrown path leading from the old laundry toward the house. He adjusted his watch, timing himself. So far, it had taken him ten minutes. Another five and the house loomed into view, massive, solid, built to last.

He stood, looking at the prize that would soon be his, contemplating that final moment of triumph when his revenge against Charlotte Parrish would be complete. He had suffered for more than twenty years, and he was only sorry that her final suffering would be so comparatively quick.

Leaving the path, he walked silently through the gardens, past the empty pool and the tennis courts, through the still-immaculately-kept *parterre* garden with its tiny clipped box hedges enclosing an arrangement of ornamental flowerbeds. Circling the big bronze dolphin fountain, he walked up the marble balustraded steps, onto the terrace. Security lights glimmered yellow from the eaves, illuminating the front of the house.

He glanced at his watch again. Twenty-two minutes. He would have to do better than that.

He was calm, collected, his heart wasn't even pounding. Pulling the pack of Camels from his pocket, he lit one and inhaled luxuriously, then took a leisurely stroll along the terrace. There was a light on in the great hall, but the rest of the downstairs windows were dark. Lamplight also glowed behind four of the curtained upstairs windows. Miss Lottie's, he assumed.

He was almost at the front door, when he heard the sound of the key turning in the lock. With a lightning reaction, he crushed the cigarette out with his fingers, ran soundlessly back along the terrace, and slipped behind the bushes outside the library window.

The old labrador lumbered out onto the terrace followed by a small, grey-haired woman in a plaid bathrobe and slippers. Buck trained the night-vision binoculars on her. She had something in her hand.

'All right, you old scrounger,' he heard her say, 'but this is our little secret, no telling Miss Lottie now.' She gave the dog the cookie, then patted its head affectionately. 'There's no wonder you're fat,' she added. The dog ate the cookie then pattered down the steps into the garden. The woman followed him and then they were out of his sight.

Buck looked speculatively at the light streaming from the open door. It was a golden opportunity: he could go in, kill his enemy, have done with it. But there were too many unknowns. He could not afford to make a mistake. He had to perfect his plan, be certain. Besides, he wanted to take his time, enjoy it.

A few minutes later, Maria walked back into the sights of his binoculars and up the steps. The dog lumbered stiffly after her. It stopped and looked directly at Buck. Then it barked loudly and began to trot toward him.

Buck froze. Now, his heart was thundering. If the dog came at him, he might be forced to make a move immediately. His mind raced ahead, planning for every contingency. He could take the housekeepr first and he might still be able to surprise the old woman upstairs . . .

'Bruno! Come here you silly old boy,' Maria called.

The dog turned its head. It looked at her, then back again at the bushes where Buck was hiding, barking loudly.

'Bruno, come here at once.' Maria was impatient. The dog looked uncertainly at the bushes for a second, then it turned and obediently followed Maria into the house.

Breathing a sigh of relief, Buck heard the heavy oak door slam, and the iron key turn in the massive old-fashioned lock that would have protected a medieval castle.

He checked the stopwatch; now he knew approximately what time Maria took the dog out, and then locked up for the night.

Lighting another cigarette he decided to wait until the lights went out, check what time they went to bed. He felt as comfortable as if he owned the place, sauntering along the terrace, smoking.

An hour or so later, the lights were turned out upstairs. Again he made a note of the time, then ran back down the steps, skirted the gravel driveway so as to make no noise, and jogged back the way he came.

Back at the car, he checked his time again. Eighteen minutes. It was way too long, and the main problem was those damn trees. He would need to come here in daylight and plot his route through the copse. He needed to get his time down to seven minutes or less, to run the mile from the house to the car.

Still, it wasn't bad for a first try. He would do it again tomorrow night, and the night after, and the night after that. Until he was ready.

28

Ellie was in the kitchen at the café, trying out a new recipe to pass on to Chan. She wore a white chef's jacket and her hair was tucked away under a chef's hat. She was in her element, cool, efficient, enjoying what she was doing.

There was something about cooking, combining creativity with the almost scientific preciseness necessary for a professional chef, that appealed to both sides of her personality. The fun-loving spur-of-the-moment adventurer in her, and the orderly, in-charge woman who knew exactly what she wanted from life and how she was going to achieve it.

With a razor-sharp cleaver and swift neat strokes, she dismembered a chicken and cut off the last wing joints. She chopped shallots, then made a *chiffonade* of spinach by removing the stalks, rolling the leaves into a cigar-shape and then finely slicing it. She did the same with fresh sorrel, then destalked watercress leaves and chervil. Throwing some butter into a cast-iron casserole, she added the shallots, the chicken and salt and pepper, then put the lid on and let it cook slowly. Next she cooked the spinach over a high heat until it wilted, then threw in the rest of the herbs. She stirred it for a couple of minutes, then added it to the cooked chicken with a small amount of cream beaten with an egg, and stirred again until the sauce thickened. Tasting it, she added a little more salt and pepper, and inspected the result, pleased.

She had come across the recipe at a little farmhouse restaurant in Provence, and with its pretty green colour and light, delicious, fresh summery taste, it was exactly the kind of thing she liked to serve.

Placing a piece of chicken on each plate, she spooned the green herby sauce over it and gave one each to Chan, Terry and Maya to taste.

'What d'you think?' She stood, hands on hips, awaiting the decision.

Maya rolled her big brown eyes, scooping up the sauce inelegantly with a spoon. 'This is heaven.'

'I know this recipe,' Chan said stubbornly. 'It's French farmhouse cooking.'

'And isn't that the best?' Ellie's eyes challenged him.

'After Chinese and Japanese, maybe.'

Terry winked at Ellie over Chan's shoulder. 'Tastes great to me, Ellie. Maybe a little more sorrel, I love that herb.'

'Me too.' She was looking at Chan again.

'It's good,' he admitted finally. 'Maybe we can do something with it. This sauce also would be good with sea bass. Or maybe crab cakes.'

'There you go!' Ellie gave him that beaming smile, pleased he'd come around.

'If it's good enough for the French, it's good enough for us,' Maya agreed.

Ellie washed her hands and went back to her marble board to prepare the pastry for the night's *tarte tatin*. She had already made a *crème brulée*, and a double chocolate *daquoise*. They also served fresh berries every night, in a delicious puddle of Terry's signature vanilla *crème anglaise*, as well as fresh-fruit sorbets. She would have loved to offer a cheese board, the way they did in France, with a tiny green salad, or fresh celery in a tall glass vase. To her, it seemed the perfect way to end a meal, but in these low-fat-conscious days, there weren't sufficient customers who would order it to make buying fresh cheeses economically viable.

Concentrating on what she was doing, she didn't hear the phone ring.

'It's for you Ell.' Maya held the phone out to her.

'Ellie here?'

On the other end of the line, Dan smiled. He loved that little rising intonation, as though she expected a wonderful surprise to happen. He hoped he was a good enough surprise to warrant it. 'Hi to you, Ellie Parrish Duveen.'

She stirred the caramel, the phone tucked under her chin. 'You're calling to tell me the Explorer is totalled and it's all my fault.'

'You're lucky, it's just a minor graze this time. I just wondered what you were up to?'

'Oh, working, slaving away.'

He said, 'I was just thinking, it's an awful long time until next week.'

'Mmmm, can you bear to wait that long for the pleasure of my destructive company?'

'I'm not sure I can. Anyhow, I was planning on being in LA later today, on business. I thought I might come by and have dinner at your place. Do you take reservations for one?'

Pleased, Ellie pushed back her hair with a floury hand. 'You'll have the best table in the house, and this time dinner's on me.'

'I guess you'll still be slaving?'

''Fraid so, the unsociable hours go along with the job. But I'll make time to have a glass of wine with you.' She thought of last night and their intimate dinner at Mollie's.

'I can't wait to taste the famous *tarte tatin*,' he said.

'It'll melt in your mouth, I guarantee it.' She was smiling, thinking about him here, in her café. In her world this time.

'Around nine, then, Ellie.'

'I'll be waiting.' She fairly sang the words, her face glowing.

Maya looked shrewdly at her. 'You look like a happy woman.'

'Who? Me?' Ellie laughed as she went back to the pastry board, deliberately not answering the question in Maya's eyes.

'So come on, Ell, tell me, was it the rancher from the boondocks?'

Ellie nodded, busy with her pastry again. 'It was Mr Boondocks himself.'

'Well, how about that. You mean I get to meet him tonight?' Maya's face was alight with curiosity. Ellie hadn't been out with a man in so long, it was almost as exciting as a date of her own.

'He'll be here at nine.' Ellie removed the caramelized sugar from the stove. Glancing at the clock on the wall, she thought that it meant she would see him exactly four hours from now. Looking determinedly away, she forbade herself to count the minutes.

'Sure you don't want to borrow the Versace?'

Maya was laughing at her, Ellie knew. 'I told him I'm working and that he'll be dining alone. This is not a date, Maya Morris.'

'Okay, okay, if you say so.'

Maya drifted off to check the tables were correctly set with flowers and cutlery, napkins and wineglasses, and Ellie glanced again at the clock on the wall. Because of experimenting with the new dish, she was running late, but there was still time to dash home and shower and change. And put on some perfume.

29

It was dusk when Buck drove up Hot Springs Road, timing his entry carefully to avoid the security patrol that serviced a neighbouring home.

He parked in the same place, clicked on his stopwatch, and jogged down the horse trail to the gate. This time he could see where he was going and he plotted his way through the copse of birch trees, zigzagging back and forth several times to find the most direct route, and hacking away the undergrowth until he had a definite path and the quickest route through the copse.

Satisfied, he waited until darkness fell, then set his watch again and jogged toward the house. He was breathing heavily when he arrived on the terrace and he decided he needed to go to a gym, work out a bit.

After deducting the time spent in the birch thicket, it had taken him fifteen minutes. Not nearly good enough. He was hoping he wouldn't have to make a quick get-away, but this time he was leaving nothing to chance. He had to be speedy.

Expecting to see Maria and the dog, he retreated to the far end of the terrace, lit a cigarette and waited. By the time she emerged, his heart had regained its normal rhythm, and he watched calmly through the binoculars as she walked down the steps with the old dog. This time, he was far enough away for it not to catch his scent, and it didn't bark. He checked the watch again. Within a couple of minutes, it was the same time as last night.

Satisfied, he waited until she went back into the house and locked the door. Then he turned and jogged silently back the way he'd come.

Back at the car he checked again. Thirteen minutes, but his

heart was thundering like a piston. Sinking thankfully into the car, he told himself he'd better get to that gym tomorrow, get on the treadmill, get in shape. Even though he didn't anticipate trouble – after all no one ever seemed to visit the house at night – he still had to be prepared for any eventuality.

He drove in darkness to the end of the horse trail and peered cautiously out into the road. It was empty. Switching on his lights, he swung left down the hill, and drove quickly back to LA.

Back at his apartment, he showered, changed into an expensive blue shirt and beige pants, downed a slug of bourbon from the half-empty bottle, then took a leisurely drive to Santa Monica.

Main Street was jammed with not a parking space to be found, and Dan was lucky to get a slot in the four-storey carpark. He slipped the car into the tight space, groaning as he noticed Ellie's yellow jeep next to him. The Explorer already looked as though it had done battle, and he didn't need any more dents and smashed headlights.

Strolling back along Main, he felt like a hick from the sticks, used as he was now to the silence and darkness of a country night. The shops were brightly lit, music blared from passing cars, people rushed past him, laughing and chattering, heading for restaurants, or stores, or clubs. An art gallery was having an opening, serving margaritas and spicy-smelling canapés to the chic crowd who'd come to inspect the artist's latest works. Dan sniffed the air appreciatively as he passed by, hoping Ellie's food was going to taste as good as this smelled. He grinned, thinking about her; she would be on her mettle tonight, out to show him her stuff. This time, *she* would be on the defensive about her restaurant, instead of him about his vineyard.

The minute he walked in the door, Maya knew it was him. He was wearing a simple white linen shirt, rolled at the sleeves, blue jeans and camel suede loafers. His eyes looked a startlingly deep blue against his tanned face, and they had a kind of wise expression as he turned to look at her; not know-it-all, just as though he had seen it all. 'Been there, done that,' she murmured, heading speedily toward him.

'Let me guess,' she said, fixing him with her gorgeous amber eyes, 'you're Dan Cassidy.'

'Guilty.' He grinned at her, and she wondered, amazed, how Ellie had resisted him for so long.

'And you must be Maya?'

She smiled back at him. 'I see my fame has spread all the way from LA to Santa Barbara County.'

'Further than that – from Arizona.'

Maya groaned, 'She told you about that?'

''Fraid so.' Dan laughed at her dismayed face. 'Maybe not in detail, but enough to know you two had a good time there.'

Maya sighed. 'Ellie's life is an open book, that woman just doesn't believe in secrets. Anyhow, welcome to Ellie's Place.' She showed him to a table in the window and handed him a menu. 'I'll tell Ell you're here,' she said, heading back to the kitchen. She couldn't wait to see her face when she told her what she thought of Dan Cassidy.

Dan looked round interestedly. The lighting was low and intimate, with little rose-shaded lamps on each table instead of candles, and a nice buzz of conversation and laughter came from the other tables. The place was three-quarters full; not bad, he figured, for a Wednesday night. He held the menu under the light, studying it interestedly.

He caught Ellie's delicate perfume, felt her lips on his cheek, and looked up, smiling. He had never been so happy to see anyone in his life. Besides, she looked delicious in her white Ellies Place t-shirt and black jeans, with her hair in a ponytail under the black baseball cap.

'Okay Cassidy,' she said, placing a bottle of wine on the table and taking the seat opposite him, 'you're on my turf tonight.'

Their eyes linked for a second. 'True,' he admitted. 'I hope you can live up to your reputation.'

'We'll see,' she said modestly, pouring wine into two glasses.

Maya appeared with a dish of *tapenade* and a basket of wonderful-smelling hot bread. 'Ellie baked it,' she informed Dan, 'it's just one of her many talents.'

He took a piece of the bread and looked at Ellie. 'So what are the others?' She looked blank. 'The talents. God, this is good.

Really good. I haven't tasted bread like this in . . . for ever. Just like our mothers were supposed to make.'

'More like Paul Poilane, in Paris,' she corrected him. 'I learned my trade there.'

'You surely learned good.' He tasted the wine and made a pleased face. 'Whose is it?'

'A neighbour of yours, Fess Parker.'

'The man knows what he's doing.' Reaching across the table, he caught her hand in his. 'I missed you,' he said, sincerely.

'You've hardly had time, we saw each other last night.'

'That's too long.'

From across the room, Maya thought they looked like a pair of lovers, alone in their window table in the rose-shaded light, lost in each other. She sighed, it was all so romantic. If only Ellie didn't blow it by getting on her 'ambition' high horse again. When would that woman learn that life was all a compromise?

Outside on Main Street, Buck saw them through the window. He'd just been about to walk into the café, but now he stopped. He took a step back, staring angrily at them, holding hands across the table, gazing into each other's eyes. *How dare she*, the voice in his head shouted angrily. *She's your woman. You will have to kill him too, if he doesn't get out of your way.*

Enraged, he turned on his heel and hurried back down the street to his car, then drove to her house. Parking on the hill, he ran across the street and let himself in with the key he'd had made. His heart thudded with that irregular rhythm as he stood for a minute in the tiny hallway, then headed up the stairs to her bedroom.

His Ellie was not a sloppy woman and everything was tidy. Picking up her pink bathrobe, he pressed it to his cheek. It smelled of her powder and perfume.

He sank onto the bed, cradling it to him. She was in his arms, pressed close to him, her scent teased his nostrils. It was almost as if she were there.

It was ten-thirty before the café quietened down and Ellie finally got a break and could sit down with Dan. He'd insisted she choose the meal for him, and she had served him herself. Simple things, because he was an uncomplicated man who knew what he liked. The white bean soup; the rack of lamb with the *persillade* crust, garlic mashed potatoes and ratatouille. And now he was about to taste her famous *tarte*.

Leaning her elbows on the table, her bottom lip caught anxiously in her teeth, she watched him pick up the fork and cut carefully into the pastry. If he hated it, she would just die . . .

Dan closed his eyes, as though he were allowing the taste to linger, then opened them. Without saying a word, took another forkful.

She leaned worriedly across the table. 'Go ahead, tell me you hate it. I can take it.'

His blue eyes looked innocently into hers. 'Was I supposed to say something?' He downed another mouthful.

She sat back in the chair. '*Beast!*' she hissed.

Dan loved it when she pouted. It reminded him of when she was a kid. He finished the *tarte*, put his fork on the plate and sighed with satisfaction. 'I could eat that all night.'

'Thanks. How about the rest of the meal?'

He could tell she was anxious. 'Best I've had since Paris.'

She looked surprised, 'I didn't know you were in Paris.' Then she blushed, furious. He was teasing her. Of course he hadn't been to Paris, he'd been too busy being a cop.

'So much for that,' she said loftily, standing and beginning to clear the dishes.

He caught her arm as she turned away. 'There's a restaurant in Manhattan. It's called Paris and the food is great.' He smiled engagingly at her. 'But this was better. Truly, a wonderful meal, Ellie.'

'Then thank Chef Chan.'

She was still huffed, he could tell. 'That was just to pay you back for what you said about my vines,' he apologized.

'*Burgeoning?*' A smile curled the corners of her mouth.

'How about having some coffee with me?' He was pushing his luck but she was weakening.

Ellie glanced round the almost empty café. 'I'll do better than that. We'll have it at my place.'

This was more than he'd expected, especially after setting her up so badly.

'I'll have Maya close up,' she said, already walking away.

He was waiting at the zinc counter, hands in the pockets of his blue jeans, when she returned. Looking at him, she thought he looked as good as she remembered him at eighteen, lean, muscular, golden-tanned.

Looking at her, he thought she looked as delicious as the *tarte* she had baked. She was wearing a little red jacket and her black bag was slung over her shoulder.

Looking at both of them, Maya thought they looked great together. And they looked even better when Dan slid his arm round Ellie's shoulders as they walked out of the café.

Leaning her elbow on the counter, she sighed, happy that Ellie had finally found someone she cared about. Not that Ellie would ever admit it. It would take a miracle, or a catastrophe, before she'd do that.

Buck hauled himself off the bed, exhausted by his passion. Replacing the pink robe carefully on the chaise near the window, he walked into her bathroom, washed his hands and dried them on the soft white towel. Then he straightened the coverlet and plumped up the pillow where his head had lain.

With one last lingering glance around his love's domain, he walked from the room, down the steps and out the front door.

There was only a single street-light and that was half a block away, leaving this section in semi-darkness. He scuttled down the little brick path and across the street, just as two vehicles turned into it. For a second he was blinded by their headlights, and quickly turned his face away.

He heard them stop, and he turned to look. He saw Ellie getting out of the jeep, and Cassidy parking the Explorer. His stomach curdled as they walked, hand in hand, into the house.

After a minute, he saw the lights go on upstairs, saw Ellie and Dan at the bedroom window. She was pointing something out to him, then she slammed it shut and pulled the curtains.

Anguished, he ran back to the car. The pain was like a stake in his heart. He switched on the ignition, drove up Ellie's street, and parked opposite. His eyes were fixed on the lighted windows. Tears were streaming down his face.

'And this,' Ellie was saying to Dan, leaning from her bedroom window, 'is why I really love this house.'

Dan peered over the rooftops, down the hill at the distant gleam of silver. He lifted a sceptical eyebrow. 'Do I assume that's the ocean?'

'Of course it is,' she said indignantly, leaning further out. 'Listen, you can hear it.'

He listened. 'All I hear is traffic.'

Ellie slammed the window shut and drew the curtains. 'And I thought you were a true romantic,' she said with a derisive snort.

The floorboards groaned as he followed her out of the bedroom and down the creaking stairs. 'You know what they say, once a cop, always a cop.' Looking at the drooping tulips in the beautiful antique urn on the console in the living room, he added, 'Besides, if I were a romantic, I'd have brought you flowers.'

'I'm perfectly capable of buying my own flowers, thanks.'

Flouncing into the kitchen, she measured coffee into the filter, poured in the water, then switched on the machine. She took a couple of the green mugs with the cherries on from the cupboard and a yellow bowl of sugar, then looked doubtfully at it. 'I don't even know whether you take sugar in your coffee.'

'Obviously I know you better than you know me.' He was leaning against the kitchen counter, thumbs hooked into the pockets of his jeans.

'That's the cop in you. You observe everything.'

'I've observed the cracks in the walls. Are you sure this place isn't going to fall down around you one night?'

She shrugged, 'Not until the next earthquake, I guess.'

'Spoken like a true Californian.' He shook his head in disbelief. 'Now I know I'm in Tomorrowland.'

'Don't worry, detective, the building inspectors told me it's only superficial damage, not structural. I believe it's moved a bit since they were here,' she lifted one shoulder philosophically, 'but what can I tell you? I like it.'

Dan liked it too. He liked the colours, and the overstuffed sumptuousness of the furnishings that lifted it from an ordinary little dwelling into a special place. *Ellie's Place*. She had a talent for creating a welcoming atmosphere, he thought, remembering the café earlier. Taking the tray from her, he carried the coffee into the sitting room.

Ellie switched on the CD player, lit the candles on the coffee table, dragged a cushion from the chair and sat cross-legged on it. Pulling the band off her ponytail, she shook her hair free, lifting the weight of it, then letting it fall.

He watched, fascinated, as it rippled back over her shoulders, glossy as a roan pony's. Her skin was translucent in the candlelight and, as she looked at him, her opal eyes reflected the flames.

Pouring coffee, she handed him a mug. 'Did we settle the sugar question?' She was smiling now, relaxed.

'I don't remember, but no sugar thanks.'

The music was Billie Holliday, gentle, her voice filled with pathos; and the room smelled of peach pot-pourri and Ellie's perfume, and good coffee. Looking at her, Dan couldn't think of anywhere else he would rather be.

'It's your turn now.' Ellie sipped her coffee, glancing up at him over the rim of the mug. 'I poured my heart – and my murky past – out to you the other night. Now I want to hear about you.'

'Warts and all?'

'Warts and all.'

'My life hasn't been as exciting as yours. In fact it was pretty ordinary, until I stopped the bullet. Dad was a firefighter. I loved it when I was a kid, the excitement of it, seeing him there at the firehouse with all the other guys in their helmets and slickers. The day they let me climb on the fire engine was the biggest thrill of my young life. Of course it didn't occur to me it was dangerous, not until I was seven, and Dan ended up in hospital with third-degree burns. Still, he survived, and went on to become Fire Chief. We were so proud of him.'

'We?' She raised her brows, enquiringly.

'Mom, my sister and I. Mom taught third grade, and Aisling

got a PhD in psychology from Michigan. She practices now, in Chicago.'

'It's a beautiful name, Aisling.' Ellie was fascinated, like a child with bedtime story.

'She was named after Dad's Irish mother. I went back to the old country with him a few years ago, to search out his family and his roots.' Dan laughed, remembering. 'Boy, I love that place. There's nothing like the Irish for hospitality, everyone's your friend. Either that or they're a relative, or they know someone who lives in California. Anyway, there were more Cassidys than we could count, and all of them seemed to be related to us.

'We toured the countryside, staying at these little offbeat inns, half of them stuck in a time-warp somewhere between nineteen hundred and nineteen fifty. I remember rolling up late one night at a rambling old place in the wilds of County Cork. It was dark and raining, and in the middle of nowhere. I half-expected to see the Hounds of the Baskervilles galloping toward us across the peat-bog. But the landlord had heard our car. He flung open the door and light streamed out. He was tall and thin as a reed with a wild mop of silver hair.

'"Welcome, welcome," he cried. "I'll have the fire lit in your room in a jiffy. And Mary Kate will be preparing yer dinner. Will a bit of fresh duckling be acceptable t'ya tonight? I killed it meself, just this morning."' Dan laughed, remembering. 'I'd never heard more welcoming words.'

Ellie was laughing too at the picture he painted.

'Our host showed us up to our rooms, and Mary Kate, who was as round as her husband was thin, with hair the colour of Guinness, was already there, putting a match to the kindling under a lump of peat.'

He glanced wryly at Ellie, 'Don't let the idea of a glowing peat fire fool you. That stuff just lurks there in the grate, smouldering sullenly and sending off smoke. Even standing with your backside up the chimney couldn't get you warm.

'Anyhow, downstairs in the kitchen the whiskey was flowing and the food was cooking, and the conversation, as always in Ireland, was non-stop. 'I'll be serving ya in the dining room,'

Mary Kate told us grandly. And was it ever grand! The place was cavernous and could have seated a hundred. It was freezing, and obviously hadn't been used in a long time, but Mary Kate lit a couple of gloomy lamps and said, "I'll just turn on a bit of music for you." It was April and the tape was Christmas carols. I guess that was the last time the dining room had been used.

'But you would have approved of the duck – golden and crisp on the outside, tender and juicy within, a mountain of *colcannon* to accompany it, and a bottle of Paddy's whiskey planted on the table to wash it down. So there we sat, dining like Brian Boru, the King of Ireland himself, serenaded by 'Oh Come all Ye Faithful' in April, chatting to our hosts like old friends.'

His smiling eyes met Ellie's. 'And that's Ireland for you,' he said. 'It's cold and rainy, but still the warmest country you'll ever be proud to visit.'

Her arms were wrapped round her knees, and she was gazing eagerly at him, wanting more. 'I can't wait to go there.'

'Then I'll have to take you, one day,' he said, lightly.

'Mmmm,' Ellie deflected that carefully. 'Tell me about your parents.'

His mouth set in a tight line and a look of sadness crossed his face. 'Mom died four years ago, breast cancer. Dad was pretty well shaken up. He'd just retired which made it even harder, but somehow he dragged his life together. He moved out of the family home and into a small apartment. Started to play golf, played poker with his old buddies. I think he was happy, or maybe content is a better word. He died last year. With what I inherited from him, plus my own savings and disability pension, I was able to buy the vineyard.' He spread his hands, palms up. 'And that's about it. The story of my life.'

She wasn't about to let him off so lightly. 'So? Where did you go to college? Who are your friends? Have you ever been in love?' She gave him a teasing sideways glance, repeating his own questions to her. He threw back his head, laughing, showing those strong white teeth that had so irritated her the first time she'd run into him. He was, she thought, looking fascinated at his strong sun-browned throat rippling with laughter, the best thing that had happened to her since . . . oh, since she had learned how to bake bread.

'College was the University of Southern California, Santa Barbara. I graduated *magna* with a degree in biology. My closest friend is an NYPD homicide detective, name of Pete Piatowsky. And yes, I have been in love.'

He was still laughing at her as he passed her his mug for a refill. She poured the coffee, handed it back to him. 'Tell me about your wife?'

'That's a very personal question.' He looked steadily at her, repeating her words this time.

'I know. But this is show-and-tell time.'

He took a sip of the coffee, thinking about Fran, remembering how he'd been so sick in love with her, he couldn't think of anything else. He couldn't breathe without her.

'God, we were so young.' He leaned toward her, elbows on his knees, his chin propped in his palms. The youthful pain was still there, in his eyes.

'We met in High School. She was the prettiest girl I'd ever seen. Small, blonde, an athlete and a cheerleader. The first time I met her, she arm-wrestled me to the ground. That girl had biceps of steel, though you'd never have known it, she was slender as a greyhound. Something just happened to my heart, it was somewhere in the pit of my stomach every time I saw her. I really knew what it meant to be "sick in love". No one was more surprised than me, when she said she felt the same way.'

Ellie could just imagine them: the small, beautiful, blonde athlete, and the tall, golden-bodied surfer. She thought, enviously, they must have looked great together.

'We were inseparable,' Dan said. 'We did our homework together, ran track together, surfed together. She was the homecoming princess and I was proud to be her boyfriend. How to explain youthful passion?' He shook his head, still not understanding the strength of the emotion of first love. 'We were nineteen when we married, and both in college. At opposite ends of the spectrum, though. I was science and she was phys. ed. While I was up all night, studying, she was up at six in the morning to go running. Teenage love in a cramped, rented, furnished apartment.'

He shrugged, looking at Ellie. 'How could it last? In a way I found freedom, though. I ditched grad school and took off for New York, full of high ideals about working to protect the good and tracking down the bad, doing my bit out there on the streets.' He shrugged again, 'Nothing in life is ever quite that black-and-white. But I was a good cop, I lived for it, and I guess in my own way I was satisfied I was doing my bit.'

'Did you ever fall in love again?' Her voice was low, sweet, understanding.

'I did, but never again, like that . . .' He wanted to add, 'until now', but it was too soon, and she was too wary. Ellie was not ready for love.

She reached across and took his hand. 'Thanks for telling me all that, Dan.'

'You think you know me now?'

Her eyes were serious as they met his. 'Somehow, I think I've always known you,' she replied quietly.

He didn't have to ask what she meant by that. He understood. They needed no preliminaries to know each other.

'It's late.' He got to his feet, thinking longingly of the many-pillowed white-canopied bed upstairs, and Ellie in it. But it wasn't the moment, wasn't the time.

'I'm glad you came tonight.' She walked with him into the hallway that was just wide enough to accommodate two people, if they stood close enough together.

'I'm glad too.' Her scent enveloped him and a strand of her soft hair encountered his lips as he brought his mouth down on hers. He held her lightly for a second as their lips clung. He opened his eyes first. 'Beautiful,' he said, looking at her.

'Mmm?'

'I could never think of the right word to describe you, but now I know. It's beautiful.'

He saw the colour rise in her face at the compliment. A real old-fashioned blush, he thought. She never ceased to surprise him.

'Thank you.' She pulled away from him and opened the door. 'Goodnight, Danny Boy.'

'Good night, friend.' He waved as he walked back down the short brick path and opened the gate. 'I'll call you, tomorrow.'

Parked in the shadows across the street, Buck saw Dan lift his hand in farewell as he walked down the path, and Ellie's smile as she waved back. The clock on the dash said three-fifteen. He was sick with jealousy, enraged with her for deceiving him. *How could she? How dare she?*

The light had been turned out in the bedroom, hours ago. Now it went on again. Gnawing nervously on his fingernails, he waited until he saw it go out again, before driving back to Sunset and his prison-like studio apartment.

The following afternoon a large bouquet of flowers was delivered to the café. Plump, creamy peonies, paperwhite narcissi, and bronze lilies. Ellie buried her nose in them. They were all scented, all beautiful. Opening the accompanying note, she read it, smiling:

'Thanks for the wonderful dinner, and a spectacular tarte tatin. Somehow, the colours and scents of these flowers reminded me of you.'

They would have place of honour on her night table and she would call him later to thank him. She couldn't wait to see him again. Next Wednesday, dinner at his place this time.

30

The following Wednesday, Ellie glanced worriedly round the empty café. It was almost six o'clock and she should be on her way to Running Horse, but Jake hadn't shown up yet.

'Are you sure you can manage without me?' she demanded, pacing.

Maya glanced up from the cash register. 'Just go, woman, while you have the chance. Did you never hear that the art of being a successful executive is the ability to delegate?'

'I'm not an executive, I'm a cook. And a waitress, and anything else I need to be. Anyhow I can't afford to delegate, I'd be out of business in a week.'

Leaving the cash register, Maya inspected Ellie's simple blue sweater and skirt critically. 'Mmm,' she said, circling round her. 'Mmm, the blue's good. A bit "missy" but not bad, considering the rural location.'

'What d'you mean, "*missy*",' Ellie said indignantly.

'It's hardly *sexy*.' Maya ran her hands through her short blonde hair, vamping. 'It's not going to knock his socks off.'

'Maybe I prefer him with his socks on. Where *is* Jake?' She glanced anxiously at her watch. 'He was supposed to be here at five-thirty.'

The first customers of the evening pushed through the door and automatically she grabbed menus and went to greet them. Maya sighed, she would never get her out of here.

At Running Horse, Florita was in the kitchen, cooking a Mexican feast. Dan stuck his head through the door, sniffing appreciatively. 'I don't know what it is, Florita, but it surely smells great.'

She smiled up at him, 'You will like, Señor, and the Señorita also.'

There was a chill in the evening air and Dan put a match to the kindling in the big river-rock fireplace, then threw on a couple of logs. He'd bought tuberoses and white lilies for the table, and their scent mingled pleasingly with the applewood and the delicious aroma of food. A Ben Webster album was on the stereo and a bottle of champagne chilled in an old galvanized tin pail nearby.

Pancho came running in from some adventure in the great outdoors, and flung himself on the rug in front of the fire, stretching luxuriously. The logs crackled, and soundbites of laughter came from the kitchen, where Florita was talking to her baby.

Dan thought, satisfied, it had come a long way from the Stephen King house of horror. Finally, it felt like home. All it needed was Ellie's presence to complete it.

'So Jake didn't show,' Maya said reasonably, at seven o'clock. 'Don't worry about it, I can cope.'

Ellie ran a hand distractedly through her hair, glancing round the crowded café. 'I knew I shouldn't have arranged this date. I've been taking too much time off lately.'

'Too much time off? I can count it on one finger. Go on, Ellie, for god's sake, just go.'

Maya urged her toward the door, but Ellie shook her head. 'I'll just call and tell him I'm going to be late.'

Dan picked up the phone on the first ring. She could hear cool jazz/blues in the background and Pancho gave a token woof. 'I'm sorry, Dan, but the waiter didn't show up, I'm going to be late.'

'Okay,' he said, smiling. 'How late?'

'It's a bit crowded now, I'll try to leave in the next half-hour. I could be with you by eight-thirty.'

'See you then.' He went to the kitchen to tell Florita there was a delay, then walked out onto the front porch and stood, looking at his property. The road curving round the hill glimmered silver in the twilight, and his newly-immaculate rows of vines marched into infinity. He could smell damp earth and applewood smoke and *chiles rellenos*. He smiled happily. Life was looking pretty good.

Back indoors, he hoped uneasily that Ellie wouldn't think the sofa and the log fire and the champagne looked like a set-up. Even though he admitted he was anticipating her visit far more than any man who was not involved should be.

At seven-thirty, Ellie grabbed her bag and went into the kitchen to check on the chef. 'Everything okay?' she asked, nervously.

'Sure!' Chan glanced up from the piece of veal he was trimming. 'What could be wrong? Except this kitchen is too small.' He whacked at the meat then let out a yell as blood spurted from his thumb. 'Jesus,' he said, 'now look what you made me do.'

'Oh, Chan,' Ellie stared horrified at the gash at the base of his thumb, then hurriedly wrapped a clean napkin round it. The red stain spread quickly through the linen. 'You'd better get to the emergency room,' she said. 'The kid can drive you. I'll take over in here.'

Maya poked her head round the kitchen door. 'What's going on?' She stared aghast at Chan's bloody hand. 'Uhuh, trouble.' She glanced sorrowfully at Ellie who already had her apron on and was heading toward the stove. 'So much for the romantic evening at the ranch.'

Dan laid his head back against the cushions, listening to the music, counterpointed by Pancho's snores. Every now and again he glanced at his watch, anticipating her arrival. The phone rang again at eight.

He picked it up. 'Ellie?' he said happily.

'It's Maya. Look, something's happened and it's a bit chaotic here. I'm sorry, but Ellie's still in the kitchen. I'll do my best to get her out of here as soon as I can. Okay?'

'Okay. Thanks for letting me know, Maya.'

He slumped down on the sofa again, sighing.

At nine, Ellie called. 'I'm sorry, Dan,' she said quickly. 'But things are impossible. I'll call you again, later.'

'Fine, that's okay,' he said.

When the phone rang again at eleven, he was mad enough at her to ignore it. He sat on the porch steps in the cool night, with the ringing vibrating in his ears. He could see Florita, through the window, clearing the dishes from the table, along with the uneaten salad and freshly-baked tortillas.

He went inside and poured himself a glass of champagne. It was too cold, and anyhow, the pleasure had gone from it. Hurling the glass to the ground, he stalked off to his office in the stables.

Shifting his mind determinedly from the elusive Ellie, he sat through the long night hours under the naked light-bulb, with only Pancho for company, studying his plans of the vineyard and reading about the new oak barrels. Anything to get his mind off Ellie and her too-busy city life, and back on his single-minded track.

31

The following evening at the café, Ellie was thinking guiltily about Dan. She couldn't blame him for not answering the phone last night, but she'd had no choice but to stay and cope. That was what she did.

Slamming dishes around tiredly, she thought maybe Chan had a point, and the kitchen was too small. Chan had taken the day off, and between them she and Terry would cope, but her heart wasn't in it.

The new kid acting as dish-washer this week suddenly dropped a few plates with a crash and she gritted her teeth, telling herself it didn't matter.

'What you need, sweetheart, is a night off.' Maya put a stack of plates on the wooden rack. 'Look, it's still early, why don't you just close up tonight? Go apologize to your fella. Or see your grandmother, or a movie. *Anything*.'

Ellie shook her head. 'How can I?

'Easy.' Maya walked through the café, locked the door, then turned the *Open* sign to *Closed*. 'It's done.'

'But I can't just close without warning. What will my regular customers think?'

'We'll tell them the chef got hurt and to try again tomorrow night. They're just going to miss you more, that's all.'

Ellie looked doubtful, but Maya could tell she was thinking about it. 'Well, that's settled,' she said, shrugging on her jacket. 'See you tomorrow, then.'

'Wait, where are you going?' Ellie grabbed her arm. 'What do you mean, *tomorrow?*'

'Didn't you hear? We're closed tonight.'

Maya's laughter drifted back into the kitchen as she strode out the door. 'Get real, Ellie,' she yelled over her shoulder. 'Get a life, woman.'

Oh, what the hell, Ellie said to herself, she was right. Chan not being here wasn't a good excuse, but it was an excuse of sorts. She told herself she could drive up and surprise Miss Lottie. But she knew what she really wanted was to see Dan.

She made good time until she got to Camarillo and then the mist began rolling over the valley, slowing her down. Fretting in the dawdling traffic, she dialled her grandmother's number on the carphone. There was no answer and a few minutes later, she tried again. Still no answer. Frowning, she pressed the off button. Could Miss Lottie be ill? But surely Maria would have called to let her know? Unless she'd had an accident and she'd been taken to hospital?

Ellie's heart lurched and she put her foot on the gas, beeping her horn impatiently as a blue Jag zipped in front of her. 'And where did that snippy little manoeuvre get you, smartyboots?' she muttered through gritted teeth. 'A big six feet in front of me.'

She thought about Dan, uncertain what to do, knowing how mad he must be at her. Dialling his number, she sat, fingers tapping nervously against the steering wheel, listening to the phone ring, unanswered. 'Where the hell is everybody this evening?' she groaned. 'Has the whole of Santa Barbara county disappeared into the ocean, or what?'

Dan walked the still-steaming mare back through the stable yard. He heard the phone ringing in the office and thought, morosely, let it ring, the mare was more important right now. Throwing a blanket over her, he slapped her on the hindquarters and sent her trotting off into the stall. The phone was still ringing.

He shrugged out of his shirt, wiped the sweat off with it, then picked up the receiver. 'Yeah. Running Horse Winery.'

Ellie grinned, relieved. He sounded winded and she hoped she'd made him run.

'This is no way to run a business. What if I were an important customer, waiting to place an order for a hundred cases?'

'Then you'd be unlucky. We don't have ten cases, let alone a hundred. And what we do have, I plan on drinking all by myself. Alone in a darkened room.'

'That bad, huh?'

'Worse.' He finished with the shirt and tossed it over the side of the stall. 'So? Where were you last night?'

'I thought you'd never ask.'

'I'm asking.'

He sounded grim and she sighed. 'Let's just say I was unavoidably detained at the café.'

'More staff problems.'

It was a statement not a question, and this time she heaved an audible sigh. 'Listen, you can't say I didn't warn you at the beginning.'

Dan leaned against the barn door. The wood was still warm from the sun and the flaking paint stuck to his bare back. He closed his eyes, imagining cool waves closing over him as he dived into the ocean, plunging smoothly through them . . . with Ellie at his side. Why was she so elusive, so difficult?

She said, 'I've taken the evening off. I'm on my way to see my grandmother, I thought perhaps we could meet later? Maybe I could make up for last night?' There was a long silence and she added softly, 'I'm truly sorry, Dan. I wanted to see you but the chef slipped and cut his thumb. He had to go off and be stitched.'

'So Martha Stewart stepped into the breach.' He pictured her trundling round the tiny kitchen, tripping over her feet, grumbling.

Ellie could hear the smile in his voice and she beamed with relief. 'I'll drop by and see Miss Lottie first. Then I could meet you.'

'I've never seen Journey's End,' Dan said, hinting.

'Then this is my opportunity to give you the grand tour. You've already met Miss Lottie, but I'll introduce you to lovely Maria, and to Bruno the dog. Then you'll have met my entire family.'

'That's it? No fifth cousins twice removed? No uncles and aunts in distant countries?'

'None that I know of.' She beeped her horn angrily again as the blue Jag darted out of the lane in front of her, then quickly back. 'You know how to get there?'

'Just drive up Hot Springs Road and look for the gates with the griffins.'

She laughed. 'See you there, Danny Boy. In about forty minutes.'

A few minutes later, she dialled her grandmother's number again. The line was dead. Peering through the fog, she wished worriedly she could get there faster.

32

The night Buck had chosen to kill Lottie Parrish was a fortunate one, weatherwise. It had been a hot day and now the sea mist was rolling in, smothering the lower part of the town, swirling through the treetops, all the way up into the hills.

He swung the BMW into the horse trail that circled the back of the property, bumping over the ruts until it was far enough from the road not to be seen. He wore a black tracksuit with the drug-pusher's Glock 27 autopistol tucked into the waistband, a padded black ski-jacket that puffed him out like the Michelin man, a black ski-mask, sneakers, and fine latex surgical gloves. The flashlight was in his pocket, and his friend the switchblade was sheathed to his calf.

A moon flickered intermittently through the mist, lighting his path as he pushed open the creaking gate near the old laundry. He jogged, stealthy as a hunter, through the copse of silver birch planted seven decades ago by Waldo Stamford, past the black empty rectangle of the swimming pool, alongside the overgrown tennis court and the once-velvet croquet lawn. Onto the stone-pillared terrace where distinguished visitors, politicians, movie stars, and titans of industry had once gathered to drink cocktails.

He stood for a moment, looking round at the playground of the rich that soon would be his. Then he walked silently along the terrace, round the corner of the big house.

He had two problems. The easier one was Maria. The second was the dog. It was slow and stiff but had a bark as loud as a young dobermann. He'd considered a piece of poisoned meat, but decided it would look premeditated; he wanted this to look like a random robbery, gone wrong.

Unlocking the kitchen door, he slipped inside, then closed it softly behind him. A clock ticked into the silence and the refrigerator loudly regurgitated lumps of ice.

In the hall a lamp glowed softly on a small table. He switched it off, easing the gun from his waistband. His sneakered feet made no noise on the thickly-carpeted stairs.

The door to Maria's room stood slightly ajar. It was empty. The sound of running water came from the bathroom, and he guessed she was taking a shower. He walked in and stood by the door, waiting.

It was hot in his down-padded ski-jacket. Sweat trickled down his back and his palms in the latex gloves were damp. He heard her singing in the shower, and tilted his head, listening. Suddenly he wanted to laugh.

Warbling 'Dixie' loudly, Maria wrapped herself in the big bath towel that had seen service for more than ten years. But as Miss Lottie always said, if you bought good, it lasted, and this certainly had. Pure Egyptian cotton that had you dry in a flash. She put on her nightdress and her plaid flannel bathrobe, thinking about the chocolate cake she'd made that afternoon. She would go downstairs and fix some tea, then they would enjoy it together in front of the television set in Miss Lottie's cosy little sitting room. They might catch one of those gossip shows Miss Lottie liked so much, and maybe the sitcom they enjoyed, *Frazier*. Then it would be early bed for both of them, as it always was these days.

Humming her little song cheerfully, she pushed her feet into her fluffy blue slippers, hung up the towel to dry, brushed her hair and rolled it into a grey-speckled knot. Then she opened the bathroom door.

The light behind her gave Buck a perfect sillhouette. He wasn't as expert with the Glock as with his strong hands, but at this range he couldn't miss. The little flame spat from the barrel, one, twice, three times.

Maria jolted backwards. She clutched at the door and stood upright for a long second while Buck debated on one more shot. Then she said '*Ohhh*', softly, and crumpled to the floor.

He nodded, satisfied. Target number one was accounted for, exactly as planned.

Along the hallway, a sliver of light shone from Miss Lottie's door. Flexing his fingers, he glided toward it. Now he could hear the TV announcer saying '*All this, on Entertainment Tonight.*'

Miss Lottie was fresh from her bath. She was wearing the new cream velvet robe and brushing her hair, counting softly to a hundred, as she always did.

She had been answering her E-mail and the computer was still switched on. The *Opus 'n Andy* screen-saver cartoons cavorted, forgotten, across the display, and the TV set blared the latest Hollywood exploits and scandals. She always had it turned up loud because Maria was getting deafer, though she would never admit to it. Besides, Miss Lottie had a fascination for the lives and doings of the glamorous celebrities on the show, though she had no idea who Pamela Anderson Lee or Drew Barrymore were.

She glanced at her old watch. It was foolish, she knew, to look forward so much to a piece of Maria's double chocolate cake and a cup of hot tea, but when one was older life's small pleasures counted for so much more. Like Bruno's morning toast and butter. She ruffled his fur fondly.

'Ah, my boy, I remember when you were just a pup,' she said smiling. 'Roly-poly, all big paws and floppy ears, and with a foolish grin on your face. Ellie fell in love with you right away, though I would have chosen the bigger dog. Perhaps I shouldn't be telling you this now, after all, I don't want to hurt your feelings. And anyway, Ellie was absolutely right, I wouldn't change you for anything.'

The door-handle squeaked and Bruno's ears pricked up. He struggled to his feet, back stiffened, staring at the door.

'Stop showing off, you silly boy,' Miss Lottie said fondly. 'It's only Maria.' She turned her head, smiling. 'Come on, Maria, you're missing the programme. What's been keeping you?'

The door swung slowly open. Her faded blue eyes clouded with concern. 'Maria? Are you all right?' She searched round for her cane. 'Where are you, Maria? What's going on?'

Bruno's mouth drew back in a snarl. A foreboding tremor shivered through Miss Lottie's veins.

Growling like a lion, Bruno hurled himself through the open door. There was a sudden popping noise. Miss Lottie heard him whimper, then he turned and staggered slowly back. His trusting eyes were fixed on hers, life fading from them, as he sank down with his head on her feet.

His blood gushed over her slippers. Miss Lottie bent, touched his soft fur, stroked him lovingly with a trembling hand. Her heart was breaking.

Lifting her head, she looked into the eyes of the masked man standing in the doorway. A tall man, huge in his padded ski-jacket, frightening in his mask. There was a gun in his hand. Pointed at her.

Anger flared in her eyes. 'You shot my dog,' she said, her voice cold as chipped ice. 'There was no need for that. He was old and harmless. If you've come to rob me, the safe is in the wall in the dressing-room, over there. It's never locked.'

'I know.'

His voice was low, almost a whisper. 'Who are you?' She stared imperiously at him, refusing to show her fear. 'And what do you want? I've told you where the jewellery is, what there is left of it. Surely there are richer houses to rob around here, than mine?' She looked down at her dog, choking with pain and anger. 'Only a coward would come into the house and frighten two old women, kill a dog . . .'

The hand holding the gun wavered. *She was meant to be afraid, terrified, begging for her life. Instead, she was telling him what to do, ordering him around, acting like she was in charge.* 'Go get her,' the voice inside his head commanded. '*Tell the old bitch who you are, what you intend to do, make her grovel. She is nothing now. And you are power.*' His blood throbbed with that power, it was zinging round his veins, pumped double-time by his thundering heart . . . He could hear it, hear his own blood pounding in his ears . . .

'Put down that gun at once,' Miss Lottie commanded. 'Take what you want, then leave my house. Though I don't know what you expect to find here.'

'I came to find you, Miss Lottie.' Buck laid the gun, obediently, on the lamp table.

Miss Lottie gripped her cane firmly as he took a step toward her. It was her only weapon and she intended to use it. She was an old woman and not afraid of dying, but she would go when her time came, and not before.

Buck wanted her to see him, to understand *who* he was. *Then* she would know fear. He pulled off the ski-mask. 'Take a good look, Miss Lottie,' he said mockingly. 'It's been a long time since you've seen this face.'

Miss Lottie stared into his dark, deadly eyes. Seconds ticked past. 'Of course,' she said at last, with a little sigh. 'I couldn't put my finger on it at the Biltmore, though I thought there was something familiar about you. Now I know, it was the eyes. You can't change those, Buck Duveen.'

'And you don't change either, Miss Lottie. Still playing the dowager queen. Only this time there are no faithful retainers, no armed guards to come running to save you.'

'You're quite wrong,' she lied firmly. 'The security patrol will be doing their rounds any minute.' But she knew there was no patrol. And no Maria and no Bruno anymore. No one to save her. She had almost nothing to lose, except Ellie. If she died, she would never see her again, and she couldn't bear that.

Buck was silent, watching her. There wasn't even the hint of a tremor in her voice. *She was still not afraid of him.* 'You old bitch.' His face was in hers. 'You had me put away for half my life, while you and the girl lived here, in splendour, enjoying yourselves.'

'You were locked away because you are mad,' she replied calmly. 'Now, I see it was a mistake, a kindness on my part that went wrong. I should have let you go to jail instead. Let you be prosecuted for the terrible things you've done. Let you be branded for what you are. *Murderer.*' Suddenly, she smashed the cane across his face.

Buck shook his head, spattering droplets of blood. Staggering back, he put his hands to his eyes, half-blinded with pain.

Miss Lottie knew there was no escape, she could not run, but she had to warn Ellie. She had only moments.

Opus 'n Andy still cavorted across the computer screen. Her fingers trembled as she found the keys and began to type *D U*

V E E E E E E. Buck's powerful hands fastened around her throat and her finger stuck on the *E*.

'*Bitch*,' he muttered, his whole body trembling with power, '*lying rich bitch*.' Her flesh was pliant under his fingers, he could feel it bruising, feel her fragile bones snapping, feel the blood in her veins slowing. But her blue eyes never wavered from his. It was as if she were mocking him, saying, 'See, even now, you can't win. I'm not afraid. *Murderer* . . . you'll never be one of us . . . *murderer* . . .'

'*Close your eyes*,' he howled, '*close your goddamn eyes, can't you?*'

But Miss Lottie did not close her eyes. Not even when she was dead.

Buck let her drop. Still trembling, he looked at her. He breathed a jagged sigh of pure pleasure. He had dreamed so often of seeing her like this.

His blood spattered over her as he dragged her into the dressing-room, then took the pearls and the few rings and brooches from the open safe and stuffed them in the pockets of the ski-jacket.

The sweat chilled on his body as he stared triumphantly down at her. Then he knelt beside her, and carved his sign into her forehead. He had won. Finally, the prize would be his.

33

The simple journey seemed to take for ever. It was dark and the coastal fog had socked in when Ellie finally swung the little car off Route 101 and headed up Hot Springs Road. Mist wreathed like grey ghosts through the trees as she drove up the long curving driveway. She had always liked the welcoming sound of tyres on gravel, but somehow, tonight, in the fog and the deep silence, it sounded lonely.

A faint light shone from her grandmother's curtained window, and she breathed a sigh of relief, guessing the phone was out of order. She parked the car, walked up the steps and tried the door. Thank goodness, tonight they had remembered to lock it. Fishing her key from her pocket she opened it and went in.

Usually, a lamp was left burning, but the front hall was in darkness. Surprised, she switched on the lights. 'Maria, hello,' she called. 'It's me, Ellie.' She waited, expecting Bruno to come waddling down the stairs to greet her. 'Maria?' she called again.

Buck opened the french windows, swept aside the gauzy white curtain, and looked out at the land that would soon be his. As if to help him, the mist rolled back and the moon flickered palely on the gardens. *And on Ellie's yellow jeep, parked in front.*

His sharp indrawn breath rattled in his throat. *He hadn't heard her drive up, he couldn't let her find him here . . . but it was too late, he could already hear her calling for Maria, her footsteps on the stairs. He stepped quickly through the french window onto the balcony.*

In the hall, silence wrapped around Ellie like a blanket and goosebumps prickled up her arms.

'Nothing's happened,' she reassured herself, taking the steps two at a time. 'They're watching TV and didn't hear me. Two old ladies, they must be getting deafer.'

'Gran, it's me . . .' Flinging open the door she almost tripped over the dog. She took a step back, her shoes sticky with blood. Bruno's dead eyes stared back at her.

'*Ohhhhh* . . .' the breath caught in her throat. '*Bruno*,' she whispered, shocked. '*Oh, Bruno* . . .' The hair at the back of her neck prickled as she dragged her eyes from him and looked warily round the room.

Entertainment Tonight was just winding up loudly on the TV, and *Opus 'n Andy* still cavorted across the computer screen.

'Gran . . . ?' Her voice wavered. She took a hesitant step toward the dressing-room, saw her grandmother's bare foot. Her eyes widened with shock as she sank down next to her, seeing the horror of her butchered face, her open blue eyes, the bruises, the blood, the matted silver hair. 'Gran . . .' she cried . . . it wasn't true, it couldn't be happening, not to Miss Lottie . . . She could hear someone whimpering, as though from a great distance.

Buck heard her cry out, a wild, thin, whimpering sound, sharp as shattered glass. He'd never heard anyone scream like that before, not even when he went to kill them. He wanted to run to her, put his hand over her mouth, stop her. He knew if she saw him he would be forced to kill her, and it wasn't time yet. Still, it would be such exquisite pain to kill the one you loved. Her chances were fifty-fifty.

Through the gap in the window, he saw her backing out of the dressing-room, her arms outflung as though she were pushing away the horror she had just seen. The window curtains belled inwards in a sudden gust of breeze and she swung round, crouching, her eyes fixed on the window.

Sweat beaded his forehead. It was moment-of-truth time. If she walked out the door, she lived. If she came toward him, she would die. The blade was cool against his palm, ready.

Ellie was frozen, her legs refused to move, she stared at the billowing curtains ... Something out there caught the light, glittering ... Suddenly the adrenalin of terror gave her feet wings and she turned and fled.

Buck sighed happily as he stepped back into the room. Tonight, his beloved Ellie lived. He heard her running across the hall, the door being flung open, the sound of the engine as she started her car.

He glanced at the silver-framed photograph on the nightstand. Ellie's eyes gazed into his, her lips curved in that dazzling smile. A smile meant just for him. Sweeping the photo into his pocket, he hurried from the room.

He ran noiselessly back down the stairs, through the hall to the kitchen. The lock clicked shut as he closed the door behind him. Keeping to the shadows, he jogged easily back across the croquet lawn, past the tennis court and the gaping wound in the ground that used to be the swimming pool. Through Waldo Stamford's carefully planted copse of silver birch, through the rusty gates near the old laundry, and back down the horse trail to his car.

He sheathed the knife, removed the ski-mask and folded it into his pocket with the latex gloves, then took off the bulky ski-parka and locked it in the trunk. Driving out onto the empty road, he was careful not to speed. He guessed Ellie had taken the quickest way back to town, and he took the upper road that followed a circular route.

Whistling his favourite tune, he was a happy man. Lottie Parrish was dead, and he had not had to kill the woman he loved.

Back at the hotel, he left the car on the street and returned to his cottage, where he showered and changed his clothes. He inspected the wound on his cheek. A couple of butterfly bandaids took care of that, then he swaggered into the bar.

Phase Three was complete and the double Jim Beam tasted like nectar that night.

34

The Explorer cruised smoothly up Hot Springs Road, and Dan smiled as he swung between the massive pillars with the griffins. Ellie was right, you couldn't miss them, they were big enough for Buckingham Palace. Too late, he saw the yellow jeep coming at him. Slamming his foot on the brake, he threw the wheel to the right. The jeep sideswiped him and, tyres screeching, skidded into a tree.

'Jesus Christ, Ellie, now I know you're crazy,' he yelled, furious.

Ellie jumped from the car, her eyes blinded with tears. It was the killer . . . she had to run . . . She heard his footsteps pounding after her, getting closer. He was almost on her . . . he grabbed her shoulder. She swung round, hand fisted, and, like a world champ, caught him a crashing blow to the jaw.

Dan grunted, as painful stars flickered before his eyes. 'What the hell's gotten into you, have you gone completely crazy?' He grabbed her by the shoulders, keeping a wary eye out for that right hook. She was fighting him off, screaming hysterically.

'No . . . no . . . no . . .'

'Ellie,' he yelled. 'Ellie, stop it.'

Something penetrated her terror-fogged brain. Fists still clenched ready to strike, she looked at him.

He could feel her trembling. 'It's okay,' he said, gently. 'You're all right, that's all that matters. It's only a car, even if it is a new one.' He smiled encouragingly at her, but there was no answering smile.

It was all mixed up in her mind, all a jumble . . . how to say it, how to tell him, the words wouldn't come out straight ... '*It's Miss Lottie ... dead ... murdered ... the dog ...*'

He was holding her away from him, looking into her eyes, unbelieving. 'Wait a minute, Ellie. Are you saying *you saw that?*'

She gulped back the sobs she knew were going to choke her. '*I saw her, I saw ... oh god, oh my god ...*'

Dan pulled her close, holding her, remembering the old ladies lived alone and were careless about security. Could they really have been murdered?

'I've got to go in there and take a look,' he told her quietly. 'I want you to stay in the car. Lock all the doors and don't make a move.'

She shook her head, afraid to be left, and afraid to go with him.

He sighed, putting his arm round her as he walked her back up the road to the car. 'Okay, but I don't want you to go in there again,' he said. She shook her head, an obedient child.

The front door stood wide open, just as she'd left it. She stood in the hall, watching him walk up the stairs to that terrible room. He was going to turn round, smile at her, tell her it was all a mistake and she had dreamed it ... she knew that was what was going to happen. She pressed a hand to her mouth to stop the scream.

Dan pushed open the door. He could smell violence even before he saw it. The dog was already stiff, its legs frozen in rigor mortis. The TV was blasting, and the computer cartoons still running, and the curtains billowed gently in the breeze from the open french window. He saw the pool of blood, the cane thrown to the ground. If he had doubted Ellie, he did no longer. He walked into the dressing-room, saw Miss Lottie's body, so pathetically small and frail. Her eyes were wide open and there was a cross carved into her forehead. *Nose to scalp, temple to temple.* He drew in a shocked breath. 'Jesus god,' he muttered.

He was too experienced a cop to touch anything or try to move her, he would leave that to the local police, and the ME. He checked the closet, the bathroom, the balcony.

From the top of the stairs, he saw Ellie waiting in the hall, her hands clasped to her trembling mouth, looking at him. 'Which room is Maria's?' he asked. She pointed to the next room.

He found Maria just outside the bathroom door. She had been shot several times in the chest. There was a lot of blood, but there was no cross carved into her head.

He went back and took another look at Miss Lottie, wondering about the link between her killing and the two hookers. The room had been turned over, the safe ransacked, but something was wrong. Two women were dead, each by a different method. If it were not for the signature, he could have sworn this smacked of a ritualistic execution-type slaying.

'It's okay,' Ellie told herself, watching him walk back down the stairs toward her. 'He's going to tell me it's okay . . .'

Dan shook his head. 'We'd better call the police,' he said quietly. 'I'm sorry, Ellie, but there's nothing much else we can do now.'

35

Ellie slumped in the front seat of Dan's badly dented Explorer
in front of Journey's End. Oddly, with lights shining from
every window, the house looked the way it used to years
ago, when Miss Lottie was throwing a *'little soirée'*, as she'd
called it. Which had meant three hundred people, dinner under
a silk-draped tent on the spacious lawns, with the scent of
roses and night-blooming jasmine on the soft summer wind.
It had meant champagne, women in gorgeous evening gowns
and jewels, handsome suntanned men in black ties. And by the
end of the evening, the charity auction Miss Lottie had organized
would have raised a great deal of money for the local hospital, or
for needy children, or some other cause dear to her heart.

Now, instead of the sleek Mercedes and limousines, squad cars
with flashing blue lights were parked in front of the portico and
fire rescue service engines glittered through the swirling mist;
ambulances with their doors agape waited for their new burden,
and the detectives' plain dark vehicles churned up the smooth
green lawn.

Uniformed officers were stringing yellow tape around what
they were calling 'the crime scene', and Ellie wanted desperately
to tell them it wasn't so. That this was their home; that Miss
Lottie and Maria were upstairs with their feet propped on the
green brocade ottoman with the bullion fringe that Bruno had
chewed as a puppy, watching *Frazier* on TV. Bruno would have
his head on Miss Lottie's knee, his eyes upraised longingly, and
soon she would feed him a few surreptitious pieces of cake, 'Just
to keep him happy.'

*   *   *

Dan was telling Detective Johannsen how he had found the bodies; that the crime scene was intact; and that the cross etched on the face linked with the hooker murdered in New York, and the one last week in LA.

'I'm trying to figure the connection between a robbery with violence and the signature serial killing of prostitutes,' he said, worriedly. 'It just doesn't make sense.'

'It's an ugly scene.' Detective Jim Johannsen had worked in the LA police department for many years before transferring to Santa Barbara. He was a veteran of violence, but there was something infinitely pathetic about the two old women and their dog, butchered so horribly. Still, he wasn't about to discuss the case with a civilian. And a witness.

A police photographer was taking flash pictures of the bodies and of the room; officers were taking measurements, ringing the patches of blood with chalk, searching for spent bullets, dusting the safe for prints, the desk, the doors, every surface; detectives were bagging other items for later investigation by the crime squad: the cane, the bloodstained slippers. Every inch of the big house would be gone over with a fine-tooth comb.

The same procedure was taking place in the room next door, with Maria. Even the dog would be taken to the morgue and the bullet extracted from its chest to be sent to ballistics for analysis.

The ME still knelt over Miss Lottie's body, doing what he had to do to establish the cause and time of death. Later, he would perform an autopsy, see what other vital information could be established from any scrapings under her fingernails as she'd fought off her attacker: minute flakes of skin, hairs, fibres from clothing. He would estimate the size and weight of her killer from the imprint of his hands on her throat, and establish whether or not he'd raped her. There was no dignity for Miss Lottie, in death.

The TV set still played loudly. Ironically, it was *NYPD Blue*.

Detective Johannsen was standing in front of the computer, looking thoughtful. 'What d'you make of this, Cassidy.'

Miss Lottie had been writing to a Rabbi Altman in Manchester,

England. The letter was chatty and charming, and a bit vague, as though she knew she knew him but couldn't quite remember.

'*Dear Rabbi Altman,*' Miss Lottie had written. '*Shalom. How pleasant to hear from you again, though I admit at this moment, I can't quite recall where we met. However, old friends are always welcome here, at Journey's End, and I feel from your letter, the goodness of your heart* ... she had broken off at that point. Underneath in caps was the name DUVEEN. Except it wasn't completed.

'Looks like her finger got stuck on the E,' Johannsen said. 'Why was she writing Ellie's name?'

Dan remembered Ellie's story about her mother. 'Her mind wasn't what it used to be. She might have been thinking of her daughter. Romany died in an auto accident years ago.'

They stared at the computer. 'You dusting it for prints?' Dan asked. Johannsen threw him a sceptical look and he held his hands up, palms out. 'Sorry, sorry. You're in charge.'

'That's right.' Johannsen's tone was mild, but it put him in his place.

Dan guessed he'd outlived his usefulness and now he could go. 'Anything I can do', he lifted his shoulders, mouth in a grim line, 'just call me.'

'I'll do that.' Johannsen was already striding across the room. 'What I'd like now, is to speak to Miss Duveen.'

Ellie was afraid to close her eyes because then she would see Miss Lottie again, see the tiny, size three narrow feet she had always been so proud of, so white and infinitely pathetic as she sprawled on the rug, her arms outflung, her pretty silver hair matted red ... '*It's not true, not true,*' her own voice screamed in her head. Groaning, she hid her face in her arms.

'Ellie?' Dan was at the open window, looking anxiously at her. 'Do you feel able to answer a few questions. It might help.'

'Okay.' Even her voice sounded different, hoarse, strange. Everything was different now. Life would never be the same ...

Detective Jim Johannsen was older, a heavy man in horn-rimmed glasses, kind, sympathetic. He'd dealt with shocked relatives in sudden death cases many times in his career, and it never became any easier. 'I'm sorry, Ms Duveen. Your grand-mother was a great woman, a true character. They don't make them like her any more.'

She nodded, eyes cast down.

'If you could, Ellie, I'd like you to tell me in your own words, exactly what happened when you got to the house.' He waited, ballpoint poised over his notepad.

She didn't even have to pause to think about it; each step was imprinted on her mind, each moment engraved on her heart. It took just a few minutes. Her voice had almost disappeared by the time she finished.

Johannsen threw her a speculative glance. 'Do you know of any reason, or of any person who wanted Miss Lottie dead?'

Dan knew instantly where his questioning was heading. Ellie was a suspect until the real killer was found.

'No. No one.'

'Thank you. I know how hard this is for you.'

Ellie's eyes followed him as he turned away, a bulky figure in a dark jacket and a gleaming white shirt. She wanted to tell him it wasn't difficult at all, that she remembered it perfectly, that she would never forget. Her hands were shaking. She looked down at them, surprised, as if they had a life of their own, and had nothing to do with her.

'It's okay, we can go now.' Dan gripped her trembling hands in his. 'I've got to get you to bed, get a doctor to give you a sedative.'

She shrank away from him. 'I'm not leaving.'

'But you shouldn't stay here, you need to get some rest.' Her face was ashen, her eyes dead with shock; even her hair seemed to have lost its lustre and hung round her tortured face in lank copper strings. He knew she wouldn't leave until her grandmother did.

The ME secured plastic bags over Miss Lottie's hands and feet, and zipped her into a body-bag to preserve any evidence. Then the old lady was bundled onto a gurney, covered with a white sheet, and carried down the stairs. Miss Lottie was leaving Journey's End for the last time.

The brilliant light from the magnificent Venetian crystal chandeliers in the hall illuminated the paramedics and the white-draped gurney like players on a stage. Ellie's tearless eyes, the pupils dilated with shock, were fixed on the slight shape under the sheet, as she followed that precious burden into the waiting ambulance. Then the doors were slammed shut and the medics walked back into the house.

When they returned, she knew they were carrying Maria. Her shape was rounder under the sheet, sturdier. Ellie had never realized how short she was, really how tiny ... it was as though, with death, people seemed to shrink ...

The next time they returned, they had the dog on the gurney. Ellie had been unable to cry for Miss Lottie, unable to cry for Maria, but now tears stung her eyes. She was out of the car, running at him. 'Bruno,' she screamed, 'oh Bruno ...'

She flung her arms round him, then stepped back with a shocked gasp. *He was stiff as a board.*

'It's rigor mortis, ma'am,' the medic explained. 'It'll wear off after a bit and he'll be just like you remembered.'

She put a hand on Bruno's soft fur, bent and kissed his dear, cold face, remembering when she and Miss Ellie had chosen him from the litter of seven. *'This is the one!'* she had said, picking him up triumphantly. So many years, so many memories, so much happiness was wrapped up in that poor stiff, furry body. Bending her head, she dropped a kiss on his sweet dog face. 'I love you, Bruno baby,' she whispered.

The paramedics glanced at each other. 'It would be better if you took a sedative now, Miss,' one said. 'It'll help you get over the shock.'

Ellie shook her head, stubbornly. She wanted to be with Miss Lottie and Maria. *They needed her. She wanted them to feel her love, her energy, her sorrow.* Awake, she was with them. Drugged and sleeping, she would be in a limbo of nothingness.

'I'm taking you home now.' Dan's arm slid comfortingly round her shoulders and she rested against him. It was an arm to be leaned against, a shoulder to cry on, a still-beating heart that offered her love and compassion.

She looked back, bewildered, at Journey's End, lit as though for a party, half expecting to hear music wafting from the windows and the sound of laughing voices. *'But this is home,'* she whispered. Even as she said it, she knew it was no longer true. It was the end of an era, and she would never live in Journey's End again.

36

Much later, Ellie lay in the tub with hot water almost up to her ears, attempting to get the ache out of her body. She felt as though she had travelled a long hard journey, climbed high, difficult mountains, run across burning hot deserts. But there were no bruise marks on her body. The pain was all inside her, and she knew it was never going to go away.

Dan had brought her to Running Horse Ranch. They had offered her brandy, coffee, wine, hot tea. She had declined everything but the tea, yet even that had failed to melt the icy numbness.

The bath water had almost grown cold when she finally climbed from the tub. Wrapping a towel around her, she caught her reflection in the mirror and saw a grey-faced woman, a woman from whose eyes the joy and sparkle had vanished. She would never be the same again.

Tugging on the Giants t-shirt Dan had given her, and his dark-blue terry bathrobe, she ran a comb desultorily through her tangled hair.

The big pine bed, piled high with pillows, looked soft, inviting, but she knew she wouldn't sleep, and nor would she submit to a sedative. She needed to be awake, needed to keep her grandmother in her head, close to her. Wandering to the window she looked out. A grey, sunless dawn was already lightening the sky.

There was a scrabbling noise at the door, then Pancho's nose snuffled through the crack. Pushing it open, he bounced joyfully into the room, but instead of leaping all over her as he usually did he sat quietly, gazing up at her.

Ellie suddenly realized that she was smiling. It was amazing, she thought, how animals and children had that universal ability to bring you back to square one, to realize that innocence still existed in this wicked world.

Climbing into bed, she lay back in the nest of pillows Florita had arranged for her. The sheets were cool against her skin and smelled of lavender, which was nicer than her own sheets which only smelled of Bounce.

The guest room was small, square and rather bare, with pegged pine floors and a tall, curtainless sash window, open to catch the breeze. There was a multi-coloured rag rug, an old green-painted dresser, a pine table next to the bed with a lamp in the shape of a bronze bear, and a large abstract print that took up a great deal of one wall. It was simple and basic, but comfortable. It felt like its owner, Dan.

Pancho leapt onto the end of the bed, turned round once or twice, then settled down, his head on his paws. Ellie closed her eyes. There was no sound and she guessed hazily it was too early yet for birdsong. Her eyelids drifted down and she fell suddenly into a dark pit of blessed oblivion.

Peeking in a short while later, Dan thought she slept like a child, her arms straight out on top of the white coverlet, her mouth slightly open. Pancho raised his eyes and looked at him, then went back to sleep. Dan closed the door softly behind him. For a few short hours, Ellie would know peace.

37

Maya was up early that morning. She had a yoga class at eight-thirty. Yawning and stretching like a sleek-muscled cat, she switched on the TV and went to take a shower.

'*LA. Today. Here is your local news. A well-known Santa Barbara woman was found murdered in her home last night, along with her housekeeper, and the family dog. Eighty-six-year-old Charlotte Parrish was found dead . . .*'

Maya swivelled round, staring at the TV.

'*. . . along with Maria Novales, aged seventy. Police are not giving out any details, as yet. Mrs Parrish was one of the city's leading social lights for decades, and her home was famous for its magnificent gardens. The crime was discovered by her granddaughter, Ellie Parrish Duveen, last night, and police are questioning her.*

'*Now for today's weather and the freeway report . . .*'

Maya's jaw dropped open and her eyes bugged from her head. For a minute, she was paralysed, then, heart thumping, she leapt for the phone.

Ellie's home number didn't answer. Of course it wouldn't, she was up in Santa Barbara. But where? Not at Journey's End, surely? Her trembling finger was already dialling the number of Running Horse Ranch.

'*Oh god, oh god, poor Ellie, poor Miss Lottie, Maria . . . oh god, oh god . . .* the words ran endlessly round in her mind.

'*Si? Señor Cassidy's house.*' Florita answered the phone.

'Is Ellie there?' Maya's fingers drummed a tattoo on the table.

'*Momento.*'

In the background, Maya could hear her calling for Dan . . . 'Dan Cassidy here?'

She breathed a shaky sigh of relief, 'It's Maya Morris, Ellie's friend. I heard the news on television, I can't get her at her home number, I'm so afraid for her . . .'

'It's okay, Maya, she's here. I brought her home with me last night.'

'Oh, thank god, thank *you* . . .' She sagged with relief. 'Is she all right? No, that's a foolish question, how can she possibly be all right? I have to see her, I'm on my way right now . . . tell me what I can do for her.' She was babbling like a crazy woman, not knowing which sentence to get out first. All she knew was Ellie was hurting and she needed to be with her.

'She's numb, Maya. It's going to be tough for her to get over it, seeing her grandmother like that.'

Maya wiped the tears away with the back of her hand. 'Oh poor, dear Miss Lottie . . .'

'I guess she could use a change of clothing, if you could bring that for her.'

'Sure.' Maya had a key to Ellie's house, and Ellie had a key to her apartment. For emergencies, they'd said, but there had never been one. Until now.

Dan gave her directions to the ranch, then said, 'We're on our way to Santa Barbara now. The police want to talk to Ellie. We'll probably be back by the time you arrive.'

'I'll get there as soon as I can. 'She hesitated, 'Dan?'

'Yeah?'

'Tell her I love her, would you?'

'I'll do that.'

His voice was steady, and she thanked heaven for Dan Cassidy as she put down the phone and hurried to get ready. At least with him, Ellie was safe.

38

The news was on all the networks as well as the local TV channels. Clicking through them, Buck sipped his morning coffee, smiling. He'd certainly hit the headlines this time.

Dunking a croissant into the coffee, he sat back, enjoying himself. The Santa Barbara channel was really going to town, with pictures of Journey's End and Waldo Stamford, standing next to President Roosevelt on the balustraded terrace, looking down at the immaculate *parterre* garden. Then there was Miss Lottie as a bride; then as the young mother whose daughter had Ellie's eyes. His stomach clenched as he thought of Ellie. He took another swig of the hot coffee. She was waiting for him, like a rose in a thorny garden. Now, all he had to do was pluck her.

He jolted upright, spilling the coffee as a picture of Rory Duveen filled the screen. They were telling about the automobile accident. There was even an old shot of the crumpled Bentley at the bottom of the ravine.

Buck glared at his father's smiling image, hating him, hating her, the beautiful woman he had chosen to marry. *The heiress*. He gave a short bark of laughter. Some heiress. The pair of them had spent it all. And Miss Lottie had gone and done the same thing. Still, Journey's End would make him a millionaire. He would be rich. And free.

There were more pictures. Of Miss Lottie as the society hostess; at charity functions at Journey's End. And finally, a picture of Ellie.

'*Her granddaughter and only living relative*,' the presenter said, '*and the one who found the body.*'

Buck remembered last night, waiting for her to come to the window and find him there. He remembered the feel of the cold steel knife in his hand, knowing that he would have to kill her. He smiled, a secret icy little smile. Her turn would come.

Meanwhile, he was checking out of the hotel, and returning to LA. He would lie low for a while, see how things developed.

39

Piatowsky was in the den of his three-bedroomed brick home, just across the George Washington Bridge from Manhattan, in suburban Fort Lee, New Jersey.

It was a pleasant room, not too big, with a bay window and a view of the small back garden. It had sand-coloured wall-to-wall berber that wouldn't show the dirt trekked in by kids; a beat-up brown leather sofa; a couple of floral chintz arm chairs; a big brick fireplace and a large TV set.

From where he sat, he could see his eldest son, seven-year-old Michel, at the kitchen table, doing his homework. The five-year-old, Ben was upstairs being bathed by his mother, and the three-year-old and the darlin' of his heart, his daughter Maggie – short for Margaretta – was curled up on his knee, one hand clasped round his neck and the other in her face as she sucked on her thumb.

'There'll be nothing left by the time you're four,' he reminded her. She rolled her big brown eyes in his direction for a second, then continued sucking. She smelled sweetly of baby powder, shampoo and clean pyjamas and he gave a happy little sigh. Sugar and spice, that's what little girls were made of, all right.

He shifted slightly so he could see his watch. Another half hour and he would have to leave. He was on the six o'clock shift tonight which meant he probably wouldn't get home until round three, or even four if they were busy. Not Angela's favourite, but there it was, she was a cop's wife. She was used to it. And in a couple of days she was taking the kids to visit her mother, in Maine, which left him free to go fishin' with Cassidy. He was kinda lookin' forward to it, seeing how the bastard was gettin' along, in sunshineland.

Maggie felt heavy on his chest and he glanced down at her. Her eyes were closed and she had stopped sucking. He smiled, clicking through the channels with the sound on low, until he found the NBC nightly news.

He didn't catch it at first; it was just another homicide out in California. Two old ladies and their dog, living alone in some mansion, near Santa Barbara.

He perked up at the familiar name of the town, looking at the picture of a handsome, frail-looking woman, and then the house. Pretty spectacular, he thought, and probably worth quite a bit. They were saying the house had been robbed, jewellery taken . . . and then they showed a picture of a lovely young woman with a big, warm smile. '*Ellie Parrish Duveen is Mrs Parrish's granddaughter and only living relative,*' they said. '*It was she who found the bodies.*'

Only living relative. Piatowsky thought of the pricy mansion and the family money she would inherit. He wondered fleetingly if Ellie Parrish Duveen had done it.

Then, cradling his daughter in his arms, he carried her upstairs to bed, kissed his wife and boys goodbye, and was on his way to the city and the night's mayhem.

40

They were in a bleak, grey room at the Santa Barbara police department. Coffee in paper cups steamed, untouched, on the table in front of them. Ellie slumped numbly in the hard chair. She felt nothing. Not pain, nor anger, nor fear. It was as if her very soul had died.

Johannsen took a sip of his coffee and glanced at his partner, detective Ray Mullins, tall, thin, dark and enigmatic, standing in the background, arms folded, watching. He cleared his throat. 'Miss Duveen, I'd like you to go over again for me precisely what your movements were last night. With exact times, if you can recall them.'

Ellie lifted dead eyes and stared at him. 'I was in my car on the 101, driving to Montecito. I was near Camarillo and it was foggy. I called Gran to tell her I was coming by to surprise her. There was no reply . . .'

Wearily, she went through her story one more time. She would tell it a thousand times, if she had to, if it would help them find the killer.

'And you arranged to meet Mr Cassidy at the house?'

She nodded. 'Yes.'

She was wearing jeans and boots, and a white oversized t-shirt that belonged to Dan, under a black sweater. She shivered, it was cold in here.

'And what was the purpose of meeting Mr Cassidy?'

Surprise flashed through her eyes, he hadn't asked her this before. 'He'd never seen Journey's End, I said I would show him around. Then we were going to have dinner . . .'

'And where was that? Did you have a reservation some place?'

She shook her head, bewildered. 'No . . . it was just a spur of the moment thing . . .'

'Miss Parrish, how long have you known Mr Cassidy?'

She ran a distracted hand through her hair, 'Maybe . . . a few weeks, I guess.'

'So he's not an old friend of the family?'

'He'd met Miss Lottie once. We had tea together.'

Johanssen's eyes met those of Mullins again. His voice lost its softness, it was firm, even harsh. 'It's my understanding that you are the sole remaining family member. That in fact, you stand to inherit Mrs Parrish's entire estate. Is that true?'

She nodded again, puzzled at the unexpected tack the questioning was taking. 'Yes, but . . .'

'That would be quite a motive for murder?'

She sat back, shocked. '*You can't think I killed her?*' Her voice had a rising tone of horror. Unbelieving, she slumped down again, shaking her head. '*Oh no, no, no, no . . .*'

Mullins fished a packet of Luckys from his pocket. 'Cigarette, Miss Parrish?'

She didn't hear him, her heart was breaking all over again. It was awful, horrible, impossible they could believe she would do such a thing . . .

'No one has suggested you did anything, Miss Parrish. It's just a line of questioning we have to pursue.' Personally, Johanssen thought it likely. Somehow the robbery scene didn't sit right. He had the impression that there hadn't been much jewellery to steal, nothing of great value anyhow, certainly not enough to butcher two old women for. Though there was no use trying to figure what happened to men's minds under those circumstances. Not these days, when they would put a bullet through a store owner's head for a couple of bucks.

'I'd appreciate it, Miss Duveen, if you'd accompany us back to the house. We need you to check Miss Lottie's possessions, tell us, if you can, exactly what's missing so we can make an inventory.'

She half-rose from her seat, panicked. 'Back to that room?'

'It might be helpful in finding the killer.'

Ellie wiped the tears away with the back of her hand. 'I'll do anything for that,' she agreed. Johannsen was already out of his chair. 'But I want Dan to come with me.'

He could have lived without that one. 'Sure, okay, bring him along if it makes you feel better.' He hadn't completely dismissed the pair of them as murderers from his mind.

Ellie held tightly to Dan's hand in the squad car as they raced along Cabrillo Boulevard. The palm trees ruffled in the breeze and the sun sparkled on the blue sea, everybody looked the same, normal. Past the bird sanctuary on the left where Miss Lottie used to like to take her binoculars and keep score of any new arrivals. Past the beautiful cemetery on the right with its view of the ocean, where Ellie's mother and father lay side by side next to Waldo Stamford, and where soon her grandmother would join them. Past the freeway entrance into Coast Village Road. Then the left turn into Hot Springs, the familiar curves in the road as they drove up the hill.

'You okay?' Dan looked worriedly at her as the car turned between the massive griffin gateposts. She nodded, but her hand clung to his and her usually soft mouth was clenched in a tight line. He knew she was holding herself in control by a hair's breadth. It wasn't easy, what she was going to do, but she'd insisted on doing it, even though he'd told her she had a right to say no.

A pair of uniformed officers guarded the gates and there were more at the front door. The yellow crime-scene tape was still in place, a dozen cars were parked outside and men hurried purposefully in and out of the house.

For the first time in her life, Ellie did not feel as though she were coming home. All that Journey's End had meant to her – her grandmother's home, her mother's, and hers – now was nothing.

Johannsen and Mullins were waiting for them on the steps. 'This way, Miss Duveen.'

Mullins ushered her inside, as though she didn't know the way. He walked in front of her up the stairs. As she followed each tread was a death knell through her heart.

'This way, Miss Duveen.' Johannsen held back the door.

'I'm doing this for you, Gran,' Ellie told her as she walked

into that terrible room again. '*I'll help you, I'll help find who did this to you, I promise I will.*' But it was hard, it was so hard. The brownish stain on the rug was her blood, she had lain here, lost her slipper there . . . this was where Bruno died . . .

'We found the door to the safe open, Miss Parrish. Do you know of anyone else who had a key, besides your grandmother?' Johanssen was brisk, businesslike in his dark suit and white shirt.

She shook her head again, 'Miss Lottie never locked it. She said she had nothing worth stealing. And anyhow who would want to take anything from an old woman?' Her voice cracked, and she steeled herself again.

'Can you tell us exactly what is missing?'

She peered inside the safe. 'Her pearls . . . it was an eighteen-inch rope of twelve millimetre southsea pearls . . .'

Johannsen's brows rose. 'Worth a small fortune in themselves.'

'I suppose so, but Miss Lottie had had them for so long, since she was eighteen, I don't think she ever considered their value. I doubt they were insured.' She fingered the pearls at her own throat. 'I don't imagine mine are, either. They were just family pieces, treasured for their memories more than their value.'

Johannsen looked disbelieving. 'What else?'

'Her diamond engagement ring, a round solitaire, very old-fashioned. I've no idea how many carats, or what it's worth. Maybe her attorneys will know. A couple of smaller diamond rings, and a sapphire. Some antique brooches, pearl earrings, a pair of diamond drops. That's about it, but as I said, Mr Majors at Majors, Fleming and Untermann in Santa Barbara will be able to help you with the details.'

'Take a look around, Miss Duveen. Tell us if you spot anything else missing.'

Averting her eyes from the bloodstains, Ellie looked round at the familiar objects that had formed part of her grandmother's life for as long as she could remember. The pair of Egyptian malachite obelisks on the ornate gilded mantel; the French ormolu clock with the three fat cherubs she had liked so much when she was a child, giving them names: Fatsy, Patsy and

Cupid. The crystal and silver knick-knacks; the old photographs. Her gaze lingered on the night table where Miss Lottie kept her favourite picture of Ellie, taken just after she'd returned from Paris with a bunch of cooking diplomas and a world of experience behind her. Her eyes widened in surprise. 'The photograph is gone.'

Johannsen hurried forward. 'What photograph?'

'It was of me, in a silver frame. Gran always kept it by her bedside. She said when she woke in the night, I was always there, smiling at her . . .'

'Anything else, Miss Parrish?'

'No, nothing else.' Weariness settled over her like a heavy blanket. She took one last long look around the room that had meant so much to her, then turned and walked swiftly away. She knew she would never see it again.

She was silent on the drive back to Running Horse, her head back, her eyes closed. The damaged Explorer grunted as Dan gunned up the crumbling blacktop lane that led through the vineyard to the house. Without opening her eyes, she said, 'Sorry.'

He glanced sideways at her. 'Sorry for what?'

'For smacking up your car. Again.'

'That's okay, you're forgiven.' His mind was on the missing photo. There were more valuable things in the room, so why would a thief take Ellie's picture? Not just for the silver frame, he was sure of that.

In the house, there were a dozen messages on the machine; from Ellie's friends; from the Parrish family lawyers and accountants who had been in contact with the police. From Chan and Terry and Jake. From Maria's relatives in Guadalajara. And from Piatowsky.

'Remember me?' he said. 'I'm the old bastard that's coming to visit day after tomorrow. Better get that bed warmed, and the women.' He laughed. 'Just jokin' around, pal, just jokin'. Meanwhile, I hope you're helping solve that juicy murder out your way? Sounds like those guys could use a bit of help. Give me a call.'

Ellie was sitting on the sofa, looking helplessly at him. 'I have to call Maria's family. And what about the funeral? What shall I do?'

'Why don't you let me take care of it all for you?'

'Would you?' She was so pathetically grateful.

'Will you trust me with it?'

Ellie reached out, touched his face. 'You're my friend. I'd trust you with anything.'

Even though it was sunny out, she looked cold, and Dan put a match to the fire, then knelt and slipped off her shoes. Swinging her legs up onto the sofa, he wrapped a blue horse blanket round her, then called Florita to bring hot tea.

He took her fingers and kissed them, just as a car squealed to a stop outside.

'Ellie, Ellie . . .' Maya raced up the steps, flung herself across the porch and through the door. She stood in the hall, glancing wildly around, a bunch of summery flowers clutched to her black-lycra chest. 'There you are.' She ran past Dan and grabbed Ellie. 'Oh baby, baby, I love you, I'm so sorry . . .'

Their tears mingled as they held each other, sisters of the heart, sobbing their sorrow and pain away. Dan picked up the bunch of flowers and took them to the kitchen for Florita to find a vase. He would tell her they had another guest tonight, and that she should make something light and appetizing for dinner.

Then he went to the office and called Piatowsky.

41

Piatowski was pushing an ancient lawnmower around the strip
of grass that, along with a small paved patio, a couple of spindly
Japanese maples he'd planted two years ago, and Angela's
precious roses, plus the kids' playhouse he'd built himself –
an effort involving many treks to Home Depot and an ultimate
understanding of why he was a cop and not a carpenter – was
the entire garden. A low grey sky threatened rain and a chill
wind blew off the river. Swinging the mower round, he decided
he was definitely looking forward to California.

The cellphone rang and he flipped it from his pocket.
'Yeah?'

'Piatowsky, it's Dan.'

His mouth widened in that snaggle-toothed grin that made
him look like a kid, instead of a mature Manhattan detective.
Dropping the mower, he ran a hand through his thinning,
windswept blond hair. 'Just thinkin' about you, out there in
the sunshine. I'm freezin' my ass off here in N'Yawk.'

'I'm glad you're coming out here.'

He caught the serious tone in Dan's voice. 'What's up?'

'A friend of mine's in trouble. Her grandmother was killed
last night. At her mansion in Santa Barbara. I get the feeling the
police suspect her of doing it.'

'The old lady in Santa Barbara? Yeah, I heard about it.'
Piatowsky hesitated, 'How good a friend is she?'

'As good as it gets.'

He knew Dan was talking romance here. He would need
to tread carefully. Clearing his throat, he said, 'Dan. I kinda
wondered about that myself. I mean, she's the only living relative

of a rich old lady who's been murdered. It's a logical chain of thought, for a cop.'

'Not a chance,' Dan said grimly. 'I'd arranged to meet her there. I was *there* at the scene, immediately after she found them. This is one woman who really loved her grandmother, she'd been more like a mother to her. And the housekeeper was more than just that, she was family. Even the dog got it. The safe was robbed, he took her jewellery, turned the place over. Have you been into work today? No? Then you won't have heard. Okay, get this, Piatowsky. She was strangled. And he'd left a signature. The same cross as on the Times Square hooker.'

'Jesus.' Piatowsky was stunned. 'But it was a robbery with violence . . . our man wouldn't go for that. It's not his kick.'

'Exactly. So do we have a copycat?'

Piatowsky shook his head. 'Makes no sense to me. What evidence have they got?'

'Nothing yet, that I know of. Forensics are working on it. My guess is the autopsy will exonerate Ellie. It needed a lot of brute strength to do what the killer did to the old lady. The housekeeper was shot though, and the dog. The robbery looked fake to me, like a set-up, you know? To cover up something else. In fact, if you ask me, this was a planned execution. And our signature killer is someone with an obsessive compulsive disorder. It's like a ritual, carving his sign on his victims.'

'Kinda odd, that,' Piatowsky said. It definitely was not the norm to have two different methods of killing at a single crime scene. 'Unless there were two of them.'

'Two killers? You could be right . . .'

He heard Dan sigh at the other end of the line. 'I sure could use you out here, Piatowsky.'

'Moral support, huh?'

'More than that. We have to solve this crime.'

'Okay fella, don't sweat. I'll be there tomorrow. Plane gets in at 11.30, United.'

'I'll be there.'

As he rang off, Piatowsky thought regretfully about the fishing and the long lazy evenings on the front porch, sipping cold beer and enjoying all that clean, fresh country air.

Somehow, he got the feeling this visit wasn't going to be quite like that.

He pushed the mower one more length of the lawn, then the heavens opened. Sighing, he told himself that at least in California the sun would be shining.

42

Florita was bustling round, setting the long refectory table for dinner. Somehow, though she never looked hurried, she moved fast, her plump feet in red flats twinkling, her full red skirt swishing pleasantly as she placed a tall glass vase of fluffy green Queen Anne's Lace and orange marigolds, scarlet poppies and bright blue cornflowers exactly in the centre. Carlosito crawled behind her, clinging to her legs, trying to pull himself upright. She turned to smile at him.

'*Ay, niño*, you are such a big boy now. Soon you will walk.'

Scooping him up, she trotted back to the kitchen to check on her black-bean soup, the slow-roasted chicken, and the fresh green salad. Tortillas were already prepared and the aroma of garlic and rosemary wafted out the open windows on the breeze.

Ortega's silver-toed boots clattered on the saltillo-tiled floor as he swung through the back door. 'How is she?' His moustache bristled anxiously and, for once, there was no smile in his brown eyes.

'Not good.' Florita's glossy braid swung from side to side as she shook her head. 'She is dying inside, I can tell. *Pobrecita, ay, qué horror, qué tragedia*.' Tears stood in her eyes and she clutched the baby close to her.

'And *el señor?*'

'He is a man with a burden on his shoulders.'

They looked at each other, then Ortega gave a little shrug. 'He is strong, he can carry such a burden. Besides, he is a man in love, and there is a saying in American, *Triunfa todo el amor*. Love conquers all.'

'She has a friend here now, to help her.' Florita put the baby down and he crawled rapidly to his father. 'Tonight, though, she must eat. Then she has to sleep, get some rest.'

'I'll speak with the señor, see if there is anything I can do to help.' Swinging the baby onto his shoulders, Ortega did a little dance around the room, making Carlosito squeal with delight.

On her way downstairs, Ellie heard them. It was such a happy, innocent sound, a baby laughing. There was a wistful look in her eyes as she walked across the hall into the living room. A log fire sparked in the grate, even though it was warm and the windows were open, and she knew Dan must have lit it especially for her. There were flowers on the Mexican wooden coffee table and a bottle of white wine chilling in the galvanized tin bucket on the battered pine sideboard, that Dan had told her he'd picked up for next to nothing in a junk shop in Santa Barbara.

Walking to the tall sash window, she leaned on the sill, listening to the bird-calls, gazing at the long view down the hill. It was so peaceful, so normal. It meant, she thought sombrely, that regardless of personal tragedy life went on. Babies laughed, birds sang, dinners were prepared.

Sighing, she turned away, just as Maya appeared. They were both wearing jeans and clean white shirts. Ellie's hair was pulled tightly back from her unmade-up face, sharpening her cheekbones, emphasizing her sad, shadowed eyes and exposing the jagged white scar running across her forehead.

'We look like a modern-day Greek chorus,' Maya said, deliberately trying to lighten up, 'But at least that's better than the way we looked earlier. Is that wine I see in the bucket over there?'

'It certainly is.' Dan came in, followed by Ortega. 'Can I pour you a glass? It's the Cakebread chardonnay I like so much.'

'It will not be so good as ours.' Ortega carried a basket of logs over to the fireplace. 'Though is *very* good. I admit it.'

'And of course, you're not prejudiced.' Maya grinned, accepting the glass from Dan.

'No, Señorita, I am merely honest.'

They laughed as Dan handed Ellie a glass, and poured one for

Carlos and himself. 'Only to taste,' Carlos demurred, taking it.

'I want to drink a toast.' Ellie held up her wineglass, looking round at her friends. Her *good* friends. 'To Miss Lottie.'

Dan threw her a surprised glance, but she seemed calm and in control. They raised their glasses and drank to the memory of her grandmother.

'And now to Maria Novales, my friend, my family.'

Maya looked warily at her. She knew Ellie well enough to recognize that she was still stretched taut as a wire.

'And of course, to dear Bruno, who gave them both so many years of happiness and finally, even his life.'

Pancho wuffed as he came skidding through the open front door, followed by Cecil. Ignoring them, they headed for the kitchen and the tempting aroma of roast chicken.

'That dog's heart is in his stomach,' Ellie said, and Dan grinned. It was the first normal, every-day comment she'd made since it happened.

'The wine is excellent.' Maya was trying to keep it low key, even though the undercurrent threatened to drag them down again any minute.

'Very good, very good.' Ortega held his glass aloft inspecting the colour. 'This wine is a role model for chardonnay.'

'Señor, dinner is ready' Florita called from the hall.

'Think you can eat?' Maya looked hopefully at Ellie.

'I must. I have to be strong so I can help find the killers.'

She was being too calm, and her voice had a flat tone to it that Maya had never heard before.

'Are you okay?' She touched Ellie's arm lightly, looking anxiously at her.

'I just need to clear my head. I need to try to remember every single detail, so I can tell Johannsen. I must do all I can to help . . .'

Dan put a CD on the player and the Brahms *Violin Concerto* filtered soothingly into the room, filling the empty silence. Maya's eyes met Dan's uneasily.

'I forgot to ask,' Ellie said, as Florita ladled out the black-bean soup and passed the terracotta pot with the hot tortillas. 'What about Chan, and the café?'

'I spoke with them,' Maya replied. 'The café is closed until after the . . . until you feel better.'

Ellie thanked her, wishing her head didn't throb so much. Not even Advil every few hours had taken the ache away. She guessed it was part of the pain she had to bear now. She hardly tasted the good soup, but at least its warmth eased the tight knot in her stomach.

They heard the sound of a car coming up the hill, and looked apprehensively at each other. 'What now?' Maya said as Florita sped to answer the door.

They heard Johannsen's familiar brusque voice. 'Is Mr Cassidy home?'

'Si, señor, I tell him who you are?'

'It's okay, Florita.' Dan was already in the hall.

'Mr Cassidy.' Johannsen was formal, polite, cold. 'Is Miss Duveen with you?'

Dan's antennae alerted him to trouble. 'She is.'

'Then I have to ask both you and Miss Duveen to accompany me to the precinct, sir. For questioning in the murder of Mrs Parrish.'

Ellie was standing behind him. He heard her gasp, then she said, 'Detective Johannsen, I've told you everything I know. Everything I saw . . . if there were anything else I could do, don't you think I would be doing it?'

'I'm sure you would, Miss, but right now we would like to question you in a bit more detail.'

'They want to jog your memory, Ellie. And mine.' Dan's eyes met Johanssen's. He was used to being on the other side of this situation, he'd never been a murder suspect before. It was not amusing.

'We were just having dinner. Miss Duveen has not eaten since yesterday morning. I'm sure you'll agree it's important that she has some nourishment before the ordeal of questioning. After all, she has just lost her grandmother in the most terrible of circumstances.'

Johannsen's mouth tightened. He didn't care to be branded an unfeeling bully, but his job was his job, and Dan Cassidy knew it. 'Finish your dinner, Miss. We'll be waiting.'

Maya was standing next to Ellie, clutching her hand. 'What does he mean, he *wants to question you in more detail?*'

She sounded frightened and Dan reassured her quickly, 'It's just routine, there maybe details Ellie's forgotten, subliminal things hidden in her memory.' He wasn't about to scare the hell out of them by telling them Johannsen suspected them of murder.

Ellie sat at the table again. She spooned a little of the soup. She looked at Dan. 'Let's just go,' she said, despairingly.

'I'll come with you.' Maya was on her feet, ready, but Dan shook his head. 'Stay here, field any phone calls. I'll get back to you later, tell you what's going on.' He looked at Ellie. 'Do you have an attorney?'

'Miss Lottie does . . . did. Michael Majors lives in Montecito.'

He remembered, Majors had called today and left a number. He leafed through the sheaf of notes by the phone until he found it.

Majors was also just about to have dinner, but when Dan called and told him what was happening, he agreed to meet them at the police station right away.

'Okay.' Dan slung his arm round Ellie's shoulders, deliberately cheerful. 'Let's go tell 'em all we know.'

'Ellie,' Maya ran after her, hugged her, 'call me, when you know what's going on.'

'I will.' Ellie wished, bewilderedly, that she knew.

43

It was odd, Dan thought on the silent ride into Santa Barbara, to be sitting behind the protective screen in the back seat of a police Ford Crown Victoria he had driven so often himself. Only now he was the suspect instead of the law, the hunted not the hunter.

He ran through the facts in his mind. The two different methods of killing made it possible there were two killers. But there was also something about this murder that spoke of ritual. He could have sworn it had been planned and carried out meticulously. Despite the copycat 'signature', it was exactly like an execution. But he knew Johannsen was on a different tack.

They were back in the bare little grey room again, with Johannsen at one side of the table, Dan and Ellie at the other. Mullins propped up the wall, inhaling a Lucky, and coffee was brought in by a female uniformed officer.

'Two with sugar, two without,' she said, glancing curiously at them as she departed.

'You understand there's no pressure, Miss Duveen,' Johannsen was saying, 'This is just an informal discussion, between us.'

Dan's antennae pricked up again. 'Do I understand you are questioning Miss Duveen, and possibly myself, as suspects in the murder of Mrs Parrish?'

Johannsen cleared his throat. 'Not exactly . . .' He knew they didn't have a shred of evidence and the autopsy had proved definitively that Ellie could not have strangled her grandmother. It had to have been a man. Which indicated her partner, Cassidy. He was big, strong, powerful enough. Ellie could have shot the housekeeper while he took care of the old woman. And then she

would inherit the lot and they would both live happily ever after
. . . Also, Cassidy knew about the signature thing, he could have
done it just to throw them off the scent, send them looking for
a serial killer. Except this serial killer butchered hookers, not
old ladies.

Dan said, 'Then I suggest you Mirandize both Miss Duveen
and myself, and that we wait for her attorney to arrive.'

Johannsen sighed. He'd hoped to break her down a bit before
getting to this point. Now the ex-cop had beaten him at his own
game. He waved his partner forward, and Mullins proceeded to
read them their rights.

Ellie's stunned eyes met Dan's. 'I don't understand . . . ?'

'It's all right,' he said quietly. 'We'll just wait for Majors to
get here, then we'll go home.'

'But I want to tell you everything.' She swung round,
leaning across the table, her hands clasped tightly together,
looking at Johannsen. 'I want you to know everything, anything
that's hidden in my mind. *I want you to find who killed my
grandmother.*'

Johannsen shifted uneasily. She sure didn't look like a killer,
but then, who did? He said, 'That's all we're asking of you right
now, Miss Duveen.'

There was a knock on the door and the female officer
announced Michael Majors.

He stood in the doorway, taking in the cell-like questioning
room and Ellie hunched over the table, staring up at him. Majors
was an estate lawyer. He dealt in torts and wills and property.
This was out of his league, but he knew enough to get her out
of there.

He was a small man, youngish, in dark pinstripes and a pink
shirt his wife had bought him for his birthday. She'd thought it
was young and cheerful, but now it seemed inappropriate for
the occasion. Straightening his bold silk tie, Majors walked to
Ellie and patted her shoulder. 'I can't tell you how distressed
I am, how shocked. My deepest sympathy, Ellie. It is truly a
terrible loss.'

'Thank you. This is Dan Cassidy, my friend. And Detectives
Johanssen and Mullins.' She introduced them, her good manners

ingrained, even under these difficult circumstances, thanks to Miss Lottie's teaching.

Majors shook hands. 'Can I ask exactly why you're holding my client here?'

'We're not holding your client, Mr Majors, we've merely brought her in for questioning,' Johannsen replied mildly.

'Then I assume you've read her her rights?'

He nodded. 'I did.'

'Not at first,' Dan interjected. 'I had to ask the detective to Mirandize both of us.'

Johannsen shrugged, 'We'd not yet started questioning either of you.' But he was frowning. Cassidy was too much the tough cop, he knew every step of the game. With him here, he was going to get exactly nowhere. 'Besides, Miss Duveen volunteered to answer any questions we choose to ask. In the hope of jogging her memory, y'understand.'

Majors looked uneasily at him, unsure of his ground. 'Sure, sure, of course. If that's what she wishes.'

Ellie just wished they would all give up arguing and let her get on with it. 'I want to help you. I'll do anything I can.'

Short of dragging her out of there, Dan knew there was nothing he could do to stop her. Even though she had nothing to hide, he understood only too well how innocent words could be made to incriminate.

'Well, if that's settled.' Johannsen smiled happily. Round one to him. 'Take a seat Mr Majors. If you think we're out of line at any point, you just holler. Now, tell me again, in your own words, Miss Duveen, exactly the sequence of events last night.'

She was living through the hell all over again. She saw herself calling her grandmother from the car, the swirling fog in the valley near Camarillo, her surprise that there was no reply. Then calling Dan, how she knew from his voice he'd been running. How relieved she'd been when he'd relented and forgiven her for ruining their dinner at the ranch. How lonely the tyres had sounded on the gravel; the lamp gleaming from her grandmother's curtained window. The light out in the hall; the silence that had sent goosepimples up her arms; her own voice echoing eerily as she called for Maria. Herself running up the stairs, two at a time. Bruno's dead eyes staring up at her, his blood on the rug, on Miss Lottie's slipper . . .

Her grandmother, sprawled face-up in the dressing-room, her arms outflung, her tiny blue-veined feet, and her face . . . *dear god, her face* . . .

She saw herself backing out of the dressing-room. She was whimpering like a terrified animal . . . standing in the pool of Bruno's blood. The curtains billowing in from the french windows . . .

'*Someone was out there.*' Ellie grabbed Johannsen's hand across the table. '*On the balcony. I'm sure of it.*'

'Okay, so tell me, slowly, exactly what you saw.'

She concentrated, she had to get it right, had to tell him exactly what it was. 'I heard something, a movement, a noise of some kind. The window had blown open and the curtains were billowing in . . .' She closed her eyes, searching for it, that flicker of something that caught her attention. A glint of light in the darkness of the night outside on the balcony. 'It was the reflective patch on a sneaker,' she said carefully. 'You know, the kind runners wear so they're visible at night? It reflects the light back.' She nodded, triumphant. '*That's what I saw.*'

'And what did you do then?'

Johannsen's face was expressionless. She'd expected a smile, approval, thanks. 'I . . . well, I don't know.' She was floundering. 'I just remember running down the stairs, throwing open the doors . . . getting in my car I was . . . I was . . .'

'Miss Duveen was terrified, Detective.' Dan's voice was harsh. 'What else did you expect her to do?'

'Of course,' Majors nodded in agreement. 'Exactly. I think you will agree she did the right thing, fleeing from danger.'

'And where were you, Mr Cassidy, when all this was going on?' Johannsen eyed Dan's hands speculatively. He could easily strangle an old woman, break her neck . . .'

'I was on my way to Journey's End to pick up Ellie. We'd arranged to meet there.' Dan's voice had a weary edge to it, but he was alert, on guard. 'I'd just turned into the gates when I saw the jeep coming at me, fast. I swung to the right, but it hit me, bounced off the side and went into a tree. I saw Ellie get out. She ran down the road. She was sobbing, screaming, in shock. I thought it must be the accident, maybe she was hurt. I caught up to her. Obviously, she imagined I was the killer. She punched me.' He ran his hand along his sore jaw. 'When she finally realized it was me, she tried to tell me what she'd seen.'

'And what happened then?'

'We went back to the house. Ellie couldn't go in that room again. She waited at the foot of the stairs while I went up and looked around. I found the scene exactly as you saw it yourself. I checked the bathroom, the closets, the balcony. I did the same in the housekeeper's room. Then I called the police.'

'So there was no man in sneakers on the balcony?'

'No, sir. Not by the time I got there.'

'And how long would you estimate that was, Miss Duveen.'

Ellie looked blankly at him. Time had had no meaning. 'It was all a blur . . .'

'I estimate a max of ten minutes.' Dan was sharp, business-like.

'Thank you.'

Majors stood. 'I assume that will be all, Detective?'

'For the moment.' Johannsen sighed, he was being cut off in his prime, just as he was beginning to roll.

'If I were you, I'd be delighted with what Miss Duveen came up with. There was someone out there on that balcony, wearing sneakers.' Dan's tone made it clear he thought Johannsen had gotten a bonus and should get off his ass and get out there and find the proper suspect.

'But the sneaker man wasn't there when you got there, right, Mr Cassidy?'

'He'd had almost ten minutes to get away.'

'And would you by any chance own a pair of sneakers like that yourself?'

Dan grinned as he shook his head. 'Wrong tack, Johannsen,' he said smoothly. 'And no I don't.'

Johanssen stood, hands in his pockets. 'Goodnight, Miss Duveen, Sorry I interrupted your dinner. Thank you for being so co-operative.'

Ellie looked him in the eye. 'I did see that, you know,' she said.

He nodded, coolly. 'I know.'

She frowned, bewildered at his attitude. 'Come on.' Dan had her by the arm. 'Goodnight Johannsen, Mullins.'

Outside in the parking lot, Majors shifted his briefcase to his other hand while he felt in his pocket for the car keys. It was a Mercedes 500SEL. Black. 'Well, what was all that about?'

'That was about questioning your client with reference to a murder, Mr Majors,' Dan snapped. 'A murder in which Detective Johannsen was trying to implicate both her, and myself.'

Ellie's mouth dropped open. 'No, oh no he wasn't. He just wanted me to help him.'

'Sure.' Dan's face was grim.

'You mean he really suspects Ellie of . . . ? Majors' fair skin bloomed a hot red, and his pale eyes behind the gold-rimmed Armani glasses blinked rapidly with shock.

'What the hell d'you think he had us there for? A nice friendly conversation?' Dan thrust his hands in his pockets, leaning against the sleek automobile, looking unbelievingly at the lawyer.

'I'm . . . I'm sorry. I'm not a criminal lawyer, I deal with wills and property . . . This is not my forte, you see.'

'Then for Christ's sake get somebody whose forte it is, because your client is going to need him.'

'Yes, yes, of course, I'll do that right away.'

Ellie gave a weary sigh. 'I don't believe this, I just don't believe it. I thought it couldn't get any worse, and now look what's happening.'

'It's a storm in a teacup.' Dan put his arm round her. 'Tomorrow, we'll sort it all out.' He thanked god Piatowsky was arriving tomorrow, he surely could use his support.

'Er, can I offer you a lift back to . . . wherever you're going?' Majors looked humble now, as well as out of his depth.

Dan relented, he'd been hard on him. 'Sorry, Majors.' He slapped him on the shoulder, then looked round the parking lot, remembering they had come in the detectives' squad car. By rights, they should have taken them home again, but he wasn't about to argue that point. 'We'll get a cab, thanks.'

'I'll call one for you.' At least he could do something to help.

The taxi arrived in minutes and Majors waved a hurried goodbye, glad to exit the scene.

They held hands in the cab, sitting silently, unwilling to talk in front of the driver. Dan thought the journey had never seemed so long, and when they finally rolled up the hill, the front door was thrown open and Maya was standing on the front porch, the light streaming behind her, looking anxiously at them.

'Are you okay?'

Ellie dashed up the steps toward her. 'Oh Maya, they think I murdered Miss Lottie,' she said, and collapsed into her arms.

44

Buck was restless. He had that itchy feeling again, the way he used to in Hudson, when he needed to break out, do something. He needed to see Ellie. But Ellie was not around.

He was sitting in the car on the hill near her house, sipping a Starbucks double espresso and wondering restlessly where she could be, when two squad cars sped past him and turned into Ellie's street. Alert as a wary guard dog, he watched through the rear-view mirror.

A minute later a black Ford Victoria passed him and parked next to the others outside Ellie's house. A couple of plainclothes detectives got out and joined the four uniformed officers.

Buck lit up a Camel, got out of the car and strolled casually along the street. They didn't knock on the door, they simply opened it and walked in. His eyebrows climbed in surprise. *They were searching her house.*

Stamping out the cigarette, he walked quickly back to the car and drove down the hill onto Main Street.

It was a Saturday, hot, a beach day, and a passing parade of Venice youth drifted across the road heading for the ocean. Honking them impatiently out of his way, he sped toward the café. There were no parking spaces, but he didn't need to stop; the *Closed* sign was still visible on the glass door.

Where the hell was she? She wasn't at Maya's apartment because Maya wasn't there. They must be somewhere together. Maya would have gone to comfort her.

He drove aimlessly in the direction of Marina del Rey, his mind on Dan Cassidy. He needed to know who he was, where he lived. He had the sudden gut feeling Ellie was with him, and rage fermented like acid in the pit of his stomach. Spotting a liquor store, he made a quick, screeching turn into its parking lot, and bought three bottles of Jim Beam.

Back on the freeway again, heading towards Sunset Boulevard, he decided angrily that he would kill Cassidy if he got in his way.

The drapes were kept permanently closed at his apartment. He switched on a lamp and the TV, clicking until he found the local channel with the news. Prowling the perimeter of the small dark room he slugged bourbon from the bottle, wiping his mouth with the back of his hand, his eyes fixed on the TV screen.

The weatherman was telling what a glorious day it was going to be, if you discounted the air quality of course, and just felt those wonderful warm rays. *Take care*, he said, *this is a factor five burn day* . . .

Buck tilted the bottle to his mouth again. Goddamit! Why didn't they get on with the news, tell him what was happening with Miss Lottie, and Ellie. Ripping off his shirt, he tossed it on the floor. He kicked off his shoes, his pants. In seconds he was naked, the bottle clutched in his hands, pacing.

Where the fuck was she?

45

The United 737 dipped lower, and Piatowsky watched Los Angeles gradually emerge from the layer of yellow smog. He saw an endless grid of streets bisected by a curving snarl of freeways, dotted with turquoise swimming-pools and tall stringy palms. He hoped it got better than this.

Urban man though he was, through and through, born and raised in the city, it still seemed like a miracle to him that he could fly across a continent and in a matter of hours be in another world.

Cassidy was waiting at the baggage claim. For a guy living in sunshineland, he surely looked tired. His jaw glistened blue-black with stubble and his hair looked as though he'd run his hands through it once too often. Still, his eyes lit up when he saw him.

'Jesus, Piatowsky, am I glad to see you.'

'Yeah, likewise.' They embraced, slapped shoulders, grinned at each other.

Dan grabbed his bag and Piatowsky shouldered his fishing-rods in their black case. 'Guess there's not gonna be much fishin', but I brought 'em anyways.' Following Dan outside, he lifted his pale city face to the sun, breathing the fumes of a zillion automobiles. He grinned. 'Perfect, man, it's great.'

'Wait till you're out of the urban sprawl, then you'll know it's really great.'

Piatowsky followed him, marvelling at the long-legged women in shorts, striding confidently in front of him. 'Boy, do you know you're not in New York,' he said, amazed. 'And every one a blonde. It must be all that sun.'

They picked up the car in the lot and Dan quickly edged his way into the flow of traffic, heading down Century Boulevard to the 405.

Piatowsky shot him an assessing glance. He thought his friend looked like a guy with a lot on his mind. 'So, how're ya holdin' up?'

'You're not gonna believe this, but the local cops think maybe I did the job, along with Ellie.'

'Jesus!' He sat back for a minute, thinking about that. 'What are they basing this theory on?'

'A motive. *The* motive. Greed. We kill the old lady, Ellie inherits. We live happily ever after, in luxury.'

'Why you?'

'I've been cast as the boyfriend, an ex-cop who knows how it's done.' Dan shrugged, swinging the Explorer into the right lane and onto the freeway. 'I had the strength to strangle the old lady, while Ellie shot the housekeeper. And the dog. I had the know-how to copycat the signature to throw them off the scent.'

'They found the weapon yet?'

Dan shook his head. 'If they have, they're sure not telling me.'

'Right, right, of course they wouldn't.' Piatowsky frowned. 'But it doesn't smell right, y'know. It's too easy, too obvious. I mean how would you be dumb enough to do the deed and then find the body? You'd have had an alibi a hundred miles from here, and so would she.'

'It's an execution, Pete, I feel it in my bones.' They had both seen enough execution-type slayings in the boroughs to know the pattern. 'Maria was shot coming out of the bathrom. He must have been waiting for her. Miss Lottie was strangled, even though he had the gun and could have shot her too. I mean, why would he do that? Strangle her?'

'Kind of a vengeance thing?'

Their eyes met, then Dan shifted into the fast lane and put his foot on the gas. 'That's what I thought. But Ellie doesn't know of anyone with a grudge against her grandmother. Though there was one incident she told me about, years ago. Seems like some guy broke into the house and attacked her. Ellie was just a kid, but she was in the room and saw it all. Her screams brought the servants running, and the security guards.'

'So what happened to the guy? He do time, or what?'

'Ellie didn't know. The grandmother never told her and she said she had to forget about it, and never mention it to anyone. Up until she told me, I don't believe she'd ever talked about it. It all took place more than twenty years ago, so I'm not sure how relevant it might be.'

'Old grudges never die, they just get more bitter.'

Dan shrugged. 'I checked the security service she used then. It's no longer in business. There's no one left who knows anything about it, except Ellie. But I *saw* the crime scene. I *know* what it felt like. Y'know how you get the feeling?'

Piatowsky knew exactly that feeling; it was part instinct, part experience, part guess. Whatever, it raised the hackles and sent the mind questing further than the obvious, and that's what made a good detective.

'What about prints?'

'I guess Ellie's were all over the place, after all she was there every week. I was careful not to touch anything. Anyhow, this is the *pièce de resistance*. The cops dragged us back in for questioning last night, right at dinner time.'

Pitowsky snorted; he knew that routine. Unsettle the suspects, get 'em while they're hungry and anxious.

'Ellie wanted to help. She remembered something that had been stuck in the blur of images when she found the body. The french windows had blown open. The gauze curtains were billowing in and she thought she saw something . . . the reflective flash on a pair of sneakers.'

'*He was out there?*'

Dan nodded. 'She thinks so.'

'Then why didn't he kill her too?'

'That's the other thing. The grandmother kept Ellie's photo in a silver frame on her night table. It was missing.'

Piatowsky took a deep breath. 'Daniel, my boy, there's more to this than meets the eye. A hell of a lot more.'

'Try telling that to detective Jim Johannsen.'

Piatowsky looked shrewdly at him. 'You in love with her?'

'I didn't want to be, I've no money, no prospects, at least for a hell of a long time.'

'And what did timing ever have to do with true love?'

Dan grinned at him. 'I guess Romeo must have asked Juliet that same question?'

'Yeah, and look what happened to them. You're gonna have to do better than that, Cassidy. And if Ellie is your woman, she's gotta be pretty darn special.'

'She is,' Dan agreed, quietly. 'Believe me, she is.'

46

'It looks just like the photos.' Piatowsky stood at the top of the hill, looking back at the immaculate rows of vines, and the black-and-white cattle clustered under the shady oaks on the hill opposite. He swung round, taking in the house while Dan hauled the bags from the back of the car. 'I thought you said it was falling down?'

'It was. Where d'you think my money's gone?'

He laughed, cocking his head to one side, listening to the birdsong and the soft sigh of the wind. He said, baffled, 'Isn't it kinda quiet round here?'

'You'll get used to it. Life is better without traffic, Piatowsky, believe me.'

He nodded, he was willing to be proven wrong, but it would take a lot. He spotted two figures cresting the hill in the distance. A couple of dogs were chasing after them and, faintly, he heard their excited barks.

'Here's Ellie and Maya. And this is Pancho.' The mutt flew toward Dan, covering the ground like a racehorse, yipping madly, with Cecil bringing up the rear. They bounced up at him, then turned their lavish-tongued attentions to Piatowsky.

'Terrific, great.' He patted them cautiously. 'What kinda guard dogs are these?'

'They're country dogs, Piatowsky. They just come with the territory.'

'Yeah, well forgive me but I'm not familiar with the breed. Though they sure aren't any prettier than city mutts.' He glanced up as Ellie and Maya approached. 'But the women are,' he murmured under his breath. 'Jeez, Cassidy, you attract 'em in pairs now?'

Ellie looked tall, slender, elegant in a pale waif-like sort of way, with no make-up and her hair pulled tightly back in a knot at the nape of her neck. She was wearing white shorts and an Ellie's Place t-shirt. Maya, also unmade-up, looked fresh-faced as a schoolgirl, except for that body, encased in a brief yellow lycra tank-top and shorts. Ellie made straight for Dan.

Like a homing pigeon, Piatowsky thought, watching as he put his arm round her shoulders, inspecting her anxiously.

'Ellie, this is Pete Piatowsky, my old buddy from New York. Maya Morris, Pete.' As they shook hands, Piatowsky knew why Cassidy was in love with her. There was sorrow in her beautiful eyes, but there was also strength. This woman was wounded, but not broken.

'Are you going to help Dan find out who did it?' Maya was nothing if not direct. Her big, whisky-brown eyes fastened on his, demanding an immediate answer.

'I'll try, Miss Morris, though this is really for the Santa Barbara police department to deal with.'

Ellie stared at him. This was Dan's friend, he'd worked with him for years, trusted him. He'd said if anybody could help, Piatowsky could; nothing escaped him, he knew his job backwards. 'I'm glad you came,' she said quietly. 'And I'm sorry if all this is interrupting your vacation.'

'Don't worry, I'm the kinda guy who can never take a real vacation. I need to keep on my toes. If I miss a trick or two, there'll be some criminal out there ready to outsmart me.'

Maya laughed, linking her arm in his. 'Call me Maya, Mr Piatowsky.'

'Pete,' he said, dazzled, walking with her into the house.

Florita was waiting in the hall with the baby perched on her hip. 'Señor Piatowsky, welcome,' she said, grabbing the fishing-rods in her free hand. 'You like some hot coffee? Iced tea, maybe?'

Accompanied by three attentive women, Piatowsky wafted into the sitting room and sank onto the sofa. He figured life didn't get much better than this.

Dan saw there were three messages on the machine. The first

was from Johannsen saying that a warrant had been issued in Santa Monica, to search Ellie's house.

He closed his eyes, stunned. They were really serious.

The second was from an attorney, Marcus Winkler, who said Michael Majors had asked him to get in touch with reference to Ellie Parrish Duveen. He left a Santa Barbara number.

The third was just a long silence, then a cut-off. Wondering who it had been, Dan dialled Winkler's number. He told him quickly what was going down, and about the search warrant, then arranged to meet at three that afternoon at his offices on Anapamu Street. He went to tell the others the bad news.

'They're searching my home?' Ellie felt that clutch of fear at her heart again. 'But why? I mean, they can't be serious about this. How could anybody think, think that . . .'

Maya plopped onto the sofa, next to her, took her hand. 'It'll be all right,' she said, sounding as though she didn't quite believe it would.

Piatowsky rearranged the thinning blond hair over his scalp, glancing at Dan. 'It's just a logical move on their part,' he reassured them. 'A cop has to check out every angle, Ellie. You are just one of several lines they must be pursuing.' He hoped he was right, but there was no point in scaring the hell out of the poor woman, she'd already been through enough without this.

Dan told them about Winkler, and they agreed they would all go into Santa Barbara for the meeting.

'For moral support,' Maya said, hugging Ellie.

Ellie wondered how it had all come down to this. Instead of trying to cope with her grief and shock, she was being forced to think about her own survival. Her anxious eyes met Dan's and he smiled reassuringly at her.

'Winkler's going to sort it all out, don't worry,' he said, hoping he was right.

47

Buck punched Dan's number out again, clamping the phone to his ear, listening to it ring. It was the goddamn answering machine again. He slammed the receiver down. Wherever Cassidy was, though, he knew Ellie must be with him. He took a slug from the second bottle of bourbon, feeling it fizz through his veins like rocket fuel. He was tanked up again, powered, ready for action. But there was no action.

He stared at the TV screen, waiting for the next news bulletin. He needed to know what was going on. If the cops were searching Ellie's house, they must think she did it. He bellowed with laughter at the thought. How ironic, the doting granddaughter as the murderer.

There it was, at last.

'*The Santa Barbara police are still searching for the killer of Charlotte Parrish, society doyen, who was found murdered at her Montecito mansion two nights ago. We understand that her granddaughter, who found the body, was taken in for questioning, but was not detained.*'

Buck set the bottle down on the table, suddenly sober. *His Ellie. They were questioning her . . . they might put her in prison, then he would never have her . . .*

He strode into the bathroom, turned the shower onto cold and stood under it for a long time, until his head felt crystal clear. He dried off, dressed quickly in a blue Ralph Lauren polo shirt, chinos and sneakers.

He put the Glock automatic in the brown paper bag from the liquor store, then took the elevator down to the basement garage. Stashing the bag with the gun on the back seat of the BMW, he drove out of there and along Sunset heading west toward the freeway. *He had to find her. He had to see Ellie.*

48

Winkler was tall and thin, with a shock of black curls and intelligent brown eyes that assessed them in seconds as they filed into his office.

Dan made the introductions. There was no need to explain the circumstances, but he did fill him in on the details.

Winkler turned and looked Ellie in the eye. 'And did you kill your grandmother, Ellie?'

Her bottom lip caught in her teeth, she stared dumbly at him, too shocked to reply.

'Of course she didn't.' Maya was on her feet, fierce as a mother cat protecting her kitten. 'How dare you ask her such a question? Can't you tell, just by looking at her, that she's not capable of such a thing?' She stamped round the office, arms folded, chin sticking out, ready to do battle if necessary.

'You'll appreciate that, as a defending attorney, it's a question I have to ask my client.' Winkler was smooth, understanding. 'And yes, I believe I can tell that Ellie is innocent, but it's also my job to prove that to other people.'

'To the cops,' Maya said flatly.

He nodded. 'At the moment they don't have much to go on, except supplying a motive. As we haven't yet received the results of the autopsy, I don't know precisely how both women were killed. I called the coroner's office, and they expect to have that information later today.'

Ellie turned cold inside, thinking of Miss Lottie and Maria on marble mortuary slabs. She wished to god it were all over and she could bury them decently and return their dignity to them.

'Meanwhile, they will not be questioning you again unless I

am present. And, unless something incriminating turns up in forensics, or the autopsy, or they prove you owned the gun, they don't have a leg to stand on.'

'How long before I can have Miss Lottie back?' She was thinking of the funeral.

'Probably early next week. I think you could safely make funeral arrangements for, let's say, Thursday. Barring anything unforseeen, of course.' His shrewd eyes met hers again, then he smiled. 'And I don't anticipate that, Ellie.'

They said goodbye, and filed out of the office.

'He's a good guy.' Dan liked a man who knew his job.

'Smart, on the ball, tough,' Piatowsky agreed. 'Just what you need.'

'Feeling better?' Dan squeezed Ellie's hand, and saw her smile. It gave him a buzz, even if it was a pale shadow of her normal ear-to-ear sparkling grin.

Ellie turned to Maya. 'You should go home, get on with your life. What about Greg? He must be missing you?' She didn't want to be a burden.

'Bull. You think I'm quitting now? Greg can wait. I'm going to help with the funeral arrangements, make sure it's all wonderful, the way it should be, for Miss Lottie.' Maya was fiercely loyal to her friends.

The peace of the countryside wrapped itself soothingly around them as they drove up the road leading to the ranch. Leafy vines stretched into infinity on either side, horses grazed in lush meadows and a pair of hawks hung motionless in the clear blue sky.

'What's really disturbing is the missing photo.' Dan broke through the peace barrier, bringing them coldly back to reality. 'It just doesn't fit with the rest of the robbery with violence scenario. Nor with a murder by a killer who left a signature. I keep asking myself exactly why the killer would take it? And I come up with only one answer. It has to be someone who knows Ellie.'

Her mind went blank. 'You mean I *know* the killer?'

Warning bells were ringing loud and clear in Dan's head. 'It's like we have four different things going in this crime scene. A robbery, two different-style murders, and a thief who steal a woman's picture.' He took the bend in the narrow lane, then swerved quickly to the side to avoid the black BMW convertible driving too fast the other way.

'Fucking idiot.' He glanced apologetically over his shoulder at the two women. 'Excuse me.'

'That's okay. I often use that expression about other drivers myself.' Maya stared out the back window but the car was already gone. 'Obviously, the idiot didn't appreciate the beauty of the countryside the way we do.' Looking up the hill to the house, she thought how good a place it felt. She was glad Ellie had Dan, and the ranch to hide out in until she could face the world again.

Further down the road, Buck squealed to a stop, threw the car into reverse, backed into the narrow entry to a gated field, and spun back the way he'd come.

The Ford was winding through the vineyard toward the little house on top of the hill. He slowed down to watch, but they were too far away and he couldn't see Ellie. Frustrated, he slammed his foot down and took off again, swerving round the bends in the road, not caring who might be coming. The voice in his head was talking at him again, nagging him, urging him on. *You're omnipotent. You can do anything, have any woman . . . You have the power of life or death . . . Only you . . .*

Tyres squealing, he swung the car round again, heading back to LA.

49

The scent of Florita's cooking drifted from the kitchen and Ellie sniffed apreciatively, thinking about her café and how remote it seemed, as though she hadn't seen it in months. She sank onto the old porch swing, worrying about Chan and Terry, Jake and the kid.

'They're okay,' Maya said, catching her train of thought, just the way she always did. 'I called Chan, they understand. I said you'd take care of them when you got back.'

Ellie nodded her thanks. She heard the phone ringing and Dan disappeared inside to answer it.

He returned a few minutes later with a bottle of Stirling Vineyards cabernet, and Florita carrying a tin tray painted with pink roses, with glasses and a plate of homemade salsa, a bowl of still-warm, freshly-made corn chips, and a slab of Manchego cheese.

Piatowsky perked up. Somewhere along the way, food seemed to have been forgotten and he was still working on New York time. Leaning against the porch rail, he took the glass of red wine Dan offered, sipped it and looked surprised. He was no connoisseur, but it tasted great to him. 'Okay,' he said, giving them the benefit of his little-boy grin, 'There's a hint of blackcurrant and pepper. Round and flavourful.'

Dan laughed, 'You got it right, even fooling around. By the way, that was Winkler on the phone with the results of the autopsy.' He felt Ellie's eyes on him. He didn't want to have to say it, but she had to know the details. He gave the good news first. 'There was no rape, but Maria was killed with three shots to the chest and stomach from a range of eight or ten feet.

Miss Lottie was strangled, manually, with great force. Her neck was broken.' He saw the pain in Ellie's eyes. 'She probably died very quickly, if it's any comfort.'

She nodded, unable to speak.

'Ballistics identify the ammo?' Piatowsky took a slug of the cabernet. Things were certainly hotting up around here.

Dan nodded. 'Winkler told me they were fired from a Glock 27 automatic pistol.'

Piatowsky took a corn chip and dipped it in the fresh tomato salsa, wincing as he bit into a piece of fiery green chilli. 'So, what's next?'

Dan lifted his shoulders, looking blank. 'Beats me. Winkler says they have no evidence. We don't have the DNA results yet, but right now there's nothing to go on except supposition. And both you and I know you need more than guesswork to hang a case on.'

'Does that mean we can get on with our lives now?' Ellie had never realized the blessedness of the routine of day-to-day living, until it had disappeared.

'We sure can.'

It was as though a weight was suddenly lifted from her shoulders. She took a sip of the wine. 'This is too good to be yours, Cassidy,' she said with a flash of her old grin.

'Try me next year, kid. It'll be burgeoning.'

Looking at the two of them smiling at each other, Piatowsky thought maybe this vacation wouldn't be too bad after all.

50

Johannsen and Mullins were sitting in the black unmarked Ford Victoria, parked in the driveway at Journey's End. Giant grey clouds were sweeping across the mountains and huge raindrops splattered suddenly across the windscreen, blurring their view of the officers with German Shepherd tracker dogs, who were combing every inch of the grounds, searching for the Glock, or the knife, or for tracks, or any other clue the killer might have left.

Lightning illuminated the drenched gardens and thunder exploded overhead as though the god Thor himself were striking monsters in the skies with his giant hammer. Johannsen thought gloomily that the rain would take care of any scent the dogs might have found, plus erasing any tracks. So far, the guys had come up with zero. He could see them now, running for safety out of the trees. Shit. This case should have been cut and dried. How come he was getting nowhere?

The phone beeped. He picked it up before the second ring. 'Johannsen.'

'Good morning, sir. This is Detective Pete Piatowsky, NYPD.'

'What can I do for you, Detective?'

On the other end of the line, Piatowsky thought he sounded weary. He grinned, he knew that feeling only too well. 'I know my department has been in touch, sir, about the prostitute murdered near Times Square. The killing was very similar to the one you have here, in Montecito. Manual strangulation with mutilation.'

'A very particular mutilation.' Johannsen had spoken not only to the NY police department, but also with LA and the FBI. Everybody was getting in on his act. He thought wearily they were all beating up the wrong path; he believed he had the killers and the motive.

'I'm in Santa Barbara now, Detective, I'd like to get together with you, discuss the similarities in the cases.'

Johannsen had already discussed, endlessly. He sighed as he said, 'I can be back in my office at noon.'

'I'll see you then, sir.'

Piatowsky grinned at Dan as he dialled the New York precinct number. 'Yeah, George, it's Piatowsky here. I'm on my way to see the detective in charge of the Montecito signature killing, see if it ties in with ours and the LA hooker. Yep, I'll let you know what develops. And no, I don't think the detective believes it's the same guy, but I'm sure as hell gonna find out.' He listened, grinning. 'Yeah, you could call it a busman's holiday . . . but life's like that. I'm always where the action is. Yeah, I'll give Cassidy your best.' He looked out the window at the clouds pressing on the hilltops. 'Guess what? It's fuckin' raining'.

Dan could hear the guffaw of laughter on the other end of the line as Piatowsky put down the phone and said plaintively, 'I thought it never rained in Southern California?'

'You've been listening to too much Beach Boys. We're meeting Johannsen then?'

'*I'm* meeting Johannsen. *You* are a civilian, Cassidy. And also a suspect. The phone rang and he picked it up. 'Yeah,' he said, sounding surprised.

Dan waited for him to say who it was, but Piatowsky was pacing the floor, the phone tucked under his chin.

'Yeah,' he said again. And, 'No kidding. Okay, will do.'

He put down the phone again and looked at Dan.

'So?' Dan threw his arms out in a question.

'There's been another woman killed. In LA again. A hooker. Manual strangulation with mutilation. She was dumped in a canal in Venice Beach.'

'Well, I guess that lets Ellie and me off the hook. This time we do have an alibi.'

'Sure.' Piatowsky nodded but he wasn't convinced. 'Unless it's not the same killer.'

'Another copycat?' It wasn't unusual, Dan knew, when a particularly gruesome murder hit the headlines.

Piatowsky shrugged on the old black leather bomber-jacket he hadn't seriously expected to have to wear in sunshineland. 'Let's go, fella. I've got an appointment with your destiny.'

Johannsen was sitting legs apart, leaning across his desk with his horn-rims perched on the end of his wide nose, studying the information on the new killing, when Piatowsky was announced.

He glanced up, assessing his visitor, the way he knew Piatowsky was also assessing him. Johannsen guessed he had him pegged for a small-town cop – Santa Barbara's population was ninety thousand – and had cast himself in the role of the all-wise-all-knowing New York big-time detective. Well he was wrong. He'd been there, done that.

The casters on the old grey fabric swivel chair squealed as he pushed it back, stood and shook hands. 'Detective Piatowsky.' He waved to a chair opposite the desk. 'Have a seat. Coffee?'

The uniformed officer waited by the door for an answer.

'Thanks, but no.' Piatowsky had been through enough caffeine to jump-start a cadaver already that morning. He worked better that way, and besides Florita's coffee was a hell of a lot better than police brew. Antagonism filtered across the desk toward him and he smiled cheerfully. He couldn't blame Johannsen, it was never good having other cops muscle in on your investigation.

'I heard there's been another murder?' He shook a Lucky from the crumpled pack and lit up. It was the first cigarette he'd had since arriving at Running Horse and he was a pack-and-a-half-a-day guy. There was just something about the atmosphere in a precinct house, the electric-sharp vibes of murder and mayhem that triggered his nicotine need. Coughing, he wafted away the smoke as the detective pushed a metal ashtray across the table.

Johannsen read from the sheet of paper in front of him.

'A hooker, caucasian, blonde hair, five two, by the name of Rita Lampert. She worked the clubs, the dives off Hollywood Boulevard, was well-known to the police. The body was found in Venice Beach, in a canal at five-thirty this morning by a jogger. She'd been clubbed around the head, then strangled, and her face disfigured.'

'The same as Charlotte Parrish?'

He nodded. 'But not the same as Maria Novales.' Piatowsky raised his brows in a question and Johannsen added, 'Novales was the housekeeper. She was shot and she was not mutilated.'

'You have a theory about that?'

Johannsen nodded again. 'I think the mutilation of Mrs Parrish was a deliberate attempt by the perpetrator to throw us off the scent. He wanted us to believe it was the signature killer.' He shrugged his bulky shoulders, 'And no, I don't believe it's the same man.'

'You still working on the theory that Ellie Parrish Duveen had something to do with it?'

'I am. Probably with the help of an accomplice. Though I admit, we don't have any hard evidence as yet. A search of Miss Duveen's home revealed nothing. Forensics say that black fibres found at the crime scene were wool, possibly from a sweater, or a ski-mask. They're pursuing it further. The weapon used was a Glock 27 Automatic pistol.' He hesitated. There was one other piece of evidence that he was reluctant to talk about yet because it might prove his case. Or it might just shoot his theory all to hell. He decided against telling the NY cop about it. He shrugged, spreading his hands, palms up. 'That's about it.'

'Thanks for your co-operation.' Piatowsky stood and they shook hands.

'Why not leave me your number,' Johannsen said, smiling now, 'so I can be in touch, keep you informed. Are you staying in Santa Barbara?' He was about to recommened a nice little motel he knew, keep the co-operation and friendship thing going.

'Didn't I tell you?' Piatowsky ran a hand through the blond hairs that barely covered his scalp. 'I'm at Running Horse Ranch with Dan Cassidy. He's an old buddy of mine.

We were partners for five years, out there on the streets together.'

He gave him his best little-boy smile, but Johannsen's smile had slipped from his face as though it had never been.

51

Ellie was on the phone, attempting to pick up the pieces of her life and reconstruct it in a different framework. Michael Majors was telling her that, apart from a generous bequest to Maria that was no longer relevant, she was the sole heir to the estate.

'I can't advise you strongly enough to put the house on the market right away. Of course, keep what furniture and objects you want, but remember, the antiques will fetch a good price. And even though the house is unwieldy, and especially now that it's . . .' he'd been going to say 'tainted', '. . . especially now that it's *difficult*, the land is valuable and it should sell without too much trouble. As you know, there's not much left in Montecito, especially in a prime location like this.'

'I can't sell it. Not yet.' It was too soon to let go of her past and the memories.

'I understand, but give it some thought, Ellie. And when you decide, I'll take care of it for you.'

Ellie put down the phone thinking that everyone was taking care of something for her. She had to get a grip, 'Pull up her socks,' as Gran would have said. She'd always been a take-charge sort of person, now she had to take charge of her own life again.

Dan had already arranged everything with the funeral home and arranged for them to ship Maria's remains to her family in Guadalajara, after the medical examiner released the body.

Miss Lottie's funeral was set; all they needed was a definite date. There was nothing more to be done. Except wait and see if they were going to arrest her for the murder of her grandmother. The idea was so ridiculous, she wanted to laugh. Except it wasn't amusing, it was tragic.

Carrying her bag down the stairs, Maya saw Ellie standing by the phone in the hall, staring at it as though it were a strange, unknown object. She wondered, uneasily, whether it was safe to leave her yet, but she had a meeting with a producer interested in her new idea.

'What happened?' She crossed the hall in a couple of strides and dumped her bag on the floor. 'You okay?'

'It was just Gran's attorney telling me I've inherited Journey's End and asking if I'd put it on the market right away.'

'You can't do that yet.' Maya didn't need to be told.

The telephone rang again and Ellie picked it up. 'Running Horse Ranch.' There was silence on the line and she said again, 'Hello, Running Horse?' There was still no reply, yet she knew someone was there. Her eyes met Maya's as she slammed down the phone.

'Who was that?'

Ellie shivered. 'I don't know?' It rang again and this time Maya grabbed it. 'Who the hell is this?' she snapped. Her face turned pink. 'Oh, excuse me, I thought it was someone else. Yes, she's here. Hold on please.' She handed the phone to Ellie.

Ellie's heart sank as she recognized Johannsen's voice. 'Yes, Mr Johannsen. Thank you, yes. And thank you for letting me know.'

She was silent, listening to the detective and Maya wiggled her eyebrows questioningly at her.

'My shoe size? Yes, it's ten. Quite large for a woman, I agree, it's always been the bane of my life.' She listened again. 'Reebok Walkers DMX? Yes, I have those. White with a blue line. No, no reflective bands.'

She was listening again and Maya screwed up her eyes impatiently. Why did he want to know about her Reeboks?

'Thanks, Mr Johannsen. I'll have him call you when he gets in.' She put down the phone.

Maya was dancing with impatience. 'What was all that about?'

'The coroner has released Miss Lottie and Maria. The funeral can go ahead for Thursday.'

There was a quiet resignation in her voice and impulsively

Maya hugged her. 'I'm sorry, baby, but it'll be better after it's over. Then Miss Lottie and Maria will be at peace.'

Ellie knew she was right and she wished she could feel happy about it, or relieved, or pained. Anything. Because she still didn't feel a thing. She might as well be dead too.

'What was that about the Reeboks?'

She jolted back to reality. 'They found a print on the balcony . . . mud and blood . . . they say it was made by a Reebok Walker and they wanted to know my size.'

'You mean he thought you were standing out there on the balcony in your Reeboks after killing your grandmother? *Hah*!' Maya expressed her contempt for the police department in one short word.

'Someone was out there,' Ellie said quietly. 'I saw his foot. It was a black shoe with reflective panels that glowed when the lamp caught them.'

'Do they know what size?'

She shrugged, 'If they do, they're not telling me.'

'It's all nonsense, 'Maya slung her black leather overnight bag over her shoulder. 'I'm on my way, Ell. I'll be back tomorrow to help with the arrangements.'

'Whatever would I do without you?' Ellie was clinging on to her. It was pitiful, Maya thought, that a strong woman had been reduced to this by someone's crazy barbaric act.

'You're doing great, Ell, just great. After the funeral, you're going to feel much better. And then they'll find the killer, and the score will be settled. You wait, I promise you, that's what will happen.'

Ellie walked out onto the porch to wave goodbye. She told herself of course that was what would happen. The police would find the killer and lock him up. Her life would go on and become 'normal' again. After the funeral.

52

It was evening, and the new storm disappeared as quickly as it had come. The hot sun sparkled on the grass and the hillside steamed like a mini-volcano about to erupt. Ellie was sitting with Piatowsky on the bank of the reedy pond in back of the house, holding a fishing line, listening to the noisy flock of starlings perched in the willow tree that swept yellow-green fronds into the dark, still water.

'You sure there's fish in here?' Piatowsky reeled in his line and inspected the bait. It had not been touched.

'There's supposed to be carp.'

'Anybody ever seen one?' He glanced suspiciously at her and she laughed. It lit up her whole face and he suddenly saw her beauty. It wasn't just regular features and a smooth complexion, though hers were regular enough and her freckles only added another dimension, it was something that came from inside her. It showed in her eyes, her smile, the soft mellowness of her voice. Ellie lit up like a hundred megawatt lamp when she smiled.

'Not me,' she replied. 'But Dan swears it.'

'Huh!' His snort was derisive. 'By the way, you should do that more often.' She looked expectantly at him. 'Smile, I mean.'

Ellie reached out and put her hand over his. 'I really have ruined your vacation, haven't I?'

He stood and cast the line into the pond again, than sank back down beside her on the warm grassy bank. 'Not much could spoil this place. I think my old partner got himself a little bit of paradise right here, in California.'

'Sometimes I think that too.' Clasping her arms round her knees, she rested her chin on them, gazing wistfully at the line bobbing on the water. 'But then I remember, I'm a city girl now and I've got a business to run, employees ... customers ... I have to get back there, after the funeral,' she added.

Miss Lottie and Maria were to be buried on the same day, though in different countries. Ellie had had Majors send a cheque to Maria's family that would more than pay for a magnificent High Mass and a stone angel to guard her for ever. Later, when the estate was probated, she would send the amount Miss Lottie had left Maria or Maria's heirs, to be distributed amongst her brothers and sisters.

She pointed to the water. 'Your line's pulling ...'

Leaping to his feet, Piatowsky reeled it in. He stared disgustedly at it, he'd snagged an old boot. 'So much for Huck Finn,' he said glumly.

'Good thing it's not a size twelve Reebok Walker.' Dan plumped down beside Ellie and gave her a quick kiss on the cheek.

'What d'ya mean?' Piatowsky was all ears.

'Johannsen kept quiet about it until he knew the size. Our man on the balcony wore size twelves. That lets out Ellie and me. And it also proves someone was out there.'

'So Johannsen's gonna have to come up with a new suspect?' Piatowsky grinned happily. 'I told him he was on the wrong tack, but ya know – cops?' He lifted his shoulders in a 'who can tell, they're all crazy anyway' gesture.

'Feel better?' Dan could see from the expression in Ellie's eyes that at least he'd been able to remove one burden from her shoulders.

For a minute Ellie allowed herself to wonder what she would do without him, then she steeled herself again. '*I'm pulling up my socks, Gran,*' she said mentally, '*I can handle this, I can cope.*' *She had to go on, she had to make her business a success so Miss Lottie would be proud of her, and then she could be proud of herself. Work was all that counted now.*

She squeezed Dan's hand. He was a true friend. 'A lot better,' she agreed.

He liked what he heard in her voice, it was as though she'd gotten her spirit back. And he was relieved that, at least for now, Johannsen was off her back. But he knew it wasn't finished yet.

53

It was the kind of day California gloried in; clear blue, warm. A breeze rippled the silken surface of the ocean and, where the sun lay on it, turned it into a sheet of gold lamé. The mountains encircling Santa Barbara were draped in the softest green velvet, and across the channel the islands gleamed like pink stone. From where Santa Barbara's cemetery was, on a verdant bluff overlooking the ocean, the oil platforms ranged along the horizon might have been warships, a Spanish armada about to conquer California once again. It was definitely a day Miss Lottie would have approved of for her funeral.

'*No miserable rain and tears*,' Ellie could hear her saying. '*Let's have all the good rousing hymns, and champagne for everybody afterwards.*'

In the black limousine, slowly following the hearse through Santa Barbara's tree-lined streets, Ellie's thoughts returned to the only other funeral she had attended. She clearly remembered sitting next to Miss Lottie in a big black car, like this one, following her parents' coffins on their final journey.

Recalling how Miss Lottie had dressed her up in white organdie and shiny black patent mary-janes, as though she were going to a party, today she had chosen to wear a sleeveless white linen sheath that her grandmother had always liked to see her in. She'd borrowed a wide-brimmed black straw hat of Maya's and tucked a big, fresh, blowsy white rose into the band; and she wore black suede heels, and carried a small matching purse. As usual she had on a minimum of make-up, a brush of powder and a touch of lipstick, with big dark glasses that hid the sadness in her eyes. She guessed they made her look very LA, but she didn't care. This afternoon she would share her sorrow with Miss Lottie's friends and acquaintances, but the hurt was still inside her. She would deal with her grief, and her guilt, alone.

She felt Dan's warm hand on hers and glanced up at him.

'You okay?'

She nodded, glad he was there for her, thankful she had met him that day. Somehow, he seemed as close a friend as Maya.

Sitting opposite in the limo, Maya smiled encouragingly. She was wearing black silk, sleeveless and soft that swung round her body like gossamer, with a black lace mantilla over her blonde hair. Next to her, Piatowsky was neat in a dark jacket and tie borrowed from Dan. And Dan looked handsome and different in a blue suit.

Dan knew Johannsen would be there, and that the ceremony would be videotaped, discreetly, by the police photographer. It was not unknown for a killer to attend the funeral of his victim. It was a kind of ghoulish triumph, he supposed. Meanwhile, he would keep his own eyes open, checking on who was there, and so would Piatowsky.

'There's a kind of scent about a killer,' Piatowsky had said that morning, 'something about him just gets to that old olfactory nerve and tells you, watch out, something's wrong about this guy. If he's there, we'll know it.'

Flanked by a motor-cycle escort to hold back the traffic, the two funeral cars drove slowly down State Street, followed by a hundred others. Ellie thought how Miss Lottie would have enjoyed all the fuss as the procession turned alongside the sparkling ocean, then around the fountain and up the driveway to the chapel.

She was almost relieved when her grandmother's coffin, covered in a blanket of scented white roses, was received by Reverend Allan, who had known her grandmother for forty years. Finally, Miss Lottie was among friends.

It seemed the whole town had turned out. Many of the people were as old as Miss Lottie, and their white hair and stooped shoulders brought a pang of tenderness. Ellie could remember when they'd attended her grandmother's parties; and visited on Christmas morning when there was always open house at

Journey's End; at garden parties in summer; playing tennis; swimming; laughing and youthful. '*We've all had a good stay up at bat,*' she could imagine Miss Lottie saying. '*No regrets. It's time to move along and make room for the younger ones.*'

Everyone was there; the mayor, the council members, the Sheriff, the socialites and the celebrities who inhabited Montecito and had known their neighbour for decades. The Manager of the Biltmore, some of the waitstaff, local storekeepers and the owner of the garage who had serviced Miss Lottie's Cadillac ever since she'd bought it in 1972.

Chan and Jake were there, and even the kid had come along to show support. She saw Michael Majors and his wife; and Harrison Thackray, the accountant, the bank manager. *And Detective Johannsen.*

In his dark suit and sober tie, Johannsen was eyeing the mourners as they arrived. There were no shady-looking characters lurking around today, though. Everyone was respectable, and respectful. Still, he knew as well as any cop that most often a killer looked just like anybody else. Besides, in his view, he was looking at the killers right now.

Johannsen couldn't get the memory of the computer message out of his mind. DUVEEEEEE . . . The old lady had been trying to tell them something. Who else could it mean, but Ellie?

Buck's gaze fastened on Ellie, graceful in white, her glossy red hair in a chignon under a big black hat. He knew it was risky to attend the funeral, but felt compelled to do it. He was wary though. He prided himself he could spot a cop at fifty paces. A jailer was a jailer, whether it was in Hudson or in Folsom. He had the men in dark suits, standing arms folded at the back, pegged for detectives the minute he'd slipped into the crowd, mingling with other mourners. He was impeccably turned out, his tie was correctly muted and his polished Gucci loafers gleamed. He looked exactly like they did: the rich lawyers and bankers and businessmen. He was one of them.

It burned his gut when he saw Dan Cassidy standing with Ellie at the graveside, though. *As though she belonged to him.*

*   *   *

As the pallbearers carried Miss Lottie to her final resting-place on the breezy bluff overlooking the ocean, Dan thought you couldn't ask for a more beautiful or peaceful spot: rolling green lawns, flowers, shade trees, and the memorial plaques of the hundreds of other Santa Barbarans who had gone before, many dating back to the last century. There was a continuity in death, he thought, if you could get yourself to look at it that way. As a cop, he had always seen the worst of it: horror and tragedy and violence, like with Miss Lottie. Those deaths were not easy to accept. He saw the TV cameras focused on Ellie and hoped she wouldn't notice the intrusion. Miss Lottie's funeral had become public property.

He gripped Ellie's arm firmly as the Reverend Allan intoned, 'Dearly beloved, we are gathered here today to pay tribute to a great lady, Charlotte Amelia Stamford Parrish – Miss Lottie to all of us.'

Ellie felt herself slipping back in time. It was her parents' funeral . . . the same blanket of white roses, the same mourners, the same beautiful resting-place overlooking the ocean, and the soft sound of the waves on the shore.

'We ask the Lord to give strength to her beloved grand-daughter, Ellie . . .' the minister was praying.

Piatowsky inspected the curious onlookers peering over the wall; joggers on their way to the beach, dog-walkers, ordinary-looking people doing ordinary things. Any one of them might be a killer.

The congregation was singing now. Buck knew every hymn by heart. After all, hadn't he attended church with his mother every Sunday of his life? Until he'd decided he'd had enough, that is. Fixing a suitably sorrowful expression on his face, he listened to the minister intoning the words of a psalm.

The Twenty-third Psalm moved Ellie to tears. When she was a child and knelt at the bedside to say her prayers, Miss Lottie had taught the gentle words to her. She remembered how she had always believed that the Lord was her own shepherd looking after her personally, in his giant flock. '*Thy rod and thy staff, they comfort me . . . He restoreth my soul.*' Would her soul ever be restored? Somehow, she thought not.

The music was Handel, soft, inspiring. The Reverend Allan made the sign of the cross over the coffin. '*Ashes to ashes, dust to dust . . .*'

Buck was careful not to go too far and pretend to wipe away a tear when the minister said the words he'd waited so long to hear, but neither did he smile, which is what he wanted to do. He wanted to dance and shout hurrah. *There she goes. Good-fuckin-bye Miss Lottie. At last.*

Ellie felt Dan's arm beneath hers, his strong shoulder was there, ready for her to lean on. For a minute there was just silence. Only the soft sound of the ocean below interrupted her thoughts. Lifting her head high and straightening her back, as Miss Lottie had taught her, she took Dan's arm and walked quickly away.

Miss Lottie had always known how to give a good party, and this one at her favourite place, the Biltmore, was no exception. As always, everything was run impeccably by the attentive staff. The hotel was giving their best-loved and longest-standing client their finest send-off. A string orchestra played the show tunes that had been her favourites, selections from the twenties and *Roberta*, through the fifties and *Oklahoma*, to the eighties and *Evita*. There was champagne, of course – *Veuve Clicquot* because she'd always liked the idea of a widow drinking the Widow Clicquot's champagne; the tiny salmon and cucumber sandwiches she'd always enjoyed so much at her Monday teas, the scones and cream and fresh strawberry preserves, and the famous chocolate cake. It was, after all, four o'clock, and teatime.

A rose arbour had been erected and Ellie stood with Maya and Dan, receiving her grandmother's guests.

'It's more like a wedding than a funeral,' Maya whispered guiltily.

Ellie smiled at her. 'That's just the way she wanted it. Tea at the Biltmore, one last time.'

'Such a tragedy, my dear,' an old friend murmured sorrowfully, shaking her hand.

The whole community had been shocked by the killing, and

frightened by it. Things like this just didn't happen in tiny, sedate, upmarket Montecito.

'It's the passing of an era,' someone said quietly. 'This place will never be the same again.'

Buck had been hesitant about going to the farewell party, it was risky, he knew. But the voice in his head urged him on. *What the hell, why shouldn't you? There would be no party if it weren't for you.* Grinning at that thought, he climbed into the convertible and drove round the corner to the Biltmore. *It was true; everyone was there today because of him.*

Taking a glass of champagne from a passing waiter, Buck wandered the lawn, smiling and nodding at people he didn't know, but who thought they must know him: pausing to commiserate with some of the older ones, who supposed they must know him else why was he speaking to them. He was pleased by his own cleverness, his confidence. He could do anything. *He was power.* Taking another glass of champagne, he downed it quickly, watching Ellie under the rose arbour with Cassidy. *Exactly like a wedding couple.*

He went to the buffet table and took a couple of salmon and cucumber sandwiches, edging closer. She didn't even see him. He was the invisible man.

His heart felt as though it was bursting out of his chest with rage. The pain was crippling. Setting the plate carefully down on a table, he took a deep breath, then walked, stiffly upright, away from the crowds and into the bar. Two bourbons later, he was feeling better, and the funeral guests were departing. He collected his car, drove onto the street and parked to one side, waiting.

Ellie thanked the Manager and the staff, wondering if she would ever be able to bear to return, then got into the car.

The limo driver did not take the route past the cemetery but drove instead along Coast Village Road. Ellie turned her head to look as they passed Hot Springs Road. It was truly the end of an era.

The black limousine cruised slowly past Buck, taking Ellie away from him again, but this time he didn't follow. There was no point. As long as she was with Cassidy at the ranch, there was nothing he could do. Angry and frustrated, he knew he would just have to wait it out, until Phase Four of his plan was complete.

54

Ellie flung her black hat onto the bench in the hall as she strode wearily back into the house. Florita came running from the kitchen. Grabbing her hands, she stared anxiously into her face.

'All is well?'

'Thank you, Florita, all is well.'

Florita suddenly flung her arms round her and hugged her. '*Ay, madre de Dios.*' Letting go of Ellie she crossed herself and muttered a little prayer. 'Is better for you now, Señorita Ellie. You will see, is better it is over.'

Ellie's eyes met Piatowsky's. 'Did you see anyone who looked like a killer?'

'The only person I saw who looked suspicious was Johannsen, lurking round like a stage detective.'

'He was only doing his job.' Dan's voice was mild as he walked into the hall with Maya. 'He videoed the whole thing. He's sending it round later, wants to know if Ellie could take a look at it, see if there is anyone you might pick out. Someone you know, or a stranger, anything that might be worth him following up.' She stared at him, blank-eyed and he added, 'You don't have to do it tonight, if you don't want to.'

'Of course I will.' Ellie steeled herself. She had wanted so badly for it all to be at an end, but Johannsen didn't let up. She would do this one thing, then finally it would be over.

A little later, the four of them were sitting around the supper table. Florita was whisking round, placing steaming dishes of *arroz con pollo*, salad and freshly made corn tortillas with *salsa verde* on the table. The baby crawled after her, levering himself up the side of Ellie's chair.

'*Ay, Carlosito, no.*' She swept him up, but Ellie held out her arms.

'Come here, Carlosito, and tell me what kind of a day you've had.' He perched contentedly on her knee, twisting a lock of her long hair in his chubby fingers, gazing curiously into each of their faces.

'Better than ours, I'll bet,' she murmured, dropping a kiss on his soft black curls.

'He has hair like his father,' Florita said proudly.

Ellie thought he looked exactly like his father, and she'd bet he had all of his charm too.

'Well, at least that's over.' Maya leaned across to tickle the baby's cheek. 'Now, you can get some rest. Maybe you and I should take a little vacation? Hawaii? Or Cabo? Somewhere tropical, with soft white sand and hot sunshine?'

The baby held out his arms for his mother, and as Ellie handed him over Dan thought, enviously, it made a pretty picture: Ellie, a baby, the family dinner table, home and hearth . . . Every cliché he could think of just fit right in.

'I have to get back to work.' Ellie sounded brisk, businesslike, as though now the funeral was over she had snapped out of grief. But Maya knew her better. Ellie always took it on the chin, whether it was a doomed love affair or a death in the family.

'Then I'll come and stay with you, keep you company.' Maya didn't want her to be alone with all her bad thoughts of Miss Lottie and Maria.

'Thanks, but I've got to get on with things, on my own, or . . .' She didn't finish it, but they knew she was going to say she might not be able to.

'Sort of like getting back on the horse after you've been thrown,' Dan said helpfully.

She looked at him and grinned, almost like the old Ellie. 'Always there with an apt analogy, Cassidy.' Their eyes linked.

'Please stay.' Dan's eyes were still on hers. He spread his hands, palms up, '*Mi casa es su casa.*'

'*Gracias, señor.*' But Ellie knew she had to go back to her own life, her own world.

Johannesen and Mullins arrived after supper with the tape. They sat on the edges of their chairs, watching as Miss Lottie's funeral unrolled, bringing the pain back all over again.

The detective slowed the tape as the camera panned the crowd at the graveside. 'I'm sorry to do this, Ellie, but if you could just take a look at their faces, see if there's anything that strikes a chord, someone your grandmother might have known years ago, or a stranger?'

Ellie's eyes searched the solemn faces carefully, some were tearful, others stony, all sad. Some she knew, and some she didn't.

She shook her head, 'I'm sorry, I wish I could help.'

Piatowsky almost felt sorry for Johannsen. The case was a tough one, and random killings were the hardest to solve.

He walked out to the car with him. 'Anything I can do,' he shook his hand firmly, 'let me know.' Lighting up a Lucky, Piatowsky leaned on the porch rail, watching the red tail-lights disappear down the hill. He had a feeling Ellie hadn't heard the last from Johannsen.

The others wandered out to join him. 'Care to take a walk?' Dan was looking at Ellie. It was almost dusk and a waning moon glimmered in the cobalt blue sky. Taking his outstretched hand, she walked with him down the steps and along the path leading behind the house, to the pond.

'They look good together.' Piatowsky offered Maya a cigarette and she shook her head.

Her eyes were on Ellie and Dan. Their two tall figures blended into one as Dan slid his arm round Ellie's waist, then they turned the corner and were gone. 'They're good together,' she agreed. 'Except she's a city girl with a work ethic that won't quit and ambition as high as that moon.'

'And he's a guy seeking the simple life, Farmer Dan, lost in the countryside, up to his eyes in vines and horseshit.'

She looked at him. 'Doesn't bode well, does it?'

He gave her his special grin. 'Not all marriages are made in heaven. How about we take a walk, Miss Maya? You can tell me all about yourself, and I can tell you about the darlin' of my heart, who's probably being so spoiled by her grandmother, she's not missing her poor father one little bit.'

'I'm going to miss this place.' Sliding her arm around Dan's waist, Ellie matched her stride to his long one. She thought they fit together as snugly as if they had been made for each other.

'And I'm going to miss you.' The darkening twilit sky intensified the flame of her hair, paled her eyes, drained her face of what little colour it had. 'Sure you can't stay? Take it easy for a bit?'

It was so tempting just to be an old-fashioned woman, to collapse into his arms, let him take care of her. A part of her yearned toward that, but she reminded herself quickly that her goals were still in front of her. She needed work, and she needed success, now more than ever. 'There's no point in taking it easy, it leaves too much time to think. Besides, I have to get away from Johannsen.'

He wanted to tell her it would be difficult to get away from Johannsen; that when he wanted her, he would be down in Santa Monica in a heartbeat, ready to question her all over again. Unless he came up with another suspect, one who wore size twelve sneakers.

She was looking at him as though he might have an answer, something to take the burden from her shoulders, but he had none. She said, 'I thought I learned everything there was to know about violence, that year my parents died. Now I know I didn't. This is even worse.'

'It's over now, Ellie. Let it go. Keep the good memories and put Journey's End on the market.'

She shook her head, her mouth set in a determined line. 'I can't. Not yet. It's as though Miss Lottie and Maria are still there, waiting for me to help them. We have to find their killer first.'

They were standing by the pond, listening to the frogs revving up, getting ready to serenade the night. 'Will you come and see me, Dan? Please?'

He turned to her. Her bones were sharp under his hands, she must have lost pounds this past week. 'Of course I will.'

Her face was uptilted to his, he could smell the clean scent of her hair, her subtle perfume. Lowering his lips to hers, he kissed her gently, sweetly.

Like a friend, Ellie thought, wrapping her arms round him. A dear, good friend.

Lifting his mouth from hers, Dan murmured, 'I promise.'

55

Ellie's brand-new Cherokee was forest green, almost the same colour as the paint at the café, with black interior and plenty of room for hauling stuff. It felt smooth, peppy, luxurious, as she drove back to Santa Monica. Her old Wrangler had been a write-off, and Dan had been stunned when she had told him she had never owned a new car.

'Never?' he'd repeated, shocked that a girl from a wealthy background could claim such a thing.

'In case I'd inherited my mother's happy-go-lucky spendthrift ways and taste for luxury,' she'd explained. 'Miss Lottie believed in the old saying 'riches to rags in three generations'. She also said, 'Prevention is the mother of necessity', mixing her metaphors as usual and making me laugh, except this time there was an odd kind of sense to it.'

Dan had said she was a crazy driver at the best of times, and that she needed a safer car; but Ellie wondered nervously about Johannsen suspecting her of already spending what they knew he considered to be her ill-gotten gains. But Dan had laughed it off.

Dan was very much on her mind. He'd tried so hard to help her come to terms with what had happened, and he'd protected her from Johannsen's endless questioning. She felt closer to him than ever, especially remembering that kiss last night. As she turned up the hill leading to her house, she warned herself if she ever allowed herself to fall in love with him, it would mean trouble. There was a direct conflict in their aims in life: she was for city and success; he was for the country and serenity. They inhabited different worlds, and she wasn't ready to give up her amibitions yet. At least, not until she had made a success of her life; then, she might consider it. But by then she suspected it would be too late. She smiled wryly; her timing had never been great.

Her little house looked just the same, as though nothing momentous and horrifying had happened since she'd left it, just over a week ago. But as she turned the key in the lock and went in, it *felt* different.

It was dusty and the lilies in the big urn had died, scattering petals and pollen all over the surface of the antique console, but other than that, everything seemed to be in its place. In the kitchen, the green mug with the cherries on it from which she had drunk a cup of wild berry tea was still in the sink. She opened the refrigerator. The carton of milk had gone off. Wrinkling her nose, she threw it down the disposal, along with a half loaf of stale bread.

She heard a tapping noise and swung round, spooked. Relieved, she saw it was only a bird outside the window. Still, she was uneasy. The house looked the same, but it felt different. Telling herself it was because she knew the police had been in there, searching through her things, she trailed despondently up the creaking stairs.

Sunlight streamed into her bedroom and the air felt stale and hot. Flinging open the window, she peeled off her clothes, letting them fall where they dropped. She took a long shower, washed her hair, anointed herself with lotion and powder. All the usual things. *Then why did the place seem so different?* She sighed, as she pulled on her work uniform of jeans and t-shirt. Everything *was* different. She was alone in the world now. The only antidote for grief was work, and she had plenty of that in front of her.

She ran a comb through her wet hair, slung her big black bag over her shoulder, grabbed the car keys and was on her way.

Main Street had that early-summer feel: school not yet out, but freedom on the horizon; hot sunshine; a glimpse of the glittering blue and silver ocean down the side streets; the scent of fresh-roasted coffee and hot bread; girls in pale summer dresses and cute sandals; store windows jazzy with the latest for the season; the art galleries displaying colourful acrylics by local artists. This was her world, her life. And it was a long way from Running Horse Ranch.

The café looked sad and abandoned, with the chairs piled upside down on the tables, no flowers, no aromas of cooking, no tinkling doorbell and the clamour of conversation and music. It was definitely time to get to work.

She phoned Chan, told him they would be opening again tomorrow and discussed the menu with him. It was time for a change, she said. A summer menu. Things like stuffed zucchini blossoms and Provençal *brandade*, a smooth creamy mixture of salt cod, olive oil and seasonings. Fresh red mullet and Santa Barbara sea bass, the best there was. Lobster ravioli and fresh Sonoma lamb. And how about if she made a lavender *crème brulée* for dessert? Inspired by the summery scene, ideas were whizzing round in her head.

'Let's make it a feast, Chan,' she said, pushing her hair back excitedly. 'A celebration.'

'Sure', Chan said on the other end of the line, though he wasn't sure what they were celebrating.

Ellie knew, though. She was alive again, buzzing with energy, raring to go. She couldn't wait to get her hands in the flour and turn out a batch of good bread; couldn't wait for six in the morning and the produce market with its green and spicy smells; couldn't wait to greet her customers again. She smiled as she sat down to make a list. This was what her life was about.

The phone rang. 'Ellie's Place.'

'Hey, you're sounding good?'

It was Maya. 'I'm glad to be back. Glad to be out of that atmosphere . . .'

''I told you it would be better, after the funeral.' Maya could remember when her mother had died, ten years ago; it hadn't been easy to accept, but life went on. 'Are you sure you don't want me to stay with you? Just until you feel okay?'

'I am okay. I'm glad to get back to my house, glad to be back at work. By the way, we're opening tomorrow.'

'So soon?' Maya sounded astonished.

'What else am I going to do?'

'True. Okay, I'll be there. Talk to you later.'

Ellie wrote out her suggestions for the new menus, then put on her apron, opened the big container of flour, put some fresh yeast in warm water and stood it on the stove to prove. Soon she was up to her elbows in dough, pounding and kneading, getting ready for tomorrow.

When she left the café, at around six, the tables were already set for morning, and the dough, in big pottery bowls covered with clean cotton cloths, was left in a warm place to rise. The menu had been worked out; lists made for the produce market; orders placed for supplies. She had organized Chan and Terry and the kid, taken care of several outstanding bills, watered the plants, and made a dozen phone calls to suppliers. She was back in business.

There was a pleased smile on her face as she walked across the road to buy a sandwich for her supper. She wasn't used to having an evening to herself, alone. She would do something mindless, watch TV in bed, go to sleep early. It sounded lonely, and she found herself wishing wistfully that she'd taken Maya up on her offer to stay.

She ordered a grilled chicken sandwich on foccacia with fresh tomatoes, roasted red peppers, arugala and a touch of light vinaigrette.

Sitting alone at the table in the window, Buck watched her as she stood, arms folded across her chest, waiting. He couldn't believe his luck. Like the spider and the fly, she had just walked right into his trap.

He'd parked on the hill near her house, as usual, watching and waiting. He hadn't recognized the new green Cherokee when it turned into her street, but when he saw her get out and carry her bags indoors, his heart had pitter-pattered like a teenager's.

Of course, he'd followed her along Main Street, seen that she was returning to the café. He'd cruised around waiting for a vacant parking spot opposite, then sat there, waiting, watching. He'd seen the lights go on in the café, caught a glimpse of Ellie bustling around, setting up tables. She wouldn't need to do that much longer, he'd thought. Not when she was with him. Half an hour ago, he'd gone into the sandwich shop and ordered coffee and muffin, biding his time.

Now he got up and walked toward her. 'Ellie, I didn't expect to see you here.' His face was suitably serious, no smile, just a hint of concern in his voice.

'Oh, hi, Mr Jensen.' She was surprised, she hadn't expected to meet him there either. The guy certainly got around, he popped up everywhere.

'I was in the area, looking at some properties. I'm told it's a good investment and that the market will undoubtedly be going up. But what about you?' Daringly, he put his hand on her arm. The smooth warmth of her flesh sent shock waves through him, tightening his belly, but he had himself under control. 'I'm so sorry.' He lifted his shoulders, expressing his futility, 'Mere words are not enough. There is no way to console you for what you must have gone through.'

'Thank you, I appreciate it, Mr Jensen. I'm trying to get back to work, get on with living . . .' Her voice trailed off as she remembered their last meeting, when he'd suggested buying the house after Miss Lottie was gone. She surely hoped he wasn't going to bring that subject up now.

Buck was too clever for that. 'I'm glad to hear you'll be opening the café again. I always find that work is the best antidote. If I'm in the area, I'll stop by and have dinner.'

Ellie's sandwich was ready. She took the box and smiled goodbye. 'Sure, that'll be good,' she said, edging past him.

When she looked back from the door, he was watching her. She hurried back across the street to her car. He hadn't said a single wrong word, but there was just something about him . . . maybe Maya was right and he really was a creep.

Back home, she stood at the kitchen counter, slowly chewing her sandwich. It was very good, but her mind wasn't on it. Instead, she was thinking about sitting on the porch at the ranch, sipping wine and watching the sunset, and remembering the scent of night-blooming jasmine and roses, and fresh clean air.

Sighing, she cleared away the half-eaten sandwich, fixed herself a cup of wild berry tea, and carried it upstairs to the bedroom. She would get into her night things, put on her comfy old robe, watch TV. And wait for Dan to call.

From his position across the street, Buck saw the upstairs

lights go on, then Ellie as she opened the window and stood for a minute, looking out. She drew the curtains and disappeared from his sight. For now, he was content. Phase Four was set; everything was ready. All he needed was the right opportunity.

56

Dan was riding the frisky mare, Honey, with Piatowsky on Paradise, and Ortega on the palomino. 'Just relax,' he said, glancing sideways at his friend. 'It's a western saddle, all you have to do is sit there, grip with your thighs, and let the horse do the work.'

'So how the hell d'ya keep from falling off?' Piatowsky looked deeply uncomfortable, sliding forward in the saddle as the horse walked down the hill. He didn't get this horse-riding bit, bumping up and down on some ornery critter who was bigger and stronger than he was. 'Wish we'd gone fishin' instead,' he muttered, and heard Dan laugh.

'Next time, Piatowsky.' Dan called over his shoulder.

'Yeah, sure. If you don't have another double murder on your hands. Be just my luck.'

'It was the Señor's luck you were here,' Carlos observed solemnly. 'Otherwise he might be in the jail, and leave me to run the vineyard by myself.'

'Thanks for your trust, friend,' Dan said. 'Do I look like a killer to you?'

'That's what Ellie said, but Johannsen thinks she does.' Piatowsky gave the horse a little nudge as it veered to one side, heading for a patch of grass. The mare whinnied and tossed her head spiritedly. His eyes opened wide in alarm. 'Give me a fast car, any day,' he said, sweating, 'at least then I know whose in control.'

'Relax, Señor Piatowsky, this mare is a just a baby.' Ortega rode alongside to keep an eye on him. He knew the horse could sense she had an inexperienced rider on top and anything might happen.

'Forensics in N'Yawk have the knife tagged as a switchblade,' Piatowsky said. 'A common type, but the blade had been honed wafer-thin. Sharp as a shark's teeth, they said. It would slice through flesh like a hot knife through butter. LA already confirmed that their killer used the same weapon. If the same knife was used on Miss Lottie, Johannsen's theory goes up in smoke. And we'll know our killer is the same man.'

Dan was keeping his fingers crossed. He was driving Piatowsky back to the airport that afternoon and planned on dropping in to see Ellie. Maybe they could have dinner together, or if she were too busy, at least a cup of coffee. He would love to be able to give her the good news that the killer was the same one as in the New York and LA murders, and she was off the hook as a suspect. Johannsen had already confirmed that the bruise prints on the throat were made by a man with large, very powerful hands. They did not match Dan's.

Piatowsky thought the ride downhill was getting even bumpier. Without warning, his saddle suddenly slid sideways and he was dangling upside down, looking at the horse's feet and hanging on for dear life. He heard Carlos shouting 'Whoa, whoa', at the horse, and Dan's laughter.

'You didn't tack her up properly,' Dan told him as he leapt to the rescue. 'The saddle came loose and that should never happen.'

'Yeah, well I'm a guy who knows what to do if the fanbelt goes, but I'm a novice on a horse.' Piatowsky smoothed his thinning hair back over his scalp, thinking worriedly, of the size of the horse's feet, clopping neatly along close to his face. 'A guy could get hurt this way.'

'You'll try it again next time,' Dan promised, leading the horses back to the stables with Piatowsky limping along behind.

'Oh, sure.' Piatowsky felt safer dodging the bullets in the boroughs. He thought maybe it was time to go home.

He called Johannsen from the airport to check on the outcome of the knife. Listening, he gave Dan the thumbs up. He thanked Johannsen, told him he was on his way back to New York, wished him success in his investigation and said he would catch up with him later.

'The knife's the same one used in the other homicides, and Ellie's free and clear. Johannsen even apologized for suspecting her, said it was all in the line of duty. I guess he was right.'

Dan hadn't realized his heart was in his boots with anxiety until it bounded up again. He slapped Piatowsky on the shoulder, then hugged him. 'Thanks, buddy,' he said.

'Any time.'

'See you soon,' Dan called after him as he walked to the boarding gate.

'I'll bring the kids next time, they'll enjoy the horses,' Piatowsky called back. He was laughing as he said it.

Ellie's Place was crowded and she was run off her feet. She supposed she should be glad to have such custom, but she did wonder whether her sudden notoriety had anything to do with it. Wearily, she hoped not.

It had been difficult to sleep last night, after Dan had phoned. She'd wanted to call him back, say I'm afraid to close my eyes because of what I might see, but she knew she couldn't. She had chosen to travel this particular path alone, and she would keep that vow. Still, she was looking out for him, and when she finally saw him, it was as if a great weight lifted from her shoulders.

His deep-blue eyes inspected her anxiously as he kissed her on the cheek, and she felt that old yearning again. Dismissing it, she took him into the kitchen and introduced him to her staff. Maya was off tonight and Jake was there, helping out.

Hoping for a sign of approval Ellie watched them inspect Dan, up and down, then up again. These guys were like her family now, she thought. They were all she'd got left.

'Good to meet you, Dan.' Chan shifted the cleaver to his left hand and offered his right to Dan. 'You're keeping an eye on her, making sure she's okay, right?'

'That's right.' Under Chan's grumpiness, Dan could see he was worried about Ellie. He shook hands with Terry and the kid, and Jake.

'You ever thought of doing TV?' Jake surveyed him interestedly. 'Be great type-casting for the cop on one of those series.'

'Thanks, but no thanks. The real thing was enough for me.'

'I recommend the shrimp tonight,' Chan called after him as they left him to his cramped kitchen. 'Shrimp Chan-style, with a sorrel sauce.'

There were no tables left and Ellie sat Dan at the counter where she could talk to him, in passing. He could see she was too busy to spend time with him, and decided to have a cup of coffee, then get back. He'd call her later, make arrangements to get together.

'I've got good news,' he said, when she brought him the coffee. She looked expectantly at him. 'The knife was the same one used in the New York and LA murders. You're no longer a suspect.'

She sagged against him in relief. 'Oh thank god,' she whispered. Then, alarmed, 'But what about you?'

'Me too.'

She nodded, reassembling things in her mind now that she was a free woman without the prospect of a murder trial and jail looming over her. She knew she should have felt elated, but all she felt was exhausted.

Jake rushed past with an order and she glanced frantically round. 'I've got to go. Thanks, Dan.'

He dropped a kiss on her cheek. 'I'll talk to you later, okay?'

She threw him a smile over her shoulder, as she hurried back to the kitchen. It would be the best part of her day – and night, she thought. Because the nights were the toughest of all.

57

She was drowning in darkness, it was all around her, there was no light anywhere. Then a thin ribbon of scarlet appeared. It slid slowly toward her, undulating, spreading, widening, until it touched her skin. It smelled harsh, coppery. Now it was rising, engulfing her in heat and redness, sticky . . .

Fighting back the bedcovers, Ellie shot upright. Her heart thudded like an express train, and her skin was sheened with sweat. The faint light from the rectangle of the window showed her familiar bedroom, the reassuring shapes of the dresser, the fireplace, the nightstand. She was safe, at home.

Shuddering, she bent her head over her clasped knees. Tears stung her eyes. 'Oh, Gran,' she whispered, brokenly. 'Oh Gran, I'm so sorry.'

After a few minutes, she pushed back the rumpled bedding, put on a robe and white sweatsocks, then shuffled, still sniffling, downstairs to the kitchen.

Two weeks had passed since she'd come home. It was always the same. She worked as many hours a day as she could, hoping to be exhausted enough just to crawl into bed and fall instantly asleep. The trouble was the deep sleep lasted only a couple of hours, then, regular as clockwork, she woke at 3 a.m. with the same dream. She was drowning in blood.

Night after night, she came downstairs and fixed herself a cup of tea with shaking hands, telling herself if only she had gotten to Journey's End earlier; if only she had been more alert and realised they no longer used the alarm; if only she'd still lived at Journey's End, instead of allowing two old ladies to stay there alone. *If only . . . if only . . .*

Guilt washed over her and she sobbed into her mug of tea, clutching it to her chest for warmth and comfort as she grieved. Now, it was too late, and try as she might, she couldn't get the image of her grandmother's mutilated body out of her mind.

A long time later, she went back upstairs and stood by the open window in the deep silence of the night, listening to the distant wash of the waves on the shore. It was dawn before she returned to bed and fell, still troubled, back to sleep.

Ellie was tempted on those endless lonesome nights to pick up the phone and call Dan, yet stubbornly she resisted. But Maya noticed her shadowed eyes and air of fatigue, and the false energy with which she attacked the day's work.

'You're like a whirlwind, in constant motion,' she told her. 'You're here at six in the morning and you leave after midnight. Are you getting any sleep at all?'

'Not much. But I'll manage.'

Recognizing that determined set of the jaw, Maya knew that nothing she could say would change her mind. Ellie wasn't about to share her feelings this time; more's the pity, because if ever a woman needed a shoulder to cry on right now, it was her friend.

Even though Ellie didn't want to admit it, the highlight of her day was when she was home, in bed, anticipating Dan's nightly call.

'Just checking on you,' he'd say, and she could hear the mocking little smile in his voice.

'I'm all right,' she would reply, resisting adding, '*Now* I am. Now I hear your voice.'

Dan was busy, grafting chardonnay budwood, and getting deeper in hock to the bank. He sounded cheerful about it, as though he were enjoying the whole process, and his enthusiasm made her wish she could share it with him. But the conflict between them was clear: she was city, he was country. She had long-term career plans; and so did he. She couldn't allow herself to fall in love with him. He was her good friend, and that's the way it would stay. For ever, she hoped.

*　　*　　*

Buck had decided against going to the café again; he would stay out of the picture from now on. Mr Anonymous, that was him. But he still kept watch, following her home every night, keeping a discreet distance so she never even noticed. His plans were almost finalized. Phase Four was just about ready to go. Excitement kept him in a constant state of hyperactivity, prowling his apartment, stoking up on bourbon, stalking Sunset Boulevard checking out the women; waiting until it was late enough for Ellie to have finished at the café, when he had his nightly date with her, sitting in his car, watching her bedroom window until the light finally went out.

Dan stuffed his hands in the pockets of his dusty jeans, surveying the north slope of Running Horse Hill. It had finally been planted and wire trellising erected to lift the growing chardonnay vines higher, allowing more of that valuable ripening sunshine to get at the grapes. Satisfied, he thought that next year his vineyard would begin to look like the others around him: leafy, with clusters of golden-green grapes promising a tangy vibrant golden wine. *Burgeoning*, in fact, he thought, smiling as he remembered the first day he'd brought Ellie out to inspect the vineyard.

He hadn't seen her in a week, though he spoke to her every night, and he decided now was the time to take a break, before he went to Napa with Ortega to check on the cabernet budwood. The vines at UC Davies had not met Ortega's high standards, and they were still searching for the perfect style of grape.

He checked the time, it was almost seven. He needed to shower, change, put gas in the car: he could be at Ellie's Place before nine. Taking the cellphone from his pocket, he began to dial her number, then changed his mind. He liked to surprise her, just to see her face light up when she saw him. It gave him a little buzz of hope for the future.

The day had been warm, but with nightfall the temperature dropped and the mist slunk in, creeping over the dead, silent ocean, wreathing in haloes around the streetlights and rolling its ghostly fingers along the boulevards. Because of it, it took Dan longer than he'd expected to drive from Running Horse to Santa Monica. It was nine-thirty when he finally pulled the car into a spot opposite the café, directly behind a black BMW convertible.

The street was quiet for a change, but lights still glowed welcomingly from Ellie's Place. Feeding quarters into the meter, he walked across the road and pushed open the door.

The old-fashioned bell tinkled sweetly, reminding him of the local candystore where he'd spent part of his fifty cents allowance every Saturday morning, when he was around five years old. Only two tables were occupied, and there was no sign of Ellie or Maya.

He went to the back, pushed open the kitchen door and stuck his head round it. Ellie was cleaning up the big stoves and he could see Jake outside, catching a quick cigarette. There was no sign of Chan and Terry, and he guessed they'd already left.

Ellie hadn't heard him, and he watched her for a second. There was a look of sadness on her face, and a weary slump to her shoulders that told him the truth about how she was really feeling, despite her brave words on the phone. His heart ached for her, as he called her name.

It was there, that instant look of surprise, the warm hundred megawatt smile that lit up her whole face. When Ellie smiled, her entire body contributed to it, sending out little vibes of pleasure. He thought it was worth a two-hour drive in the fog just to see it.

'Hi there,' she said, 'this is a surprise.'

'I hoped you were going to say "an unexpected pleasure".' He dropped a kiss on her smiling mouth.

'That too,' she agreed.

The new kid with the bleached blond hair who looked like a budding rock-star, eyed them curiously from the sink where he was busy rinsing dishes. They looked good together, he thought. Kind of like they belonged.

'You must be hungry.' Ellie was already taking out pots and pans. 'I'm cooking tonight, just tell me what you'd like.' She enjoyed having him on her turf, on her terms. It put her on her mettle.

'Scrambled eggs and a toasted bagel would be fine,' he said.

She smiled at him, remembering the first day he'd come into

the café. *Her life had changed so drastically since then, it seemed light years away.* She thanked god that he'd wandered into her place, instead of one of the other dozens of cafés along Main Street. Chance was a fine thing, sometimes.

'I can't do the bagel, but I can promise you some very good rosemary bread. Are you sure that's all you want?'

He couldn't think of anything better than eggs prepared by Ellie. 'No, it's not all.' He caught her hand in his. 'I want you to join me for supper.'

'I think I might be able to manage that,' she said lightly, dropping his hand to get fresh free-range eggs from the pantry, tripping over her feet again and losing her shoe.

'Cinderella?' He was down on one knee, laughing at her as she balanced on one foot.

'Cinderella was never as clumsy as this,' she sighed, clutching the carton of eggs to her chest.

At the sink, the kid thought this was better than a movie. Even Jake was leaning against the door watching them. The kid could almost see him framing them for the camera lens, ready to direct their next action.

'Would you like a glass of wine?' She was busy stirring the eggs and he shook his head, fascinated by the efficient economy of her movements as she worked. Even fixing scrambled eggs was no haphazard 'throw it all in the pan' deal for her. She was all professional, knew exactly the quantities to use of eggs and butter and milk. Scrambled eggs, Ellie-style, would turn out the same every time. Big meal or small, she was an excellent chef.

Ellie hadn't eaten, but now Dan was here she fixed eggs for them both, gave him the basket of bread to carry, then followed him into the café with the steaming plates.

'Bon appetit, m'sieur,' she murmured. Suddenly hungry, she tucked into the eggs.

'Good,' Dan mumbled, his mouth full. 'These are truly great.' She smiled her thanks across the table. 'So tell me, Ell, how are you really?'

She lifted her shoulders, looking weary. 'It's tough to sleep. You know, that old three-in-the-morning-guilt-trip, the "if onlies" . . .'

'Whatever you're thinking, it wasn't your fault.'

'I guess not,' she sounded uncertain, shifting the eggs around her plate with the fork. Looking at the mist pressing at the café window, the spectre of nightly loneliness crushed her again, like a weight. 'Want to come home and have coffee with me?'

He nodded. 'Sure.'

Jake was taking care of the other tables; they were just leaving, paying their bills. 'I'll close up for you, Ellie,' he called from the counter. 'Take it easy for once, go home.' He'd seen how stressed out she was, and thought it was a good thing that, at least tonight, she had company. In his opinion loneliness never solved anything. Trouble shared was trouble solved, as any good LA psychiatrist would tell you, while charging a small fortune for the privilege, as he knew only too well.

Ellie beamed her thanks as they carried their plates into the kitchen. 'Would you stay on and help Jake?' she asked the kid stacking one of the big industrial dishwashers.

'Sure, Ellie.' He had a date at Victor's Club on Abbot Kinney, but, for a budding rockstar like him, he knew the girl would wait.

Outside, the dense fog pressed up against their faces and visibility was down to about ten yards. Definitely not a good driving night.

Ellie had taken the Cherokee out of the lot earlier and parked half a block from the café. 'Why don't you follow me?' Dan called, striding across the road to his car as she walked the half block to hers. 'It'll be safer that way.'

The black BMW was still parked in front of him, and he saw the man sitting in it, in the darkness. Wondering briefly what he was up to, he edged the Explorer out from behind him, waited for Ellie to catch up, then drove slowly down the silent, fog-bound road.

Ellie's cosy little lamp-lit house was an exotic oasis appearing like a mirage, out of the fog. Vanilla-scented candles flickered on the mantel and soft string music played gently in the background, the Henry Mancini orchestra with the soft, warm voice of Johnny Mathis. Ellie was pouring fragrant hot coffee. She put the mug on the low table in front of Dan.

He was sitting next to her on the sofa, his head thrown back, listening to the music.

She studied the strong planes of his face; the faint bluish hint of stubble on his recently shaved chin; the way his hair sprang so vigorously from his forehead. His muscular body looked relaxed, and dark hair crowded the shirt open at his throat. His hands were beautiful, wide, long-fingered, and with no dirt under the nails. She smiled, imagining how he must have scrubbed them after working in the fields alongside Ortega and the team of Mexican workers all week. He was such a physical man, and she liked that about him. But even a strong man looked vulnerable, somehow, with his eyes closed, his face unguarded.

Pleased he was able to be that way with her, relaxed, easy, she said, 'Black, no sugar.'

'Finally, I think you know me.' His eyes were still closed.

'Finally, I think I do.'

There was something in her voice, a silkiness he'd never heard before. Opening his eyes he looked directly into hers.

Reaching out, she ran her fingers gently through his hair. Now she had him here, she couldn't bear to let him go. 'I was just thinking,' she said, phrasing it carefully so he wouldn't get the wrong meaning, 'you can't possibly drive home in this fog. It's way too dangerous.'

'True,' he nodded, his eyes still fixed on hers.

'Then it's my turn to offer hospitality. I have pillows, blankets, you'll be comfortable, here on the sofa.'

'True,' he nodded again.

She was drowning in the deep blueness of his eyes, lured by his mouth . . . Getting a grip on herself, she stood. 'I'll just go get the blankets.'

He caught her arm, pulled her down on the sofa again. 'Stop running from me, Ellie.'

She could feel the warmth of his hands on her shoulders where he held her. His mouth approached hers and her eyes closed in anticipation. His lips were firm, gentle on hers, a butterfly wing of a kiss . . . nothing to shake her to her roots

272

. . . nothing at all to worry about . . . She felt herself relaxing in his arms.

Dan dropped those gentle kisses across the sliding curve of her cheekbone, over her eyelids, unmade-up and delicate as the paper narcissi he'd sent her; on the tip of her nose where the freckles were so close together, it looked like a Siamese kitten's. Heat flared in his groin, he wanted her so badly, but he knew she was only seeking comfort from him; she was wary of love. His tongue found the uptilted corner of her mouth, licked, tasted . . .

'Delicious,' he breathed in her ear, 'better than *tarte tatin.*'

Pleasure flickered, flamelike, in her belly. Her mouth opened under his, and she linked her hands around his neck, pressing him closer, his thick dark hair soft in her entwining fingers. The kiss deepened, she felt as though the breath were being sucked from her body, leaving her soft, helpless.

'We really shouldn't,' she murmured in between kisses, feeling his heart beating against hers.

'Give me one good reason why not.' He was nibbling her earlobe, then his mouth trailed down her throat, found the pulse fluttering there, lingered over it, then moved on to explore the smooth hollows near her collarbone.

Ellie shivered with pleasure. There's nothing wrong with taking a lover, she told herself. They were both grownups, both dedicated to their work. There was no commitment on either side, and after all, they could still be friends . . . She felt herself yearning towards him, wanting him . . .

Opening her eyes, she looked dreamily into his. 'After all,' she whispered huskily, 'we're not involved . . .'

'Mmmm, uhuh . . . Certainly not, involved.' She saw the question in his eyes, and he saw the answering heat in hers, the longing. Taking her hand in his, he guided her up the creaking stairs.

Ellie's legs refused to hold her, and she sank onto the bed. It wasn't only that it had been a long time since she'd made love, it was that she'd never felt like this before. This kind of melting tenderness combined with the heat that his eyes and his hands generated, wherever they touched, wherever they lingered.

Dan tugged the t-shirt over her head, unhooked the flimsy white lace bra, paused for a moment, glorying in the perfection of her high rounded breasts. Gently, he circled her nipples with his tongue, felt her arch with pleasure, heard her sigh. His hands smoothed the delicate skin of her back, gripped the beautiful curve of her ribcage, encircled her breasts as he devoured them. She was so sweet, so pliant under his searching hands . . . he was on fire for her but he took his time, gentling her into it . . .

She pulled off her jeans, and his heart stuck somewhere in his throat as he looked at her, so slender, so strong, so beautiful in the tiny slip of white lace that covered her nakedness. Her glossy red hair tumbled over her breasts as she lifted herself on her elbows, watching as he stripped off his clothes.

He lay next to her, ran his hand the length of her body. His palms were hard, rough, the hands of a man who worked in the fields alongside his workers, building his dreams with them, his hopes, his future . . . a future that would not contain her. Ellie thrust the thought away as quickly as it came. Right now nothing mattered except his mouth searching every curve of her body, his hands holding her, lifting her to him, his tongue seeking out magical places. She was floating somewhere outside herself, brimming with pleasure. Shuddering, she cried out his name . . .

His eyes demanded hers as he slowly lowered himself into her. She moved against him, fitting together with him as though they had been made for exactly this moment, moving to his rhythm, crying out her pleasure.

Her hands skimmed his damp flesh, and she wrapped her legs round him, urging him deeper, then she was tumbling from that great height, heard herself moan, cry out for him, shameless in the urgency of her need. And then they were falling together into that silvery space where spent passion let them lie, still entwined, for that peaceful shaky moment, still as one.

The blissful weight of him pressed her into the soft bed, his heart thundering over hers. Ellie never wanted to move, she wanted this moment to last for ever; surely it could never be so good again . . .

Levering himself up on his hands, Dan smiled at her. Her tumbled hair spread in ripples of bronze across the pillows, her opal eyes were still dark with remembered passion, and her skin felt like molten satin. He lowered his mouth to hers, kissed her lingeringly. He wanted to tell her he loved her, but remembering the wariness in her eyes, he knew he would only scare her off. 'You're beautiful,' he said instead.

'You too.' She smiled as she ran her fingers through his curling, dark chest hair. 'Was it better?'

He looked puzzled. 'Better than what?'

'Than the *tarte tatin*.'

With a great shout of laughter, he rolled from her. 'No comparison, Chef. But then, I heard you were multi-talented.'

'You too,' she said with a playful little smile. Swinging her legs over the edge of the bed, she stepped close to him, her smooth, slender body stretched against his as she slid both arms round his neck and kissed him. 'Thank you,' she whispered in his ear. Then picking up the pink robe from the chaise, she wrapped it round her nakedness.

Dan stared at her astonished. The robe was obviously old and the pink clashed terribly with her roan-pony hair. In an instant, she'd gone from passionate woman to vulnerable girl, comfortable in her schoolgirl robe.

'Hardly sexy lingerie,' she admitted giving him that startling ear-to-ear grin, her eyes alight with amusement. 'I must have had it since I was seventeen, and I can't bear to give it up.'

He shrugged, still naked, laughing at her. 'Some kids have blankets, you have a robe. It takes all sorts.'

With the tip of one finger she pushed him back onto the bed. 'Wait right there, Mr Cassidy, famous owner of the burgeoning vineyard,' she said.

Dan lay back on the pillows, his arms behind his head, thinking about the many forms love could take. This one had crept up on him, ensnared him against all logic, almost against his will. Yet he couldn't tell this woman he loved her. It was a dilemma he'd never expected to confront, and he wondered how in hell he was going to get around it.

Music swelled again from the wall-speakers, soft lyrical, Antonio Carlos Jobim and strings, then Ellie appeared in the doorway, clutching a bottle of Vin Santo, two small glasses and a box of almond biscotti.

She perched on the bed next to him. 'It must be the home-maker in me,' she said, 'or maybe the chef, but I feel compelled to feed my man.'

'I like it.' He sat up, took the bottle from her, opened it, poured the rich dessert wine. Raising his glass to her, he sipped, 'It makes me feel wanted.'

Ellie's heart felt featherweight in her chest, it was fairly singing with happiness. Her room, her whole house, felt different with Dan in it. His strong masculine presence chased the ghosts of the night away, and his warm, sensual body gave her the gift of pleasure – and love. Though she didn't want that, not yet.

Smiling, she said, 'Open your mouth and close your eyes, and see what Ellie will send you.' He obeyed and she popped a small almond cookie between his lips. 'Delicious,' he muttered. Their eyes linked again, remembering.

He watched her sip the sweet wine and, unable to resist, he leaned closer and ran the tip of his tongue across her lips, tasting her. She was too much, too tempting . . . He caught the glass from her suddenly nerveless fingers, placed it on the night table, pressed her back against the pillows.

She lay, her slender arms over her head, her beautiful eyes soft with wanting, as he slowly unfastened the belt holding the pink robe together. Then she was naked before him, and it was starting all over again.

Buck sat in the car, staring at the lamp-lit upstairs window. Tears streamed down his face. He didn't know a heart could contain this much pain. He would have to kill Ellie, now. He started the car and drove like a madman, through the dense fog, back to Sunset and the apartment. Bolting the door, he hurled himself round the room, flailing his fists against the walls, howling his despair.

His upstairs neighbour, a young guy watching a loud music video, lowered the sound for a second, listening. He shrugged, wondering what channel the horror movie was on, then turned up the sound again.

58

They awoke simultaneously to the un-drunk wine and the biscotti scattered across the floor. Sunlight streamed through the curtains, casting a golden haze over their entwined bodies.

Still warm with the glow of their lovemaking, Ellie shifted her head to look at him. Her eyes met his and she smiled. 'Morning, friend.'

Her lazy voice wrapped like spun-sugar around Dan's heart. 'Morning, Chef,' He ran a finger tenderly across the curve of her cheek. 'Tea or coffee, ma'am?'

'I'll get it.' She swung away from him but he grabbed her, held her down against the pillows.

'Oh no, this time I play chef. Just tell me what you'd like for breakfast. I'm a man who can find his way around any refrigerator.'

She giggled, struggling against him. 'All you'll find in mine is a couple of lemons and a bottle of champagne.'

'What, no muffins? No home-baked bread? No eggs or blueberry pancakes?'

His look of astonishment made her laugh. 'I know, you're wondering what kind of chef I am?' she said. 'The truth is I always grab a cup of coffee en route to the produce market.' She jerked bolt upright. 'My god,' she added, pushing him away and leaping from the bed. 'I'm supposed to be down there now, picking up the fruit and vegetables for tonight.'

Dan heaved a loud sigh, as she dashed into the bathroom and turned on the shower. It was back to business again, back to the café. Her life. Her world. 'You mean you're going to send me out coffeeless, into the cold, cold morning?' He leaned, naked, against the bathroom door.

''Fraid so. 'She peeked at him from the shower, admiring the view. 'That's life, Mr Cassidy, as they say.'

For a second, he contemplated joining her in the shower, but she'd already switched moods and he could feel her mind was on the day in front of her. He threw her a towel as she stepped from the shower. Wrapping it around her, she scooted past him.

'It's all yours,' she called, as though he were a college roommate sharing the only bath. But Dan saw the laughter lurking in her eyes. He caught her arm, pulled her back and kissed her firmly.

'What was that all about?' She was laughing as she stepped away from him. He thought it was worth anything, even being thrown out in the early morning without coffee, just to hear her laugh again.

Ten minutes later, they were both showered, dressed and out on the street. 'Careful, the neighbours,' she warned, smiling, as his mouth covered hers again. 'Talk to you later.'

Eyes narrowed, he watched her back the Cherokee out of the garage. He gritted his teeth as she swung quickly left, until it almost touched the Explorer.

She leaned from the window, laughing at him. 'Nerves of steel, Cassidy, that's what you've got.' Then with a casual wave, she shot off like a rocket down the hill.

He was smiling as he drove along Main, looking for Starbucks. Hot coffee and a good woman were all a man needed, he decided. Or should it be the other way around. Either way, he was winning.

The dream had not gone away. It returned that night, when she was alone again, and the night after that, and the next. Somehow, she coped with it better, though. Now, when she woke, sweating and trembling, she imagined Dan was with her, felt his strong masculine presence in her room, in the darkness. She knew all she had to do was pick up the phone, but he'd called her every night since they'd made love, and she hated to wake him this late, with her fears.

Lack of sleep was taking its toll though, and she didn't know what to do about it, except to keep ploughing on. Work and more work was all that counted. And the fact that, soon, she would see Dan again.

59

The café was busy that evening, and that suited Ellie just fine. The more work she had to do, the less time she had to think, and maybe tonight she would finally sleep.

The doorbell announced new arrivals and she gathered up her menus and went to greet them. They were regulars and the routine was easy. She brought them red wine and a basket of her warm crusty bread, then suggested the night's specials: crab spring rolls with ginger and fresh mango chutney, and rack of Sonoma lamb.

Watching her, Maya thought Ellie was doing okay, though she had the sense not to keep on asking. After all, what else was Ellie going to reply except, 'Sure, I'm fine?'

She rubbed her aching jaw anxiously, her wisdom tooth was acting up again, she was sure it was impacted, the pain was getting really bad.

'If you don't want a face like a full moon, you'd better get yourself to the dentist tomorrow,' Ellie advised in passing.

'Dentists terrify me, all that whining machinery and needles, and the steel probe they tap on the crater in your molar, asking does that hurt? *"Oh no, Mr Dentist, only when I scream."* I admit I'm a coward,' she added, following Ellie into the kitchen.

'Okay, so be a coward and lose your looks.'

Maya knew she was right. 'I'll go tomorrow, first thing,' she agreed, finally.

'Take the day off, you'll need it. Make that two days. I'll get Jake to pinch hit for you. If you can still speak, call me afterwards.'

'Sadist.'

'Don't worry, I'll be round later, with chicken soup and champagne, though of course, you'll have to drink them both through a straw.'

Ellie glanced round her domain. The kitchen smelled great tonight. Chan was just removing a couple of racks of lamb from the oven, ready to be served with rosemary roast potatoes and tiny green *lentils de Puy*, cooked in the juices and stock. A couple of Ellie's pear *tartes tatins* waited on the butcher's rack, and Terry was stirring a pan of vanilla *crème anglaise*.

Everything was under control and she breathed a pleased sigh of relief. With a full house, all she needed was trouble in the kitchen.

It was close to midnight when the last couple left and she finally latched the door and turned the sign to *Closed*. She looked at Maya, sprawled in a chair, holding her aching face in her hands. 'Go home,' she said, 'you look terrible.'

'Thanks, I appreciate that remark.' Maya looked sorry for herself. 'But maybe I will go, if you think you can manage without me?'

Ellie handed her her jacket and purse. 'You're going to be so happy to see that dentist tomorrow, you won't believe it.'

The phone was ringing and she pushed Maya out the door and picked it up. 'Ellie's Place.'

'I thought I'd give you a call, see if you were still slaving.'

Her heart lifted at the sound of Dan's voice. 'I'm still slaving. How about you?'

'I'm leaving for Napa tomorrow, early. Carlos and I are going to inspect a few vineyards, see what we can learn, maybe buy some rootstock for the north slopes. I'll be back in a couple of days, though. I thought I'd come down and visit you?'

Ellie closed her eyes, imagining him in her little house, and how it would change the dark mood, the long, crawling sorrowful hours of the night, the grey dawns, filled with guilt. 'I'd like that.'

'Good. Are you going home now?'

'Soon,' she glanced at her watch. 'Don't worry, I'm okay.'

'Promise me?'

'I promise.'

'I'll call you from Napa.'

'Okay.'

'So, take care, Ellie . . .'

'You too, Dan.' She almost said *love you* as she rang off, but caught herself just in time.

Feeling better, she busied herself with the routine chores; putting the day's receipts in the safe; whisking cloths off tables, tidying the counter and cleaning out the coffee machine. It was close to two o'clock and the fog was rolling in again when she finally left.

Only a single car drove past as Ellie sprinted down the misty street. The four-storey parking lot was shadowy and silent, and she found herself wishing nervously that she'd taken her car out earlier and put it on a meter near the café.

Her footsteps rang in the silence as she hurried into the elevator, and pressed the button for Three, staring down at the floor to avoid reading the graffiti. It jolted to a stop and she stepped forward, waiting for the doors to open. Nothing happened. She glanced at the indicator. It was stuck between Two and Three.

She jiggled the button, panicked at the idea of being stuck, alone, at night. The elevator still didn't move. Frantic, she pressed every button, sighing with relief when it finally jolted slowly upward again. Only this time it went right past the third floor.

'Stupid thing,' she muttered anxiously. When it stopped at Four, she shot out and ran to the heavy steel door leading to the stairs. She wasn't going to take a chance on the elevator again, she would walk down one flight.

She heard a noise behind her. She hesitated, her hand on the doorknob. There it was again. Only now it sounded like footsteps. Fear rushed hotly up her spine and she turned and fled down the stairs. She emerged, breathless and panicked, on the third floor, frantically searching the bottom of her bag for her keys. *Where were they? Her car was all the way over on the other side. He must be looking for her. There wasn't enough time to get there, find her key, start up the car and get out*. The elevator door was open, she jumped in and pressed the button for the ground floor.

She sagged against the wall as it began to descend, her heart pounding. She must get out of the carpark, run the half block to Main, get help. She would be safe, out there . . .

It stopped again, on Two.

'Oh god, oh god. This can't be happening.' Clutching a hand to her mouth, terrified, she told herself that whoever it was couldn't possibly *know* it was her in the elevator. Maybe he would think it was someone else coming to pick up their car? Maybe there *really was* someone else coming to pick up their car . . .

Crouching against the scarred steel wall, she strained her ears, but all she heard was the pounding of her own heart. She tried to remember the lessons she'd taken on how to protect herself in a mugging. 'Don't panic,' she told herself, taking a deep breath, 'it's the worst thing you can do.'

The elevator began to descend again. Breathing a shaky sigh of relief, she took an eager step forward as the doors slid open.

He was waiting for her, masked, his arms outspread, holding back the doors. The knife in his hand glinted icily under the white fluorescent light.

For a breathless second, her eyes met his. Then she flung her purse at his feet. 'Take it, please, just take it. I don't know who you are, I won't say anything. Just let me go.'

Her usually deep soft voice was shrill with fear, and Buck smiled. 'It's not your money I want, Ellie,' he whispered.

And then he grabbed her.

She could smell his sweat, feel his breath on her face, his powerful arms gripped her closer.

'*Bastard*.' Adrenalin and anger suddenly gave her a crazy strength. Twisting round she slammed her elbows into his chest. His grip loosened and she swung round again, kicking, aiming for the knees, the groin. He reached for her and she raked her nails over the face in the mask. She was strong with anger, spitting, scratching, biting.

Buck was sweating with the effort. Grabbing her ponytail,

he yanked it back, hard. Ellie yelped as he dragged her to the floor.

He was kneeling over her, pinning her arms down. She stared up at him, frozen with terror, saw his bunched fist coming at her: then a terrible pain. Her eyes rolled back in her head and she was unconscious.

Winded, Buck scooped her in his arms. He grabbed her purse, pressed the up button and exited on the fourth floor. The BMW was the only car there. He tossed her into the trunk, placed a pillow under her head, arranged her limbs neatly, then covered her with a blanket, and slammed down the lid.

In the driver's seat, he pulled off the mask, wiped the sweat from his brow and smoothed back his hair. Still breathing heavily, he drove down the ramp, out of the unmanned carpark, onto the empty street.

Phase Four was complete. He was home free, and Ellie was his. Until death did them part.

60

The following morning, a heavy marine layer hung, thick as Halloween cobwebs, over the Napa and Sonoma Valleys. Driving the rented Chevy past fog-shrouded acres of immaculate vineyards, Dan thought they might be in Bordeaux. Or, passing the magnificent *Domaine Carneros* chateau that was a copy of the Taittinger family's eighteenth-century *Chateau de la Marquetterie*, they could even be in champagne country. And everywhere were rows of young grapes: cossetted, watered, fed, stroked.

'All this for a bottle of wine,' he said to Carlos, impressed.

'Ah, but a good bottle, Señor.' Carlos was happy surrounded by vineyards, and he would have been even happier at harvest, when the heavy scent of ripe, freshly picked grapes hung in a winy haze over the countryside.

'Do not forget Señor, wine-making was always a peasant occupation,' he said. 'For centuries simple farmers made their own wine; they drank it every day.' Twirling his moustache thoughtfully, he added, 'And naturally, with my help, Señor Dan, you will have the best wine in Santa Barbara County.'

'This simple peasant farmer's betting on it.' Dan grinned, as Carlos continued a running commentary on the vineyards they were passing. This one was good but not great; that one had an off-season last year, a bad crop; this had improved its quality; and this one was experimenting with *sangiovese* grapes to make an Italian-style wine.

As he turned the Chevy into the gates of a winery noted for its superior cabernets, Dan glanced enviously at the immaculate rows of vines stretching into infinity; at the well-tended gardens and the famous sculpture park; the art gallery and the soaring redwood tasting rooms.

'One day,' he told himself, sipping the oaky richness of the wine, 'one day Running Horse will be like this.' He could picture it perfectly. The burgeoning vines, the gardens, the wine-tasting room. There was even a restaurant. Nothing pretentious, just a little French café, with a tall, red-haired young woman at the stove, baking her famous *tarte tatin*.

He wished suddenly he'd asked Ellie to come with him, it would have given her a break from the pressure and they could have been together. He should have suggested it last night, she'd sounded so tired, so unlike her former buoyant self. But it wasn't too late, he would call her when he got to the hotel and ask her to join him, they could stay an extra day or two and Carlos would go back to keep an eye on things.

He smiled, picturing them together amongst California's great vineyards and restaurants. Sipping a glass of Mondavi cabernet, he wished she were there already.

61

Maya was in bed that afternoon, propped up with pillows because, lying down, her face felt as though it had been hit by a ten-ton truck. Upright, it was only a five-ton impact. Hoping to take the pressure off, she wrapped a red bandana round her throbbing jaw and tied it on top of her head in a bow, then caught sight of herself in the mirror opposite. She groaned.

'So much for making me go to the dentist, Ellie Parrish Duveen,' she mumbled through rubber lips. *Now*, she had a face like a full moon and the pain was even worse. And she couldn't call Ellie on the phone to complain, because she couldn't even speak.

Anyhow, why hadn't Ellie called her? Some friend! She slid a couple of painkillers through her numb lips, then lay back, praying they would put her to sleep for a while so she couldn't feel anything. She guessed Ellie would call later.

62

At five-thirty that evening, Chan was in the kitchen, rattling pots and pans around, and grumbling to Terry. 'So where is everybody today? Ellie's not here, Maya's not here? How am I supposed to manage this place on my own?' He slammed the cleaver angrily into a lamb shank he was preparing for braising. 'Where the hell is everybody?'

Terry was used to his tantrums. 'Maya had her wisdom teeth out today. I guess Ellie's with her, she said something about chicken soup and champagne.'

'They are drinking champagne while I run the place for them?' Chan snorted angrily. 'Who's gonna serve, that's what I want to know?'

Terry removed the baked Idahos from the oven, wincing from the heat as he split them and began to scrape the fluffy potato into a large steel bowl to be mashed with pesto. 'Jake's coming in, for Maya.'

'And who's coming in for Ellie?'

'She'll be here later, I guess,' he said, intent on perfecting what he was doing.

Chan chopped his lamb shanks viciously. Suddenly, he wiped a tear from his eye. 'Poor Ellie,' he muttered. 'Such a tragedy, terrible, terrible. So I run the cafe for a night, so what?'

Jake bounced cheerfully through the kitchen door. 'Evening, guys.' He hung his jacket on the rack and tied on his white waiter's apron. 'What's doin?'

'Ellie's not here.' Chan was in charge now. He arranged the lamb shanks in a roasting pan, sprinkled them with chopped garlic, fresh rosemary and thyme, then put them in the hot oven for ten minutes to brown the marrow bones. 'You got a friend who could help out?'

Jake looked surprised. Ellie was always here, rain or shine. 'Sure. What's wrong, is she sick?'

'I guess it's her grandmother,' Chan shrugged. 'Sometimes it must get to her. Sometimes, she can't cope, that's all.'

Jake nodded, already on the phone to his friend. He'd seen Ellie bending under the strain.

'Maybe she'll call,' Chan said, flinging chopped tomatoes into a hot pan and watching them sizzle. 'Later.'

63

There was a white-hot light flickering inside Ellie's head. She groaned, twisting from side to side, trying to escape it, longing for the darkness of oblivion. The pain throbbed behind her eyes, it pressed loudly against her ears, nibbled with sharp little rat's teeth at her brain. Slowly, the light faded to a pallid uneven grey as she swam back to consciousness.

She was lying on a soft bed, staring up at a wood-planked ceiling. The pillow beneath her head was white satin, the coverlet white lace, threaded with pink ribbon. There were fluffy white rugs on the floor, a dressing-table with a flounced lace skirt and swags of pink ribbons; a pair of white satin mules, trimmed with marabou, waiting by the side of the bed for her to slip her feet into them.

She wondered if she had died and this was a motel in hell. Then she caught sight of her swollen face and blackened eyes in the dresser mirror. And she remembered.

Trembling, she swung her legs over the side of the bed and stood up. She was still fully dressed in her black jeans and white Ellie's Place t-shirt, but her boots and jacket were gone. She stared round. The room was panelled in dark wood, oppressive, like a coffin. She looked for a window. *It was boarded up.* She darted to the door. *There was no handle.* She ran like a scared rabbit into the tiny adjoining bathroom. *There was no window, and no exit.* Back in the bedroom, she tugged at the wooden planks covering the window, but they were solidly nailed on. She put her eye to a crack. She could see nothing.

Her breath came in a long shaky sigh. She had no idea whether it was day or night. No idea where she was. No idea who it was holding her captive.

Panicked, she took in the details. There was no TV, no radio, no telephone. The latest magazines were lined up on the night table, but no newspapers. There was a bottle of Evian, a plastic glass, a Powerbar, and a blue bowl with Fuji apples.

Sliding open the closet door, she stared at the collection of clothes. Dresses, sweaters, jeans, lacy nighties, shoes. She checked the labels. *They were all her size.* She ran to the dresser, yanked open the drawer, stared, horrified, at the sexy underwear. Looking up, she saw the bottle of *Eau d'Issey* on top of the dresser. *Her perfume.* The Bobbi Brown lipstick in Nude, *her colour.* On the bathroom shelf she found her favourite bath oil, her lotion, her powder . . .

He knew every intimate thing about her. He must have stalked her, been in her home, gone through her closets, her drawers, her personal things. He'd touched her life with his filthy hands. And he'd created this fluffy travesty of a romantic rendezvous specially for her.

Her knees buckled and she sank onto the pink velvet boudoir chair, staring at her own terrified face in the mirror. 'Oh, God,' she whispered, as realization overwhelmed her, 'Oh God, please get me out of this.'

64

Dan and Carlos were in a small hotel, whose cute decorative theme was grapes. They were stencilled on the furniture, rampaged across sofas, and tiled the bathroom walls. Dan thought a guy could get drunk, just looking at them.

It was seven before he got a chance to phone Ellie at the café. He knew it was her busy time, but he just had to hear her voice, tell her he missed her, and that he'd call again later.

'Ellie's Place.'

His brows lifted in surprise at the sound of a man's voice. 'Is Ellie there?'

'She hasn't come in yet. This is Jake, can I help you?'

'Hi, Jake. Do you know where she is?'

'I guess she's with Maya. She had her wisdom teeth extracted today, Ellie's probably doing the visiting angel bit.'

Dan grinned, 'Okay thanks. I'll call her again later.'

He was still smiling, thinking about her, as they left for a restaurant called *Terra*, and a dinner he knew she would have enjoyed.

He called the café again at ten, but Ellie hadn't been in, and she still hadn't called to say where she was. He asked for Maya's number, then dialled it, drumming his fingers impatiently on the table, waiting for her to pick up.

'Hi, you've reached me, but I can't speak to you right now,' Maya's voice said on the answering machine. 'Leave me a message though.' There was a snatch of heavy metal music, then the tone.

Frustrated, Dan cut off, then dialled Ellie's home number. She didn't answer. He shrugged, she was probably still with Maya, and Maya wasn't answering because she couldn't talk. He'd try her again later, at home. Switching on the TV, he clicked through the channels.

At eleven he tried her number again, and again at midnight. There was still no answer. Hands thrust into his pockets, he paced the hotel bedroom, counting the grapes on the patterned carpet. Where the hell was she?

He called again at one. Then two.

He didn't sleep that night.

65

Ellie seemed to have been sitting in that hellish room, in the rose-shaded lamplight and brittle silence, for hours. Her head throbbed, her eyes burned, and her ears buzzed with the strain of listening for him.

She heard the key in the lock and her heart seemed to shrivel, then stop. The door creaked slowly open.

Frozen, she stared at her abductor, reflected in the mirror. He was still wearing the ski-mask. He walked toward her, reached out, touched her arm. She shrank back, her flesh crawling, eyes wide with terror.

Buck ran his fingers gently along the soft, creamy skin he had so often dreamed of touching. 'I'm glad to see you're feeling better, Ellie,' he said, in a rough, low whisper. 'I apologize for having to hit you but you left me no option. I assure you, I would have preferred it if you came quietly.'

His whispered voice triggered a memory somewhere in the caverns of Ellie's panicked mind, yet she couldn't place it.

'My dear Ellie,' he went on silkily, 'I've brought you to this lovely place because I want you to be happy. Can't you see how nice I've made it for you?' He didn't want to frighten her with his passion, he'd give her a couple of days to adjust and get used to him.

Walking to the closet he flung back the door, 'Look at the pretty dresses, all in your size, and I hope, your taste. As you can see, I've thought of everything. But if there is anything else you need, all you have to do is tell me, and it's yours.'

She stared numbly up at him, and he added, gently, 'I have

our life together all planned, Ellie. You will want for nothing. You'll live like a princess.'

His hand trembled with desire as he touched her arm again, but he controlled himself and strode back to the door. He turned, looked at her. 'All I want is for you to be happy,' he whispered. '*Here, with me.*'

But it wasn't all he wanted. He thought pleasurably of the time she would have to die. When he had had his fill of her, then he would have to do it. Because his revenge must be complete, and he must take his reward. Journey's End, and all it meant to him.

Ellie ran after him; stuck her nails in the crack in the door, trying to prise it open, but it was locked. Panicked, she swung round, palms flattened against it.

He was insane. She'd read about people like this, obsessives who stalked their human prey like animals. They thought they belonged to them, that their own sick lives were intertwined with their victim's.

Closing her eyes, she conjured up Dan's strong face. His blue eyes were looking into hers, smiling in that mocking kind of way they always did when she did something crazy. *That was it! Dan was a cop, he would know what to do. Dan would find her.*

She sank into the pink chair, holding his image close to her. Minutes passed. Then there was the sound of the key in the lock again. Her eyes flew open.

Buck wheeled in the room service cart, complete with white linen cloth and a white rose in a silver bud-vase. He arranged a chair for her.

'Tortilla soup,' he said, wafting off the silver dome covering the food. 'Olive bread, the kind you like. Cold roast chicken, with a green salad. And a bottle of your favourite wine.'

He took a corkscrew from his pocket, opened the wine, then poured a little into the glass for her to taste. 'Madame?' he stepped back with a courtly little bow. She said nothing and he sighed as he walked back to the door.

'Please enjoy it, Ellie,' he said in that low rough whisper.

'Believe me, I mean you no harm. All I want is for us to be together.'

She stared sullenly at him and he gritted his teeth, angrily, reminding himself it would take time. In a couple of days, she would come round. Didn't they say women always fell in love with their captors? He locked the door securely behind him.

The finality of the key turning in the lock chilled Ellie's blood. She was his prisoner and he meant to keep her that way. For ever. He'd just said so. It was him and her, together.

She had to get out of here.

She ran to the table, picked up the knife. It was sterling, from Cristophle. The wine goblet was Baccarat, the plates Limoges. The food was exactly what she liked, and the wine, *Chateau de Peyrelle*, a favourite.

Hunger gnawed incongruously at her stomach. She had no idea of how much time had passed since she was abducted, no idea how long it had been since she had eaten, but suddenly she was starving.

She took a piece of bread, held it to her mouth. *Maybe he was a poisoner? Or the food was drugged, so he could rape her more easily?* Dropping the bread, she backed away. Her knees buckled and she sank into the pink chair again. She put her head in her hands, and tears trickled through her fingers. '*Oh Dan,*' she whispered, '*please, please help me. Please find me.*'

But then she remembered, Dan was a homicide cop. What he found were bodies.

66

Time ticked slowly past. Each minute seemed like an hour, each second an eternity as Ellie waited for him to return. She washed her face and looked longingly at the shower, but didn't dare take off her clothes in case he came back. Naked, she would be even more vulnerable. Besides, he might be spying on her. The idea sent a shiver through her and she stared apprehensively at the ceiling, looking for hidden cameras.

Sitting in the pink chair again, she wondered if Maya had discovered she was missing. But then she remembered, Maya had gone to the dentist; she wouldn't be back for a couple of days. And Dan was in Napa with Carlos. But surely Chan would try to call her at home, say, hey, where are you? What's going on? She shook her head. She doubted it. Chan knew she was wrecked, and he'd been going out of his way not to upset her. Tears spurted from her eyes.

Nobody would even have missed her yet. Nobody was looking for her. She was on her own.

She must have dozed off because the sound of the key in the lock woke her. Her swollen eyes flew open and she jerked upright in the pink chair, watching warily. He was standing in the doorway. Immediately behind him she could see a small hallway with a naked lightbulb dangling overhead. She wondered if it were night time.

Buck's mouth tightened angrily behind the mask; she hadn't even tasted the wine he'd bought specially. Without a word, he wheeled the cart back to the door and locked it behind him.

She had to get out of here. Panicked, Ellie ran and peered through the crack, but she couldn't see anything. She lay flat on the floor, and pressed her face into the thick pile carpet, peeking through the tiny gap under the door, but all she could see was a thin sliver of light.

She flung herself onto the fluffy satin and lace bed, staring helplessly up at the ceiling, remembering how strong he was. He was big, powerful, vicious, and she was no match for him. Her heart sank like a stone. There was no escape.

67

Dan was on the phone to Ellie at six the next morning, then again at seven. 'It's no good,' he said to Carlos, 'I have to get back.'

Carlos knew a worried man when he saw one, and he also knew a man in love. 'Don't worry, Señor,' he said, as they sped back to San Francisco and the airport, 'everything's gonna be all right. Trust me.'

Dan wished trusting Carlos was all it took, but he had the uneasy feeling that something was terribly wrong.

Three hours later, they were back at Running Horse Ranch. The red light flickered on the answering machine in the office. Praying it was her, Dan punched the playback button.

'This is Chan from Ellie's Place. Do you know where she is, because I cannot open the cafe again tonight, by myself? I need to hear from her. Please call me.'

'Where the hell could she have gone?'

Carlos' brow furrowed as he thought. 'She loved the grandmother. She is disturbed, unhappy, grieving. She would maybe go back to Journey's End?'

'Why didn't I think of that?' Dan was already searching in the drawer for the key Ellie had left there.

The ornate iron gates were shut, but Dan told himself it meant nothing; Ellie might easily have closed them behind her for security.

Already, weeds were sprouting in the gravel driveway, the lawns looked overgrown and shaggy, and the beautiful dolphin fountain was silent. The windows glinted dully in the weak sunlight, and the front steps were littered with leaves. Journey's

End looked cold, empty, forbidding. And Ellie's Cherokee was not there.

Dan ran up the steps and pressed the bell. He could hear it ringing loudly inside, but somehow, he knew no one would answer. Hurrying round the corner, he unlocked the kitchen door and went in. Everything was neat and in place. There were no dishes in the sink, no half-empty mug of tea on the counter.

Their footsteps rang hollowly on the stone floor as they strode into the hall. Everything looked the same, and yet it didn't. The house felt as dead as a long-closed museum.

'Ellie?' His voice rang loudly in the silence. 'Ellie? Are you here?' Taking the steps two at a time, he flung open the door to Miss Lottie's room.

Violence still hung heavily in the air, like a sinister presence. The room had been cleaned but brownish bloodstains showed faintly on the pale green Aubusson rug. Down the hall, he could hear Carlos opening and shutting doors, calling her name. He shook his head, he knew it was futile. Ellie would not have come here.

There was only one other place she could be. At home.

Traffic flowed easily on the freeway and an hour later, he exited at Las Virgines, and made a right onto Malibu Canyon. He got lucky, the road was virtually empty, and soon he was driving down PCH to Santa Monica. He called Chan on the carphone, just to check.

'She's not here,' Chan said, sounding desperate. 'Tonight, we cope, but not tomorrow. Maybe tomorrow, I quit.'

'Don't quit,' Dan said determinedly, as he turned into Ellie's street, 'she'll be there.'

A couple of little kids were kicking a red ball around in the garden of the house next door. The street looked quiet, normal, an everyday scene. In a second, he was pressing the bell, hammering his fist on the door. The dead silence was ominous. Taking a step back, he gazed up at the bedroom window. 'Ellie', he yelled.

The kids next door stopped their playing and came and hung over the fence.

'Nobody's there,' the tow-headed boy said.

'Have you seen Ellie today?'

'No, sir. She hasn't been round for a while. Usually we see her and she gives us cookies. Mom said she shouldn't do it, but she said she can't resist.'

Dan grinned, that sounded like Ellie. Then reality took over again. 'Thanks, guys,' he said, already back in the car.

The phone was ringing. Pressing the TV mute button, Maya searched for it under the litter of Kleenex and magazines, her eyes still on Fred and Ginger, foxtrotting in white tie and tails and applegreen chiffon, in *You Were Never Lovelier*.

She picked it up. 'I'm in pain. Who is it?'

'Maya, it's Dan Cassidy.'

She grinned, surprised. 'Well, well, the rancher who managed to get Ellie off the straight and *very* narrow. I guess she's with you, waiting to apologize. She was meant to be here, with chicken soup and champagne. Some friend, huh? Deserting me in my hour of need.'

'Maya, no one has seen Ellie in two days. I was hoping she was with you.'

Maya switched off the TV. There was a sinking feeling in the pit of her stomach. 'You're kidding.'

'I wish I were.'

'But I haven't seen Ellie since the night before last. I left her at the café.' Maya could see her now, handing her her jacket and pushing her out the door, then turning to pick up the phone. There was a catch in her voice as she said, 'Oh, Dan, where can she be?'

She could tell from his answer, he wished he knew. 'Take it easy,' he said, 'she's okay, I'm sure of it. We'll find her. I'm on my way to the police now.'

'Call me,' she said desperately. 'Tell me what's happening.'

'I will.'

He rang off and Maya stared at the blank TV screen. Ellie and she were like twin sisters, she knew what Ellie was thinking almost before she knew it herself. And in her heart she knew that Ellie was in trouble.

68

Detective Mike Farrell of the Santa Monica Police Department, was a humourless, methodical man who believed every question had a logical answer, if you were smart enough to find it. He had thinning dark hair and a waxy complexion that spoke of too many doughnuts and late nights.

'People go missing every day in California,' he said, twisting a ballpoint pen endlessly through his stubby fingers.

Dan nodded. 'But how many of them have had their grandmother murdered, only weeks before?'

Farrell sat up straight, ballpoint poised over the worksheet. 'You dating her?'

'We saw each other. But Ellie worked hard, she was at the café six nights a week.'

'So you saw her on the seventh, the day God said all men should rest.'

With an effort, Dan kept his temper in check. 'I saw her on Mondays.'

Farrell scribbled the information on the sheet.

'She datin' anyone else? Maybe you didn't know about?'

'No.'

Farrell grinned. 'That's what they all say.'

'Jesus Christ, man.' Dan banged his fist angrily on the table between them, 'A woman has disappeared. Her grandmother was murdered three weeks ago. This is no ordinary missing person.'

Farrell pushed back his chair, looking steadily at him. 'Did you ever think of this scenario?' he said, in his slow southern drawl, 'Maybe the grandmother's death, combined with hard

303

work and responsibility has been too much for her? Maybe she's just cracked, walked away from it all? It's been known to happen.'

Dan thought about that steely core of self-reliance that fuelled Ellie's ambitions; the resilience that got her through the long hard days; the courage that had made her pick up her life and go back to work, instead of languishing at Running Horse. 'She's not a quitter.'

Farrell nodded, satisfied. 'Then we'd better get out there and look for her.'

69

Detective Farrell weaved the unmarked black Ford through the clogged Santa Monica traffic, then turned up the hill to Ellie's house. There were no kids playing outside this time and the street was quiet. A squad car pulled in behind him as he and Dan got out and walked up the little brick path and pressed the bell. It rang with the same hollow sound as at Journey's End.

Farrell had the search warrant in his pocket and he motioned to the waiting officer to break the lock. They fanned out on the ground floor as Dan ran up the creaking stairs.

Ellie's room was neat. The bed was made up, and her favourite old pink chenille robe, the one she'd put on after they had made love and that clashed with her hair, was flung across the chair by the window. In the bathroom, the t-shirt she had slept in was in the laundry hamper. The towels hanging on the rail were dry and so was her toothbrush. There were no droplets of water in the sink and the soap had not been used. Ellie had not been home recently.

The 'Closed' sign was up at Ellie's Place and a squad car was parked outside, lights flashing. Chan, Terry, Jake and the kid were sitting round a table with Farrell, while a couple of police officers stood by. A lamp shone on the green-checkered tablecloth, and Dan was leaning against the wall in the shadows, arms folded, listening while each said what they knew. It wasn't much.

'I saw her Friday night,' Chan repeated one more time. 'Here, at the cafe. It was very busy, people stayed late. I cooked the last meal at eleven, then I left.'

'I finished up a half hour later,' Terry said. 'Then I ate dinner in the kitchen. I left after midnight, when the last couple finally went home.'

Jake was almost enjoying the scene, it might have been a TV movie of the week, even the lighting was good. 'I wasn't there Friday,' he said, 'I only come to help out occasionally, when they need me.'

The kid ran his hands nervously through his tousled blond mane, thinking of the joint in his pocket. He hadn't bargained on the cops. 'Then I finished the cleaning up. I left when Maya did.'

'Maya?' Farrell looked questioningly at Dan.

'Ellie's friend, she works as a waitress here.'

'Maya had a bad toothache that night.' Terry explained. 'Usually she stayed to help Ellie tidy up.'

'That's right.' The kid remembered. 'I heard Ellie tell her to go home, and then the doorbell chime as she left. I was just on my way out the kitchen door myself.'

Farrell fixed his bland gaze on the kid. 'Then you were the last person to see Ellie that night.'

The kid swallowed hard, red in the face with panic. 'Jeez, I never thought of that. I don't know, maybe somebody else came in . . .'

'Where did you go, when you left the cafe?'

'To Victor's, a club on Abbot Kinney.'

'They know you there?'

'Oh, sure, I go there all the time.' He was sweating now.

'Then someone will have seen you, maybe know exactly what time you were there?'

'Sure, oh, sure . . .' He surely hoped so.

Someone was hammering on the door, and Farrell swung round, staring at the woman peering through the glass.

'It's Maya.' Terry got up and unlocked the door for her.

Maya practically fell inside, she was in such a hurry. Her face was still swollen and her eyes were red from crying. She was un-made-up and dishevelled, in black tights, boots and an oversized brown sweater. Her short uncombed hair stuck up like fluffy golden chicken feathers.

She grasped Detective Farrell urgently by the shoulder, 'Have you found her yet?'

'No, miss, not yet.' He looked her up and down, assessing her. 'You are Maya Morris?'

'And who are you?' Maya was impatient, imperious, scared.

Dan took her arm. 'Maya, this is Detective Farrell. He's going to help us look for Ellie.'

She stared at him, then suddenly her face crumpled and she sank into a chair, her hands over her eyes. 'Oh god, where is she? I shouldn't have left her here, alone. It was late, I should have stayed with her . . .'

Dan rested his hand comfortingly on her soft blonde hair, 'Do you know where Ellie usually parked her car?'

She lifted her head, looked blearily at him. 'In the multi-storey lot, a couple of blocks away. I told her she shouldn't, it was too lonely there at night, but there's only two parking slots out back and she said they were for the chef and the help. Usually, if it got too late, she'd get the car out and put it on a meter, right here on the street. But she hadn't . . . that night . . .'

70

Dan felt like a rookie cop again, driving in the detective's Ford to the parking lot. It was still early, only eight o'clock and the lot was almost full. People turned their heads to look as the two squad cars squealed to a stop and cops piled out.

Farrell told his men, 'We're looking for a recent model green Cherokee, licence number 3CVB28. You can't miss it.'

They didn't. It was there on the third floor, locked and empty, just the way she had left it on Friday. Dan knew then they were in serious trouble.

He had to give Farrell credit, though, he moved fast after that. In minutes, there were cops all over the place, intercepting owners coming to collect their cars, questioning them about who they were, whether they used the lot regularly, had they been here on Friday night? Dan knew the value of the hard slog of police detective work. Disheartened, he left them to it and went and checked into Loews Hotel in Santa Monica.

In the bar, he ordered single malt scotch, then sat sipping it, gazing at the television screen, oblivious to the other customers. The Lakers were playing but he couldn't summon up any interest. His mind and his heart were on Ellie, as he went over the scenario again. Over, and over.

The good whisky warmed his stomach, but he felt powerless, wondering what to do next. When the Lakers game finished, the ten o'clock news came on.

'*News just breaking of a well-known Santa Monica café owner's disappearance*,' the newsreader said. '*Ellie Parrish Duveen, whose grandmother was brutally murdered at her Montecito home, just weeks ago, has not been seen in more than two days. Police are out searching for her now and foul play is considered a possibility.'*

Dan's stomach clenched as Ellie's smiling face appeared on the screen, and the announcer described her, then said the police were asking for the public's cooperation. Anyone who had seen her, or knew her whereabouts, should contact the Santa Monica Police at the following number . . .

Dan drained the whisky. He paid the check, went to his room, and got Piatowsky on the phone.

'So, what's new?'

Piatowsky was bored, it was a slow night at the eleventh precinct.

'Ellie's missing. I believe she's been abducted.' Dan filled him in quickly on the details.

Piatowsky had never heard him sound like that; bitter, desperate. He thought of Ellie, imagined if it were Angie, or one of his kids . . . how he would feel.

'You think it's the same guy?'

'Possibly.'

'I'm getting the red-eye outta here, I'll be with you tomorrow early.' He hesitated, 'Dan . . .'

'Yeah?'

'It's not looking good . . .'

Dan's heart was falling like a stack of cards into the pit of his stomach. He knew the truth when he heard it.

'Just hang in there Cassidy.'

Dan put down the phone. He would hang in because he had to. He had to find Ellie.

71

It must have been morning when he came to visit again, because this time he brought breakfast.

He smoothed the white cloth, arranged the chair for her. 'There's juice, granola, low fat milk, wholewheat toast, butter, and blueberry preserves. Fresh coffee is in the thermos jug.' He looked at her. 'Please, enjoy it, Ellie,' he said quietly. Then he left her alone again.

The smell of coffee and toast taunted her. She wanted it so badly, she could almost taste it. Getting up, she opened the bottle of Evian and took a long drink, then she ate the Powerbar in three ferocious gulps, like a child with stolen candy.

Feeling stronger, she did a few Yoga stretches, then sat in the pink chair, waiting.

He was back a while later to remove the cart with the uneaten food. Ellie watched him through hooded eyes, but this time he didn't look at her, didn't speak.

She lay on the bed, counting off the minutes, trying to figure out what to do. Her head still throbbed and she got up and looked in the mirror. Her hair was a wild tangle, her eyes blackened, her jaw a swollen blur of purple-yellow bruises. She washed her face, found the Clinique moisturiser she always used in the cabinet, and smoothed it on. She brushed her teeth, rinsed her mouth, and dragged a comb through her tangled hair. She longed for a shower and fresh clothing but balked at the idea of putting on the sexy lace underwear he'd bought.

She was sitting in the pink chair, as usual when he returned with the room service cart and dinner. At least now, she knew approximately what time of day it was.

He removed the silver dome, then turned his masked face to her. 'Chicken soup, Ellie,' he said in that throaty whisper. I thought you might find it soothing. Some French bread, a green salad. A little wine.'

He waved his hand at the table, showing her the good food, the fresh rose in the silver vase, the fine linen, the crystal and porcelain, and the beautiful sterling flatware. 'Please enjoy it, Ellie,' he said again, sounding sincere.

Ellie thought his voice sounded cultured, educated. She remembered her grandmother's golden rules for life: good manners, consideration for others, unselfish behaviour. There was no way she could fight him, but maybe she could play a psychological game with him. Act nice, try to talk her way out.

'Thank you,' she said quietly. 'You're very thoughtful. The soup looks good.'

Buck's eyes narrowed, then he smiled. He had outsmarted psychiatrists for a couple of decades; reading Ellie was easy.

'I advise you to eat it, you'll need your strength.' Taking out the corkscrew, he began to open the wine.

'Why are you treating me so well?'

He glanced up. 'Why do you think?'

She didn't want to think about the answer to that. 'But you hit me, you hurt me.'

'I told you, I had no choice, you wouldn't come quietly.'

'How could you expect me to.' She was struggling to keep the tremor from her voice. 'I don't know you, I can't even see your face.'

'You will, when the time is right. For now, I suggest you eat the food.'

Her eyes followed him to the door. He did not turn round. '*Who are you?*' She was desperate, frantic. *She had to know*.

He turned, smiled at her behind the mask. 'I'm your friend, Ellie,' he said. Then he locked the door again.

She couldn't take it any longer, she just couldn't take it. She was on her feet, banging her fists against the door, howling with rage and fear.

Listening to her, Buck heaved a pleased sigh. It was a small revenge, but nonetheless sweet. He had locked Ellie in a cage, exactly the way he had been locked up by her grandmother. Now it was her turn to beat the walls, her turn to howl. This time, *he* was the jailer.

Drained, Ellie sank back into the chair. She stared at the food displayed appetizingly in front of her. She was weak and starving, and no longer cared if it was poisoned. Her hand shook as she lifted the glass, took a sip of wine, then a piece of bread. It stuck in her dry throat, choking her. She drank a little more wine, forced down a little of the chicken soup, another piece of the bread. Then she lay back on the bed and waited to see if she were going to die.

Another hour dragged by. She prowled the room restlessly. He should have been back by now, checking on her. Had she been here two days? Or three? Surely Maya must have missed her by now. Dan would be home, he'd be calling her. And Chan couldn't run the restaurant on his own, he'd be frantic, trying to contact her . . .

Angered at her own helplessness, she snatched up the Baccarat goblet and hurled it at the wall. It shattered loudly into a hundred pieces. She hurled the Limoges plates after it, then ran to the closet, grabbed the clothes and flung them to the floor. She tugged an armload of sexy lingerie from the dresser and threw it on top of the clothes, and stomped on them. Then, inspired with rage, she grabbed the bottle of red wine and emptied it over the white satin and lace bed.

She stared, wild-eyed at the spreading red stain. *It was her dream come true, the blood seeping through the bed, engulfing her* . . . She began to scream, thin high-pitched screams of fear and anguish, and helplessness.

Buck came running. He looked at the broken dishes, the spilled wine, the ruined bed, all the pretty things he had bought specially to please her. The guards in the Hudson Sanitarium would have recognized the icy expression in his eyes, the dead chill in his voice, the involuntary flexing of his strong fingers.

He circled the bed toward her. Ellie took a quick step back, her eyes fixed warily on him. He came closer. Another step and her back was against the wall, there was nowhere else to go. He was so close she was breathing his minty breath.

His hands were on her breasts, his body thrusting against hers. She felt him tremble, felt his excitement. *'No,'* she was pinned against the wall, twisting her face away, *'no, no, no . . .'*

Behind him, she saw a crack of light; he had left the door open. The sudden glimpse of freedom gave her a crazy strength and she slid down through his arms, grabbed his legs and pulled. He crashed down next to her. Scrambling to her feet, she made a dash for the door. He caught her arm, dragged her back.

The beautiful Cristophle silver fork sparkled in the lamplight. In a flash it was in her hand. She felt the soft, sinking sensation as the fork went into his flesh, heard his great roar of pain. He staggered back, blood trickling from his eye socket. She was running.

'Little bitch,' he snarled, agonized, but even wounded, he was still fast. He grabbed her, slapped her hard across the face. Her head slammed back against the wall, but she didn't cry out this time. She just stood there, looking at him.

She was looking at him just the way her grandmother had. Loathing him, despising him. As though he were nothing.

He looked round for something to tie her up with. Jerking the lamp out of the wall socket, he bound her wrists behind her back with the flex. He stood looking at her for a minute, then he pulled the switchblade from his pocket.

Time stood still as Ellie stared at the cold steel that she expected would destroy her. But instead, he cut the flex from the lamp.

Breathing heavily, he slowly eased the mask over his bloody face.

For a long horrified second she stared at him. 'Ed Jensen,' she whispered, unbelievingly. 'But *why?'*

Without answering, he turned and walked from the room.

He'd left the door open and she stared blankly at the rectangle of white plaster wall that led to freedom. *Why him? Why? Who was he?*

He was back in seconds, with a length of cord. He tied her

ankles, then cut away the electrical wire and re-tied her wrists behind her back with the cord.

He looked at her, trussed like a helpless chicken. 'Oh, Ellie, Ellie, what a foolish woman you are,' he sighed. 'Don't you know you can't win?' Then he hefted her in his arms, carried her down the corridor into another room and flung her onto a sofa.

Her face was pressed into the cushions, but she could still hear him close by, panting with the effort. Then his footsteps disappearing.

Cautiously, she turned her face to the light.

She was in a log cabin. Through the window opposite, she could see a mountain range and a hazy grey sky. There were no other houses, no neighbours, no sound of children playing, no dogs barking. Only trees and silence. *She was somewhere in the mountains, somewhere nobody would ever find her. They wouldn't even find her body, because she was sure now, Ed Jensen was going to kill her.*

He was coming back, dragging something, huffing as he carried it into the room. She watched from the corner of her eye. It was a large wooden crate, the kind used by movers. He came over, picked her up, carried her across and dropped her into it.

Helpless, she folded up in the bottom like a broken doll, knees bent, arms twisted behind her back. Lifting her head, she stared up at his blood-stained face. Their eyes met. Then he fastened down the lid.

Ellie heard the hammer striking on the nails. Heard him walk across the floor. Then the slam of a heavy door. The click of the lock behind him. And then there was only darkness.

72

Dan was at the airport early, waiting for Piatowsky.

'Am I glad to see you,' he grabbed his bag.

Piatowsky thought he looked like a man who hadn't slept in two nights; rumpled, with a blue-stubbled jaw, his hair standing on end from the dozens of times he'd run his hands frantically through it.

'What's the score?'

'Zero to us.'

'Go over the whole story with me again,' he said as they crossed through the busy airport traffic to the carpark.

'There's not a lot to tell. She was last seen at the café Friday night, around 12.45. Alone. The café was not robbed, it was locked and all was in order. Her house had not been broken into, nothing was disturbed there.'

There was a catch in Dan's voice as he remembered her bedroom, and the pink robe that clashed with her red hair.

He manoeuvred the Explorer into the stream of traffic. 'Her car was in the four-storey parking lot, just where she'd left it. Also locked. Somewhere between the café and the carpark, she just disappeared into thin air.' He glanced grimly at Piatowsky. 'I'll bet the bastard knew where she worked, what her hours were, where she parked. He lay in wait for her, I know it.'

'There had to be a motive. How about rejection? Unrequited love? Are there any ex-boyfriends around? Anybody she gave the brush-off to who didn't take it kindly?'

'She never told me about anyone being crazy in love with her. She said she hadn't time for love – and that included me.'

Despite the circumstances, Piatowsky grinned. 'Okay, how about obsession?'

Dan threaded through the traffic on Century, honking impatiently at a driver who cut in front of him. 'I guess it's possible, but she works all the time. Who's been around her enough to become obsessed by her?'

'Let's try revenge.' Piatowsky lit up a Marlboro Light and Dan glared at him. He stubbed it out. 'Sorry, I didn't realize this was a no-smoking zone.'

'You mean maybe someone had a grudge against her?'

'Yeah, like someone who worked at the café.'

'She and the chef fought all the time, but that was out in the open. The others liked her, enjoyed working there.' Piatowsky had the unlit cigarette clamped between his lips, and Dan added wearily. 'If you don't give that up, you'll be dead at forty.'

'I'm forty-two already. So, who would gain by Ellie's death?'

The word *death* sent a jolt down Dan's spine. 'She owned nothing of great value, except the string of pearls she always wore, and I'll bet no one even knew they were real. That just leaves the house and the antiques.'

'*And* twenty prime acres in one of the richest little communities in California. Worth quite a few million, I'll bet.'

Dan remembered how Ellie had not been able to bring herself to part with the house. 'It's as though Gran and Maria are still here,' she'd said, 'waiting for me to help them. We have to find their killer first.' Now, he wished with all his heart that she had put it on the market right away, let go of her memories, good and bad, and gone on with her own life. Because he knew in his heart that Piatowsky was right and that Journey's End had something to do with Ellie's disappearance.

He said, 'This is the third day. What are her chances?'

Piatowsky knew the statistics. He was being kind when he said, 'Fifty-fifty. But there's always hope.'

They went directly to the Santa Monica Police Department and met with Detective Farrell. Piatowsky told him of his involvement, via the signature murder in Manhattan. He sensed

Farrell was not thrilled to see him, and he figured, rightly, he didn't want him interfering and bringing in the FBI.

'So far, this is a local incident,' Farrell said, sitting behind his desk, twisting the ballpoint through his fingers. 'Meanwhile, officers are out on the streets showing Ellie's photograph, asking if anyone has seen her. Her face is on every television newscast. Helicopters are out searching the canyons, and the Montecito division is searching the house and grounds, one more time. There's not much more we can do, right now,' he shrugged, still twirling the ballpoint.

'He's like a fuckin' baton twirler,' Piatowsky said, disgruntled, to Dan later in the hotel bar. 'The only thing he's not discussing is motive.'

'That's because he believes he's dealing with a random killer, a psychopath.'

'And you don't believe that.'

Dan shook his head. 'There's a plan to all this, Pete, I know it.'

'And a good cop always trusts his instincts.'

Dan sipped his beer morosely. 'Ellie told me she had no other relatives. No cousins twice removed, no aunts and uncles in far-off countries. So who would stand to benefit by her death?'

'The Parrish lawyers would know.'

'You remember Majors? Majors, Fleming and Untermann, attorneys of Santa Barbara.'

'I'll call him. They're not going to give away the family secrets to a rancher, but they'll talk to a cop.'

He went to make the call and Dan glanced at his watch. Time was ticking away fast. He, too, knew what the statistics were in abduction cases.

Piatowsky was back ten minutes later. He sat down and finished his beer in a long gulp. 'Ellie was right, there are no more Parrishes to inherit Miss Lottie's estate.'

'Come on.' Dan was already striding across the room.

'Where are we going?' Piatowsky hurried after him.

'To Makepiece and Thackray, accountants to Lottie Parrish. To see who exactly she was supporting, before they made her cut them off without a dime.'

73

The opulent offices of Makepiece and Thackray were in a Century City skyscraper. The leather chairs were the colour of good wine, the carpet a muted grey, and the desks, weighty and expensive. Piatowsky thought that just watching the sleek young receptionist walk across the room was a pleasure that must cost.

'If these guys were my accountants, I'd want to know how they could afford to live better than I can,' he muttered to Dan, under his breath.

The smart receptionist was obviously not used to having a detective on the premises, and nor was Mr Harrison Thackray. He was in his fifties, tall, suntanned, unsmiling, with a mane of well-coiffed silver hair.

He shook their hands, and invited them to sit. His desk was big enough for two, and meant to show who was in charge. Dan let Piatowsky lead.

'Detective Piatowsky, NYPD,' he flashed his ID. 'I'm involved in the investigation into the disappearance of Ellie Parrish Duveen.'

'Terrible, terrible,' Thackray shook his head. 'After what happened to Miss Lottie, god knows this is just too much.'

'Mr Thackray, do you know of anyone who stood to gain by Ellie's death?'

He looked surprised. 'I do not.'

'Ellie said that her grandmother supported various charities and she'd been forced to give them up recently. Do you have a list of those charities, sir?'

'I do.'

'We'd like to take a look at that, if you don't mind.' Thackray hesitated and Piatowsky gave him his benign, little-boy smile. 'Just checking, that's all, y'understand?'

Thackray understood that he had no choice. He pressed the intercom and told his secretary to bring the Parrish file, then he glanced at his Cartier watch. 'I have a meeting in five minutes, gentlemen. Perhaps you'd care to use the boardroom, while you look through the file.'

The richly panelled boardroom with its red-leather swivel-chairs, hunting prints, and antique walnut partners' table, was as cosy as a gentlemen's club. 'I could move in here, easy.' Piatowsky swivelled his chair, like a little kid. He handed the list to Dan. 'Go ahead, partner. You know more about this than I do. I'm only the key that got you in here.'

The list was a long one. They were mostly women's names, and Dan guessed they were old friends Miss Lottie had helped. There was also the children's ward at the local hospital, the animal shelter, and various other local charities, plus a substantial sum divided annually between deserving causes that she picked herself. Tucked away near the bottom of the third page, was a name that triggered a memory.

He glanced up. 'You heard of the Hudson Sanitarium, in Rollins?'

'The maximum-security facility for psychos? Yeah, I was there once, to interview a nut about a murder. Heavy-duty guys in there, you don't mess with them. What's Lottie Parrish doing involved with a place like that?'

'That's what I'd like to know.' Dan shuffled through the papers until he found the right one. 'She's been paying the bills for someone in there for years. More than twenty, according to this.'

He found the page, read on. He looked at Piatowsky. 'Remember, when we saw the dead hooker, I said check out what nut they'd let out of prison recently? Well, he didn't get out of prison. He got out of the Hudson Sanitarium, because his fees weren't paid. And his name is Patrick Buckland Duveen.'

Their eyes met, remembering the name DUVEEEEEEE . . . on Miss Lottie's computer. 'Bingo!' Piatowsky said.

74

The flickering neon sign just off Highway 101 caught Buck's eye, 'The Avalon Motel,' in scarlet and green letters with the 'O' missing in Motel. Swinging the BMW down the off ramp, he doubled back until he found it.

It was a low, shabby, wooden building with a shingled roof. A twenty-five-watt bulb glimmered over each door, casting more shadows than light, and there was only one other car parked out in front. It was exactly what he needed.

He checked in the driver's mirror. His right eye was practically closed and there was blood on his sweatshirt. He tugged it over his head, revealing a black t-shirt underneath, then wiped the dried blood from his face, smoothed his hair and put on his dark glasses. The switchblade was in his palm, just in case of trouble, as he walked into the miniscule office.

'Evenin'.' The old man behind the counter dragged his gaze away from *Jeopardy* on TV and gave him a cursory glance. 'Rates are twenty-nine dollars, check-out time's eleven, and there's coffee-making facilities in the room.'

'Fine.' Buck handed over the cash.

He put the money in a drawer and plucked a key from the wallboard behind him. 'You wanna receipt?'

'No.'

'It's room 23, on your left.'

Buck parked in the slot outside room 23. He unlocked the flimsy door that he could easily have opened with a good kick, and switched on the overhead light. The thin brown carpet was stained, the orange chenille bedspread had seen decades of wear, and the room smelled of age and motel air freshener. It was a long way from the Biltmore.

Flinging his keys onto the bed, he stripped off his clothes, then went and stood under the shower.

The hot water felt sharp as needles on his wounded eye, but he barely noticed. He was thinking of Ellie, locked in the crate. Anger sent his pulses racing again, he should have killed the little bitch right then and there. But he couldn't, he needed to torture her, he needed revenge. He whimpered, suddenly distraught. *Besides, he loved her.*

After a while, he stepped from the shower, dried himself on the skimpy towel, got dressed again and went out in search of a liquor store. Half an hour later, he was lying on the bed, drinking Jim Beam from the bottle. The fifteen-inch black-and-white TV set flickered opposite, but he wasn't watching. He checked the time, Ellie had been locked in the crate almost five hours. He took another swig of the bourbon. He hoped she was enjoying it.

There was no light where she was, no sound, no air, no space to move. Time had lost all meaning. The hot, salty tears had long since dried on Ellie's cheeks, she couldn't even cry any more, she was reduced to a small terrified creature, locked in a box, abandoned and left to die. Claustrophobia was crushing her chest, her throat was tight with panic, her hair drenched with sweat.

She shifted a fraction of an inch and the rope cut cruelly into her ankles. She was in a foetal position, knees under her chin, head bowed, with her arms twisted behind her back. The pain in her shoulders was excuciating, but at least it kept her from falling into unconciousness. She needed to stay awake, stay alert. *If she wanted to live . . .*

Her calf muscles were locked in a cramp, and she moaned. She'd thought she couldn't stand any more pain, but by now it had become part of her. It was just something else she had to bear. *If she wanted to live.*

Apathy settled over her like a heavy grey cloud; she wasn't even sure if she did want to live any more. Each breath took so much effort, so much pain.

Dan's strong image floated in front of her eyes. He was so close she could see the faint stubble on his jaw, see the darker flecks in his blue eyes, the firm set of his mouth. The mouth that had kissed her so tenderly ... was it only a short while ago? Longing for him made her weak; she could smell the sharp masculine scent of him after they had made love, feel the dampness of the sweat on his back under her skimming hands; she could almost taste him, she wanted him so badly. The warmth of him, the safety of his arms, the security of knowing he cared. She told herself again, that surely by now he must be looking for her. He was clever, an ex-cop, he would know what to do.

But how would he ever find her in this godforsaken place? No one would ever find her. *She might as well be dead.*

Cold air filtered sparingly from tiny holes in the side of the crate, and she twisted her face to them, searching for breath.

She had almost died once before. She remembered it perfectly now. Her father's smile, and the way her mother's gaze had linked with his when the car went into that final spin. Now, she understood that her father knew he was going to die, but bravely, he'd kept on singing. She could hear him, it was as if he were here, in the room, with her ... *'Onward Christian so-o-o-o-ldiers, Marching as to war ...'*

Her voice wobbled as she joined in, in a low husky, treble ... *'With the cross of Jesus Going on before ...'*

322

75

Hal Morrow was not surprised to get a call about Buck Duveen; he'd been half expecting it ever since he'd watched him walk out the door, a free man, a few weeks ago. Nevertheless, what he heard shocked him.

'I didn't know about Charlotte Parrish's death,' he told Dan. 'But I've no doubt he did it.'

'How was he related to the Parrishes?'

'Hold on a minute, all this happened more than twenty years ago, I have to bring myself up to date.' Morrow shuffled through the papers in front of him. 'Ah, now I have it. Buck is the son of Rory Duveen by a previous marriage. Later, Rory married Charlotte Parrish's daughter, Romany.'

Dan's shocked eyes met Piatowsky's. 'So Buck is Ellie's half-brother.'

'Right,' Morrow said. 'I have the full story here. Apparently, he'd gone to Journey's End to try to claim his father's inheritance, but his father didn't have any money. That belonged to Romany, and she had spent it. There was nothing left, and anyhow, if there had been, their daughter Ellie would have inherited it.

'He went crazy and tried to kill Charlotte Parrish, but the child, Ellie, was in the room. It was her screams that brought the servants running. Mrs Parrish refused to press charges against him. Buck had the same father and the same name as her granddaughter, and she refused to taint Ellie publicly. Instead, she had him committed. Clinically, the man is a psychopath. He is violent and deranged, and absolutely capable of the crimes you've described.'

'Then why the hell did you let him out of there?' Dan couldn't hide the anger in his voice.

Morrow sighed regretfully. 'Believe me, I wish I hadn't. But this is a private facility, when the money wasn't paid I had no choice. I also had no evidence that he'd committed any crime. The state facilities were not willing to take him, they're overcrowded as it is, and funding has been cut . . .'

'He fell through the net.'

Morrow nodded. 'Exactly. But I do have a recent photograph of him, plus I can tell you he is a big man. Six-three, weighs around two-twenty, has a wiry build, a pale complexion and copper-red wavy hair. He has dark eyes that look almost black, and he's very strong.'

Dan put down the phone and looked at Farrell. 'There's your motive,' Farrell said, twirling the ballpoint, and looking sombre.

Irritated, Piatowsky averted his eyes from the twirling pen. If Farrell didn't put the fuckin' thing away he might do something drastic to him.

'With Miss Lottie and Ellie out of the way,' Piatowsky tried to phrase it delicately, 'Buck might legitimately claim the estate, as the last of the Parrishes and Duveens. After all, he was, *is*, Ellie's half-brother.'

No one said it, but they all knew Buck would need Ellie dead in order to claim the estate. Without a body, the case could hang fire in the probate courts for years.

'So why didn't he just kill her, there at the café? Or at the carpark?' Piatowsky was pacing the floor. 'If he needs a body, why has she disappeared?'

Dan thought of Ellie's photograph, stolen from her dead grandmother's room. 'Because he's in love,' he said quietly. 'He's obsessed with her. He must have watched her, stalked her, known her every move. Buck Duveen has *all* the motives. Gain, revenge, passion, obsession. All we can hope is that he hasn't killed her. Yet.'

76

Ellie's Place was closed, not because Chan had quit, but because with Ellie missing none of them had the heart to go on.

Farrell had summoned the staff one more time, and they were sitting around the table with cups of unwanted coffee in front of them, passing the colour copy of Buck Duveen's photo around, racking their brains to remember if they had seen him.

Chan, Terry and the kid knew nothing; they rarely saw the customers, and Jake swore he would have remembered. 'I always notice the faces,' he added.

Maya studied the photograph intently, wishing with all her heart she could say, yes I know him. But she didn't. 'There was a guy came in once or twice, kind of hanging around Ellie. But he didn't look like this.'

Dan's ears pricked up. 'What *did* he look like?'

Maya frowned, she wanted to get it right. 'He was very tall, good-looking I suppose, in a strange sort of way. I mean he had this pale skin . . . and dark hair with a moustache. He always wore dark glasses, kind of cool steel frames. I didn't like him, and I told Ellie I thought he was a creep.'

'She knew him?'

'Oh yes, she said she'd met him at the Biltmore. She laughed, said he was just lonely, that's all. But I thought there was something odd about him, he was cocky for a lonely guy, swaggering about the place . . .'

Dan shoved the picture in front of her nose. 'Put a moustache on this face, Maya. Put on the dark glasses, the dark hair. Tell me, are we close?'

Maya stared again at the photo. Then she nodded. 'His name is Ed Jensen.'

Dan threw his head back, his eyes closed. *The young Lothario.* 'That's our man,' he said in a steely voice. 'I'd bet my life on it.'

The Manager at the very proper Biltmore was not used to having police detectives question him, but when he heard it was about Lottie Parrish, and Ellie, he softened. A few minutes later, Farrell had the Miami address and telephone number. 'He always paid the hotel in cash,' he said, dialling the Miami number. 'No credit card.'

Maya nodded, dabbing her eyes with a Kleenex. 'He did the same here at the café, paid cash. And left a big tip.' She shuddered. Thinking of Ellie in his clutches she began to sob again.

Terry poured more coffee. 'Come on, hon, drink up,' he whispered encouragingly. 'Remember, it's not over until the fat lady sings.'

Miami was giving Farrell a hard time, refusing to part with any information.

'How do I know who you are?' the young woman on the other end of the line asked.

Red-faced, he retorted, 'You will in just a few moments, ma'am, when uniformed officers arrive in a squad car. Maybe then you'll give them the information.'

Slamming down the phone, he grabbed a jelly doughnut from the box of Winchell's he'd bought, then paced the room, munching angrily. 'Okay, you guys,' he said with his mouth full. 'Thanks for your help. You can all go home.' He looked sympathetically at Maya. 'Thanks, honey,' he added. He was a good guy at heart.

'I should have thought of him earlier,' Maya realized, panicked. 'I should have known.'

Dan shrugged. 'I saw him too, and I didn't make the connection. He was respectable, well-dressed, pleasant.'

'A good actor,' Jake said.

'A sociopath,' Piatowsky corrected.

326

They picked up their belongings and filed silently out the door. Dan took Maya's arm, 'I'll call you, soon as I know anything.'

She gazed bleakly at him. Her beauty had disappeared and she looked like a tear-stained child. She nodded her thanks. 'I'll be home, waiting.'

Piatowsky hated taking a back seat and letting Farrell do the work, but this was the other guy's turf. He and Dan sipped yet another styrofoam cup of police brew, hanging around until Miami got back to them.

The information came up on the computer screen: The Jensen Property Development Company did not exist; the business address was just a service, and the cheque received in payment was Ed Jensen's. His bank was the Santa Monica branch of First National.

Minutes later, after a hurried consultation with the FBI, they had the information from the bank that the funds in Ed Jensen's account had been transferred by the Madison Avenue branch of the Bank of America, from the account of Buck Duveen. They also had Jensen's social security number. Farrell checked. It was a fake.

He sat back in his chair, twiddling the ballpoint. 'Now all we have to do is find him,' he said, smiling.

77

'You've gotta eat, gotta get some sleep.' Piatowsky was sitting opposite Dan in the hotel bar. They were drinking Glenfiddich and the basketball game was roaring from the TV screen. Dan's stubble was becoming a beard and his hair looked as though it had been raked through once too often. 'At least, take a shower,' he sighed. 'Buy yourself a clean shirt.'

Dan ran his hands through his hair one more time, slumping wearily back in his chair. 'I can't stand not doing anything. All I can think of is her. I hear her voice in my head. I close my eyes and see her, smiling at me . . . God!' He stared bleakly in front of him.

The Lakers game was over and the news came on. Buck Duveen's face was on the TV screen. '*Suspect In The Case of Missing Heiress, Ellie Parrish Duveen*,' the newsreader said, his voice weighty with seriousness.

How Ellie would have hated it, Dan thought, grieving silently inside as though she were already dead. Then he reminded himself of Terry's words to Maya: *It's not over until the fat lady sings*. No one was singing yet. There was still hope, there had to be.

'You're wrecked.' Piatowsky finished his drink, stood, then hitched up his pants. 'Come on.'

'Where are we going?'

'To get a burger, and figure out our next move.'

It all sounded positive, except Piatowsky had no idea what their next move was going to be.

Dan chewed the burger without tasting it, staring blankly down at his plate. He drank the Coke, then glanced at Piatowski, watching him. 'Thanks.'

'You're welcome. So? Where d'ya think he'd take her?'

Dan frowned. 'There has to be some special place, somewhere that meant something to him . . .'

The cellphone rang, and he answered quickly. It was Farrell.

'Just wanted to fill you in. We traced Duveen's mother. She was murdered when he was still in college. Strangled. There was a cross carved in her head. He inherited everything she had, and it was a fair bit. After the sale of the house, around a hundred thousand. He was never a suspect and the case is still open.'

78

Buck woke from a deep, drunken sleep. His head felt stuffed with lead and the sound of the TV grated like a steel file across his raw nerves. Slowly, the newscaster's voice penetrated the fog in his brain.

'This is the face of the man suspected of abducting the heiress, Ellie Parrish Duveen. He is six-feet-three-inches tall, pale complexioned, with red hair, possibly dyed darker. He has dark brown eyes and may also have a moustache. You are looking at a photo of the way he usually looks, when not disguised. And this is an artist's concept of the way he looked when last seen.'

Buck jolted upright. He stared at the tiny screen, saw his own face, looking at him.

'The suspect's name is Patrick Buckland Duveen, aka Ed Jensen, and he is also being sought in connection with the death of Charlotte Parrish, the missing woman's grandmother, and her housekeeper, Maria Novales. As well as in the strangulation and mutilation deaths of three prostitutes. This man was recently released from a high-security mental facility and is known to be a violently deranged criminal. The police wish it to be known that he is armed and dangerous, and they ask the public not to approach him. If you have seen this man, or know where he is, they ask you to call the following number, right away.'

Leaping to his feet, Buck pounded his fist furiously against the wall. *He'd thought he'd beaten them all. He thought he'd won and the prize would be his.*

He flung on his clothes and made for the door. The pain clamped down suddenly in his chest. He leaned against the wall, gasping. Blood pounded in his ears and his chest was bursting.

Pulling himself together, he stumbled from the room, into the car, and drove back up the mountain.

Ellie was so tired, but she couldn't let herself fall asleep because she was afraid she would never wake up. Never see the blue sky again; never feel the warmth of the sun, taste good wine; kiss Dan Cassidy . . .

'*Onward Christian so-o-o-o-ldiers, Marching as to war, With the cross of Jesus . . .*'

Buck stood in the open doorway. *She was singing, her voice low, husky, cracked. It was their father's favourite hymn, the one they had played at the funeral, when they buried him.* Well, now they could sing it at *her* funeral.

Grasping the hammer, he strode across the room.

Ellie stopped singing and lifted her eyes. She could hear the wood splintering, as he hacked the nails out.

'Oh, Daddy,' she whispered, '*I know you love me. If you can hear me, please help me now. Please, Daddy, help me . . .*'

The lid was wrenched back and light streamed in, blinding her. She could hear him panting, then he dragged her from the crate. Her cramped muscles refused to unlock and she fell to her knees. She couldn't move, couldn't see. She was helpless, waiting for the blow that would finish her off.

The Lord is my shepherd, I shall not want, He maketh me to lie down in green pastures . . .' Her brain flickered in and out of reality. *She was a child again, safely tucked up in bed; she had just said her prayers and Miss Lottie was reading the beautiful psalm to her . . .*

Buck stared at her kneeling on the floor. At her long tangle of red hair, at her once-graceful body, and her bloodied limbs where the rope had cut into her. His golden girl: dirty, wounded, beaten. The moment was perfect.

Dropping to his knees, he pushed her down, straddled her, pressing himself urgently onto her. His strong fingers fastened around her throat, squeezing. Panting with excitement, he waited for her to scream, to excite his passion by begging, fighting him off as he took her. Just the way she had screamed in his dreams of revenge, all those long years locked away in Hudson.

Ellie waited to die. She only hoped it would be before he raped her. Her thoughts drifted between the Christian soldiers and the Twenty-third Psalm, between God, and her father, and her grandmother. And Dan, who symbolized life and love . . .

Buck's hands were trembling. *She was not frightened enough, not screaming, not begging for her life. It was no good, he couldn't get hard . . .*

The acrid smell of his stale sweat was in Ellie's nostrils as he picked her up and carried her across the room. Then they were outdoors and she was dragging cool fresh air into her lungs. He flung her onto the cold leather seat in the back of the convertible. She wondered why he hadn't killed her yet.

The fresh air began to revive her. Her blood was circulating again and she was in an agony of pins and needles. *But she was alive.*

The convertible lurched from side to side as they swung down a steep mountain road. He was driving dangerously fast. Suddenly, he swung the wheel all the way to the right. The car went into a spin, tyres shrieking.

Ellie screamed, her head reeled and for the second time in her life she saw herself hurtling from a car, spinning through the air, crashing down the mountainside.

The car stopped, its wheels quivering on the brink of the ravine. Buck turned and looked at her. His dark eyes were malicious. 'Recognize this place, Ellie?'

And suddenly, the memory that had lain dormant in the back of Ellie's mind for more than twenty years was a memory no longer.

79

The last time she had looked into those eyes she was five years old and he was crouched over the hood of her father's white Bentley, parked in the shade of the tall pepper trees. There was something in his hands, a tool of some kind. She had asked him, interestedly, what he was doing, and he'd quickly slammed down the hood. He'd put his finger to his lips, smiling at her.

'Shhh, it's a secret,' he whispered, glancing cautiously round to see if anyone was coming. He took her by the hand and walked rapidly away from the parked car. 'It's a surprise for your mother. Now don't you go telling on me and spoiling it, will you?'

He stared menacingly down at her. Frightened, she turned her face away, shuffled her feet. 'Oh, no,' she muttered.

'You do know how to keep a secret, don't you?'

'Of course I do,' she retorted, upset. 'I kept my Christmas presents secret, even though I was bursting to tell.'

'Well, this is the same. Only now we both have to keep the secret. Okay?'

'Okay.' She pulled her hand away from his tight, hot grip.

'Promise.'

'Promise,' she repeated, reluctantly.

'Cross your heart and hope to die.'

She crossed her heart and said she hoped to die, and he burst out laughing at some joke she didn't understand.

'Goodbye then, Ellie.' He let go of her hand and she turned and ran from the shady pepper trees, down the hot sandy lane, back to her mother

She remembered it all now, clear as day. Her father was

holding up his glass in a toast. She could see the sunlight gleaming through the amber-coloured beer, sending off little sparkles that dazzled her sun-struck eyes. He was singing, of course, 'Return To Sorrento', one of his Italian favourites. Ellie followed his gaze to her mother, saw the love in their smiling-linked eyes. They were so happy, it was just the two of them, and she felt suddenly excluded from their magic world.

Jumping down under the table, she crawled past rows of feet until she came to her mother's expensive little white lizard-skin cowboy boots. Winding her arms around her mother's legs, she wriggled upwards like a worm.

Romany lifted the red-checked tablecloth, peeked down at her. 'So that's where you are,' she said, smiling. 'I missed you.'

And then everything was all right in Ellie's world again.

Until an hour later, when everything had changed.

80

'You killed them,' Ellie said. 'You fixed the brakes on their car.'

Buck nodded, smiling lazily. He had her now.

'*Who are you?*'

'You don't know? Then let me introduce myself. I'm Buck Duveen, your half-brother.'

Ellie's mind went blank with shock. She had known Rory had been married before, but she hadn't known he had a son, never knew he existed.

'Rory was my father too. He had everything, and I had nothing.' Buck shrugged. 'With them out of the way, I stood to inherit their fortune. And with you out of the way, I would be the sole remaining heir. Unfortunately, I've had to wait more than twenty years to complete my task.'

Ellie closed her eyes, unable to look at the cold evil in his. He had smiled at her just like that, in the library that night, when she had seen him trying to kill her grandmother. Sickened, she knew he had finally completed *that* task.

Buck's expression changed. He looked longingly at her. 'There's need for you to die, Ellie. You know I love you. I'd look after you, you would be my own perfect princess. We could have such a wonderful life together. All you need do is say the word.'

She lifted her eyes. 'And what word is that, Buck?'

'Yes,' he said softly.

'*Murderer.*' She spat the filthy word at him.

His eyes glittered angrily, then he turned away, gazing across the ravine, his fists clenched, his face an expressionless mask. And Ellie knew she had signed her own death warrant.

'*Oh, daddy,*' she prayed, '*I hope you are waiting for me, out there. I hope you can send God to punish your evil son.*'

She thought, despairingly, of Dan, whom she would never see again. '*Dan,*' she said, in her heart, '*I know I never told you this, but I hope you'll understand. I do love you. I was just too busy, too determined to succeed, too set in my priorities even to allow love into my life. Oh, I hope you will know, I hope you will think, "Well, you know, she really did love me." Oh Dan, Dan, my friend . . .*'

Buck switched on the ignition, and Ellie opened her eyes for her last glimpse of blue sky, her last look at life.

Then the car swerved back onto the road, and they were heading, too fast, down the mountain again, skidding round the bends, tyres screaming.

She was not dead because Buck Duveen had another plan for them.

81

Dan looked at Piatowsky. 'Let's walk.'

It was cool and moonless, but Santa Monica's Third Street Mall was still crowded with young people, dining at cafés, window shopping, or just hanging out. Their eyes scanned the crowd with the cop's automatic reaction, but their minds were on Buck Duveen.

Leaving Third Street, they walked to Ocean Boulevard, and strolled along the seafront, amongst the palm trees and the homeless. Dan didn't even see them and for once he was indifferent to their pain. His own was too great.

Piatowsky walked silently beside him. He understood what he was going through and he had no words of encouragement. The outlook was bleak.

In his mind, Dan was running through everything he knew about Buck Duveen and his connection with Ellie. Buck had wanted revenge, he'd wanted Journey's End. And he was just crazy enough to take her back there . . .

'Let's go,' he said abruptly.

Piatowsky stared wearily after him. 'Where now?' he called.

'Journey's End.' Dan was running. 'Where it all began.'

82

When he reached the foothills, Buck stopped the car. He dragged Ellie from the back seat, opened the trunk and flung her in.

Ellie turned her head away, refusing to give him the pleasure of her pain and fear.

Without a word, he slammed down the lid.

Claustrophobia hit her again. *She was trapped. It was hot, dark, cramped. She couldn't breathe.* Sweat soaked her hair, her back. She closed her eyes tightly, she must get a grip. *She must think.*

He was speeding again, flinging her from side to side as he took the bends. She felt a sudden sharp pain, blood trickling down her arm. She wondered hazily how badly she was hurt, then realized it no longer mattered. *She was going to die anyway.*

Anger rocketed through her. '*I don't want to die. I refuse to die.*' She was screaming now, surely someone would hear her, there was just a chance if he stopped at a light. But in minutes her voice was reduced to a rasping whisper.

She moaned, wearily. All these years she had prided herself on being a strong independent woman, and look at her now. Reduced to nothing. She couldn't even scream.

'*But I will not die, I will not die . . .*' She kicked her feet, angrily twisting them against the rope until her flesh was raw.

She paused, panting. Blood still oozed slowly down her arm, and she recalled the sharp edge that had inflicted the gash. Shuffling round, she felt for it with her fingers. She was bent over in a cramped V and the pain was unbearable, but she had to try. *She wasn't going to die . . .*

Her fingers explored the object behind her. It was a spade. *The spade with which he meant to bury her.*

Sobbing, she pushed her bound hands back and forth over the sharp edge, not caring if she slashed her wrists . . . better to die that way than to feel his hands on her throat, strangling her, raping her . . . The pain in her shoulders was intolerable, but she pressed harder.

Suddenly, the cord snapped. She slumped forward, tears of relief flowing down her face, massaging her burning wrists.

Hunched over, she wriggled round some more, grabbed the spade and began to saw at the cord binding her ankles. Sweat dripped into her eyes, she could see nothing, only feel. The car kept on swerving round the bends, making it difficult to keep the sharp edge on the cord. Oh god, it would never break, never . . . She chopped savagely at it, harder, harder, until the blood ran over her feet. *At last, she was free.*

By now, the air was thick, dense, moist. Each breath was a gasp that failed to fill her burning lungs. She knew she didn't have much time left.

She shuffled round in the cramped space until she was kneeling, the spade gripped in both hands. *'I'm not going to die, I'm not going to die, I'm not going to die . . .'* She repeated the reassuring mantra over and over, hoping that he would stop soon, and that her strength would hold out.

The Explorer ate up the miles, but Dan was aware of every minute ticking away. He had to find her, it was up to him, she trusted him . . .

Piatowsky sat silently next to him, wondering if the Highway Patrol were around. The Explorer wasn't technically a police vehicle but he could always claim he'd commandeered it. Anyhow, he didn't have the heart to stop Dan speeding.

Dan was on the phone, telling Carlos what was happening. 'Get the key to Journey's End from the drawer in the office, the one in the table. Meet me there,' he checked the clock on the dash, 'in half an hour. Park halfway up the drive. And Carlos, leave your lights off.'

Piatowsky glanced at him. 'You really believe she's there?'

'Where else would he take her? Besides, I feel in my gut he'll return to the scene of his crime. Journey's End and all it means, is what he really wants. I'll bet he's dreamed of it, all those long years in Hudson.' He shrugged wearily. 'It's our only chance.'

Ellie was counting off the minutes. Finally, the car rolled to a stop. She heard the engine idling, smelled petrol fumes, guessed they were at a stoplight. The car pulled away again, drove smoothly to the next light, and the next. They must be passing through a town.

Wiping the sweat from her brow with the back of her hand, she listened for the sound of other cars. Maybe she could bang on the trunk with the spade, attract their attention. But she could hear no other cars. Then they made a left turn and began to climb a hill. She lifted her head, alert.

She knew every bend in that road. Now, she knew where he was taking her.

The tyres crunched on the gravel, then the car stopped. She heard him get out, heard the door slam, his footsteps coming closer. The trunk lid swung slowly up.

Screaming, she slammed the spade into his face. He was clutching his head, yelling with pain, his face a mask of fury and blood. She fell from the trunk, scrambling quickly to her feet. He was coming at her, powerful arms outstretched.

'*Oh, god, oh god, help me, please* . . .' She swung the spade again, it crunched sickeningly against his skull, and this time he dropped to the ground.

The adrenelin of fear gave her legs wings. She was running for her life. But she was weak, her muscles leaden from the hours in the cramped space. She couldn't keep up this pace for long, she would have to hide.

'Bitch,' he was screaming, 'Bitch, like your whore of a mother . . . rich bitch like your whore of a grandmother . . . *you are dead.*'

She veered off the drive, weaving her way through the trees, stumbling over exposed roots. Her breath was coming in short hard gasps, her heart thudded somewhere in her throat . . . *she was not going to die . . .*

She stopped, waited, listening for him. It was pitch dark and she slipped deeper into the copse, wincing when a fallen branch cracked loudly under her stumbling feet. She leaned back against a tree, her heart thundering, lips pressed tightly together so he wouldn't hear her breathing.

He grabbed her by the throat.

Buck was buzzing with that electric surge of power. Even wounded, he was indomitable. She was pathetic to think she could beat him, he was smarter than her. Smarter than all of them.

Ellie could feel the heat of his breath on her cheek, the cold steel of the knife at her throat, his blood trickling stickily down her neck.

'*You are dead, Ellie Parrish Duveen,*' he whispered, pressing the knife deeper.

She closed her eyes, waiting . . .

'Walk,' he commanded.

She stumbled in front of him to the house, stood trembling while he fumbled with the kitchen door. Then he pushed her inside and locked it behind them.

There were no lights, but Ellie knew her old home so well, she could have walked through it blindfolded without bumping into a single piece of furniture. The silence of the familiar rooms felt soothing. She was exhausted, wounded, frightened. There was no fight left in her. 'If I'm going to die,' she thought, wearily, 'I'd rather it were here, where my good memories are. Where I began.'

Buck hustled her in front of him into the library. He switched on a lamp, his dark eyes glittered icily as he looked at her.

'Kneel.' He pointed to the place near the desk. She stared mutely at him with those big opal eyes. '*Kneel, I said.*' He threw her to the floor, pressed her face into the beautiful red silk Turkish rug.

Now he had Ellie Parrish Duveen at his mercy. And he had no mercy left to give her.

83

The rusty pickup squeaked up the driveway, with Cecil, the brown mutt, and Pancho swaying in the back. It was pitch dark and Carlos peered through the window looking for the Explorer. It wasn't there yet and he parked halfway as Dan had instructed, then paced around, waiting.

A few minutes later, he heard the sound of a car turning into the gates. Crouching behind the truck, he eyed the vehicle warily, nerves crackling. It was the Explorer.

Pancho leapt out of the pickup, dancing on his hind legs and yipping loudly. Carlos shushed him quickly as he climbed back into the cab and followed them up the long gravel driveway.

Light glowed behind the curtained library windows, and a black BMW was parked outside.

Piatowsky reached for his gun. They were taking no prisoners tonight. 'You called it right, Cassidy,' he said.

Buck lifted his head at the sound of tyres on the gravel. Panic flickered in his eyes. He could kill her now, have done with it. But then his revenge would not be complete. Like this, they might catch him, and he had vowed he would never be a prisoner again.

They were hammering at the front door now, calling Ellie's name. Hefting her in his arms, he carried her upstairs to the grandmother's room and threw her on the bed, then went back and locked the door. Now they were alone.

He tugged the cans of lighter fluid from his pocket. He'd meant to use them to incinerate the car when he'd done with it. Now, he emptied them across the carpet, the furnishings, the hallway. Then he lay on the bed, next to her. She stared wide-eyed at him, like a cornered rabbit with a ferret.

'I really loved you, Ellie,' he said. Then he kissed her.

His tongue forced her mouth open, his hands explored her breasts, travelled down her body. She wanted to scream, to vomit, *she wanted to kill him*. She lunged back and fell off the bed, heard him laughing as she crawled to the window and tugged desperately at the catch. It was locked. Her fingers groped for the key. *It wasn't there.*

Trapped, she turned and looked at him, caught the insane gleam in his eyes as he tossed the match to the floor. Then, with a great whoosh, the room burst into flames.

Dan saw her, a dark shape against the hot red glow. 'He's torched the place,' he yelled. 'Ellie, Ellie, break the window, jump.' But Ellie couldn't hear him, couldn't see him, didn't even know he was there.

Carlos sped off in search of a ladder. Piatowski was running for the pickup. He drove it back along the terrace and positioned it under the balcony. Dan vaulted into the back, then climbed onto the roof of the cab. An old fig tree grew up the wall, it would give him a handhold, if it would take his weight.

Grasping the thickest branch, he hauled himself up. It creaked ominously, and he leapt for the balcony rail, hanging by one hand, suspended in space. Sweat beaded his forehead, he could feel himself slipping . . .

Buck was bursting with laughter, delighted with his cleverness. He had won, and the prize was his.

Through the smoke, Ellie saw his mad eyes lit red by the flames. He reached for her, dragged her back into the room. The smoke was choking her, searing her lungs, the whole world was going black. She was dying after all.

Suddenly the window exploded inwards. Fuelled by the oxygen the room roared into an inferno. Ellie's brain was hazy, her eyes unfocused . . . for a minute she thought it was Dan standing there.

Quick as a panther, Buck lunged for Dan's heart, but the gun was faster than the knife. It spat once, twice.

Piatowsky levelled it at Buck again. He fired at him one more time, to make sure. He jerked backwards, like a puppet with the strings cut, then dropped to his knees.

Buck's world was full of pain. A million knives pierced his chest. He looked at Ellie, lying on the floor in front of him. The flames were licking at her long red hair. It was burning like a halo, around her beautiful face. 'Ellie', he whispered, smiling, 'Ellie . . .'

Dan beat out the flames with his hand. He picked her up, put her over his shoulder. 'Let's get out of here.'

Carlos held the ladder steady as they climbed carefully down, and laid Ellie on the cool grass. Looking at her, Dan didn't know if she were dead or alive. Piatowsky was already on the cellphone, calling for paramedics, the fire rescue squad, the police.

A terrible howl split the night, and they looked up.

Buck was crouched at the window. The pain was clamping down in his chest like a mighty sword. With a tremendous effort, he hauled himself to his feet, his strong arms gripped the window frame. He looked like a great bird of prey, wings outstretched. Behind him was only scarlet heat. In front of him, an abyss of darkness.

That buzz of power was humming through him. He was alive as he had never been before, every part of him in an agony of pain. It was almost beautiful. Then the sword thrust through his chest again. Flinging back his head, he howled like a wolf. Just the way he used to in Hudson, when the guards would say, 'There goes Buck Duveen again. It must be full moon.' Only now there would be no more full moons.

He was still howling when he fell backwards, into the flames.

84

Dan had not budged from Ellie's hospital bedside, all night. They had bandaged his burned hands and kept telling him to go home, that she'd had a strong sedative and would sleep for hours, but he had refused to move. Piatowsky had gone to get some sleep, after dealing with Farrell and Johannsen, as well as calling Maya to let her know Ellie was okay.

The slight mound of Ellie's body under the white sheets reassured Dan that she was still with him, in the land of the living. Her bruised face glowed yellow and purple; antiseptic gauze covered her singed arms, and they had cut off what was left of her beautiful, long red hair. She looked like a little boy, sweetly sleeping.

Her face had such a look of innocence, it wrenched his gut when he remembered how close it had been. He still didn't know what had happened in the time she had been abducted, and he sighed deeply, hoping it would not scar her soul for ever. She had already been through so much.

Ellie had never dreamed of such peace, such sweet silence, such a soft pillow. *It smelled of hospitals.* Panicked, she opened her eyes. Dan's face swam into view and she relaxed. She knew everything was all right.

'Hello, friend.' Even raspy, her voice was sweet as spun sugar, deep as rich chocolate.

Dan threw his hands up helplessly. 'I'm afraid to touch you. And I want to kiss you, so badly.'

The big grin was the same. 'Go ahead, friend,'.

He leaned across and brushed his lips lightly over hers.

'Mmmmm, soft as a feather,' she sighed.

'Consider that feather a down payment.'

Ellie wiggled her eyebrows in a question; it was about the only bit of her she could wiggle. 'A down payment? On what?'

'On future kisses, and . . . oh hell, enough of this friend stuff. I need you, woman.'

'Oh?' Even drowsy, she couldn't resist teasing him. 'For what, exactly?'

'Let me think.' He ran a hand through his dishevelled dark hair, frowning. 'To run the tasting room at Running Horse. Maybe open a café there, nothing pretentious, you understand. Just a little French kind of place, sawdust on the floor, green checked tablecloths, great food . . .'

Ellie heaved an enormous sigh, wincing as the pain hit her. 'Dammit, Dan Cassidy, any woman could do that. Where do I figure in all this?'

'Right in the middle,' he said, smiling. 'I can't live without you, Ellie Parrish.'

Her sigh was happy this time, but the sedative was kicking in again and her eyelids drooped. 'Right in the middle of your life,' she murmured. 'Exactly where I want to be.'

His lips brushed hers again as she drifted, contentedly, back to sleep.

Dan was smiling as he watched over her. He knew that what had happened would have to be spoken of later, addressed, resolved. It would take her a long time to recover from something as terrible as this, but with his help, and the peace and quiet of Running Horse Ranch, they would survive. His car might be a wreck, but his life was great. He had no regrets.

They were the winners.